GORGEOUS GROOMS

Helen   Trish   Anna
BIANCHIN   MOREY   CLEARY

Mills & Boon, an imprint of Harlequin (UK) Limited, Eton House, 18-24 Paradise Road, Richmond, Surrey TW9 1SR

AUSTRALIA: GORGEOUS GROOMS
© Harlequin Enterprises II B.V./S.à.r.l 2013

The Andreou Marriage Arrangement © Helen Bianchin 2010
His Prisoner in Paradise © Trish Morey 2010
Wedding Night with a Stranger © Anna Cleary 2010

ISBN: 978 0 263 90589 2

010-0313

Printed and bound in Spain
by Blackprint CPI, Barcelona

THE ANDREOU MARRIAGE ARRANGEMENT

ARRANGEMENT

Helen
BIANCHIN

THE AUSTRALIA COLLECTION

March 2013

April 2013

May 2013

June 2013

July 2013

August 2013

Helen Bianchin was born in New Zealand and travelled to Australia before marrying her Italian-born husband. After three years they moved, returned to New Zealand with their daughter, had two sons and then resettled in Australia. Encouraged by friends to recount anecdotes of her years as a tobacco share farmer's wife living in an Italian community, Helen began setting words on paper and her first novel was published in 1975. An animal lover, she says her terrier and Persian cat regard her study as as much theirs as hers.

CHAPTER ONE

ALESHA sat in stunned silence as the lawyer finished reading her late father's will.

Surprise didn't even begin to cut it.

What had Dimitri Karsouli been *thinking* in selling a twenty-five-per-cent share in the Karsouli Corporation to Loukas Andreou?

Worse…gifting Loukas a further twenty-five-per-cent share. Representing several hundred million dollars on today's market.

Subject to marriage.

The breath caught in her throat as realization hit. Dear heaven. Her father had *bought* her a husband?

It was beyond comprehension.

Yet she was all too aware how her father's mind worked; it didn't take much to do the maths.

A year ago Alesha's disastrous short-lived marriage had formally ended in divorce from a man who had professed to love her…only for her to discover to her cost that Seth Armitage's main goal had been a stake in her father's fortune and a free ride on the gravy train. It had devastated her and angered her father…more than she had known.

Dimitri, out of a sense of parental devotion, had clearly conspired to arrange what he perceived to be a fail-safe liaison for his daughter via marriage to a man who had his total approval. A man of integrity, trust, possessed of astute business nous, and a worthy companion.

Loukas Andreou, the inflexible omnipotent head of the Athens branch of the Andreou Corporation, whose financial interests included shipping and considerable ancillary assets worldwide.

Loukas, whose father Constantine had been Dimitri's lifelong friend and associate…a man whose powerful image sprang so readily to Alesha's mind, it was almost as if his presence became a tangible entity in the room.

In his late thirties, attractive, if one admired masculine warrior features, with the height, breadth of shoulder and facial bone structure that comprised angles and planes. Loukas had brilliant dark eyes and a mouth that promised much.

Sophisticated apparel did little to diminish an innate ruthlessness resting beneath the surface of his control.

It was utterly devastating for Alesha to even begin to imagine what had possessed Dimitri to revise his will to include a clause stipulating his bequest of the remaining fifty-per-cent share in the Karsouli Corporation to his only child, Alesha Eleni Karsouli. This bequest was conditional on a marriage taking place to Loukas Andreou within a month of Dimitri's demise, thus ensuring a one-hundred-per-cent joint *family* ownership, thereby securing the corporation and ensuring it would continue into another generation.

'A court of law could rule the marriage stipulation as invalid,' Alesha voiced.

The lawyer regarded her thoughtfully. 'While there would be a degree of sympathy regarding that specific clause, your father's instructions were very clearly defined. I counselled him to reconsider, but he was adamant that clause should stand.'

Alesha stifled a startled curse beneath her breath.

Dimitri had known how much Karsouli meant to her, how she'd lived and breathed it for as long as she could remember. Absorbing every aspect, studying for degrees at university to ensure she acquired the relevant knowledge, the edge…aware the word *nepotism* didn't exist in her father's vocabulary.

He knew too the pride she'd taken in working her way from the ground up to her current position of authority.

It had been a foregone conclusion his only child would assume control upon Dimitri's demise.

And he had, Alesha conceded, gifted her that…with strings attached. Conditions aimed to protect Karsouli, and her. Especially *her*.

To attempt to force her into a marriage she didn't want was the ultimate manipulative act, and in that moment she could almost hate him for it.

Two days ago she'd weathered the funeral service at the chapel. Walked behind the hearse to the grave site. Stood in silent despair and grieved as the ritual played out.

Aware of Loukas Andreou's presence…imagining he'd flown in from Athens to attend Dimitri's funeral as a mark of respect. And totally unaware of any subterfuge.

She could walk away; ignore the marriage clause, resign from the Karsouli Corporation and seek a position in a rival firm.

Except she was a Karsouli, born and bred, legally reverting to her maiden name after her failed marriage. Hadn't her father groomed her to rise to her current position? Conditioning her to believe it didn't matter she was female; women in the twenty-first century held positions of power, and he'd given her no reason to suppose otherwise.

Dimitri Karsouli had ruled his life and his business interests with an iron fist in a velvet glove, earning him a corporation now worth a fortune.

His father before him had come from humble beginnings in Athens, and, fostering an idea presented to the right person at the right time, initiated the founding office in Athens of the Karsouli Corporation. Dimitri, his only son, had followed in hallowed footsteps, living and breathing the business and injecting it with new ideas, broadening its scope and extending it onto a global market.

Dimitri had married and moved to Sydney and had sought to have his own son continue, except his marriage had gifted him a daughter, born in difficult circumstances that had rendered his wife unable to produce another child.

A beloved daughter, Alesha, who had become her father's pride and joy, especially when she proved she'd inherited his business acumen and sharp mind.

Privately educated and exclusively schooled, Alesha had graduated from university with honours in a business degree, and had entered Karsouli in a lowly position, rising in the ranks through hard work and dedication.

Her one error in judgement had been to marry in haste, against her father's wishes, a man who, while playing a part to perfection during their brief courtship, had revealed his true persona within hours of leaving the wedding reception.

A painful time, when divorce and a handsome pay-out had been the only option. Especially so, as it was compounded by her mother's losing battle with a virulent form of cancer.

Alesha's adamant refusal to consider marriage at any future stage became a bone of contention between father and daughter. Now, by a conditional clause in his will, Dimitri was bent on manipulating her into matrimony with a man of whom he approved. A man of Greek descent. Someone who had his utmost trust…to take the reins of Karsouli and lead his daughter into the marriage bed.

Dimitri had to be smiling in his grave, assured Alesha would never concede to losing what she loved most in life…the family firm.

In that respect she'd inherited her father's genes. His bloodline was so strong, the desire to achieve, to succeed, to prove her worth beyond doubt, irrespective of gender.

'This…*scheme* has Loukas Andreou's approval?'

The lawyer spread his hands in a telling gesture. 'I understand he has indicated his consent.'

'It's outrageous,' Alesha uttered with considerable heat. '*Impossible*,' she added for good measure. 'I don't want to marry *anyone*.'

Loukas Andreou had been welcomed into her parents' home on the few occasions he'd visited Sydney. She'd dined in his company, and met up with him in Athens on the occasional trip to Greece with her parents. Combining business with pleasure…or so she'd thought at the time.

Now, she wasn't so sure. Even *then*, had Dimitri sown the seeds of a possible future marriage?

Loukas Andreou. The man was a force to be reckoned with in the business arena…and the bedroom, if rumour had any basis in fact.

Old money. His great-grandfather, so the Andreou biographical details depicted on record revealed, had made his fortune in shipping. A fortune added to by each succeeding generation.

The Andreou consortium owned two Greek Islands, property, residences in most European cities, and there was the private cruiser, the Lear jet, the expensive cars…the women.

The media followed and tabled Loukas' every move, embellishing the smallest fact with gossip.

Tall, well-built frame, dark hair, ruggedly attractive facial features…he unsettled her. Almost as if he saw far more than she wanted anyone to see.

There were some secrets she'd buried so deep, no one would uncover them. Ever.

'How long has Loukas been aware of the contents of my father's will?'

'It's something you'll have to ask him.'

She would…at the first opportunity!

Alesha glimpsed the faint lift in the lawyer's brow.

'You have two clear options,' he cautioned quietly. 'Agree to the marriage…or disagree. I strongly advise you not to make a decision until you've spoken with Loukas Andreou.'

She stood and indicated the consultation had reached a conclusion. The lawyer accompanied her into the lobby and pressed the call button to summon a lift.

Alesha gritted her teeth together in a need to prevent the urge to scream as the lift transported her to ground. *Why* had her father conspired to do what he had?

Except she knew precisely why.

Hadn't Dimitri's own marriage to her mother been deemed a satisfactory liaison benefitting both families?

Love? If it happened, well and good. If it didn't, affection, *family* was enough to make a contented life.

Surprisingly, her parents had shared a good marriage. A little volatile at times, she reflected, remembering Dimitri's voice raised in anger over some relatively minor conflict with her mother. A woman who'd stood her own ground and given back as much in kind. Had they shared a grand passion? Perhaps. Great affection, certainly.

Alesha had wanted the grand passion, the love generated by two souls in perfect accord. She'd thought she'd found it with Seth Armitage…only to discover he'd very cleverly

played a cruel game, and her marriage was nothing more than
a travesty. One she escaped from almost as soon as the ink
had dried on their marriage certificate.

Dimitri, to give him his due, hadn't vented with *I told you
so*. He'd been supportive, caring.

Yet it hurt unbearably that behind the scenes he'd been con-
spiring to cement her future and the future of Karsouli. Worse,
somehow, was Loukas Andreou's complicity.

To think she'd accepted his condolences, shared his
presence during the funeral service, suffered his silent watch-
fulness…and he *knew*.

Dear Lord in heaven.

Was she the only one who'd been in ignorance?

At this very moment, was Loukas Andreou already putting
plans in motion to assume prime position within Karsouli?

Or had he already done that, skilfully lining everything up
to ensure any hiccups would be only minor? And if he had, how
could she have missed *seeing* it? Surely there should have been
something, even subtle, that would have alerted her attention?

Yet even on brief reflection, she failed to pinpoint any one
thing.

The Sydney skyline was slightly hazy in the prelude to
evening dusk, the harbour assuming a darker hue as ferries
left a white churning tail as they transported some of the
city's workers to the northern suburb of Manly. Her apartment
formed part of a large old double-storeyed home in fashionable Double Bay, whose interior had been completely re-
structured into four self-contained two-bedroom apartments.
Modern state-of-the-art appliances blended beautifully with
the deliberate styling of the previous century.

It had given Alesha immense pleasure to add furnishings
to complement the era…large comfortable sofas, antique fur-

niture, exquisite lamps and beautiful Oriental rugs, large squares and runners providing an attractive foil for the stained wooden floors.

Home, for the past two years. *Hers*, alone.

Something completely different from the modern house gifted to her on her wedding day. A home she'd legally tussled over with Seth, along with his claim for a half share, together with a half share of the assets she'd brought to the marriage.

A slight shudder scudded down the length of her spine as she garaged her car.

Seth, the handsome charmer who'd played so skilfully into her hands…and who, once vows legalized their union, with his ring on her finger, had dropped the pretence he'd so carefully fostered.

Even now with hindsight, she had trouble relating the charmer to the hard, calculating monster he became.

It's gone, done and dusted, Alesha dismissed as she entered the spacious foyer and trod the stairs to her apartment.

She was whole again, mentally and physically. Dating wasn't on her agenda…hadn't been since she'd walked out on her marriage. She had friends…a trusted few whose company she valued.

Life, until her father's death a week ago, had become settled, predictable, *comfortable*.

Now it was about to take a backwards flip into the uncertain, and instinct warned she'd need all her wits to cope with whatever lay ahead.

Marriage to Loukas Andreou?

If it happened, it would be on *her* terms.

She entered the apartment, ditched her bag, laptop, toed off her stilettos, then padded into the kitchen and filched chilled water from the refrigerator.

A leisurely shower, then she'd fix dinner…and plan her strategy.

Conditions, she elaborated as she shed her tailored suit, stripped to the skin and walked naked into the en suite.

A paper marriage; separate bedrooms; separate private lives. They'd work together in harmony; confer and co-ordinate their social diaries in order to entertain and grace the requisite social functions.

Alesha adjusted the water dial and stepped beneath the generous spray, collected delicately scented gardenia soap and attempted to match her marriage strategy to the man Dimitri had deliberately selected as her *second* husband.

'Hell's teeth,' she muttered with unaccustomed ire. She didn't *want* a husband!

On the occasions she'd shared Loukas' company, he'd been attentive, an interesting conversationalist, knowledgeable, intelligent, focused.

Sexy, a silent imp added, in a leashed, almost primitive manner that hinted at much and promised more.

Alesha closed her eyes, then slowly opened them again. *Where had that come from?*

Oh, for heaven's sake, admit it. There had been a time when she'd wondered what it would be like to have his mouth close over her own, and savour, taste…persuade. To lean in against his body and absorb his strength, and discover…*what*? Attraction, *more*?

She'd caught a sense of it, become fascinated by him, even curious…aware he met with her parents' approval. A man of independent wealth and substance. Attentive, watchful, almost *waiting*, she reflected. For what? For her to make the first move?

Except she hadn't. Instinctively aware if she did, there would be no going back.

Perhaps, she allowed in retrospect, Dimitri had begun to hope, to plan…even then.

Except Seth had already been on the scene, sweeping her off her feet with glib words and false promises. Words and promises she had believed to be genuine, in spite of her parents' caution.

From beautiful to battered bride in the space of a heart-beat…okay, *weeks*, Alesha corrected grimly as she closed the water dial, caught up a towel and wrapped it round her slender curves.

Leading, she admitted, to the most painful months of her life as she had weathered the aftermath, regained her self-respect…*dammit*, her very identity.

Together with a resolve never to allow anyone to get close enough to earn her personal trust again. A fact she'd set down in stone, with a frozen heart and a cool, determined brain.

The evening stretched ahead, and one she'd choose to fill after a light meal with a few hours spent on her laptop, catch the late news on television…then bed.

It seemed like a plan, albeit a familiar one as she swept the length of her hair into a careless knot, donned underwear before adding comfortable jeans and a singlet top.

The message light was blinking on her answering machine as she entered the kitchen, and she crossed to the servery, took up a pen, pulled the message pad forward and pressed the *play* button.

"Alesha. Loukas Andreou." His voice was deep, husky, with a slight accented inflection that curled round her nerve-ends and tugged a little. It wasn't a feeling she coveted, and she drew in a calming breath as she noted down the number he recited. "Call me."

A soft curse emerged from her lips, and she rolled her eyes in silent self-castigation. He wasn't wasting any time.

So make the call. The sooner she dealt with him, the better.

He picked up on the third ring. 'Andreou.'

'Alesha,' she informed him matter-of-factly.

'Have you eaten?'

'I'm about to.' It would take only minutes to assemble a salad and enjoy her solitary meal. 'Why?'

'I'll collect you in ten minutes.'

Who does he think he is? *Don't go there.*

'If you're issuing an invitation,' she managed silkily, 'it's polite to request, not demand.'

'I'll make a note of it.'

Was there a smidgen of mild amusement apparent in his response?

'Ten minutes.' He cut the connection, and left her silently fuming and on the verge of calling back to insist she meet him at a nominated venue.

Except it would seem petty, and not the action of a woman in control. Or one determined to treat this meeting with prosaic common sense.

There was the need to change. Comfortable well-worn jeans, a casual top, her dark hair caught in a careless knot and anchored there with a large clip, bare feet, and no make-up didn't comprise fitting attire in which to dine out.

There was a part of her that felt inclined to slip her feet into trainers, collect her car keys, wallet, and leave.

Except her absence wouldn't achieve a thing.

So, get over it, she admonished silently as she changed into tailored trousers and a buttoned blouse. She added a dash of colour to her lips, fixed her hair, then selected a fashionable jacket and slid her feet into killer heels.

Her intercom buzzed as she collected a clutch purse, and she picked up, clarified Loukas Andreou's image on the security monitor, then uttered a brisk—'I'm on my way down.'

His height and breadth of shoulder seemed vaguely intimidating, his hard, strong-boned facial features arresting in the early evening light. Black tailored trousers, a white shirt unbuttoned at the neck, and a black butter-soft leather jacket lent a casual sophisticated look…one she knew to be deceiving, given the power he wielded in the business arena.

'Loukas.' Her greeting was polite, almost formal as dark eyes seared her own, and for a moment she experienced the strangest feeling that time stood still. Then it was gone.

'Shall we get this over and done with?'

Was that a faint edge of humour apparent, or simply a trick of the light? She couldn't be sure in the brief instant before he stood to one side and indicated the black Aston Martin parked in the forecourt.

She walked at his side to the car, aware of his close proximity as he opened the passenger door and saw her seated before crossing to slip in behind the wheel.

There was an unwanted sense of nervousness she strove hard to hide as he fired the engine and eased the powerful car onto the road.

A shared meal, during which she'd state her perspective, negotiate…and hopefully resolve the terms of Dimitri's will to their mutual satisfaction.

In a short space of time Loukas drew the Aston Martin to a halt at the entrance to the Ritz-Carlton hotel and organized valet parking.

Pleasant choice, Alesha approved, having dined in the restaurant on a few occasions.

Except once inside the foyer Loukas indicated the lift.

'My suite will afford us some privacy.'

Her nerve-ends coiled in painful protest at the thought of being alone with him. 'I'd prefer the restaurant.'

'And risk public scrutiny?' he elaborated quietly. 'Possibly be overheard or photographed discussing a private matter?'

The fact that he was right didn't help much. Speculation would run rife soon enough when Loukas Andreou's continued presence in Sydney was noted. Especially when his extensive shareholding in Karsouli became known.

There was little she could do but acquiesce, albeit with some reluctance, duly observed, she noted as she bore Loukas' slightly hooded gaze as they rode the lift to his designated floor.

You can do this, a silent voice bade as she watched Loukas swipe a card and usher her into his suite. Loukas had her late father's trust. Otherwise Dimitri would never have structured his will the way he had.

Would he?

Dear God, how would she know…for sure?

With both parents gone, she had become very selective in whom she chose to confide in. Not even Lacey, a dear friend from childhood, knew everything about her first marriage. Some details were too personal…too hurtful to divulge.

'Relax,' Loukas drawled. 'I'm not about to hit on you.'

Alesha directed him a level look. 'I would deal with it if you did.' Hadn't she trained hard to effectively do so?

He shrugged out of his jacket, tossed it onto the large king-size bed, then he undid the cuffs on his shirt and turned them back twice, revealing muscular forearms sprinkled with dark hair.

'Can I take your jacket?'

'I'm fine, thanks.'

'Why don't you take a seat?' He indicated a comfortable chair. 'Would you like something to drink?'

'Can we pass on the social niceties and go straight to the matter at hand?'

He regarded her carefully for several long seconds, and she glimpsed a muscle tighten at the edge of his jaw.

'By all means,' he concurred with deliberate indolence. 'Then we'll eat.'

Alesha was so tempted to vent. Anger had built to a point where throwing a hissy fit would at least relieve some of her angst. Yet, conversely, it was probably exactly what he expected of her.

'The terms of my father's will are unconscionable.'

He didn't pretend to misunderstand. 'Apropos the marriage clause?'

'You *agree* with it?' Her eyes widened measurably. 'What manner of man are you?'

'One who prefers to embark on marriage with an honest foundation at its base.'

The look she gave him should have shrivelled him on the spot. Except it had no effect whatsoever.

'Oh…*please*. Let's not forget the primary focus.'

'Karsouli?'

Alesha allowed herself a faintly bitter smile. 'Dimitri's trump card.'

Loukas offered a thoughtful look. 'Perhaps.'

She stilled, suddenly alert. 'What are you saying?'

'Dimitri made a few errors in financial judgement in recent months.'

Her shock was real and barely masked. 'I don't believe you.'

'The global economic climate worked against him, so too did his failing health.'

Failing health? 'He was killed in a car accident.'

Loukas' gaze didn't waver. 'Your father risked heart failure unless he agreed to undergo heart transplant surgery. He refused, and bartered a deal with me to safeguard Karsouli.' He waited a beat. 'And you.'

No. The word echoed as a silent scream, and the blood chilled in her veins.

Oh, dear God.

'Karsouli needed a large injection of cash in order to remain solvent.'

'How much?' The demand almost choked her.

'Half a billion dollars.'

That much?

Selling off a twenty-five-per-cent share represented the injection of cash. The gift via Dimitri's will, conditional on marriage, would have been a sufficiently attractive enticement.

Karsouli would survive and flourish beneath Loukas Andreou's skilled leadership.

Of which she would become a joint partner and director. There was just one major snag… In order to achieve both, she had to agree to marry Loukas Andreou.

Two pluses versus one minus.

Alesha took a deep calming breath…not that it had any effect. 'I'll need to verify those facts.'

'Of course. I have certified copies of relevant documentation for you to peruse.'

Somehow she didn't expect any less of him. Even given the advantage of his father's success, Loukas appeared very much an achiever determined to forge his own destiny, both professionally and personally.

She accepted the paperwork, took time to read and absorb the data, aware of a sinking heart with every page.

The slim hope there might be a mistake disappeared as she was forced to face the inevitable.

With care she placed the papers onto the table, then met his hooded gaze. 'Why did you sanction Dimitri's terms?'

One eyebrow lifted. 'The truth? His request coincided with a promise I had made to my own father to marry and provide an heir.'

'How noble,' Alesha accorded sweetly. 'To sacrifice yourself out of duty and family loyalty.' She sharpened a figurative barb. 'Were none of the many women who attach themselves to you suitable wife material?'

His features assumed musing cynicism. 'No.'

'What if I choose to contest the marriage clause?'

His eyes speared her own, dark with dangerous intent, and belying the quiet purpose in his voice.

'Should you refuse, the purchase will fall through. I'll sell the twenty-five-per-cent shares comprising Dimitri's bequest, and you will be placed in an invidious financial position.'

Forced to take on a partner and possibly face a takeover bid. Thereby losing everything her father had achieved. All she'd lived and breathed for as long as she could remember.

Anger, resentment, dammit—*grief*, welled up inside. So many emotions…consuming, invasive, and in that moment uncontrolled.

She stood and turned towards the door. 'Go to hell.'

CHAPTER TWO

'I SUGGEST you *think* before you walk out that door,' Loukas cautioned with dangerous quietness. 'Or the *hell* you'd consign me to will be your own.'

His meaning was icily clear, and had a sobering effect.

Pride and anger held no place in Dimitri's diabolical scheme.

Walk…and Alesha would lose the *one* thing she considered to be the most important entity in her life.

Could she trust Loukas? Dear heaven. If not him…*who*?

At least he had a vested interest in Karsouli; he possessed the skill and expertise to assume dual directorship; add considerable financial resources…

It was no contest.

Except she was damned if she'd give in easily.

For the space of a few seconds she closed her eyes, then opened them again, took a deep calming breath and turned slowly to face him.

There was an inherent strength apparent, an entity that went deep beneath the surface. An indomitable sense of power that made him both an invaluable ally and feared adversary.

But as a husband? *Lover?*

An instant recall of what she'd suffered at Seth's hands sent apprehension feathering her spine.

Don't go there.

One man's manic proclivities were not those of all men.

Unbidden, her teeth worried the inner fullness of her lower lip.

Yet how could she *know* for sure?

Seth had played the perfect part as loving fiancé, adoring new husband…until she had refused to concede to his demands.

A sudden bleakness clouded her eyes. A shadow of pain which appeared so fleetingly Loukas almost missed it, and his gaze narrowed.

'If the deal didn't include *marriage*, I'd be ecstatic.'

'Nevertheless, it does.'

'Unfortunately.'

On some level she *got* the loyalty thing. Matchmaking suitable partners from two eminently suitable families. A little devious manipulation added to the mix, and *voilà*…the convenient marriage scenario intended to safeguard the family fortunes and ensure the continuation of a dynasty.

'Yes or no, Alesha.' His expression was unreadable, his eyes dark and unwavering as they regarded her.

It had to be *yes*. There was no way she could countenance Karsouli slipping ignominiously between the cracks to disappear in the belly of iniquity.

'I have no choice but to agree, subject to certain conditions.'

There was a strength apparent in her demeanour, a determination he could only admire given she'd taken a king-hit about the true state of her father's corporation.

'Name them.' His voice held a silkiness she chose to ignore.

'I retain my position in Karsouli.'

Loukas inclined his head in agreement. 'Naturally.'

Now for the cruncher. 'A separate suite of rooms in whatever home we share.'

His gaze narrowed. 'Your reason being?'

She kept her eyes steady on his. 'A personal preference.'

'Based on?'

'A need for my own space.'

He regarded her in silence for several timeless seconds. 'The same bedroom, separate beds.' He waited a beat. 'Until you feel comfortable sharing mine.'

As if that were going to happen any time soon. 'It isn't fair you get to dictate all the terms.'

'Be grateful I've conceded one of them.'

But not for long. Apprehension rose like a spectre, and for one wild moment she wondered at her sanity in aligning herself with a man such as him.

'So, on that basis, I should fawn at your feet and express undying gratitude?'

A faint quirk lifted the corner of his mouth. 'For saving Karsouli?'

'Of course.' Her response held a certain dryness that didn't fool him in the slightest.

Honesty, at a cost. With no attempt to hide it beneath any number of platitudes. Strength and a degree of fragility, he mused, made for an intriguing mix.

Loukas retrieved the in-room dining menu, opened it at the appropriate page and handed it to her. 'Choose what you'd like, and I'll order dinner.'

Food? The mere thought of ingesting anything was enough to send her stomach into immediate revolt.

'I'm not hungry.' What was more, she wanted out of here. Away from this forceful man who held her fate in his hands.

She caught up her bag and slung the strap over one shoulder. 'I should leave.'

His eyes seared hers. 'We're not done.'

She took the few steps to move past him, only to come to a halt mere inches from where he stood. 'Yes, we are.'

'We'll share a meal, discuss wedding arrangements and relevant details, then I'll return you to your apartment.'

Alesha tilted her head a little. 'So…sit down, be quiet, and bow my head in polite servitude?'

She could almost swear she caught a faint gleam of humour on his handsome face, but then it was gone. 'I doubt the latter two form part of your repertoire.'

'How perceptive of you.' Sweet, she could do sweet, although it was impossible he missed the faint edge apparent in her voice.

Loukas offered her the menu. 'Choose, Alesha. Or I'll order for you.'

A starter would be all she could manage, and she selected one, then attempted to tune out as he picked up the phone.

A difficult feat, when the fine edge of awareness curled around her nerve-ends and heightened the tension she experienced in his presence.

A sophisticated strategist, he bore the persona of a man well versed in the ways of humankind, with the ability to see through any deliberate orchestration.

Had anyone tested his control…and escaped unscathed?

Stupid question. Why even go there? Loukas Andreou was an entity unto himself…indomitable, inviolate, and utterly ruthless.

But what of the essence of the man…as a friend, lover, husband? Would he be capable of gifting a degree of affection? *Caring?*

Or would she merely become a trophy wife…soothed by an enviable lifestyle and expensive gifts? Her life a mere facsimile?

The question had to be, was retaining Karsouli worth a

marriage she didn't want to a man who placed financial assets above all else?

Get over yourself, she denounced in silent chastisement. You thought you had *love* first time round, only to discover to your cost that it was nothing more than a nebulous dream.

At least marriage to Loukas would be unclouded by sentiment. A business arrangement she entered into with her eyes wide open…nothing more, nothing less.

Their meal, when it arrived, was beautifully presented, although Alesha barely tasted a thing as she forked morsels of food with mechanical precision.

'I have the application for a special licence,' Loukas informed her as they shared coffee. 'It requires your signature. I foresee the marriage ceremony going ahead on Friday.'

'This Friday?'

His eyes seared her own. 'Is that a problem?'

You're joking, right?

'Why the hurry?' she managed, and quelled the sudden onset of nerves playing havoc with her stomach as he queried reasonably,

'Why delay?'

Sure, and she was ready for this?

Take a *reality* check. A week, a month—even a year down the track, and she'd still never be *ready* to embark on another marriage.

Yet ever present was the instinctive knowledge there would be no second chance with Loukas if she reneged.

'Give me the application and a pen.'

She attached her signature with a sense of fatalism, then she reached for her shoulder bag, slid the strap over one shoulder and purposely made for the door. 'I'll call a taxi.'

Loukas stood, filched his jacket from the back of the chair, then he hooked it over one shoulder and reached the door ahead of her.

Okay, he could accompany her to the lift, except when it had been summoned he accompanied her into the electronic cubicle.

Courtesy was a fine thing, she acknowledged as they reached the ground floor, and she turned towards him prior to moving across the foyer. 'Goodnight.'

Without a further word she crossed to the concierge desk and made a polite but firm request, which was negated by Loukas' presence.

'The lady is with me,' he informed the concierge, and followed it with a request for his car to be brought up from valet parking.

Alesha opened her mouth to deny it, only for Loukas to direct her a piercing look. 'Don't argue.'

'There's no need—'

'Yes, there is.'

It was ridiculous, and her eyes flashed dark fire before she lowered her lashes to hide her anger at his high-handedness.

'Did you have to behave like a dictatorial ass?' Alesha demanded the instant he eased the sleek Aston Martin out onto the street.

'That's a first.' His drawled comment held a tinge of humour she chose to ignore.

'So, bite me.'

'Aren't you in the least concerned I might bite back?'

She was unprepared for the faint sensation feathering over the surface of her skin as it stirred something deep inside she had no wish to disturb.

She didn't offer so much as a word during the short drive to her apartment, and she reached for the door-clasp the instant the car slid to a halt at the kerb.

Cool, polite words born from instilled good manners emerged from her lips. 'Thanks for the ride.'

She didn't wait for his acknowledgment, nor did she look back as she swiped her card at the main entry and hurried into the foyer.

It was a relief to enter her apartment, tend to the lock and security system.

Home. A place uniquely *hers*, where she felt safe, secure.

But not for long, a tiny voice taunted. All too soon her life…*everything* would change. She slipped off her stilettos, then discarded her jacket. It wasn't late, and she was too tense to consider retiring to bed.

Television, watching a DVD, or work were three options, and she retreated to her bedroom, discarded her clothes and donned cotton sleep trousers and a singlet top before cleansing off her make-up. Then she slotted in a DVD and settled into a comfortable chair with the remote.

It was almost midnight when the credits rolled, and she switched everything off, then made her way to bed…surprisingly to sleep until the alarm roused her early next morning.

Maintaining a routine gave focus to the day, and Alesha donned sweats, slid her feet into trainers, tied back her hair, exited the apartment building and broke into a steady jog en route to a local gym.

An hour's workout helped diminish her stress levels, and she returned home with renewed vigour to shower, breakfast, then dress for work.

The executive power suit, minimum jewellery, hair smoothed into an upswept style, a light touch with make-up, killer heels…and she was good to go.

Laptop, briefcase, shoulder bag…check.

Minutes later she slid behind the wheel of her silver BMW, engaged the engine, then made her way to the main arterial road leading into the city.

Traffic at this hour was heavy, and making it through electronically controlled intersections without at least two enforced stops was rare.

Consequently it was almost eight when Alesha took the lift from the basement parking area to a high floor in the tall modern building housing the Karsouli Corporation.

A luxurious office suite with prime views over the inner harbour, expensive carpeting, sparkling glass, executive furniture and expensive works of art adorning the walls.

Dimitri had enjoyed displaying the acquisitions earned by his success. Ongoing consultations with a prominent interior decorator ensured *ostentatious* didn't figure in the scheme of things.

Alesha didn't want anything to change. In fact, she'd insist on it. Karsouli would remain Karsouli in honour of her father's memory, his years of hard work.

'Good morning.' Her smile held genuine warmth as she passed through Reception and trod the wide passageway leading to her office.

A greeting she repeated as her PA rose from behind a desk with the day's scheduling in hand.

'Mr Andreou requests your presence a.s.a.p. An executive meeting will be chaired by Mr Andreou at ten in the conference room. Department heads are currently being advised. I've noted everything in your diary, and printed a copy for your perusal.'

Alesha took the offered schedule, skimmed it, and her eyes widened fractionally.

Loukas was wasting no time in setting several contingency plans in motion.

'Thanks, Anne. You can alert Mr Andreou I'll be with him in ten minutes.'

'I understand there is some urgency to his request.'

Sufficient for Anne to issue the caution? All hail the new chief? Except the partnership with Loukas was equal. And *damned* if she'd drop everything and rush to his bidding!

'Ten minutes, Anne.'

She took every one of them before entering the large office Dimitri had occupied for as long as she could remember...and tamped down the faint resentment she experienced at seeing Loukas seated behind her father's desk.

'You wanted to see me?' The polite smile she summoned didn't reach her eyes as Loukas rose to his feet and moved forward to close the door behind her.

An action that sent the nerves in her stomach into a tangled knot.

He indicated a leather chair. 'Take a seat.' Whereupon he crossed to the desk to lean one hip against its edge.

She continued to stand. 'I hope this won't take long.'

'You'd have preferred a memo relaying I'm due in Melbourne late this afternoon to head an emergency meeting before flying on to Adelaide, then the Gold Coast?'

'You require my input?'

'Personally or professionally?'

A trick question? 'Professionally, of course.'

Of course. His eyes narrowed a little as he took in the red power suit, the killer heels, the upswept hair, and his fingers itched to loosen the pins holding the elegantly contrived knot in place.

Her choice of apparel made a statement, one she'd deliberately sought to portray, he noted silently. And wondered why she'd thought it necessary.

Because she felt threatened by him? Perhaps she had cause, professionally.

'The current state of Karsouli requires swift action, and formal meetings with each of the men who head the corporation's three out-of-state offices are imperative. Personally, not via conference call.'

Alesha didn't give him the satisfaction of verbally agreeing with him. 'When will you be back?'

'Late Thursday evening.'

'I trust you'll keep me posted. Is that all?'

One eyebrow quirked a little. 'There's the matter of our wedding details.'

Her stomach executed a painful somersault, and it took considerable effort to remain calm. 'Email me the time and venue.'

'Wolseley Road, Point Piper.' He offered the number. 'Friday, four o'clock in the afternoon.'

A slight frown creased her forehead. 'That's a private residence.' Situated amongst Sydney's most expensive real estate.

'My home, which is currently in the final stages of redecoration.'

Sufficient money could achieve almost anything…and obviously had. It explained his preference for temporary hotel accommodation.

'There's also the legalities attached to the union,' Loukas relayed smoothly. 'We have an appointment at three-thirty this afternoon to tend to the necessary paperwork.'

Ensuring everything was neatly tied together before he flew out to Melbourne, she perceived, and attempted to quell the feeling she'd boarded a runaway train from which escape would involve irreparable damage to life and limb.

'Fine.'

'There's nothing you want to add?'

A whole heap in verbal castigation…none of which would do any good! Instead, she managed a stunningly sweet smile. 'Not at this moment.'

She turned and made for the door, only to discover he was there before her, and she attempted to ignore his close proximity, the musky tang of his cologne, the sheer sensuality he managed to exude without any seeming effort at all.

Assuring herself she was immune didn't quite cut it. Nor did likening him to *all* men.

Loukas Andreou stood alone, a male entity that defied categorization.

So where did that leave *her*?

Right now…out of here!

'Ten in the conference room,' Loukas reminded her silkily as she exited the room.

A meeting he chaired with the type of ruthless strategy that left no room for doubt his proposed restructuring of Karsouli would be immediate and far-reaching.

Details were provided in individual folders placed in front of the attending executives, who were each given forty-eight hours in which to submit approval, reservations…or otherwise.

It took considerable effort on Alesha's part to contain her resentment and present a neutral front when she wanted to silently rage at his high-handedness.

She managed it, *just*, until Loukas called the meeting to a close, and she bore the carefully polite glances as the executive staff filed past her as they exited the room.

Questions would follow by the long-serving personnel, concern expressed by those whose tenure was more recent…and she'd do her best with damage control.

But *now* she had a bone to pick with the self-appointed man in control.

With care she closed the door and crossed to where Loukas stood assembling paperwork into his briefcase.

'How dare you initiate changes without consulting me?'

She resembled a pocket virago, Loukas noted. Dark eyes flashed with anger as she sent him a venomous glare. 'My father—'

'Allowed his emotions to rule, and didn't keep you apprised of the reality.'

'You can't just terminate—'

'Dimitri kept performance details on file of every employee.' He handed her a memory stick. 'Study them in my absence, together with my recommendations, and we'll confer on my return.'

'And if I don't agree?'

'We'll discuss it.'

'*We* will?' The fine edge of sarcasm was evident. 'Should I express gratitude at being slotted into your busy schedule?'

His cellphone beeped and he checked the screen. 'I need to take this call. Three-thirty, Alesha. My office.'

The temptation to throw something at him was uppermost, and she deliberately held his dark gaze, glimpsed his recognition of her intent, together with his silent threat of retribution.

For a timeless few seconds the air between them pulsed with electricity, a perilous force so overwhelming she almost forgot to breathe.

Then he activated the call, effectively dismissing her.

Panache, control, she possessed both, and she turned away from him and exited the room, closing the door with an imperceptible click behind her, when she would have delighted in slamming it. Except the door was carefully weighted to avoid anything other than a smooth, almost silent action.

She wanted badly to vent, and she would the moment she had him alone, she promised as she crossed to her office.

Three-thirty couldn't appear soon enough!

CHAPTER THREE

ALESHA spent what remained of the morning attending to the immediate business at hand, and chose to have her PA send out for a chicken and salad sandwich with mayo on rye and a double-strength latte.

Something that became a working lunch eaten at her desk as she accessed computer data, inserted reference notations, took phone calls and instructed Anne to clear an hour between three-thirty and four-thirty.

The adherence to punctuality was something Alesha considered important…personally, and professionally. And *this* was business, she qualified as she allowed time to freshen up before presenting herself at Dimitri's…dammit, *Loukas'* office on time.

He stood close to the plate-glass window with its cityscape view of the inner harbour, cellphone at his ear in quiet conversation as he gestured she take a seat.

Contrarily she opted to remain standing, and she caught his faint gleam of amusement as he continued conversing in French…with a woman, from the light tone of his voice.

A lover? Past or present? Certainly a *close* friend.

She told herself she didn't care…and, in truth, she didn't. So how did she explain the sudden warmth flooding her veins, the slow invidious curling sensation deep within?

Because she envied the woman his affectionate attention?

Oh, *please*. Get real. She no more wanted another man in her life than she wanted to fly over the moon.

Especially not *this* man. Impressive, too powerful, *too much*.

A slight shiver feathered the length of her spine. *Way* too much on a personal level.

Why not call it as it was? The forceful Greek exuded a magnetic sexuality that verged close to the primitive.

The sensual promise was *there*, almost a tangible entity, and for one wild moment she wondered what it would be like to be ravished beneath his hands, his mouth…dear God, his possession.

Soul-destroying. Utterly. Completely.

Enough already, she upbraided silently. Focus on the here and now.

Dimitri's office had undergone a few changes. State-of-the-art electronic technology replaced the standard desktop her father had preferred, several files were stacked at the end of the desk, an MP3 player. Tidy, but very much the workspace of a busy man.

'Shall we leave?'

Alesha cast Loukas a deceptively cool glance as he pocketed his cellphone, collected a briefcase, laptop, and indicated she precede him from the room.

'I'll meet you at the lawyer's office,' she indicated as the lift transported them down to the underground parking area.

'We'll go together in my car.'

'It might be easier if I follow you.'

The lift doors slid open and Loukas shot her an analytical look as they entered the concrete cavern. 'Are you determined to debate me on every issue?'

The air sizzled with a tension she refused to define. She

should cease and desist, but there was a dangerous imp sitting on her shoulder bent on mischief and mayhem.

'My apologies.' She offered him a sweet smile. 'I tend to forget most women merely *exist* to do your bidding.'

'But not you.' His drawled response held a tinge of humour.

'No,' she managed with a degree of dry mockery. 'However, in this instance I'll concede and get a taxi back to the office when we're done.'

They reached the Aston Martin and he unsecured the locking mechanism to the doors, the trunk, deposited his briefcase and laptop, then closed the trunk. 'I'll drop you off before I continue on to the airport.'

'It's out of your way.'

'Get in the car, Alesha.' His voice held a silky quality that boded ill for further argument.

She slid into the passenger seat and waited until he moved in behind the wheel before posing with deliberate sweetness, 'Are you always so appallingly arrogant?'

He ignited the engine. 'Whenever the occasion demands.'

Inner-city traffic and numerous electronically-controlled intersections ensured it took fifteen minutes to cross town, a further five to find a parking bay beneath the lawyer's office building.

Alesha was conscious of Loukas' studied look as he jabbed the call-button summoning the lift, and she tilted her head a little as she held his gaze.

'What?' she challenged. 'My mascara is smudged? Too much bronzing powder or not enough?'

'Faultless.' His silky drawl held a tinge of amusement as the lift drew to a smooth halt.

'While you resemble the quintessential male,' she responded an instant before she preceded him into the spacious reception area.

Within a very short space of time she'd sign documentation detailing precise legalese pertaining to the terms outlined in Dimitri's will. A pre-nup covering every known contingency.

Copies of which she'd already perused.

So why *now* were the nerves in her stomach tying themselves in knots?

Because each step she took brought her closer to a marriage she didn't want. To a man she had no choice but to trust on every level.

Sure, she could opt out. Except losing Karsouli was too heavy a penalty to pay.

Consequently she listened to the lawyer's clarification, the reassurance he felt beholden to relay.

When he was done, she took up a proffered pen, signed where indicated, then solemnly watched as Loukas attached his signature.

'I consider it an honour to act as a witness to your marriage on Friday. Dimitri would be very pleased with this outcome.'

Alesha managed a faint smile at the lawyer's words.

What about *her*? Didn't she count? Or was she merely a pawn in a diabolical game?

Don't go there. It's done.

Almost.

Next step…marriage.

She preceded Loukas into the lift and pressed the 'ground' button on the instrument panel.

He stood too close as he chose 'basement', and when they reached street level he merely bypassed her command and sent the lift down.

Her mouth tightened and she cast him a fulminating glare…which had no effect whatsoever.

'Give it up,' Loukas advised as the lift doors slid open and he indicated the black Aston Martin.

He waited until they were both seated before engaging the engine. 'Can I leave the choice of second witness with you?'

There was only one person she'd consider asking. Lacey Pattison, lifelong friend and trusted confidante who had, ironically, acted as chief bridesmaid at her first wedding. 'Yes.'

Was there such a thing as the sound of silence? If so, it seemed to hang heavy in the car's interior as he negotiated city traffic before easing the car into the kerb adjacent the office tower housing Karsouli.

'You have my cellphone number if you have any concerns.'

She met his dark gaze with equanimity. 'Is this where I wish you a safe flight?'

The edge of his mouth quirked a little. 'I'll be in touch Thursday evening.'

'I might be otherwise engaged with a male stripper at a very private "hen" party.' *As if.*

'In which case, have fun.'

That was it? No macho follow-up?

'Not quite.'

He read minds?

The next instant he leant forward and took her mouth with his own in a slow evocative kiss that drained the breath from her body…and then some.

There was no demand, just a sense of intent…*his.*

Then he straightened, and his eyes narrowed at her faintly dazed expression, the sudden paleness of her cheeks.

In one fluid movement she released her seat belt, caught up her bag and slid out from the passenger seat before crossing to the building's foyer without so much as a backward glance.

It was only as she rode the lift that she permitted herself to reflect.

The feel of his mouth on her own lingered, and she pressed light fingers to her lips.

What was that?

No matter how she viewed it, there had been nothing to prepare her for the unexpected sensuality evident...or her reaction.

The unbidden need to deepen the kiss was merely a transitory figment of her imagination, she dismissed as she entered Reception and moved into her office.

The phone call to Lacey resulted in a barrage of rapid-fire questions, to which only truthful answers would suffice.

'Okay,' Lacey said with deliberate calm. 'We've covered the *who, why, when* and *where*. I've done the *ohmigod* thing. Now it's down to basics. What are you going to wear?'

'I'm sure there's something suitable in my wardrobe.'

'We'll go shopping tomorrow afternoon.'

'Lacey—no.'

'*Yes*. Double Bay.' She named a place. 'I'll be there at three.'

'I don't finish until five.'

'You're the boss. Leave early.'

'You're impossible.'

'Yes, I know. That's why I'm your friend. *Three*, Alesha. Don't be late. We have a lot of ground to cover in a short time.'

She opened her mouth to protest, except the faint click indicated Lacey had already hung up.

The next morning Alesha went into the office early,

declined a lunch break and collected Lacey mid-afternoon to shop for *the* dress.

'Coffee first, double shot of caffeine, double sugar,' Alesha determined as Lacey indicated one of a few streets in exclusive Double Bay where boutiques offered designer wear with exorbitant price tags.

'Darling, *no*.' Lacey gave her a *don't mess with me* look Alesha recognized from old. 'Dress first, coffee later.'

'I need sustenance.'

'Delaying tactics,' Lacey dismissed. 'We're shopping for your *wedding dress*. Something that cannot be rushed. We need to *look*.'

'*One* boutique,' Alesha stated firmly. 'I choose, try it on, present plastic, we leave.'

Lacey's smile was pure imp dressed in steel. 'You think?'

Alesha achieved an expressive eye-roll. 'I *knew* inviting you was asking for trouble.'

'Precisely why you displayed *some* sense,' came the airy response. '*Chill*,' her friend commanded as they paused outside a small boutique with one model displayed in the window. 'Let's go inspect the merchandise, shall we?'

She uttered an expressive sigh. 'I don't think—'

'You don't *need* to think while I'm here to advise and guide.'

'That's what concerns me.'

The vendeuse greeted them with refined politeness, whereupon Lacey launched into her verbal spiel.

'White, of course.'

'Ivory,' Alesha corrected.

'Full-length,' Lacey insisted.

'Mid-calf.'

'Stunning.'

She did the eye-roll thing. 'Simple.'

'Perhaps it would help if you tell me something about the venue, the reception, the number of guests,' the vendeuse suggested.

'A civil ceremony held in a private home with two witnesses.'

'Ah. I see.' There was a faint click of the fingers as she accurately appraised Alesha's slim curves. 'I think I can offer you something suitable.'

The design was fine, the colour was not.

'It's a very pale blush.'

'Thank you, but no.'

The second boutique had the perfect gown, Chanel…except it only came in black. Alesha considered, only to be firmly outvoted by Lacey. 'You are *not* getting married in *black*.'

'Hey, whose wedding is this, anyway?'

'Yours, and just because it's not traditional, doesn't mean we won't do it *right*. Agreed?'

Lacey had a point. 'Coffee,' Alesha insisted.

'Soon, promise. Let's go.'

'Heaven forbid…*where*? I thought we had a one-stop deal.'

Lacey took hold of her arm and led the way to the car.

'Get in and drive.'

'It had better be good.'

Doing it right was achieved in a beautiful little boutique that sold vintage designer gear. Gorgeous gowns in cream, ivory…and Alesha sighed as she caught sight of sheer perfection. A slim-fitting gown in layered ivory and pale champagne silk, accented by a fine pin-tucking edged with narrow lace.

'Delicate strappy sandals with killer heels,' Lacey advised. 'Minimum jewellery, just diamond ear-studs. Maybe a bracelet.'

Alesha removed the gown, handed it to the sales person, endeavoured not to blink at the price, presented plastic and minutes later walked from the shop with a signature-emblazoned glossy carry-bag.

'Strappy sandals,' Lacey insisted. 'Then we get to have coffee. OK?'

'Thanks.' She gave her friend an impulsive heartfelt hug. 'I couldn't have done this without you.'

A light bubbling laugh emerged as Lacey initiated a high-five gesture. 'Who else, when we've been friends since for ever?'

'Sisters in every way but by blood.' *There* for each other, the first one to call.

It was later as they sat sharing coffee that Lacey adopted a serious expression. 'You so deserve to be happy.'

Alesha smiled. 'Wisdom over double-shot lattes?'

'Loukas is a good guy.'

She slanted an eyebrow. 'And you know this…because?'

'I've met him, remember? He made a lasting impression.'

Alesha took time to sip her coffee. 'That's supposed to be reassurance?'

'He's hot. Those eyes. That mouth.' Lacey gave a lascivious sigh. 'Yum…and then some.'

'*Yum?*' she queried with quizzical amusement.

'Uh-huh.'

A wicked smile widened her lips. 'I think you need food. Plus, I owe you, big time. Let's do dinner…my treat.'

Lacey laughed with delight. '*Where?*'

'Your choice.'

'Reckless. Definitely reckless.' Lacey allowed a few seconds' deliberation. 'Italian. There's this little restaurant that serves divine pasta to die for. It's the other side of town.'

Alesha rose to her feet and paid the tab. 'Let's go.'

It became a wonderfully relaxing few hours as they enjoyed fine food, a glass of wine, reminisced and laughed.

True friendship was something to be treasured, and Alesha entered her apartment at evening's end with a lighter heart.

The familiar nightmare came out of nowhere in the early pre-dawn hours, vivid, almost *live* in its intensity, and she woke breathing hard, her body soaked with sweat.

She reached for the bedside lamp and the room glowed with light.

Dear God.

She lifted a hand to her face, almost expecting in that instant to feel the heat, the swelling, the *pain*. Except her cheeks were cool, and for several long moments she worked at slowing her breathing, her rapidly beating pulse.

A silent voice prompted… *You're fine.*

In the here and *now*…and alone.

With one smooth movement she cast aside the covers and padded out to the kitchen, brewed tea, then she subsided into a comfortable chair and channel-surfed until she found a comedy and didn't move until the dawn gradually lightened the sky from indigo to pearl grey.

Then she hit the shower and dressed. Breakfast was yoghurt and fruit with a reviving shot of caffeine, before she fixed her make-up, gathered her laptop, bag, keys, and drove into the city.

Focus, concentrate on the day, Alesha urged as she rode the lift to the high floor housing Karsouli.

As days went, this one soon became a doozy, with her PA calling in sick, the replacement hesitant to take any initiative, minor delays resulting therefrom, and a laptop that decided to crash at a crucial moment. Fortunately the auto-save function ensured only a small amount of data was lost, but it took time to get the system up and running again…time that became increasingly scarce as the day progressed.

Consequently she skipped lunch, alternated coffee with bottled water, and made do with a banana mid-afternoon.

Running on empty was not advisable, and coupled with loss of sleep it tipped her into headache territory with increasing intensity.

At five she was tempted to give up, except another hour—two, tops—and she'd put the day's work to bed. Given international time-zones, the data would be accessible, and any delay minimal.

She was almost done when her cellphone buzzed, and she automatically picked up...something she rarely did without first checking caller ID.

'Alesha.'

There was no mistaking that deep, faintly accented voice. 'Hi.' As a greeting, it was sadly lacking.

'I'm on my way up.'

So he was back...and *here*. He'd said he'd call, but she hadn't counted on seeing him. Nor did she expect the slow curling sensation to begin deep within.

She wasn't alone in the building... There would be others staying back catching up on work, the cleaning staff.

Minutes later he was there, his tall frame filling the aperture, and unbidden her pulse kicked into a faster beat as he moved into her office.

'Working late?'

His voice was deceptively mild, his eyes faintly hooded as he took in her pale features, the dark circles beneath her eyes. She looked beat, almost fragile, and at a guess she was harbouring a headache.

Alesha deliberately focused her attention on the computer screen. 'And you're here...why?'

'I need to collect a file which hasn't been uploaded into the computer system.'

A mark against Dimitri's recently reassigned PA?

Her father had expected efficiency…but not to the level demanded beneath Loukas' direction.

'Tough day?'

Like you wouldn't believe. 'I'm almost done.'

'Good. You can share Chinese with me.'

She lifted her head and saw the paper sack he placed on her desk. 'You brought food?' Her stomach did a slow roll in anticipatory pleasure.

'I missed lunch.' And opted out of an in-flight meal that failed to provide sufficient sustenance to fuel a minimum four hours' work. Following an intense few days of meetings, staff reorganization, and ironing out several kinks in the Karsouli infrastructure.

He thrived on brokering high-powered deals, but Karsouli was personal. Aware of the need for a different approach from the *slash and burn* techniques for which he'd gained a formidable reputation.

The necessity to input a few hours' work didn't faze him. What he hadn't expected to see when he entered the office building's underground parking area was Alesha's silver BMW stationary in its parking bay.

Loukas heard her faint sigh as she hit *save* and closed down. With deft movements he snapped open the various containers and handed her a set of chopsticks.

'Eat.'

She did, with evident enjoyment. 'Thanks. This is so much better than a boiled egg and salad.'

'No girls' night out?'

'The male stripper called in sick.' Her response was slick,

and she was almost sure she caught a faint gleam of humour apparent in his dark eyes.

'No replacement available?'

'Unfortunately.'

His presence unsettled her. There was something about him...a dangerous sexual chemistry combined with a primitive earthy quality that promised much.

It filled her with a curious tension, combining reluctant anticipation with a sense of trepidation.

Which seemed crazy. She didn't even *like* him.

Or was that due to an emotional shutdown...hers? A case of 'if you don't think about it, it won't happen'.

Some chance.

She should leave.

With that thought in mind, she gathered her jacket, her laptop and briefcase. 'You have work to do.'

He stood up. 'I'll see you down to the car.'

'That's not necessary.'

He merely slanted an eyebrow and indicated she precede him. 'I consider it is.'

She was tempted to argue. Instead she summoned a sweet smile. 'How...' she paused, then added with delicate intent '...kind.'

Her eyes widened as he trailed light fingers down her cheek in an unexpected gesture that stole the breath from her throat.

'Get some sleep.' Then he dropped his hand, and she stood still for a few heart-stopping seconds before brushing past him.

Thankfully the lift doors opened the instant she pressed the call-button, and she moved in ahead of him, then stood in silence as the cubicle transported them swiftly down to basement level.

It took only minutes to reach her car, and she released the locking mechanism, slid behind the wheel, engaged the ignition and drove towards the ramp leading to street level without a backwards glance.

Traffic in the inner city had eased from its peak-hour exodus, and she reached her apartment with a sense of relief.

A hot shower, attired in sleepwear, a cup of tea plus a couple of painkillers in hand, she curled up in a comfortable chair to watch TV for an hour or two before she retired for the night.

On the edge of sleep came the intrusive knowledge that tomorrow she would marry Loukas.

Share his home, his bed, eventually.

How long would he allow her solitary occupation in a bed next to his own? A few nights…a week?

Did it matter?

She told herself she didn't care. Sex was just…sex. In the dark of night she could simply close her eyes and wait for the act to be over.

How difficult could it be?

CHAPTER FOUR

Two wedding days three years apart, Alesha mused as she put the finishing touches to her make-up. Each so completely different they were at opposite ends of the spectrum!

Having *done* the full bridal thing with designer dress, four bridesmaids, flower girl, page boy, the church, several hundred guests, the tiered wedding cake and exclusive reception with her marriage to Seth, the prospect of a civil ceremony by a celebrant held in the grounds of the groom's Point Piper home with Dimitri's lawyer and Lacey as witnesses seemed a breeze by comparison.

So why was she a mass of nerves?

'You look gorgeous.' Lacey's compliment was genuine, and should have acted as reassurance. Instead the nerves inside Alesha's stomach twisted into a tighter ball.

'Thanks.'

Lacey looked at the overnight bag resting at the end of the bed. 'Is that all you're taking with you?'

'It's enough for the weekend.'

'Darling,' Lacey chided. 'You're *moving* in with Loukas. Permanently. You need to *pack*.'

'I'll shift some of my stuff tomorrow.'

'Hello?' The admonishment held a degree of musing scepticism.

Arguing with Lacey was a losing battle as her friend flung open wardrobe doors, drawers, and quickly transferred a varied assortment of apparel into a suitcase.

'Okay, we're out of here.'

Second thoughts? She had a few! Primarily, relating to her sanity!

Yet as tempting as it would be to bail out, there was the overriding knowledge that she'd *agreed* to this marriage. What was more, she'd signed legal documentation confirming it.

So *suck it up,* Alesha chastised as she negotiated traffic and headed towards suburban Point Piper, with Lacey following close behind.

Loukas' home was positioned behind a high wall and entered between stylish gates that opened onto a curved driveway leading to a double-storeyed mansion whose imposing entry was guarded by two massive ornamental-studded wooden doors.

She brought the BMW to a smooth halt behind a late-model four-wheel drive, and Lacey parked directly behind her.

No sooner had she cut the engine than both entry doors opened to reveal Loukas in the wide aperture.

His tall, broad-shouldered frame attired in an immaculate dark suit appeared slightly intimidating as he moved towards her.

There was little she could do to control the sudden fluttering inside her stomach as he held open the door for her to emerge.

'Alesha.' His close proximity, his dark watchful gaze merely accelerated her nervous tension, for soon, within the space of an hour or less, she'd enter into a legal union with this man…and her life would change.

Concern as to just *how* it would change affected her more than she imagined possible.

Would Loukas suddenly assume another identity within hours of the wedding...as Seth had?

The mere thought was enough to send an element of fear shivering the length of her spine, and the smile she summoned appeared over-bright and failed to reach her eyes.

Did he notice? She hoped not.

The faint sound of an engine caught her attention, and she turned slightly as a vehicle slid to a halt behind Lacey's car.

'The gang's all here.' She kept her voice light as Lacey joined them, followed closely by Dimitri's lawyer.

Loukas ushered them into a spacious foyer whose floor featured beautiful marble tiling in a large circular star-burst design, above whose centre an exquisite crystal chandelier provided prisms of light.

Antique tables, exquisitely crafted chairs, wall sconces, paintings, graced an area whose focal point was a sweeping double marble staircase featuring ornate wrought-iron balustrades leading to an upper floor balcony that divided into two separate galleried wings showcased by matching ornate wrought-iron balustrades.

'Come through to the lounge,' Loukas directed with ease. 'Everything is set up there.'

Alesha moved on autopilot, so acutely conscious of his presence at her side that she barely noticed the beautiful sofas and chairs, the amazingly high ceilings.

Instead she focused on the small table with its exquisite lace-edged linen cloth, the votive candle, a delicate spray of cream orchids, and a leather-bound Bible.

Introductions complete, the celebrant conferred with the lawyer, exchanged small talk, then she opted to begin the ceremony.

You can do this.

As an affirmation, it didn't begin to scratch the surface!

Almost as if he knew, Loukas captured her hand and held it loosely within his own.

To prevent her sudden need to escape? It was a moot point!

Alesha heard the solemn beautifully spoken words, and on some level she took them in, and managed to recite the vows that united her with Loukas in matrimony...aware his vows held a calm solemnity that was lacking in her own.

He slid a wide diamond-studded ring onto her finger, surprised her by lifting her hand and brushing the ring with his lips, before offering a ring for her to slip onto his finger.

He was prepared to wear a wedding ring?

Her fingers shook a little as she slid it on, and his hand covered hers as he used a little pressure to slide it home.

'It gives me great pleasure to pronounce you husband and wife.' The celebrant bestowed the gathered foursome a pleasant smile. 'And introduce Alesha and Loukas Andreou.' Loukas lifted both hands and cradled Alesha's head, then he covered her mouth with his own in a fleeting sensual caress.

Oh, my. There had to be some explanation for the slow curl of sensation unfurling deep within her. Almost as if her body was at variance with the dictates of her mind.

How could she even begin to think what it would be like to have him invite a more intimate touch, to feel his hands on her body, his lips tasting an evocative trail, teasing, encouraging her response.

The question had to be *could* he succeed? When she'd left Seth she'd locked the door to her emotional heart and thrown away the key. And vowed never to allow another man to get close.

Alesha became conscious of Lacey's laughter as she was enveloped in a hug; the voiced congratulations from the lawyer, the celebrant; Loukas' hand resting against the back of her waist before he released her to open the champagne cooling in an ice bucket.

Smile, a silent voice prompted. You're supposed to be happy. The future of Karsouli is secure, and your future is safe...if *safe* could be attributed to the man whose ring she now wore.

So play the game expected of you. *Pretend*. Haven't the past few years provided plenty of practice?

Consequently she accepted a flute of champagne, smiled at the toast Lacey proposed to happiness and a blessed future, and managed to nibble a proffered canapé from a silver platter presented by Loukas' housekeeper, Eloise.

The celebrant took her leave, and conversation flowed with ease for a while until the lawyer indicated a pressing engagement and Lacey followed suit as she pressed a light kiss to Alesha's cheek before turning to Loukas.

'Take good care of her.'

'I intend to do so.'

Together they moved through the foyer to the main entrance where Loukas opened the door.

'Drive carefully.'

'Always.'

There was the sound of heels tapping along the driveway, the beep of a security remote, followed by the solid clunk of a car door closing and the purr of an engine as Lacey drove away.

Alesha watched as the car eased down the driveway, saw the accented red of brake lights as Lacey slowed at the gates, then the car disappeared from sight.

She was extremely conscious of the man who stood at her side, his easy movements as he closed both doors and activated the security system.

The house...*mansion*, she corrected, seemed incredibly large, not to mention an unknown entity, for, although she assumed the bedroom suites were situated upstairs, she had no idea precisely which wing contained the master suite.

Loukas indicated the curved staircase. 'Eloise will have transferred your bag upstairs.'

'Is this the part where you give me a guided tour?'

'You'd prefer to explore on your own?'

She crossed to the staircase and began ascending the wide marble stairs, aware he joined her. 'I might get lost.'

'It's quite simple. Personal suites and home office situated to the left, guest suites to the right. Ground floor, formal and informal lounge and dining rooms, media, home theatre, kitchen, utilities. Lower floor, gym, entertainment room, indoor pool. Outdoor pool. Self-contained flat for staff over detached garages.'

They reached the gallery and turned to the left. 'It's a large home for one man.' An observation that incurred his steady appraisal.

'A man who has very recently acquired a wife,' he reminded silkily.

Loukas opened a set of double-panelled doors to reveal a spacious master bedroom, containing two king-size beds.

So he'd kept his word.

She told herself she should be relieved...and she was. Except sharing the same room implied a certain intimacy with which she felt distinctly uncomfortable. There were two separate en suites, two dressing rooms and a recessed alcove furnished with two comfortable chairs and standard lamps.

It was, she had to admit, incredible. Luxurious, with spectacular views over the harbour to the cityscape. Magic at nightfall when the city was lit up and varied coloured neon flashed with advertisements atop many of the inner-city buildings.

He shrugged out of suit jacket, dispensed with his tie and loosened the top button of his shirt.

For a moment she caught her breath at his intention, and he glimpsed the fleeting apprehension evident before it was quickly masked.

'You might want to change into something less formal.'

She reminded him of a skittish foal in an unfamiliar environment…one who had experienced fear, possibly damage, with every reason to mistrust.

'Eloise has unpacked your bag.' Loukas indicated the dressing room she would use. 'Tomorrow we'll shift the remainder of your belongings.'

'I can manage on my own.'

'You won't need to.'

So give up the independent streak, accept two pairs of hands are better than one, and some masculine strength for the bag-carrying is a *good* thing.

Slipping into something more comfortable depended on what items of clothing Lacey packed, and she crossed into her allocated dressing room to check the meagre assortment.

Jeans didn't cut it, but tailored trousers with a cotton top would do.

Minutes later she emerged to find Loukas standing close to the wide expanse of glass taking in the panoramic scene.

The white shirt accentuated the impressive breadth of his shoulders, and his shirt cuffs had been folded back to rest midway up his forearms, lending a casual air.

Deceptive, she knew, for he could move with the silent stealth of a primitive cat and reduce an adversary to speechlessness with a few sentient words.

She watched as he turned towards her, and the breath caught in her throat.

He was someone she'd known for a number of years, as the son of Dimitri's closest friend, a man whose company she'd shared with her parents' friends and business associates on a few occasions at various social events. Instinctively aware, even then, that when he played, he played to win…in business, and with women.

Through circumstance he'd won Karsouli…together with her as part of the package.

'Shall we go eat?'

Food wasn't foremost on her mind, although she sipped excellent vintage wine, sampled succulent morsels from no less than three courses, while engaging in meaningless conversation.

The economic state of the nation and the world's foremost leaders made for interesting debate and carried the hour with relative ease. Something for which she was immensely grateful.

'Do you still have regular contact with Lacey?'

Alesha wondered if Loukas' query related to genuine interest, or merely a shift to the more personal.

'Regularly,' she answered lightly. 'We share dinner each week, occasionally take in a movie. Go shopping together.'

'I seem to recall you were a keen advocate of tennis. Do you still play?'

'Not as often as I used to.' She took an appreciative sip of fine wine. 'Do you still travel extensively?'

'My father prefers to remain in Greece these days.' He affected a slight shrug. 'Andreou has offices in London, Milan and New York, and I alternate between each of them while overseeing the main office in Athens.'

'And now you've added Sydney to the equation.'

One eyebrow lifted in sardonic query. 'That still bothers you?'

'I have no alternative but to accept it.'

'It's a little late to change your mind.'

'How are your parents? Your sister Lexi?'

'They're well. My mother is on various committees, which consume some of her time. Lexi designs handcrafted jewellery and has a studio in the Pláka.'

'And your Aunt Daria?' It was a polite query and resulted in a musing smile.

'She remains a force to be reckoned with.'

Plain-spoken to the point of bluntness, Alesha remembered as she recalled a visit to Athens with her parents several years ago when they'd spent time with Angelina and Constantine Andreou.

'That appears to take care of family and friends,' Alesha managed lightly. 'Should we move on to the more personal? The master breeding plan, perhaps? I trust you're aware the male sperm determine the sex of the child?' She spared him a pseudo-intelligent look. 'I refuse to bear any blame if we produce only girls.'

Alesha glimpsed his faint smile. 'Why, when their mother is a fine example of what women can achieve?'

'An attempt to soften me up for the inevitable consummation?' She was heading down a dangerous path, and she silently damned her runaway tongue.

'The chemistry we share bothers you?'

Bother was too tame a description!

'And chemistry is an automatic guarantee for satisfaction between the sheets?'

What is the matter with you? a silent voice screamed inside her head. Are you *insane*?

'Did your ex gift you that?'

She silently damned herself for metaphorically opening a vein. 'You expect me to answer such a question?'

He was silent for several seconds…seconds during which she found it difficult to hold his gaze. 'You just did.'

It would be so easy to tell him to go to hell, and she almost did. Except sanity ruled her tongue and she maintained a dignified silence. He had depth of character, a silent strength that had been lacking in Seth…although she hadn't seen it at the time.

Blinded by what she imagined to be love, Alesha decided with cynicism. Seth had played his part well…as she'd soon discovered.

This, her second wedding night, was so vastly different from that of her first wedding when she'd been surrounded by family and friends, and filled with love for her new husband and barely containing a breathless excitement for the night when she and Seth were alone.

A faint bubble of cynical amusement rose in her throat to remain unuttered.

She'd thought being in love resolved everything, except it hadn't. The magical wedding night she'd imagined didn't happen due to her new husband imbibing vintage champagne a little too freely. And the sex had been…less than she'd imagined it would be. Afterwards, when she had refused to give in to his demands that they upgrade their home and lifestyle, and allow him an unlimited expense account, the sex had become a punishment she had endeavoured to avoid…to her cost. And she'd walked away, vowing never to be taken in by another man in her lifetime.

Yet here she was, a few hours into a second marriage she didn't want to the man of her father's choice. Sharing the same room in separate beds…for how long? One night…two?

After all, in the dark of night, sex was just…sex. No big deal. Right?

So why did she feel like a cat treading hot bricks?

Because instinct warned she was way out of her depth with a man of Loukas' calibre. There was something about him, an intrinsic, almost raw sexuality that bordered on the primitive.

Intoxicating, brazen, shameless.

A part of her ached for the experience, while sanity cautioned she might not survive with her emotions intact.

It was almost a relief when Eloise entered the dining room to clear the table, and Alesha elected tea in preference to the strong espresso Loukas favoured.

How soon could she conceivably offer an excuse and retire to bed? Another hour or two? Did Loukas have anything planned?

A tiny bubble of laughter rose in her throat. *Sure*...like they'd settle comfortably in the media room and watch a movie on DVD?

Resorting to cynical humour was a defence mechanism she chose to employ against an increasing onset of nervous tension.

'I have a few international calls to make.' Loukas studied her expressive features, and it was almost as if he knew the pattern of her thoughts. 'Maybe an hour or two ahead of me on the computer as the business day begins in Europe.'

Her relief was palpable, and she only hoped it wasn't evident. 'Sure. Go for it.' She stood and moved away from the table, aware he did the same, and she preceded him from the room, then headed for the upper level.

Tomorrow she'd familiarize herself with the house and its several levels...but for now she ascended the curved staircase and made her way along the gallery to their suite.

Her choices numbered many: a leisurely soak in the spa-bath; slipping into bed with a book—if she could locate one. Sliding between the covers of one of the two beds and attempting to sleep.

As if she'd be able to do that, when every nerve in her body would be alert and tuned into Loukas' appearance.

Two beds…would he sleep alone, or choose to share her own?

Hell. She didn't even know *which* bed was his.

What if she selected the wrong bed and he took it as an invitation to share?

Dammit, since when had she become so ambivalent?

Since her separation and divorce from Seth, she'd regained her independence, healed, and forged a reputation as a confident savvy young businesswoman who'd earned her rightful position as Dimitri Karsouli's colleague.

Very little, if anything, fazed her. Certainly not a man of any calibre…except Loukas.

She'd stayed away from him, careful not to show so much as a glimmer more than mere friendship. Aware, even from the first moment she'd met him that he was more than she could handle.

Light and dark, mesmeric…possessed of a sensual power that electrified and frightened. Because she instinctively knew he'd want it all…the heart of a woman, her body, her soul.

And she couldn't *be* that woman. Didn't want to be *absorbed* so totally that there was nothing left except him.

Now, she didn't know. So much had changed. *She* had changed.

No longer did she believe in love. At least, not the happy-ever-after enduring kind that lasted a lifetime.

Nor did she intend to place her trust in any man.

Once burned by flame, it was the height of foolishness to toy with it again.

For timeless minutes she stood taking in the superb furnishings in the spacious suite. Despite the luxurious accoutrements there was an underlying air of comfort that held appeal. The muted colours aided relaxation, and she wondered if they'd been a deliberate choice by the interior decorator responsible for creating the refurbishment.

Decisiveness had to be a plus, she perceived as she collected sleepwear and moved into the en suite where the spa-bath beckoned invitingly.

Mellow, she coveted the slow slide into the kind of relaxation that aided an easy sleep. Hopefully way before Loukas entered the room, so she wouldn't be aware of his presence until morning…and maybe not even then, if he rose early to make use of the downstairs gym.

Heaven, Alesha breathed as she sank into the warm bubbling water and positioned her head against the cushioned rest.

Ten minutes, she allowed…then she'd switch off the jets, release the water, dry off, and slip into bed.

It was almost midnight when Loukas closed down the laptop and muted the desk lamp. He'd spoken to Constantine in the Athens office, liaised with two colleagues in Paris, another in Rome. There'd been data to peruse to which he added his input, and the stock markets.

He lifted his arms and stretched, easing out the kinks in his shoulders, then he sat in contemplative silence for several long minutes before rising to his feet.

In the kitchen he filled a glass with chilled water, drank it down, then he checked the security system and moved quietly upstairs.

The master bedroom suite bore the softened light from muted lamps, and it took only a brief glance to determine both beds were empty.

A slight frown creased his forehead as he crossed to the en

suite, knocked quietly, and when there was no answer he opened the door.

For a moment he stood taking in the scene...the soft pulsing jets in the spa-bath, the slender feminine form whose facial features in repose looked peaceful, almost childlike and bare of artificial enhancements.

Her soft, slightly parted mouth almost begged the touch of his own. Fine, almost porcelain skin moulded delicate bone structure, a perfect nose, and long natural eyelashes fanned out from petal-like eyelids.

He moved quietly towards the bath and switched off the jets, then he collected one of several large folded bath-towels and spoke her name.

There was no sign she heard him, and his gaze skimmed over her slender curves, the soft swell of her breasts with their tender peaks, the delicate waist, flat stomach with its slim gold pin with a strategically placed diamond attached to her navel. A cheeky jewellery accessory that winked and gleamed beneath the water's surface.

He felt the stirring of arousal, and banked it down.

'Alesha.' His voice was firm, and he caught the faint flutter of her eyelashes. 'Wake up.'

He saw the moment his words penetrated her subconscious, the sudden upwards sweep of her lashes as she came awake, and the stark mix of startled surprise and fear in the depths of her eyes the instant before she recognized him and gained the reality of her surroundings.

'It's after midnight,' he said quietly. 'You fell asleep.'

Loukas glimpsed her attempt to control the fleeting expressions chasing her features, saw the embarrassment change to indignation as she automatically used her hands to shield the vulnerable parts of her body.

'Leave the towel and go…*please.*'

He was tempted to release the water, scoop her out and wrap her in the towel, then carry her to bed. *His.*

Except when he took her, it would be because she wanted him, not an act she conceded out of duty or mere compliance.

He might be many things, and he'd been called on several…but he stood by his word.

So he did as she requested and closed the door behind him, then he shed his clothes, took a cool shower, and slid between the sheets to lie with his arms crossed behind his head.

He watched idly as she emerged into the bedroom attired in cotton sleep trousers and a singlet top, looking impossibly young.

A slight smile widened his generous mouth as she avoided meeting his gaze, and he waited until she slipped beneath the covers before closing the lamps.

'Goodnight.' His voice was an indolent drawl in the darkness, and he only just heard her muffled response.

CHAPTER FIVE

ALESHA woke to light filtering through partly closed shutters along the wall of glass facing east.

For a brief moment she felt slightly disorientated by her unfamiliar surroundings, then memory surfaced as she cautiously examined the spacious room.

Specifically the large bed next to the one she'd occupied through the night...and she experienced a sense of relief to find it empty.

She brushed a hand through her hair and checked the time, saw it was almost eight, and hurriedly slid from the bed before gathering up fresh clothes and disappearing into the en suite to complete her morning routine and dress.

Jeans and a stylish tee sufficed, and she caught her hair in a ponytail, added gloss to her lips, then she made her way downstairs to the kitchen.

Coffee would be good, breakfast even better, and she entered the spacious, beautifully appointed kitchen to discover Eloise stacking the dishwasher, with no sign of Loukas in sight.

'Good morning.' Alesha kept it light and offered a warm smile, which the housekeeper returned in kind.

'It's a lovely day,' Eloise added. 'What can I get you for breakfast?'

'If it's okay with you, I'll make coffee, and just grab some cereal and fruit, and take it out onto the terrace.'

'I can easily prepare a cooked breakfast if you'd prefer.'

'Thanks, but cereal is fine.'

There was something infinitely relaxing in looking out over the harbour. Small and large craft sprinkled the sparkling Port Jackson waters; tugboats guided a massive tanker towards the wharves, while ferries cruised the distance between the city and Manly.

The cityscape bore tall modern high-rise buildings in varying architectural designs, their plate-glass windows glinting as the sun rose in the sky.

No matter where she'd travelled, Sydney was *home*. The place of her birth and education. It held *familiarity* for her. Memories, all of them good...until Seth. And just as she emerged whole and healed, she was flung into the unknown again by her father's hand.

'Finish your coffee, then we'll collect the rest of your belongings from the apartment.'

Loukas had the silent tread of a cat, and she replaced her cup down onto its saucer with care before she turned to meet his gaze.

Attired in jeans and a chambray shirt, he bore a deceptively casual air that was the antithesis of the man he'd proven himself to be.

It was the eyes, Alesha perceived. Dark silken depths that were too perceptive for anyone's peace of mind...especially hers.

Oh, why not admit it? He unsettled her, increasing her vulnerability to a point where she felt constantly on edge in his presence.

'I can manage to do that on my own.'

'You don't need to.'

'What if I prefer to?'

'Give it up, Alesha.'

She tilted her head and held his gaze with equanimity. 'I was unaware taking your name meant alienating my freedom of choice.'

He rested a hip against the edge of the table and leant towards her, not exactly crowding her in, but close…too close.

'You prefer the difficult route to a simple one?' He waited a beat as her eyes darkened at his proximity. 'Or do you merely enjoy debating me?'

She resembled a startled foal whenever he encroached on her personal space, and his gaze narrowed fractionally as the pulse at the base of her throat began to visibly thud.

'You lucked out if you want a subservient wife who will agree with your every word.'

'It should make for an interesting life.'

Her smile was deliberate. 'You think?'

Loukas stood to his feet. 'Collect your keys, then we'll leave. Presumably you've forgotten one of Dimitri's charitable causes is hosting an event this evening and our presence is expected?'

He glimpsed the conflicting emotions pass fleetingly across her expressive features before she managed to control them. 'I doubt you packed a suitable gown.'

She hadn't. Neither gown nor shoes, nor evening clutch.

Surely she had the event entered in her diary? Yet she'd neglected to check…understandable given her father's sudden death, the funeral, Dimitri's will. Dammit, her *marriage*.

But *tonight*? She could have put in a token appearance even with Loukas as her partner as a matter of respect. But wearing Loukas' wedding ring, how long would it take for the inevitable question to arise? The speculation?

Dear heaven, the need to maintain some form of pretence as Alesha *Andreou*?

She didn't want to go there…at least, not so *soon*. Yet she'd been raised with a strong sense of duty, a respect for bona fide charitable causes, and this evening's fundraiser was indeed a special one, fostering a terminally ill child with the opportunity to fulfil a much revered wish.

Alesha gathered her crockery and flatware together and deposited both in the kitchen before she ascended the stairs to collect her keys.

She caught sight of Loukas waiting in the foyer as she re-entered the upstairs gallery, and she ran lightly downstairs.

'I'll be a while.'

It was a parting shot, a last-ditch attempt for independence that failed miserably as he swung open one of the two solid-panelled doors and indicated the four-wheel drive parked in the driveway.

'Let's go.'

She threw him a fulminating look that had no visible effect whatsoever, and they rode the distance to Double Bay in silence.

The apartment was exactly as she'd left it, and she became extremely conscious of Loukas' presence as he overrode every objection she made.

Okay, so she'd transfer all her clothes, shoes and personal possessions. Any decision about the furniture and the apartment itself could wait. The practical side voted she maintain it as was. Logically, she should lease it out.

Except it bore her personal stamp, with everything carefully chosen to create a perfect blend of muted colours, a kitchen to die for, beautifully elegant furniture and furnishings.

Hers alone…a sanctuary representing a personal triumph

through darkness to light, the re-emergence of strength and resolve.

'I'll clear the tallboy and dresser drawers while you take the wardrobe.'

She looked at him askance.

He intended to gather together her personal stuff? Lingerie, briefs, bras?

'I'll take care of those.'

Except he was already there, opening a drawer and scooping up pastel silk thongs, satin briefs, lacy bras and transferring them into a packing box.

'Must you?' she flung with exasperation, barely quelling the urge to hit him.

His husky chuckle incensed her, and she reacted without thought, aiming the shoe she held in her hand with accuracy, only to watch in stunned disbelief as he fielded it and placed it down with care.

His smile was still in place, but the expression in his dark eyes sent chills scudding the length of her spine.

'You want to play?'

Not the sort of game he had in mind, and she silently damned her foolish action. 'I don't *do* sex in the middle of the day.'

One eyebrow lifted in cynical humour. 'You prefer furtive foreplay beneath the cover of darkness?'

As Seth had? Ensuring any strike came without warning, and the advantage became his?

In the animal kingdom, she qualified, Seth was akin to a reptile—while Loukas came from an entirely different species...primitive, highly sensual, and infinitely dangerous. A very sexual man, whose reputation with women was legend.

And now he was hers.

Or more accurately...she was *his*.

Something moved in her eyes, then was quickly gone.

Loukas' gaze narrowed as he glimpsed the fine hold she had on her emotions, and how unaware she was that he could so easily read them.

Just what was it about her brief marriage that had changed her from a delightful young woman possessed of an engaging personality into someone who rarely laughed and shied away from men?

Abuse? Physical, mental…or both?

The extent of his anger at the possibility surprised him, and he banked it down as he turned his attention to the next drawer. 'Let's get this done.'

Methodical placement of clothes being her *thing* made for easy transference from wardrobe to packing boxes, and she focused on the chore at hand while attempting to ignore Loukas' presence.

Difficult, she acknowledged, when he was *there*, a physical entity that filled her with an edgy awareness and made her supremely conscious of every breath she took.

Tonight…she really didn't want to think about the evening, or how much it would cost her to play an expected part at Loukas' side. To smile, converse and *pretend*.

You'll be fine, Alesha silently assured herself as she slid the zip fastener home on an exquisite gown in deep emerald green whose off-the-shoulder design hugged her slender curves. She opted to leave her hair loose, and employed the skilful use of make-up to highlight her eyes and accent her generously moulded mouth.

Six-thirty for seven meant leaving the house at six, and she attached diamond studs to her ears, added a matching pendant on a slim gold chain, only to have the clasp prove difficult.

'Problems?' Loukas crossed to stand behind her, and she held her breath as his fingers brushed her own as he slid the clip into place.

The exclusive tones of his cologne teased her senses, and she stood still, unable in those long seconds to do anything but breathe.

He seemed to surround her, a magnetic force that caused her body to pulse, irrespective of the dictates of her brain.

For one wild moment she wondered if he knew.

Dear heaven, she hoped not.

'Ready?'

She stepped away from him and collected her evening clutch. 'Yes.'

As ready as she'd ever be, she vowed silently as the Aston Martin swept through streets slick from an early evening shower.

She'd done this before, many times. Attending various functions in the company of her parents, and partnering Dimitri after her mother's death.

So what was the big deal?

You can do this, Alesha assured herself again as Loukas slid the car to a halt adjacent the main entry of one of Sydney's prestigious hotels.

With smooth efficiency the concierge arranged valet parking, and she entered the hotel foyer at Loukas' side.

A magnificent wide staircase curved to a mezzanine level where guests were gathered in the spacious lounge adjacent the grand ballroom.

Uniformed waiters and waitresses offered canapés, champagne and orange juice.

Smile. Do the meet-and-greet thing, comment on the attendance, assure Karsouli's continued support to members of the charity committee…and refer any awkward questions to Loukas.

Simple. At least it should have been.

Except she neglected to factor in Loukas' constant company, the touch of his hand at the back of her waist, the effect his warm smile had on her equilibrium. Dammit, their projected togetherness.

It was inevitable the wide diamond-encrusted wedding ring on her left hand would eventually capture attention. Coupled as it was with the plain gold band Loukas now wore, conclusions were reached and the more emboldened requested confirmation.

The news spread, with almost comical circumspection if one was inclined towards cynical amusement.

'Darling, how wonderful happiness should evolve from such recent sadness.' Words expressed by the charity committee member were genuine, and Alesha accepted the air-kiss, the obligatory hug as others followed.

Men, captains of industry, who took the opportunity to shake Loukas' hand and offer congratulations. And women, some of whom expressed their affection a little more enthusiastically to Loukas than the occasion demanded.

Two in particular, known for their flirting skills and love of high-living.

Alesha assured herself she didn't care when the exquisite blonde melded her body close and wound her arms round Loukas' neck.

To his credit, he moved his head so the intended kiss brushed the edge of his jaw, and he summoned a faint smile as he disentangled the blonde's arms.

A sparkling laugh, the hint of a moue, then the blonde turned towards Alesha. 'Darling, he's delicious. If you hadn't snared him first…' The words trailed to a halt, with no doubt of the implication.

Darling, Alesha was sorely tempted to redress, you'd have been most welcome. Instead she offered a sweet smile, and barely managed to contain her surprise as Loukas lifted her hand and brushed his lips to her sensitive palm.

For a brief moment the room and everyone in it faded as her eyes locked with his, and the air between them seemed filled with electric tension.

Then he smiled, and curled her hand within his own. 'Fortunately, she did.'

Oh, my…*what was that*?

Playing the part, a tiny imp taunted. And he does it so well.

'Pity,' the blonde voiced with seeming regret. 'We could have had fun.' With a pretty wave of her hand the blonde turned and melted into the crowd.

'You can let go now,' Alesha managed quietly, attempting to pull free without success, for he merely threaded his fingers through her own. She kept her voice light and a smile in place. 'Must you?'

'Yes.'

He glimpsed sudden pain darken her eyes, then it was gone.

It was perhaps as well the ballroom doors opened and the assembled guests converged towards the three main entry points.

Their table held prominent position, and the usual speeches included gratitude for previous funding together with a plea for the guests' continuing generosity.

The drinks flowed, entertainment was provided between each of the three dinner courses, and it wasn't until coffee was served that there was the opportunity for any lengthy conversation.

A DJ set discs spinning at one end of the ballroom and provided a mix of music. A time of the evening when some of the older guests began to leave, and the younger set filled the adjoining floor-space.

'Shall we?'

Dance? With him?

She had, on a few occasions in the past. Way past, when her life had been uncomplicated and she'd viewed the future as a journey of discovery.

Following her separation from Seth, the only male she'd chosen to dance with had been her father...occasions when she'd felt protected, *safe*.

Loukas and *safe* didn't equate.

In the name of heaven, *get a grip*. She was in a room filled with people, and she was being too ridiculous for words.

'Sure, why not?' she managed simply.

Except being held by him was far from simple. Even in killer heels she was conscious of his height, his restrained strength and his sexual energy.

One hand lingered at the base of her spine, and she barely controlled a faint shivery sensation as his thumb brushed a gentle pattern over the delicate bones.

If he sought to soothe, the caress had the opposite effect, and she dug her lacquered nails into his hand in a silent plea to desist.

A fruitless exercise as he drew her close, splaying the hand at her spine to hold her there.

Worse, the DJ selected a slow, seductive number and the lights dimmed low, providing a level of intimacy that made her want to pull away from him.

She tried, without success, and everything within her co-alesced and became one highly sensitized ache. It made her want something she'd thought she once held in her grasp...only to be cheated as her emotional dreams were smashed into a thousand pieces.

Please, she silently begged. I can't do this.

I want my life back…the one I carefully rebuilt for myself. No emotional ties, no room for disappointment and heartache.

'I think we've managed a sufficiently convincing display,' Alesha offered evenly, and wondered if Loukas had any idea of the effort it had cost her not to tear herself away from him.

'You've had enough?'

Enough of *what*? Being held intimately close to him? Playing pretend? Why not go for broke and include *both*, with emphasis on the former?

He sounded mildly amused, and she deliberately stood on his foot.

'I'm so sorry,' she said sweetly.

'No, you're not.' He eased her to the edge of the dance floor, then began leading the way to their table.

The 'goodnight' thing took a while, and it was a relief to leave the ballroom and descend the stairs to the hotel foyer.

The concierge summoned their car, and within minutes the Aston Martin appeared in the forecourt.

Alesha slid into the passenger seat, fastened the seat belt, then she eased her head against the cushioned rest and closed her eyes.

Home, bed. And, mercifully, a restful sleep.

Except home was no longer her apartment, and it was late, which meant Loukas probably was unlikely to run an electronic check of the world markets before heading for bed.

'Headache?'

Her eyelids lifted and she turned towards him. It would be so easy to say *yes*, and she almost did. Except honesty had her shaking her head.

The night cast the car's interior with a shadowy light, throwing his profile into stark angles.

He was something else. Sophisticated, powerful…yet beneath that persona lurked a man she found difficult to fathom. Content, apparently, to enter a loveless marriage and sire progeny sans emotional involvement.

What was it with that?

She knew all the issues. Hadn't she agreed to them? Although *agree* didn't enter the equation. Choice had weighed heavily against her.

A situation that pushed her to the edge and kept her there.

'You handled the evening well.'

His silky drawl curled round her nerve-ends and pulled them to breaking point.

'While you excelled.'

'A compliment?'

She looked at him carefully. 'Of course. What else?'

'I doubt your foot's deliberate aim was accidental.'

'Really?' Alesha managed sweetly.

Loukas smiled. She was a refreshing change from the women who formed part of his business and social entourage. Women who knew how to please and were forthcoming in offering to share his bed.

Easy pickings, he reflected without shame. Aware few, if any, had any thought beyond the advantages of his wealth, the gifts, the travel, the media attention his presence gained.

It was after midnight when he garaged the car and reset the security system.

Alesha made for the staircase, reaching their suite ahead of him, and she slipped off her heels, removed her ear-studs and reached for the clasp holding her pendant in place.

Stiff, it still refused to release, and she muttered an unlady-like oath beneath her breath.

'Let me.'

She hadn't heard him enter the room, and she held her breath as his fingers brushed her nape. Within seconds he freed the recalcitrant clasp and dropped the pendant into her palm.

'Thanks.'

His eyes were dark, slumbrous, as he laid a finger beneath her chin and tilted it. 'So...thank me.'

The wayward pulse at the base of her throat began its rapid thudding beat, and her eyes flared as he lowered his head down to hers.

'Don't—'

Whatever else she meant to utter didn't find voice as his mouth took hers in a kiss that grazed her lips with sensual promise, warm, caressing with deliberate intent as he sought her response.

One hand shifted to cup her nape while the other slid to the base of her spine and he drew her in against him.

Awareness flared as he deepened the kiss, his tongue an erotic force that sent the blood sizzling through her veins, flooding her inner core with a piercing sweetness until she became lost...wanting, *needing* on some subliminal level to superimpose a different image from the cruel taunts she'd received beneath Seth's hands.

It would be so easy to close her eyes and let whatever happen...*happen*.

She felt him reach for the zip fastening on her gown, sensed the slow slide as the silk slithered down her body. All she wore was a satin thong brief, and the breath hitched in her throat as he cupped her breasts and began exploring their contours, stroking each tender peak until she became powerless against the pleasurable sigh emerging from her lips.

His mouth possessed her own...persuasive, evocative, as his hand shaped her waist, then slid low to seek her swollen clitoris.

Unbidden, she arched against him, unaware of the sensual sound she made as he skilfully brought her to climax, held her there, then he probed her silken heat in readiness for his possession.

It was the intrusion that brought her to a shuddering halt, and she froze, catapulted into a stark reality where past and present images merged and became one.

Panic born from fear lent her strength as she wrenched her mouth from his own, before she railed her fists against his shoulders in a bid to be free of him.

The air in her lungs escaped in tortuous gasps as he released her, and she could only look at him in shocked dismay.

Her lips parted, but no sound emerged, and she hugged her arms together, emotionally bereft and unable to control the way her body began to shake.

Dear God. She wanted to run and hide, except escape wasn't the answer. *Hell...* what could she say?

Any explanation would take her to a place she didn't want to go. Yet how could she not?

Her eyes widened as Loukas lifted a hand, and she instinctively took a protective backward step...a reaction that brought his narrowed gaze.

He caught the stark fear evident before she successfully masked it, and he fought against a silent rage as he reached for his discarded jacket and placed it carefully round her shoulders.

'I'm sorry.' Her voice was little more than a whisper as she instinctively caught the edges and hugged them close, barely registering the jacket was way too large on her slender frame.

Not nearly as regretful as he felt, Loukas perceived. For more reasons than the one she presumably referred to. The ache in his groin would subside...eventually. Her issue with intimacy was something else.

It placed a different emphasis on her previous short marriage, and he silently damned the man who'd clearly mistreated her.

'I should have—' she began, only to have him place a gentle finger over her lips to still anything further she might have uttered. *Warned you*, she finished silently, stricken with a host of ambivalent emotions, the overriding one being a mix of guilt and shame.

'Don't,' he said quietly.

She wanted to escape into the en suite, don nightwear, then slip beneath the bedcovers and summon sleep. Except her feet refused to obey the command of her brain.

'I'll go sleep in another room,' Alesha offered, and felt the light brush of his fingers over her lips.

'No.'

How much would it take to lie in a bed barely a few metres from his own, and not be vividly aware of how close she'd come to the sexual act?

To recall in intimate detail the touch of his mouth on her own, the trail of his hands, and how he'd aroused her emotions to fever pitch.

Until she'd freaked out.

Oh, dear God.

How could she have come so *close*...only to freeze like a frightened virgin?

She almost wished he'd overridden her physical protest and consummated the marriage. Then she'd have got past the dread, the fear...*hell*, the stark memory of that last night beneath Seth's vicious hands.

At the very least, she owed Loukas an explanation...

Oh, please, she derided silently. Like he wouldn't already have reached the right conclusion?

Hadn't she consulted therapists and talked the talk until she knew every angle? Every possible scenario?

She'd thought she'd conquered her fear of intimacy after Seth…but then she'd never tested it. Preferring to lead a celibate life, and refusing to date.

Tonight was the closest she'd allowed any man to come…and look how that had ended? Disaster *plus*.

Even thinking about it filled her with shame…and guilt.

Move forward.

Sure, like that would happen any time soon given her reaction just now?

She shivered beneath the warmth of his jacket, and she lifted one hand, then dropped it back to her side with an awkward gesture. 'I need to—' Escape. Move away from him and the almost electric tension filling the room before—*what*? She said something foolish? Trite?

Go, a silent voice bade. And she did, heading into her en suite without a backward glance.

She took care to close the door carefully, then she removed the jacket and laid it over a chair before crossing to the vanity.

Studiously avoiding the mirror, she removed her make-up, brushed her teeth a little too vigorously, then she pulled on sleep-wear, took a deep calming breath…and re-entered the bedroom.

And found it empty.

There was a sense of relief as she crossed to the bed she'd occupied the previous night, and she slid between the sheets, dimmed the lights, then closed her eyes.

To sleep, hopefully.

Except images filled her head, past and present, merging into a scrambled mix that entered her subconscious with tortured clarity, rendering her helpless as the mental reel spun out.

CHAPTER SIX

LOUKAS dragged a hand through his damp hair and reached for a towel.

A shower had eased some of the muscular tension, but not the slow-burning anger existent, for there was a part of him that wanted to physically harm the man whose mistreatment had seeded fear in the woman he'd married.

There was a word for it. And legal redress.

The question was whether Alesha had pressed charges.

Possibly not, in a bid to avoid publicity.

His eyes narrowed as he pulled on boxers…nightwear he rarely donned. The women he'd bedded were comfortable with their nudity, as well as his own.

What in hell had Alesha's ex done to turn a confident outgoing young woman into someone who had serious issues with intimacy?

Rape…physical abuse? *Both?*

His hands clenched into tight fists at the thought of her being subjected to either.

And paused momentarily to wonder why it affected him to this degree.

Had Dimitri known of his daughter's mistreatment?

Subdued lighting greeted him as he re-entered the bedroom, and his gaze swept to the slender form beneath the covers of the bed adjacent his own.

Was she asleep…or merely contriving to give that impression?

Loukas slid between the covers of his own bed, closed the lights, then lay quietly as he reflected on his every move since their arrival home from the fundraiser.

She had kissed like an angel…and he was willing to swear her reaction to his touch had been genuine.

Until she had panicked and fought against him with a desperation born of fear. Hardly the action of someone who'd sought counselling and emerged whole.

It was a while before he slept, and he came sharply awake at a soft beeping sound that had him reaching for the security sensor unit.

The glass door leading onto the terrace was unsecured, and the heat sensor detected a human form occupying a chair.

He moved quietly to his feet, checked the adjoining bed and discovered it empty.

The luminous dial on his watch showed it was several minutes past three.

Alesha? It had to be, and he extracted jeans and pulled them on, then added a tee shirt, before going in search of her.

With sure movements he crossed the gallery and ran lightly downstairs.

Subtle garden illumination provided sufficient light for him to see the slight feminine form curled up on one of four cushioned cane sofas nestled around a glass-topped table.

He made a point of ensuring she heard his approach, and he caught the quick movement of her hands as she brushed each cheek before turning towards him.

Tears?

Somehow the thought of her needing to retreat out here to cry alone touched a place in his heart he'd previously considered beyond reach.

The night air held a faint chill, and he sank down onto the sofa beside her.

'Unable to sleep?' He kept his voice light, and caught the slight shake of her head.

'I didn't mean to wake you.'

'The security sensor,' Loukas corrected. 'It beeped an alert when you opened the external door.'

His features were shadowed in the half-light, and in the distance the city breathed life with its coloured neon billboards, street-lighting…casting a dappled reflection over the dark inner harbour waters.

In a few hours the indigo sky would begin to lighten as dawn emerged, providing colour and substance to the new day.

'It's peaceful out here,' Alesha offered, aware her voice was edged with tiredness. Hardly surprising since she hadn't slept at all. Yet she didn't feel inclined to move.

Nor did she particularly want to converse. The silence of the night, the solitude it offered, acted as a soothing balm, and most of all she simply wanted to close her eyes and let it wash over her, cleanse a little and ease the ache deep inside.

There was a psychological process she needed to travel, a series of steps that would lead her from the dark back into the light, and it was better she took them alone. Then she could sleep.

'Go back to bed,' she said quietly. 'I'm fine.'

Sure she was.

'Please.'

It was the *please* that reached him, but he merely looked at her. 'I'm not going anywhere.'

Okay, so she'd pretend he wasn't there.

Difficult, when his presence acted as a compelling entity impossible to ignore. He radiated innate strength and vitality…a dramatic mesh, even in repose, that made her incredibly aware of him.

Fool, she denounced in silent self-castigation. Why…*why* did you go into orbit, when you'd mentally conditioned yourself to have sex with him?

Now you've created a wedge…oh, call it as it is…an emotional physical *chasm* so deep and wide, it'll be almost impossible to breach.

There was a part of her that felt inclined to urge him to take her to bed and…just *do* it.

Sure. Like he was going to risk her freaking out again? What man would be willing to risk rejection after being so convincingly repelled?

How could she explain that as much as she'd wanted his possession…somehow at the crucial moment Seth's angry image had superimposed Loukas' own.

'Did your ex rape you?'

His voice was quiet, steady…yet she flinched from the words, and it took a few long moments to gather herself together.

'Rape conjures up a picture involving violence.'

Loukas took hold of her hand and threaded his fingers loosely through her own. 'Sex between consenting adults should be consensual. Not a demand or used as a punishment.'

The shadows helped. His closeness provided security. And he deserved to know some of it. All of it, eventually, but for now some of it would be enough.

'Seth played a convincing part,' she began quietly. 'He fooled me, but not my father, who was against the marriage from the start.' She couldn't look at him. 'It began almost as soon as we were married, with insults at first—about my lack of spine in demanding a substantial salary package, perks. When I refused to comply, he became…rough.'

Loukas kept his voice even, in spite of the anger building inside him. 'He hit you.'

'Yes.'

'More?'

'Some,' she admitted, and heard the breath hiss between his teeth.

That any man could hurt her…dammit, *harm* her physically and emotionally enraged him. Yet if he showed any sign of it, she'd retreat even further behind the barrier she'd erected in self-protection.

She needed time to trust him, and he could give her that…even if it killed him to do so.

Meanwhile, it wouldn't be difficult to discover the date of her first marriage, and uncover any hospital records…if any of her injuries had required hospital attention.

It became a matter of importance he discover as much as he could about what had transpired during her brief marriage. Better that, than push her for details she was reluctant to share.

For how else could he help resolve her issue with intimacy without all of the facts?

'If it's okay with you,' Alesha managed quietly, 'I'd prefer not to go into it any more tonight.'

This morning, he amended.

So where did they go from here?

With extreme care on his part.

The immediate agenda had to be a return to bed.

Soon the sky would begin to lighten, the birdlife stir and twitter with sound, and car engines would herald workers begin their trek to commence an early shift.

Dawn's break would bring men and women out for their early morning run, and the day would begin.

Sunday indicated recreation and relaxation for some. The beach, time spent cruising the inner harbour waters, following cultural pursuits, entertaining guests, sporting activities.

Maybe she'd give Lacey a call and suggest they share part of the day together. Shop a little, linger over a latte at one of their favoured cafés.

There was pleasure in the thought, and a sense of encroaching drowsiness…something she fought, unaware of Loukas' thoughtful gaze as her eyelids slowly drifted down.

For several long minutes he viewed her softened features, noted her even breathing, then he rose quietly to his feet and carefully lifted her into his arms.

She didn't stir, and he carried her easily into the house, reset security, then he took her upstairs to their room.

He breathed in the clean smell of her hair combined with the soft drift of her perfume, and tamped down the stirring of desire.

Feelings he hadn't expected to experience, born from an emotion he consciously chose not to explore.

The covers were thrown back on the bed Alesha had occupied, and she uttered a faint protest as he relinquished his hold.

With easy economical movements he shed his jeans, tee shirt, snapped off the bed-lamp and slid into bed beside her.

With extreme care he enfolded her slender body close in against him, felt her stir, and he soothed a hand over her hair…again and again, until a soft sigh emerged from her throat and she relaxed against him in sleep, her cheek resting into the curve of his shoulder.

He could offer her safety, and hold her through the night. Be there for her, and help soothe her fears.

* * *

Of the many social functions Alesha had attended in the past, tonight's fundraiser took precedence, and was one in which she maintained a personal interest.

Children who'd suffered abuse at the hands of those who professed to love them. Adults, whose trust they deserved, yet failed to receive. The varying shades of grey to the deepest black, covering circumstances too grim for the average person to comprehend.

Tonight a few children's plight would be highlighted in order to touch the guests' hearts and persuade them to give generously.

Alesha chose a black bandage-design gown that hugged her slender curves and showcased delicate-textured skin. She confined jewellery to a slender gold necklace with matching ear-studs and bracelet, and black killer heels completed the outfit.

Minimum make-up, with emphasis on her eyes, she opted to leave her hair loose in a soft feminine style.

The event drew a pleasing number of guests, and she stood at Loukas' side sipping champagne, acutely aware of his close proximity.

He portrayed the man he was…sophisticated, urbane, highly intelligent, successful. And he wore the verbal labels with ease, comfortable in his own skin with little, if anything, to prove.

And he was hers.

Well, not in the truest sense…yet. She bore his name, wore his ring, and she…liked him.

Admit it, you find him stunningly attractive. Sexy…incredibly sexy, she amended. And there was a part of her that craved the intimacy she instinctively rejected.

So why did she feel as if she were treading eggshells,

aware she consciously watched everything she said, every action, in case it was misconstrued.

At work, home, and on social occasions such as this when she played the part of recently married *happy* wife.

A young woman who, by all accounts, should be ecstatic to be bedding one of the most eligible men on planet earth.

'Penny for them?'

She tilted her head and gifted him a teasing smile. 'Not for sharing, at any price.'

Loukas' mouth curved a little, and the hand resting at the base of her spine brushed a light trail up her back to linger at the lower edge of her nape.

Sensation spiralled through her body, and it took conscious effort to hold his dark gaze.

Dear heaven, she was almost flirting with him…for real. Not the best idea, given the tenuous quality of their relationship.

Yet it was fun, almost *safe*. Although was it? If you played with fire, you tended to get burnt.

So chill, and don't risk conflagration.

Their table was well placed, the company stimulating, and the food delectable.

The speeches held a poignancy that speared her heart, and her eyes clouded…for she could envisage so much more than the mere words conveyed. At one point her fingers tightened into a fist, and her lacquered nails dug into her palm. No one should be a victim of abuse…dear heaven, especially never a child.

Almost as if he sensed her torment, Loukas placed his hand over hers until she released her grip. His silent presence and strength comforted her and she gave him a tentative smile and returned his hold on her hand, suddenly glad he was there with her this evening.

The entertainment for the night comprised a designer

fashion showing, with elegant models parading the catwalk, followed by an auction of the garments with a generous percentage gifted to the charity.

It lightened the evening, with the auctioneer really getting into the swing of it, encouraging bidders to raise the stakes.

One gown caught Alesha's interest, a deep red silk with spaghetti straps attached to a beautiful ruched bodice and a soft floor-length tiered skirt.

Loukas indicated his bid, and escalated it by increments until it reached an exorbitant amount and the one remaining bidder pulled out.

Alesha leaned towards him and said in a subdued but scandalized voice, 'Are you crazy?'

'It's a worthy cause.' His voice held a teasing indolence as he brushed his lips to her temple. 'And the gown is perfect for you.'

Oh, my. For an instant the room and everyone in it faded into nothing as his eyes locked with her own, and something violently sweet coursed through her body.

His mouth curved into an easy smile, almost as if he knew.

'Thanks.' On impulse she pressed her lips to his cheek…at least that was her intention, except he moved and her mouth met his own, and a light kiss became something else as he savoured her briefly before lifting his head.

Colour filled her cheeks, and he trailed light fingers over the soft heat, then skimmed over one shoulder to rest at the edge of her waist.

'Dear Alesha,' a light feminine voice intruded. 'So nice to see you happy in your new marriage.'

Recovery was swift as she summoned a smile and turned towards the woman who'd stopped by to offer congratulations, only to have her heart sink.

Nicolette de Silva had a reputation for lacking tact. Even

the kindest amongst her coterie of friends admitted Nicolette didn't *think* before she opened her mouth.

'Her brief liaison with that terrible man was a disaster,' Nicolette confided to Loukas. 'But then, of course, you know about that?'

'Naturally.' His voice was smooth as silk. Sufficiently so that most people would immediately cease pursuing the subject and move on.

'There were rumours, some of them extreme.' Nicolette offered a conciliatory smile. 'I believe Seth Armitage tried to sell his side of the story to the media, but nothing came of it, isn't that right, Alesha?'

Alesha's fingers clenched beneath the cover of the table-cloth, and she tensed as Loukas again took her hand in his and traced soothing fingers across the pulsing veins at her wrist.

Support? Whatever, it felt...pleasant, comforting.

A double whammy, she admitted silently as the action increased her pulse-beat and made her increasingly aware of him.

She tried to tell herself she was immune to gossip. Three years on she'd heard it all...first and second-hand. The inquisitive comments she chose not to concede or deny. The false expressions of sympathy. Each a quest for information she refused to give.

'There's no point in rehashing old history,' she managed quietly. 'Don't you agree?'

Nicolette looked momentarily distraught. 'I'm so sorry. I didn't mean to upset you.'

The weird thing was she meant it.

'Apology accepted.'

'Please do enjoy the rest of the evening.'

'We shall.'

'Red will look stunning on you.'

'Thank you.' Inherent poise enabled her to conduct a perfectly sincere conversation with one of the women sharing the table. 'It's a gorgeous gown.'

'Everyone bid. The fundraiser has proven to be an enormous success.'

'Yes, it has.'

'My condolences for the sad loss of your father. He was a wonderful man.'

It was easy to agree, and Alesha turned to offer Loukas a slow sweet smile. 'Coffee, darling? The waiters are circling the tables as we speak.'

She was something else, Loukas perceived. Brave when it mattered, yet so hauntingly vulnerable on occasion.

Was he the only one who glimpsed what lay beneath the protective façade she'd created?

It was almost midnight when the evening came to an end, and guests began making their way into the foyer. Air-kisses were exchanged, invitations issued and the need for diary dates to be checked and acceptances confirmed.

The concierge ordered cars to be fetched with military precision, and Alesha experienced a sense of relief as the Aston Martin appeared at the hotel entrance.

Home...not exactly *home*, but the place she shared with Loukas seemed almost welcome. Even better was the prospect of shedding her clothes and slipping into bed to sleep.

If she could just erase the vivid images portrayed on screen during the evening. If she had been alone in her apartment, she would have watched a DVD and lost herself in a light comedy until sheer tiredness forced her into bed.

Except she was no longer alone.

There was a part of her that wanted to become lost in the seductive touch of a man. To be held close and feel the trail of his lips as he explored her body. Experience the joy of intimacy without the fear of cruelty.

Not just any man...Loukas.

If she'd wanted an affair to expunge unwanted memories, she would have sought one by now.

Dammit, what was she waiting for?

Love?

Oh, *please*. The emotion only existed for such a brief period of time in the real world...didn't it?

The kind that changed lives and lasted a lifetime, one man for one woman, twin souls meant only for each other...that was a beautiful fantasy with little basis in reality.

Since when had she become so cynical?

A hollow laugh rose and died in her throat, for she could pinpoint the date, the time almost to the minute.

The car turned off the New South Head Road into Point Piper, and reached the magnificent set of gates guarding the entrance to Loukas' mansion.

A modem released the gates and simultaneously lit the curved driveway as he eased the Aston Martin towards the garage.

A sense of restlessness invaded her body as she ascended the stairs...a feeling she attempted to dismiss without much success on entering the master suite.

She became extremely conscious of Loukas' presence as he shed his jacket, then loosened his bow tie.

Smooth easy movements that were uncontrived as he moved to free the buttons on his dress shirt...and she focused on discarding her evening shoes, her jewellery.

All the time she was acutely aware of him...the faint thud as he removed his shoes; the almost undetectable slide of a zip fastening and the soft slither of material as he freed trousers.

The image of his tall, near-naked frame was hauntingly

vivid. Hell, she had no problem visualizing the impressive breadth of his shoulders, the superb musculature tapering to a sculptured waist and lean hips.

Would there ever be a time when she could feel sufficiently confident to seduce him? Boldly explore and tease until he groaned beneath her touch?

To have him reach for her in the night and gift him the freedom of her body...to exult in untold pleasure?

She drew in a ragged breath, then released it slowly. Oh, for heaven's sake...*stop*.

Get rid of the dress, gather up your sleepwear, escape to your en suite, remove make-up, brush teeth, fix hair into a ponytail...then go to bed.

She did all that and re-entered the bedroom to find Loukas stretched comfortably beneath the covers, arms crossed pillowing his head.

'Goodnight.' Her voice sounded slightly strangled even to her own ears as she slid between the sheets and he doused the lights.

'Sleep well.'

As if that were going to happen any time soon.

Perhaps if she lay perfectly still and conjured only pleasant thoughts...

Except nothing helped, and her thoughts assumed a kaleidoscopic mix that subdued the colours and brought Seth's image into stark black and white focus.

Go away. A silent entreaty, harsh only in her mind, had no effect whatsoever.

There was a need to remain awake, for at least then she retained a measure of control. If she slid into sleep all control would be lost and his image would emerge to haunt her as it had too frequently in the past.

She needed to win...she *had* to.

Yet slipping from her bed and joining Loukas in his took more courage than she possessed, for what if he mistook her for a former flame...or, worse, he rejected her?

So much for that plan.

Afterwards Alesha had no memory of when her subconscious led unerringly into the familiar nightmare. She only knew she was fighting to escape...crying out as she shielded her face from the stinging slaps, the harsh bite of cruel hands pinning her down, the sound of her name on his lips.

Then she came sharply awake to a room flooded with light...a room different from the one she'd occupied in her mind, and the man leaning close to her wasn't Seth.

It took one brief horrifying moment to shake free of the starkly intrusive images, and she was barely conscious of the concern evident in the dark eyes of the man watching the range of fleeting emotions chase her expressive features before she gained the control to mask them.

Loukas lifted a hand, saw her eyes flare with sudden fear, and swallowed the curse that rose to his lips as he smoothed a wayward lock of hair behind her ear, then let his hand trail along her jaw to cup her chin and press a thumb to her quivering mouth.

There seemed no past, only the present, and words fell from her lips without conscious thought. 'Please...'

She looked stricken as the realization of what she said sank in, and she lifted her hands in a defensive gesture as he dispensed with them and drew her close.

His skin was warm against her cheek, and she felt a hand cradle her head as the other slid low over the back of her waist.

It felt good...*he* felt good, and she breathed in the scent of him, the faint traces of soap, cologne and the muskiness of man.

His hand brushed a path over her spine, rested briefly at

her nape, then slid slowly down in a slow soothing pattern that did much to settle her ragged breathing.

She didn't want to move, and she instinctively lifted her arms to link her hands together at the back of his neck.

He grazed his lips over her cheek, nuzzled her ear, then eased his mouth down to savour the curve at the base of her neck…and sensed the breath hitch in her throat.

A hand shifted to her waist and gently slipped beneath the sleep top to skim the warm skin as he traced a path to her breast, cupped it, then brushed the tender peak until it swelled to his touch.

With care, he deepened the kiss, tasting, exploring the inner texture, the sensitive tissues as he encouraged her response. Her body jerked as he took her lower lip into his mouth and bit down gently, and she moved restlessly in his arms, seeking more, *wanting* so much more.

With care he eased the cotton top high, and when she didn't resist he removed it completely.

'Beautiful,' Loukas said gently as he shaped each breast, then soothed their softness before lowering his head to caress one tender peak as it hardened into a swollen bead that begged to be suckled.

Her body arched against his own, and she cried out as he took the peak into his mouth and used the edge of his teeth to heighten her pleasure.

There was satisfaction as her hands began their own discovery, shaping his shoulders, sliding slowly down the bunched muscles to his forearms, before moving to his ribs, where, once there, she trailed light fingers over his chest, toyed with the tight buds, then slipped to frame his waist.

His breath caught as she leaned in and placed her lips over one tight bud…and drew it between her teeth, only to release it and trail a path to his navel, explored a little, and sighed when he pulled her down onto the bed and took her mouth with his own.

Frankly sensual, he plundered at will, hungry, almost demanding as she matched him in a primitive oral dance where she became lost…totally lost in the magic he evoked.

There was no sense of time or place…only the man, and she whimpered in protest as he began easing back, softening his touch until his mouth drifted gently over her own, then he lifted his head and regarded her carefully.

Alesha had no coherent thought as her emotions went into meltdown.

Dear God, what had just happened here?

She couldn't tear her eyes away from his, almost as if she were held captive by the smouldering heat…the intense passion, unrestrained and primitive in that instant. And the control, leashed, but easily broken by a careless word or gesture on her part.

'Your call.'

CHAPTER SEVEN

HE COULD come so close, yet stop if she asked him to?

How could he do that? Ohmigod…how could *she*?

'Please.' The word whispered from Alesha's lips, a fragile sound barely lucid in the stillness of the night.

His eyes were dark…so dark, she became lost in their depths as he brushed a thumb-pad gently over her lower lip.

'Do you know what you're asking?'

She did, on some subliminal level. Yet she couldn't stop, for it was as if she were being driven by an inner force that left her powerless.

'Yes.' As proof she sought his mouth with her own, and held on as he took possession in a kiss that made her forget everything except his touch, the hunger…and the innate knowledge she didn't want him to stop.

With care he eased off her sleep trousers, taking his time as he trailed gentle fingers over the surface of her skin, then he cupped one ankle and lowered his head down to brush his lips over the delicate arch.

Slow, he wanted slow and easy, building the tension, stoking the passion until he filled her sensual world.

It became a voyage of discovery, learning what caused her

breath to hitch, the pleasurable sigh as he explored her breasts, savoured the sensitive curve at the edge of her neck…the way her body arched when he palmed the highly sensitive place between her thighs.

He felt the faint sting of her nails as her fingers bit into his shoulders, and he reciprocated with a teasing bite to the soft underside of one breast.

Naked, he saw her eyes widen as her hand brushed his arousal, and he glimpsed her brief panic, then it was gone as he took possession of her mouth in an erotic kiss that brought a purr of pleasure.

It was then he trailed his mouth in a slow caress down her throat, felt the slight vibration as he lingered there before he began grazing a sensual tasting towards her navel, circled his tongue round the diamond pin, then traced an evocative path to the intimate folds guarding her sensitive clitoris.

He felt her tense, then utter a faint sob as he bestowed the most intimate kiss of all, taking infinite care as her tension built, urging her high until she reached the brink…then he held as she fell.

And glimpsed the tears well in her eyes, the soundless movement of her lips as she struggled to find the words, and he trailed gentle fingers over each cheek, dispensing the warm moisture.

It was more, so much more than she believed it possible to experience, and she cradled his face and urged it towards her own as she sought his mouth in a kiss so expressive there was no need for words.

She felt mesmerized by the darkness in his eyes, the passion clearly evident as he moved over her, and she managed a strangled plea to turn off the light. Only to have him shake his head.

How could she explain that in the darkness she hadn't had to witness the hatred of the man who'd only married her for material gain? A man who had used sex as a punishment.

'Loukas—'

'Open your eyes,' he chided gently. 'I want you to see me, only me, and know who and what I am, and the pleasure I can give you.'

'Please. I—'

'Trust me, *agape mou*.' His mouth closed on her own as he positioned his length and eased in, careful to ensure she could accommodate him before filling her completely.

At first he didn't move, almost as if he sensed she needed to absorb his possession, and her eyes widened as he shifted his weight and began to withdraw, only to increase the pace as her vaginal muscles caught his rhythm and matched it, until he took her high…so high she could only cling to him and experience the ride.

She felt alive. Acutely sensitive to every nerve in her body. This…*this* was how it was meant to be.

Not just sex…something so much more.

Body, mind, and spirit coalesced into one entity to provide a sensual magic.

Electrifying, primitive, exquisite.

She wanted to thank him, except she couldn't find the words for what she wanted to say.

Instead she lifted a shaky hand and placed it against his cheek, then brushed his mouth with her own.

She expected him to withdraw, and she gasped as he caught her close and rolled onto his back, taking her with him.

A slow smile curved his lips as he eased her into a sitting position astride him, and he took in her pink cheeks, the gleaming brown eyes dreamy with lingering passion. The softly parted mouth swollen from his kisses, the tousled hair framing her face.

His hands clasped her waist, and he used each thumb to trace a light pattern over her stomach…and felt her quiver beneath his touch.

This is the aftermath? Alesha mused as she felt him swell inside her. A spiral of sensation curled deep within and rose through her body…sensuous, consuming, *witching*.

His eyes held hers, and she was unable to look away as he began to move, taking her with him as she held on and joined him in a ride that held her spellbound with intense pulsating pleasure.

It was almost more than she could bear, and he drew her trembling body close and pressed his lips to her temple.

He murmured words she didn't quite catch as he nestled her head into the curve of his shoulder, and she lay there, too emotionally spent to move.

She must have slept, for she became aware of a warm body close to her own and the drift of fingers trailing a light path over the slender curve of her waist.

Her eyes flew open, and for one agonizing second her body tensed…then she recognized the bed, the room, the man who held her.

She lay perfectly still as memory of the night filled her mind, and she swallowed the sudden lump that rose in her throat.

'Look at me,' Loukas commanded gently, and when she did he captured her chin, giving her little option but to hold his dark gaze.

Her mouth quivered, and he brushed the pad of his thumb over its sensitive fullness.

'What do you want from me?'

'Whatever you choose to give.'

It wasn't the answer she expected. 'Last night—'

'Was beautiful,' he completed, and saw the soft pink colour her cheeks.

It had been all about her…her pleasure, her orgasm. What would he say if she told him it was her first?

A sudden thought swept her eyes wide. Ohmigod…he couldn't know, surely? She'd been blind with ecstasy, totally out of herself. Had she cried? Please, dear heaven, she didn't scream?

Was this where they conducted a post-coital report?

Should she thank him?

For what?

A miraculous melting of her frozen emotions?

Like one sexual encounter would do it?

Staying here quiescent was madness. He'd take it as an invitation for *more*, and, besides, daylight filtered through the shutters.

His hand slid to her stomach…her *bare* stomach. A touch that made her aware she wore nothing beneath the bedcovers, and she shifted as he traced her ribcage, only to pause as he encountered a small hard lump on one rib, followed by another.

Alesha uttered a distressed sound as Loukas discovered the scar lesion beneath her breast, the legacy of a vicious bite.

'Don't.' Except she was too late to prevent Loukas from peeling back the bedcovers, and any move she made to escape from the bed was easily stalled.

'Are these *it*?' Loukas demanded in a dangerously soft voice. 'Or are there more?'

More. Cracked ribs, long healed.

Her eyes met his, hardening to obsidian shards. Anger rose from the deep well in which she'd buried it. She drew in a shuddering breath. 'Let me go.'

And let her escape to curl into a foetal ball alone? 'No.'

Only her father knew she'd summoned a lawyer from a hospital bed and filed for divorce. And paid Seth to get out of her life so she could rebuild her own.

'You want me to admit I was a blind fool and should have listened to my parents' caution?' She was like a runaway train, unable to stop. 'That I should have realized much sooner that it was the Karsouli wealth he wanted…not me, and that the entire engagement and lead-up to the marriage had simply been an act?'

Loukas wrapped his arms around her slender form and drew her in against him, sheltering her even as anger against the man who'd hurt her consumed him. To think of her as the victim of one man's uncontrollable rage almost undid him.

A shiver shook her slender frame as she felt his muscles tense. 'Please.' She couldn't remain where she was, naked and vulnerable.

'Stay,' he said gently.

What of her own emotions? He'd awakened something inside her she hadn't known existed. Feelings that tugged her heartstrings and made her think of the impossible.

And that would never do.

She'd given her heart once, only to have that love blow up in her face. There was no way she'd risk gifting her heart again.

Yet it felt good to be held curved in against him. His warmth surrounded her, the beat of his heart solid and even against her back. His arms offered a protective haven, and on an early Sunday morning there was no need to rise, shine and prepare for a day in the city.

Alesha spent the morning at her apartment, checked with Reception for any mail, made a few phone calls, one of which enlisted the continued services of her cleaning lady…another to Lacey suggesting they spend the afternoon at Darling Harbour.

The day was cool, the skies grey with the threat of showers, and she chose to don designer jeans, a tee shirt over which she pulled on a thigh-length knitted jacket, and she fixed a belt low on her hips. Knee-length boots completed the outfit.

By chance she found a convenient parking space not too far distant from where she'd arranged to meet Lacey, and after exchanging an affectionate hug they made for a nearby café and ordered lattes.

'So,' Lacey began. *'Tell.'*

Alesha lifted an eyebrow. 'As in?'

'This is Lacey, best friend, confidante…remember? I have your happiness at heart.' The look she offered held thoughtful concern as she queried quietly, 'Are you?'

Prevarication wouldn't work. Lacey would see through it in a second. 'Happy? It's early days.'

'Yes, I guess it is. So…moving right along?'

The benefit of friendship was being in tune, and they were, instinctively aware when to pause or pursue a subject.

'Let's focus on you.' Alesha took an appreciative sip of her latte.

'Too boring.'

'Elucidate. Life, John, work?'

'He wants the ring, house in the burbs, kids.'

'And you don't?'

'I've known him for ever. We fit together well. But I want more than just…contentment. Warm and fuzzy is fine twenty or more years down the track. But now?'

'Try adding some excitement.'

'Did that, and all I got was the *look*. You know the one…like have I suddenly flipped?'

'I'm almost afraid to ask.'

Lacey leaned in close to confide, and a few minutes later Alesha didn't know whether to roll her eyes or laugh. 'Subtle—not.'

Afterwards they wandered the various shops, boutiques and stalls, sharing company with an eclectic mix of people. Girls sporting boho chic, guys dressed from top to toe in black; a television personality with his wife and children; tourists. As well as the social set enjoying a late leisurely lunch in the restaurants overlooking the inner harbour.

Dusk was encroaching as Alesha headed towards Point Piper, and her pulse quickened to a faster beat as she garaged the car.

Loukas' black Aston Martin was parked in its customary bay, and she entered the foyer, then headed for the staircase.

There was a need to shower and change before dinner, and she walked into the master suite, only to pause at the sight of Loukas in the process of shedding his clothes.

Fluid muscles moved and flexed beneath smooth olive skin…superb musculature honed to a peak of physical fitness.

Heat unfurled deep inside her with the memory of what they'd shared during the night. How his mouth had devoured her…the touch of his hands, the movement of his body within her own. Oh, dear God, the sweet ecstasy he created within as he played her with unhurried grace, urging her high until she shattered in his arms.

There was a part of her that wanted to cross the room, lean in close and lift her mouth to his and seek the wickedly sensual slide of his tongue as it explored, tantalized…and possessed.

At that moment he turned, and dark eyes speared her own as a smile curved his generously moulded mouth.

'How was your afternoon with Lacey?'

'Great.' She consciously swallowed as he freed the zip fastening on his trousers and dispatched them. 'We explored Darling Harbour.'

What was she *doing* standing here watching him undress like a fascinated voyeur?

An impertinent imp silently taunted, *Because he's well worth the look.*

Alesha turned away, suddenly cross with herself, and she tugged off her boots, freed the belt and discarded her woollen jacket.

She heard the faint buzz of an electric shaver and relaxed a little. If she moved quickly, she'd be able to shed her jeans and tee and reach her own en suite before Loukas finished shaving.

Minutes later she activated the shower, shed bra and briefs, then she stepped into the large marble-tiled cubicle, caught up soap and began sliding the scented tablet over her body.

Her skin felt sensitive, *alive*, in a way it never had before, and each movement of the soap brought a vivid reminder of his touch. If she closed her eyes, she could almost believe he was *there*.

To have her every waking thought filled with his image after one night in his bed was crazy. Yet try as she might she couldn't shake him from her mind.

A faint groan emerged from her throat minutes later as she closed the water dial and caught up a towel.

Don't think…in the name of heaven don't let your mind slip back and compare the past with the present.

Yet how could she not?

Sex with Loukas had been mind-blowing. Except it hadn't just been sex, it had been *intimacy*, at a level she hadn't previously experienced.

A shaft of sheer sensation spiralled through her body at the mere thought…

Oh, *move right along*, why don't you? Focus on the prosaic. Get dressed, go join Loukas for dinner, indulge in pleasant conversation…and escape in due course with the need for an early night.

Rethink that excuse, or he might take it as an invitation to join her in bed. Time spent on her laptop, catching up with email, work…that should do it.

Act…you're good at it, she admonished as she forked delicious morsels from her plate.

Did Loukas guess she was harbouring a conflicting mess of nerves? Possibly. He was an intelligent man, and way too astute for her peace of mind.

Why should she feel so acutely sensitive…on edge, and extremely conscious of him? Dammit, she could still *feel* him inside her, his penetration so deep and all-consuming her vaginal muscles quivered on mere reflection.

Oh, hell. Now she was *really* losing it.

Somehow she managed to get through dinner, and when she was done she excused herself on the pretext of work.

Loukas let her go, his gaze thoughtful as he watched her leave the room. She was like a cat treading hot bricks, at odds with herself, *him*.

He tamped down the inclination to go after her. Instead, he refilled his cup with coffee, then took it into his home office and participated in a conference call with the Andreou Athens office, issued orders, and faced the possibility he might need to personally deal with the problem.

It was late when Alesha closed the laptop down and headed towards the master suite, only to find it empty.

She completed her nightly routine, discarded clothes for sleep trousers and top, then she stood hesitantly unsure whether to occupy Loukas' bed or her own.

There was a part of her that wanted the comfort of his arms, his body and the pleasure he could gift her.

'One or the other,' Loukas declared from the doorway, startling her. 'But we share.'

She turned and offered him a level look. 'What if I choose not to?'

'We sleep together,' he drawled. 'With the emphasis on sleep.' He pulled his shirt free, tended to the buttons and reached for the zip fastening on his trousers, shed them and crossed to his en suite.

Alesha slid into bed, her own, closed her eyes and pretended to sleep, only to unconsciously tense as she sensed the bedcovers shift and Loukas joined her in bed.

'Sleep well, *agape mou*.'

His voice held quiet amusement, and she refrained from uttering a word in response.

Within minutes his breathing steadied, and she silently cursed his ability to fall asleep so easily.

At some stage she must have succumbed, for she woke at dawn feeling warm, secure...and aware she lay gathered in against a hard male body.

Had she moved in the night...or had he?

Did it matter?

The question was how she could extricate herself without waking him. A mission in itself, given his arm lay heavy across her waist.

It was a nice feeling.

Nice? Oh, please. The word didn't even begin to cut it. It felt so good, so *right*, there was a part of her that wanted to remain where she was, curled in against him.

Safe, secure, *here* where she was meant to be.

Where she wanted to be.

To touch him, lightly, with her lips, the tips of her fingers…to watch him stir, become aware, awake. And see his mouth curve into that sensual smile he did so well, the soft gleam appear in those dark eyes…and have his mouth close over hers in the prerequisite that would lead to early-morning sex.

Whoa. What was happening here?

Being held in his arms was one thing…sex, a whole different ball game. One she didn't feel sufficiently equipped to play. At least, not yet. But just for a moment, while he slept, she savoured the luxury and let her mind wander to possible maybes…until reality surfaced.

So, just shift his arm, and move. What's the big deal?

But what if…? Oh, hell.

'I can almost hear your mind working.'

So much for thinking he still slept.

'Then you'll know I want out of this bed.'

She was almost certain she sensed his soft laugh. 'I can't persuade you to stay?'

'No.'

'Pity.' He removed his arm and rolled onto his back as she escaped from the bed, taking pleasure in watching her cross the room.

A beautiful young woman, who came alive beneath his touch, wondrous at the measure of her response, yet tentative about losing her inhibitions.

There was a part of him that wanted the opportunity to physically thrash the man who'd treated her with such deliberate mercilessness.

Except there was a better, more subtle way to inflict pain. He had the resources, the influence, the knowledge.

All he needed to do was set the wheels in motion.

CHAPTER EIGHT

PEAK-HOUR traffic into the city seemed more hectic and hazardous than usual, and Alesha silently cursed her independence in refusing to ride in to the office earlier with Loukas.

It set the day on a wrong foot; her laptop refused to boot up, her PA called in sick, and almost anything that could go wrong...did.

Worse, her BMW developed a puncture en route home at day's end and the spare happened to be flat. Enlisting the help of an automobile service took wait time, together with the need to have the car towed to an approved workshop, where she called for a taxi to take her home.

Loukas arrived as she paid off the driver, and she grimaced a little.

'Don't ask,' Alesha declared as he reached her side. 'You really don't want to know.'

He examined her pale features, the tenseness apparent as he cupped her chin and tilted it. 'You weren't in an accident?'

Her eyes met his with fearless disregard. 'No.' Without preamble she relayed the puncture, the flat spare.

'You should have called me.'

It simply hadn't occurred to her to do so. 'Why? I took care of it.'

He touched a light finger to her lower lip. 'Next time, call.'

He'd been concerned about her?

'Maybe.'

'Do it, Alesha.'

He cared? Really cared enough to worry about her safety? No other man, with the exception of her father, had shown such concern.

Loukas managed to surprise her, when she least expected it, and whatever frustration the day held dissipated to nothing.

'Okay, I will. I promise.'

Standing so close to him was beginning to affect her, and she moved around him, entered the foyer and ran lightly upstairs.

She thought wistfully of the spa-bath, a scented candle or three, and muted soothing music. Except it wasn't going to happen. Instead she'd settle for a leisurely shower.

On reaching the master suite she discarded her outer clothes and entered the en suite, loosened her hair, set the water dial to medium, then she shed bra and briefs and stepped into the large tiled stall.

Heaven, she determined as the water cascaded over her body, and she reached for shampoo, lathered her hair, rinsed and applied conditioner, then she reached for the scented soap…only to freeze as the glass door opened and Loukas joined her.

Splendidly naked…as if he'd be *clothed*, a wicked imp taunted…he loomed large in the confines of the shower stall.

Shocked surprise didn't cover it. Without conscious thought her hands moved to act as an automatic shield.

'Modesty, *agape*?' Loukas drawled with musing humour as he caught up the soap and began smoothing it along her arm.

'Why are you doing this?' Her voice sounded strangled, even to her own ears.

'Sharing your shower?' He turned her away from him and tended to her back, using long strokes that eased over her bottom and slid down to her knees…then crept up to encompass her shoulders. When he was done, he caught hold of her shoulders and turned her to face him.

'Don't.' It was a heartfelt plea he chose to ignore as he shifted her hands and palmed her breasts, lightly examined their soft fullness, then slid to the curve at her waist before slipping to the intimate vee between her thighs.

The brush of his fingers caused her body to arch, and she balled one hand into a fist and aimed for his chest.

Except he deftly fielded it before it could connect.

For a wild moment her eyes seared his own, and her lips formed a soundless gasp as he brought her fisted hand to his mouth and lightly brushed his lips across her knuckles.

His eyes were dark, heavy with lambent warmth, and she gave a startled cry as he clasped her shoulders and began to massage the taut muscles, easing in to loosen the kinks.

It felt so *good*, and she sighed as he rendered a similar treatment to her back, easing up to her neck to knead and soothe until she relaxed completely beneath his touch.

Not content, he massaged her head, and she closed her eyes and let her mind drift until he shifted her beneath the beating water to rinse the suds from her hair, her body.

Alesha turned to face him and swept her hands over her face to dispense the excess water.

'Better?'

'Much,' she admitted. 'Thank you.'

The stress of the day had diminished, together with the loosening of tense shoulder and neck muscles. Although there was a need to escape the confines of the shower stall…and the man who stood far too close for her peace of mind.

A wet naked man who with just a look could cause her body to go into sensual meltdown.

Did he know?

She hoped not. After Seth she'd vowed never to allow another man to get beneath her skin...*ever*.

Yet Loukas was steadily invading her senses, *there*...a strong magnetic force who managed to arouse feelings she hadn't known she possessed.

For one wild moment she wondered what it would be like to let go...to feel sufficiently secure to initiate sex and soar together in mutual delight. To gift him every sensual pleasure and *know* they were twin souls meant only for each other.

How emotionally freeing that must be.

Loukas glimpsed the faint wistfulness apparent, the fleeting emotions...and wondered if she knew how well he read her expressive features.

There was an urge to lift her high in his arms and take her, here, now. He could, easily. Except he wanted more than her mere compliance.

A quick coupling in the shower, invigorating as it would be for him, wouldn't be her idea of fun...yet. He was treading delicate ground, with the need to earn her trust...completely and without reservation. Something that required time, patience and care.

'I should go.' Did her voice sound as awkward as she felt?

His mouth formed a faint smile. 'You could stay and return the favour.'

Run the soap over his body? Reach for him?

'It's easy,' Loukas encouraged gently as he placed the soap in her hand and covered it with his own.

Her eyes flared as he brought the soap to his chest and

began easing it in a slow circular pattern extending to his throat, the tops of his arms and down to his waist.

Easy? How could this kind of intimacy be *easy* when she'd never indulged in it before?

Especially when the man was Loukas…who steadily with every day and night that passed seemed to extend the boundaries in their marriage.

Worse, she found herself increasingly in a state of ambivalence…alternating longing for his tenderness, the promise of something more, yet nervously reluctant to accept it.

The nerves in her stomach tightened into a painful ball as memory provided vivid recall of Seth's unfeeling cruelty, both verbal and physical.

Don't…the word screamed silently inside her head. Don't bring your ex into the equation. There's no comparison between Seth and Loukas.

Focus on the now. You can do this.

Slowly, in gradual increments, the stroking of soap combined with the hiss of hot water cascading from the dual shower heads began to have a soothing effect, and there was a sense of pleasure verging on eroticism evident in washing a man's body.

Not any man. Loukas, she admitted with a degree of surprise.

Alesha avoided meeting his gaze as sensation flared deep within and began to pulse through her veins as fascination combined with reluctant admiration for his superb musculature, defined and sculpted by physical fitness. The slender waist, the lean hips…dear God, the size of him in a state of semi-arousal.

Surely he wouldn't take the soap there…except he did, much to her embarrassment, although to be fair he kept it clinical and he released his hand from her own as he turned to present his back.

Not that it made much difference, and for a brief few seconds she was strongly tempted to throw down the soap and escape.

Instead, she began smoothing the soap across the expanse of his shoulders, noting the flex of powerful muscle tone as she swept long strokes down to his waist and back to his shoulders until she'd covered every inch.

He possessed a tightly shaped butt…cute, she accorded, then she stilled in shock at the thought she might actually be deriving a degree of enjoyment in washing him.

When she was done he turned to face her, and colour flooded her cheeks as she saw he was fully aroused.

Ohmigod… *Chill*, she bade silently as she endeavoured to keep her breathing steady. It's just a normal male reaction.

Didn't *his* ministrations with the soap have a similar effect on you?

Had that been the object of the exercise?

She needed to get out of here *now*.

One wrong move…

'I'm sure you can manage the rest.'

With that, she stepped around him and pushed open the glass door, filched a folded towel from one of many stacked on a nearby rack and wrapped it round her slender form before collecting another to deal with her hair.

Alesha was dressed when he emerged, and she spared his impressive frame a quick glance. A white towel hitched at his hips accentuated his olive-toned skin, and her pulse quickened as he discarded it and pulled on briefs.

'I'll go check on dinner.'

They enjoyed a pleasant meal, sipped wine, and indulged in easy conversation. Loukas was a skilled raconteur, and she began to relax…until he mentioned the need to return to Athens for a short period of time.

'Business,' he relayed.

'How long will you be away?'

'We,' Loukas corrected, and saw her lips part in disbelief.

'You want me to go with you?'

'It's an opportunity to reconnect with the family.'

Alesha had met his parents and his younger sister several years ago when she'd accompanied her parents to Greece. Then she'd been a carefree young woman of twenty, in love with life, establishing her career with Karsouli and studying for an honours degree in business management.

A lot had happened in the intervening years. Now she was Loukas' wife, an equal partner in Karsouli, and all too aware Loukas' parents knew the facts surrounding their son's marriage.

How could she refuse…and on what grounds?

'We'll take an evening flight out tomorrow evening.'

So soon?

Athens. At this time of year the temperatures would be similar, with autumn in one country and spring in another.

There was a part of her that looked forward to visiting the city again. The ancient and the new, the sense of history.

Playing the newly-wed wife beneath the keen eyes of Loukas' family was something else.

'I'll take these through to the kitchen and load the dishwasher.'

Loukas joined her, and set up the coffee-maker, then when it was ready he filled two cups, placed one on the servery and leaned a hip against its marble edge and spared her a discerning look.

'We'll stay at my home in suburban Kifissia, then spend a few days on the island.'

Okay, she could do this. Like she had an option?

'Pack light. My mother and sister will undoubtedly plan at least one shopping expedition.' He shifted to his full height and indicated his coffee. 'I'll take this with me and work for a few hours.'

A full day at the office and packing with lightning speed ensured Alesha didn't have time to *think*...which had to be a bonus.

Loukas, on the other hand, juggled everything with admirable expertise, filled a carry-on bag with essentials, and offered a musing smile as she queried, 'Is that all you're taking?'

'I have clothes in each of my homes.'

Of course. 'You lead a charmed life.' Not exactly fair, when he worked long hours between office and home, and achieved more in a day than most men accomplished in a week. What was more, he managed to do so with exemplary ease.

He crossed to her side, slid a hand to her nape and kissed her briefly, but with a thoroughness that left her catching her breath.

'Relax.'

Like she could do that when he invaded her senses and melted her bones?

He made her think of the impossible...only to dismiss it out of hand. They had a marriage. The beginnings of affection...maybe. It was enough. More than she'd expected. So why did she feel as if her emotions were spinning out of control?

Ridiculous, she chided silently as she tossed cosmetics and perfume into a bag and slotted it into a suitcase.

She caught up her shoulder bag. 'Shall we leave?'

A chartered Lear jet awaited them at Sydney airport, and, once airborne, Loukas opened his laptop and focused on work, while Alesha did likewise.

Although her father had preferred to travel via a commercial flight, she admired the advantage of a chartered jet whose interior held luxurious recliner sleep chairs, together with designer office accessories enabling a corporate high-flier to work in comfort.

For the duration of the flight they both spent large slices of time on their laptops, ate, slept and took the occasional break.

Alesha found it stimulating to discuss Karsouli on a one-to-one basis; to present a few of her ideas for its future...proposals Dimitri had listened to, but not implemented due to lack of capital—something she hadn't known at the time.

The strategies Loukas intended—some of which were already in place—had her approval, and she could only applaud his long-term plan to return Karsouli to its former power amongst a global industry.

His keen mind, intelligence combined with a certain ruthlessness to elevate him sharing equal prestige with some of the world's known financial peers.

Qualities that offered a different perspective to the man who'd taken on the husband role...in a business arrangement that, for her, was becoming increasingly personal with every passing day.

Night, she corrected. For she couldn't deny she found comfort as he held her through the night. To stir in sleep, and have him reach for her. The feel of his lips against the soft-beating pulse at the base of her throat. Just *knowing* he was there.

And the sex...more, so much more than she'd ever dreamed possible. Wondrous, exciting, magical.

But that's all it is, she reminded herself. Good sex is just...good sex, and not to be confused with a deeper emotion.

So…enjoy the ride and don't question the motives?

Fine, if you could separate the prosaic from the illusion.

After all, what was she to him other than a partner in every legal sense?

It was late afternoon when the Lear jet touched down in Athens, and they emerged to balmy sunshine, passed through Customs to be met by Loukas' driver, Cristos, who transported them via limousine to suburban Kifissia where luxury homes surrounded by trees and beautiful gardens exuded wealth.

Alesha's eyes widened slightly as the limousine turned into a gated entrance and eased to a halt outside the entrance to a double-storeyed palatial mansion.

'My home base,' Loukas informed her as he led her into a large marble-tiled foyer where a middle-aged housekeeper, whom he introduced as Hera, greeted them. Cristos followed with their luggage.

'It's beautiful,' she complimented simply. Elegant, she added silently as he led her upstairs to their bedroom suite. Rich furnishings, solid furniture, imposing mirrors and artwork adorning the walls.

A very large home for one man, she perceived, although fitting given he headed the Andreou consortiums and doubtless entertained…business associates, as well intimate dinners *à deux* with women.

Had any of his former mistresses shared his home?

And what if they had? His past was his own.

He'd vowed fidelity…the question had to be whether he intended to abide by it.

Emotional introspection following a long international flight, comfortable though it had been, did not make for a good mix.

What she needed was a leisurely shower, a change of clothes, dinner and a good night's sleep…in that order.

The spacious bedroom suite held one bed, albeit king-size, two walk-in robes with adjoining dressing rooms, two en suites.

Alesha opened her bag, extracted fresh underwear, tailored trousers and a knit top, then she entered the en suite Loukas indicated as her own, ignored the temptation to linger overlong, and chose to sweep her hair into a careless knot atop her head, vetoed make-up with the exception of lip gloss and emerged some ten minutes later to discover Loukas in the process of pulling on a cotton shirt over chinos.

Heeled sandals lent her height and aided confidence, she added silently as she slid them on.

Hera had prepared a delicately flavoured moussaka, a greek salad, with fresh fruit to follow, and Alesha declined coffee in favour of tea, lingered over it and endeavoured to fend off an increasing weariness while experiencing envy of Loukas' apparent vitality.

How did he do that?

'Why don't you go up to bed? I have a few calls to make before I call it a night.'

It was all too easy to acquiesce, and she cast him a musing smile as she rose to her feet. 'Goodnight.'

'Sleep well.'

She did, almost as soon as her head touched the pillow, and she was unaware of Loukas' presence as he slid in beside her, or that he curved her in close against him.

Alesha murmured indistinctly as she slid into the dream, subconsciously aware the sound moved to a purr of pleasure as lips nuzzled the sensitive curve between her neck and her shoulder. Mmm, *nice*.

So, too, was the gentle drift of fingers over the delicate slope of her breast, and her mouth relaxed into a winsome smile as the tender peak hardened beneath their touch.

She shifted a little, unconsciously arching her body as the hand slid to her waist, explored the diamond pin at her navel, before tracing a pattern over her stomach.

A husky sigh emerged from her throat as a mouth fastened over one breast and gently suckled, sending sensation spearing through her body, and she groaned softly in the need to beg for more…only to give a satisfied moan of pleasure as deft fingers slid to the apex between her thighs and found her throbbing clitoris.

If this was a dream, she didn't want it to end, for the pleasure was so acutely intense it almost transcended into reality.

Afterwards she couldn't pinpoint precisely when she became aware of emerging consciousness…only that she did, and she reached for him.

'At last you wake, *agape mou*,' Loukas murmured with a husky chuckle.

'Uh-huh.' She captured his head and framed it as she sought his mouth with her own in a piercingly sweet kiss that touched him more deeply than he thought possible.

It unleashed a primitive hunger he fought to control as he shaped her body and entered her in one unrestrained thrust, absorbing her startled cry as her vaginal muscles gripped his hardened length.

For several seemingly long seconds he remained still, gentling his mouth into an erotic supplication, then he began to move, slowly at first as he took her with him, her increasing urgency matching his own as they became consumed by electrifying passion.

Incandescent, primal…she cried out with the force of it,

and held onto him, almost afraid to let go in case she shattered into a thousand pieces.

It was almost as if her whole body vibrated with the aftershock of sensation that was more than just sex.

Dear heaven, she couldn't even find the words to describe how she felt as she buried her mouth in the curve of his neck.

She was barely aware of the soothing brush of his hand along her spine, or the touch of his fingers working a tactile massage at her nape.

There was no sense of the passage of time…just the slowing of her ragged breathing as she became consumed by a sense of dreamy peace. Too emotionally spent to do more than close her eyes and drift easily to sleep.

Loukas slid from the bed as the dawn lightened the sky, then showered; freshly shaven, he dressed in business attire and crossed to the bed and stood looking at his wife's softened features.

She slept curled to one side, a hand tucked beneath her cheek…rested, replete, her generous mouth slightly parted in the semblance of a smile.

He felt his body stir, and he banked down the urge to take her mouth with his own.

Except it wouldn't stop there, and regrettably there wasn't time. Cristos waited in the limousine to drive him into the city where he'd connect with Constantine, field a call from his mother, and attempt to vet the social activities Angelina had undoubtedly planned during her short visit.

Beginning with this evening's family dinner held in his parents' home.

Would Alesha recall he'd informed her of the invitation as she rested in his arms through the early morning hours?

Possibly not. Rather than wake her, he'd leave a message

with Hera, call between meetings, and issue Cristos with instructions to accompany her wherever she wanted to go.

Alesha woke late, discovered she was alone, and gave a startled yelp as she checked the time.

Nine? Half the morning gone…and where was Loukas?

Then she remembered, and she shifted the bedcovers, took a shower, dressed in casual wear and made her way downstairs to the kitchen.

Hera relayed Loukas' message, then she made fresh coffee and offered croissants, fresh figs, Greek-style yoghurt, and currant bread with honey.

Alesha chose the figs and yoghurt, washed them down with coffee before taking a walk in the grounds.

The day was warm, the air stirred by a slight breeze, and she admired the meticulously kept garden borders framing beds filled with floral blooms.

Loukas' mansion nestled against a hillside and offered a stunning panoramic view of the city reaching to the port of Piraeus.

The place of her parents' birth, where they had grown up and married before choosing to relocate in Sydney.

There was a sense of timelessness, of an ancient age, often violent, as rulers fought for power and glory.

She moved away, and heard the insistent ring of her cellphone as she paused to admire the swimming pool with its blue mosaic tiles, ornamental cupids at placed intervals spouting plumes of water.

The sound of Loukas' deep, slightly accented voice sent her pulse into a quickened beat.

'A quick call to say I'll be caught up all day and not in until around seven,' he enlightened her. 'We're due at my parents' home at eight.'

'I'll ensure I'm ready.' She waited a beat. 'Tough day?'

'Nothing I can't handle.' He paused to speak to someone. 'I'll see you tonight.'

An event Alesha prepared for with care, electing to wear classic black, killer heels, and subtle make-up with emphasis on her eyes. Hair—upswept or loose?

'Loose,' Loukas declared as he entered the bedroom and shrugged out of his suit jacket, then pulled his tie free.

'You think?'

He crossed to where she stood and framed her face, then kissed her. 'Shame you're already dressed. You could have shared my shower.'

'Not enough time.'

His eyes gleamed. 'I could always ring ahead and say we'll be delayed.'

'But you won't.' A wicked smile curved the edges of her mouth. 'Besides, I prefer a lover with a slow hand.'

He trailed light fingers down her cheek. 'You'll keep.'

Constantine and Angelina resided in the southern suburb of Voula, in a luxurious home located at the top of Panorama.

Cristos deposited them at precisely eight, and no sooner did the limousine draw to a halt than the front door opened to reveal Loukas' parents, who moved quickly down the wide steps to offer an affectionate greeting before ushering them into a spacious foyer where a vision in black stood poised at the base of an elegant staircase.

Lexi, Loukas' young sister, all grown up in her early twenties, tall, dark-haired, impeccably dressed…the antithesis of the defiant teenager Alesha remembered from five years ago.

'Hi.' Lexi hugged him. 'You've given me the best gift of all…a sister.' She turned towards Alesha. 'Welcome.'

'Thank you.'

Lexi offered quietly, 'Thia Daria is waiting in the lounge to offer a formal greeting.'

Constantine's sister…a dour spinster, Alesha recalled, with an acerbic tongue, and wondered if perchance she'd mellowed a little since the last time they'd met.

Not a smidgen, if the woman's severe expression was any indication.

'So,' Daria began imperiously. 'You are the pawn Dimitri offered to save his wretched soul.'

Oh, my, this had all the portents of being a *fun* night.

'Hardly his soul.' She met the older woman's steely gaze and held it. 'He took that with him.'

'I speak the truth.'

'A truth I'm very aware of,' Alesha offered calmly. 'Did you imagine otherwise?'

'Loukas is my godson. As the only male Andreou of his generation, I consider it is of vital importance he has taken a wife worthy of bearing his name.'

'While I consider the importance lies with Loukas' ability to share equal partnership in Karsouli.'

Lexi clapped her hands lightly. 'Well fielded.'

Constantine indicated a collection of comfortable sofas. 'Please, be seated. I'll open the champagne.'

'I prefer ouzo.'

Naturally, Alesha conceded, Daria would take pleasure in being contrary. Was it a game? Maybe two could play…

Over dinner, perhaps.

A delicious meal prepared especially by Angelina, comprising several courses…tasty samples of various seafood dishes, followed by mouth-watering sweet honey and nut pastries and fresh fruit.

It was during dessert that Daria made an announcement in

the form of a statement...no one could possibly term it a suggestion, Alesha decided a trifle ruefully.

'You have denied your family the pleasure of participating in your wedding. A ceremony will be repeated here in Athens. Tomorrow,' she determined firmly, 'we will shop.'

'A reaffirmation of your marriage vows,' Angelina declared with enthusiasm. 'All that is required will be the documented proof the marriage has already taken place.' Her eyes sparkled. 'There will be guests...a party.' She paused for a few seconds. 'Afterwards you will take Alesha to the island for a few days,' she concluded.

Oh, my. The light touch of Loukas' hand on her thigh caused her to look at him askance.

'A charming idea.' His eyes speared her own. 'Alesha?'

That was right...throw the ball into her court! Like she was going to refuse? 'Charming,' she agreed. In a moment of inspiration she turned towards Lexi. 'I'd love it for you to be my attendant.'

'Done,' Loukas' sister concurred with delight. 'Which means I get to join in the shopping expedition.'

'It will be my pleasure. My gift to you both.' Constantine beamed as he sank back in his chair. 'And now we shall adjourn to the lounge and Angelina will bring the coffee.'

It was almost midnight when Loukas summoned Cristos and they took their leave.

Alesha settled into the rear seat of the limousine as Loukas joined her, and she sat in reflective silence as Cristos traversed the driveway.

Loukas reached for her hand and brought it to his lips. 'You managed very well.'

His features appeared as shadowed angles in the evening's

darkness, illuminated by passing street-lighting and the beam
of oncoming traffic.

'Your aunt is a lioness.'

'Yet beneath the surface lies the heart of a pussycat.'

'You're kidding me?'

'You're now part of the Andreou family. One Daria guards
with her life. You will discover she is generous to a fault,'
he relayed quietly. 'And very caring towards those who earn
her trust.'

'You could have warned me what to expect.'

'Perhaps,' Loukas conceded. 'But would it have made any
difference?'

No. For how could she have disappointed his parents,
Lexi…Daria, even, if she'd indicated a reaffirmation of her
wedding vows was too much to ask?

'So we get to do it…when?'

'I imagine my mother and Daria already have the details
in hand.'

Alesha didn't doubt it for a moment.

Sleep didn't come easily, and she sighed a little as Loukas
drew her close and brushed his lips to her temple. 'You want
me to help you sleep?'

'Depends what you have in mind,' she managed in a voice
husky with tiredness.

'If I promise to do all the work?'

'Uh-huh.'

'I assume that's a *yes*?'

His light teasing held a sensuality that warmed her blood and
sent it pulsing through her body. 'What are you waiting for?'

A faint chuckle emerged from his throat as he sought the
softly beating pulse at the edge of her neck, savoured a little,
then his lips trailed a path to her breast, suckled there, and

moved low to create the sort of sensual havoc that demanded release...hers, by him.

He gifted it to her, eventually, and caught her as she climaxed. Then he held her for what remained of the night, sleeping as she slept until dawn crept over the horizon and gave birth to a new day.

CHAPTER NINE

LOUKAS' words 'have fun' echoed in Alesha's mind as Cristos drove to Voula, collected Angelina, Daria and Lexi, and headed towards one of several elite shopping areas in the city where designerwear graced exclusive boutiques.

Angelina and Daria quibbled and clicked their tongues as one gown after another was submitted for their approval…or not. Mostly it was not.

'Don't despair,' Lexi encouraged quietly. 'They both have excellent taste.'

And no regard whatsoever to cost, Alesha perceived, and gave up figuring the exchange conversion.

By comparison, it made shopping for *the* dress in Sydney with Lacey seem like a breeze.

'Lunch,' Daria announced. 'After which Cristos will take us on a tour of the city until the shops reopen.'

Although Alesha had explored some of the tourist sights with her parents during her last visit to Athens, it proved interesting to revisit familiar places and hear a different perspective of the history. Tales passed by word of mouth through the generations, doubtlessly distorted by the passage of time, but there was a sense of admiration that some of the buildings had been painstakingly assembled without benefit of machinery so long ago.

To pass over ground trodden by an ancient civilization, where the blood of her ancestors had been spilt, and heretics were put to death.

Modern roads, homes, industry now covered ground that had once been barren. If one possessed an overly vivid imagination, it was almost possible to hear the thunder of galloping horses, the roar of men as they went into battle, the clash of swords.

A return to the city streets where some of the most famous shops were located ensured forays into a few, where recognition of the Andreou name resulted in almost obsequious attention.

'Today we look, we compare,' Angelina confided. 'Anything of particular interest we request a twenty-four-hour reserved hold. Tomorrow we return and decide.'

It was late when Cristos departed from the Andreou home in Voula and headed north to Kifissia.

All Alesha had to show for the day was one glossy designer-emblazoned bag.

She thanked Cristos when he deposited her outside the front door of Loukas' home, greeted Hera on entering the foyer, then she ran lightly upstairs to their suite, toed off her shoes, undressed and ran a bath where she luxuriated in a leisurely scented soaking before emerging to dry off and don a towelling robe.

Loukas entered the room as she caught the length of her hair and twisted it into a loose knot, which she fixed in place with a large clip.

'Hi, you're home,' she offered as he crossed the room to her side. The mere sight of him, his presence, invaded her senses, and her insides felt in serious danger of melting into an ignominious puddle as he framed her face and took her mouth with his own in a lingering kiss.

'You shared an enjoyable day?'

Alesha rolled her eyes. 'Do you have any idea how the female members of your family *shop*?'

'That bad, huh?'

'Don't you dare laugh,' she threatened.

'I wouldn't dream of it.' He rested light hands on her shoulders. 'Which ache the most…feet or shoulders?'

'Both,' she said succinctly, and almost groaned as his fingers sought out the kinks and knots and began to ease them with an expertise for which she could only thank him.

Heaven…he could have been a masseur in another life.

'Should I ask how many purchases have been made?'

'Shoes,' she offered. 'Even though I have a perfectly suitable pair of my own.' She lifted a hand, then let it fall to her side. 'Your mother has offered me her lace wedding veil.'

'I believe it's exquisite.'

'I thought this would be *simple*.'

'Shopping to my mother, Daria and Lexi is an art form,' Loukas assured her solemnly. 'And accorded due reverence.'

'Tomorrow we take up where we left off.' She turned slightly to look at him. 'There's no chance I can take a rain check and spend the day with you in the city office?'

'It would be more than my life is worth.'

'You're kidding me? The powerful omnipotent Loukas Andreou bows down to the three women in his life?'

'Four,' he corrected with an amused smile. 'You neglected to include yourself. And shopping, in this instance, is of the utmost importance.'

'I shall think of ways to make you pay,' she threatened with dire emphasis, and heard his husky laugh.

'Sounds interesting.'

'Is this second wedding, for want of a better word, scheduled to happen *soon*?'

'Early next week, I believe.'

'You mean, you don't know for sure?'

'Tuesday has been mentioned.'

She could do this. The trick was to be more assertive and not allow the Andreou women to make *all* the decisions.

'Is there any social engagement I should be aware of?'

'A fundraiser on Saturday evening for a worthy charity Andreou has sponsored for a number of years.'

Consequently attendance would be expected together with the gift of a sizable donation. Which meant an Andreou bride would garner considerable interest.

But then, hadn't Loukas also drawn attention as her husband at a similar charitable event Karsouli supported in Sydney?

Wealthy tycoons were known to donate generously to worthy charitable causes. Most chose to give something back, with time and money for those genuinely in need. Committees organized events, provided entertainment and a three-course meal including alcoholic beverages…and charged accordingly.

It gave the social elite an opportunity to select designer gowns, wear their jewellery, be seen and the chosen few to appear in the media social pages.

'How was your day?' She hadn't thought to ask, and he removed his hands as she turned to face him.

'Busy. Constantine is considering semi-retirement. It means reshuffling a few executive staff, selecting suitable replacements and aligning a technical infrastructure I can oversee from Sydney.'

'And you're okay with his decision?' It would mean a heavier workload, possibly a reasonably regular commute between Sydney and Athens.

Would she accompany him? Somehow the thought of remaining in Sydney alone didn't hold much appeal. She'd miss his presence...sharing her bed, the pleasure of his touch through the night. Dammit...she'd feel as if a part of her were lost.

For a moment she couldn't think. Where had that come from? It meant she cared...when she'd silently sworn not to become emotionally involved.

A hollow laugh rose and died in her throat.

Sure, like that isn't the joke of the year!

'It's inevitable, given he's reached his early sixties.'

For a moment she looked at him blankly, for she'd lost the thread of their conversation.

She glimpsed the faint gleam in his dark eyes as he lifted a hand and traced light fingers down the vee of her robe, loosened the ties at her waist, then he shaped the slight weight of her breasts.

'Beautiful,' he complimented gently. He lowered his head and brushed his lips to each in turn, then he sought the faint scar beneath one sensitive peak, caressed it...and sensation speared through her body.

'You're wearing a new perfume.'

'It's soap,' she managed in a slightly strangled voice, and felt his mouth curve into a smile. 'Gardenia,' she added and gasped as he lifted his head and took possession of her mouth.

Magic, sheer magic, she registered dimly as she threaded her fingers through his hair and leant into the kiss, gifting as well as taking, absorbing everything he chose to give...and more.

It wasn't enough. She needed him, all of him, naked, skin on skin, his body fused with hers in a primitive mating, uniquely and exclusively *theirs* in a way there could never be another for either of them.

Was that *love*?

Lust, certainly. But surely love was a different entity, involving trust and fidelity.

And she couldn't love him…could she? Hadn't she sworn never to let another man get beneath her skin and steal her heart?

Yet Loukas was *there*, a constant in her thoughts, her mind. He managed to make her feel different, almost special. Was it merely a practised act in order to lull her into a false sense of security?

Sadly, she didn't know…and there was a part of her that didn't *want* to know. For to discover it was all a charade would hurt her more than she imagined possible.

And that, she recognized, was an admission in itself.

With effort, she eased back from him a little, aware he didn't attempt to dissuade her.

'You should go shower and change,' Alesha managed quietly. 'Or we'll be late for dinner.'

He touched a finger to her slightly swollen mouth. 'And that would never do, hmm?'

'I'm sure Hera has gone to considerable effort.'

Without a further word she crossed into her dressing-room, shed the robe, selected fresh underwear, and chose tailored trousers and a fashionable blouse…reappearing into the bedroom to find it empty and the sound of the shower running in Loukas' en suite.

Dinner was a pleasant meal, during which conversation didn't lag…although afterwards Alesha retained little memory of what they'd actually discussed.

Loukas excused himself on the pretext of work, while she used her laptop to catch up with emails and respond to one of Lacey's that had landed in her inbox that morning.

It was late when she retired to bed, and even later when Loukas joined her. For a moment she lay perfectly still, unsure whether he'd reach for her or not…and when he curved her close in against him she wasn't sure whether to be relieved or peeved when his breathing slowed and acquired the steadiness denoting sleep.

The following few days were filled with shopping, and it came as a relief when the Andreou women conceded contented satisfaction in having achieved their objective.

Alesha had to admit they showed excellent taste in fashion, and she couldn't fault their suggested choices.

'Now you can relax,' Lexi confided as Cristos delivered them to Voula late Friday afternoon.

You *think*? Alesha posed silently.

With the charity fundraiser the following evening, the reaffirmation of marriage vows and party planned for Tuesday, *relaxing* wasn't a state she'd reach any time soon.

Daria, as Loukas had predicted, had mellowed considerably during the past few days, and it was possible to catch a glimpse of the woman beneath the severe exterior.

Angelina proved to be the quintessential mother, who had learnt to accept her son and daughter as adults in an adult world, and gained the wisdom to step aside from the strict parental role and respect them as equals. An admirable quality that Alesha found endearing.

Lexi's engaging personality made her easy to like, so too did her determination to strike out on her own.

'Loukas *is* Andreou. My talent lies with fashionable jewellery, specifically design. I have a studio in the Pláka, and a small degree of success. This year has brought exposure, and I will soon need to take on another staff member.'

'So when do I get to see some of your designs?' Alesha asked as they shared coffee in the lounge after a dinner Angelina had insisted she share when Loukas had called to say he would be dining with associates and not due home until late.

'I'll give you the link to my website, and we'll fit in a time for Cristos to bring you to the studio before you return with Loukas to Sydney. Sound good?'

'I'll look forward to it.'

It was almost eleven when Cristos delivered her home, and her cellphone beeped as she headed upstairs.

'Another hour, *agape mou*,' Loukas relayed in his slightly accented drawl.

'I'll probably be asleep.'

'In which case I'll wake you.'

The mere thought of being woken by him sent delight slithering down the length of her spine. 'If you must.'

His soft chuckle almost undid her.

Alesha undressed and headed into the shower, set the water dial to hot and let the heat soothe away the stress of the day as she lathered her body with the gardenia-scented soap…and attempted to convince herself the choice had nothing to do with Loukas.

Caught up in reflective introspection, she attempted to analyze when her emotions had begun to change from reluctantly accepting the marriage…to wanting it to work, to be real.

To love, and be loved in return? Was that too much to ask for?

Yet love couldn't be bought. It was built on emotion, and deserved the utmost care.

In a moment of self-indulgence she let her mind wander to the years ahead…children Loukas would lift high in the air and laugh with in their tender years, be fiercely protective of as they grew, and encourage to achieve in all areas of their lives.

Wishful thinking didn't mean it would happen, and with

fresh resolve she closed the water, caught up a towel and dried off before donning sleep pants and a singlet top.

On the verge of sleep she heard the faint click as Loukas closed the bedroom door, the soft rustle of clothing being discarded, followed by the sound of the shower.

Long minutes later he slid beneath the covers and reached for her, turning her easily in his arms as she caught his head and brought his mouth down to her own in a hungry kiss that stirred his senses to fever pitch.

This…*this* was what he'd consciously anticipated as he'd wined and dined three associates while negotiating a deal. One that had taken skilled strategy and patience to achieve.

Now he wanted to bury himself in the sweet sorcery of a woman's body. Not any woman…*this* woman.

To pleasure her until he sensed the soft purr in her throat as she arched her body against his own. The faint moan of capitulation as he nuzzled the sensitive hollow at the curve of her neck. Her reaction to his touch, the intimacy they shared…and the joy of mutual orgasm.

On the edge of sleep he gathered her close, soothed her when she stirred and held her through the night.

Alesha dressed with care, aware the silk chiffon gown with its ruched bodice in deep sapphire hugged her slender curves and highlighted the texture of her skin. The diagonally cut skirt flowed gently to rest at her ankles, and her heeled pumps and evening clutch were a perfect match.

Jewellery was restricted to a diamond pendant, ear-studs and matching bracelet.

She ensured her make-up was understated with emphasis on her eyes, a touch of bronzing powder and a soft neutral lipstick and gloss.

'Beautiful,' Loukas complimented as she prepared to precede him from the room, and she threw him a faintly teasing look.

'Thanks.'

Her eyes sparkled as she subjected him to a sweeping appraisal.

Attired in a black evening suit, fine white linen shirt and black bow tie, he looked far too compelling for any woman's peace of mind...especially hers.

'I guess you'll do.'

His soft laughter curled round her heartstrings and tugged a little. 'Damned with faint praise.'

Together they descended the staircase and moved to the front entrance where Cristos waited with the limousine.

'Anything more and you'll get a swelled head,' she said solemnly as she slid into the rear passenger seat. Her pulse leapt as he captured her hand and held it for the duration of the drive into the city.

The hotel hosting the event had to be one of the city's finest, Alesha perceived as she stood at Loukas' side amongst the mingling guests sipping champagne.

Men of varying ages wore formal evening wear while the women sparkled...literally, in jewellery worth a fortune.

She became aware her presence garnered speculative interest, and she tilted her head a little, kept a smile in place, and maintained an expected pretence.

It was something of a relief when Constantine, Angelina, Daria and Lexi joined them.

'The rescue team,' Lexi enlightened her quietly as she leant forward to brush her lips to Alesha's cheek. 'You look gorgeous.'

'Same goes.' A genuine compliment as Loukas' sister wore

a stunning gown in fire-engine red that showcased her figure with breathtaking style.

Daria looked regal in black, while Angelina had opted for delicate shades of lilac.

'Would you like a rundown on some of the guests?' Lexi queried lightly. 'Or would you prefer to form your own impression?'

'You think it'll make a difference?'

'Not in the slightest,' Lexi assured her. 'Although I shall warn you of any impending danger.'

She couldn't help a faint laugh. 'Loukas' ex-girlfriends?'

'Plural? You're quick. One in particular.'

'Do I get a name?'

'Iliana,' Lexi informed her with droll humour. 'Model, filthy rich, and hunting Loukas. Expect a cat-fight when she discovers he's taken.'

'As she will?'

'Darling Alesha. News travels fast.'

So it did, in any city in the world. Why should Athens be any different?

'Approaching from the right,' Lexi voiced softly several minutes later. 'Wearing black and white.'

Stunning, tall, incredibly slender, with exquisitely assembled facial features, luminous dark eyes and a mouth that promised much.

Oh, my. Perfection personified, Alesha conceded as Iliana drew close.

'*Kalispera.*'

The greeting included each of them, but the model's attention rested solely on Loukas.

'Iliana.' His voice held a coolness that was ignored.

'You have a relative join you tonight?' The assumption held

a teasing lightness that wasn't reflected in her eyes, and Alesha was willing to swear all three Andreou women drew in their collective breaths.

'My wife, Alesha,' Loukas relayed in a silky drawl, and merely compounded the situation by taking hold of Alesha's hand and raising it to his lips.

'How…adventurous of you, darling,' Iliana arched, 'when a legal commitment was never on your agenda.' She paused to summon a slight, deliberately fake smile. 'Although there is the duty to produce an Andreou heir.'

The woman was all feline with vicious claws, Alesha perceived, and doubtless ate unsuspecting men for breakfast.

It posed the question as to how deeply involved she'd been with Loukas.

Even the thought of the model's sinuous body wrapping itself around him made Alesha feel slightly nauseous.

She gave herself a mental shake. *Get real.* He's no celibate. It's a given there have been women…probably scads of them. So what?

But *Iliana*?

How could she hope to compete?

'Do you not speak?' the model posed with the glitter of revenge momentarily apparent in her dark eyes.

'When I have something to say.'

She sensed Lexi's faint smile, and mentally braced herself for Iliana's next verbal parry.

'It doesn't bother you that Loukas and I are intimate friends?'

'Should it?'

'Enough.' One word, quietly delivered, but only a fool would ignore the steel beneath Loukas' silky voice.

Daria offered a comment in her own language…words Alesha had no difficulty in comprehending.

The evening didn't improve as Iliana boldly took her place at their table, ignored Daria and Angelina's telling looks as she proceeded to stake a claim for Loukas' attention.

To his credit he mostly ignored her, adhering only to polite civility as the occasion demanded.

Yet it made for unnecessary awkwardness, and doubtless aroused speculation amongst many of the guests present.

Alesha recalled the words of a famed socialite who advised... *'Don't get mad, darling—get even.'*

So she smiled, conducted animated conversation with their table companions, and managed to cast Loukas an adoring look or three during the meal.

It helped that he played a similar part, although there was a bad moment when Alesha and Lexi used the powder room, and Iliana entered as they were about to exit.

Alesha witnessed the gleam of satisfaction in the model's eyes, and mentally prayed a verbal war could be avoided.

'Very clever of you, darling, to land a fish of Loukas' calibre. What bait did you use?'

'Public displays are a trifle tacky,' she ventured as Iliana initiated a confrontation. 'Don't you think?'

'Are you pregnant?'

'Iliana,' Lexi said quietly. 'You're in danger of making a fool of yourself.'

Alesha placed a placating hand on Lexi's arm and held the model's gaze as she asked evenly, 'Is there a point to this conversation?'

Hard eyes raked a damning appraisal. 'You're quite pretty. But don't think your marriage will last. Loukas is an intensely sexual animal. I doubt you'll satisfy him for long.'

'You think? Perhaps I should thank you for the advice and

suggest more creative positions…' she paused deliberately '…in places other than the bedroom.'

The colour leeched from Iliana's face, then flooded back as her hand flew towards Alesha's face.

A move Alesha stalled with galling ease. 'Don't,' she warned quietly.

'Or you'll do…what?'

'This.' She sought the right nerve and the model's legs buckled, sending her sliding to the floor.

With incredible calm she turned towards Lexi. 'Shall we leave?'

'My God,' Lexi breathed in stunned surprise as they gained the ballroom and headed towards their table. 'Where did you learn to do that?'

She bore Lexi's speculative look. 'It's a long story.'

'That's what I thought.'

Loukas' gaze seared her own as she slid into her seat.

'Problems?'

'Interesting question. Would that be singular or plural?'

'Iliana.'

'Astute of you.'

Lexi leaned forward. 'Alesha was magnificent.'

His eyes didn't leave her own. 'Indeed?'

'You had to be there,' his sister relayed.

'That particular Jezebel needs to be taken down a peg,' Daria opined sternly, whereupon her niece grinned unashamedly.

'*Thia*, Alesha did…literally.'

'Good.'

A backhanded compliment from Loukas' dour aunt? Accompanied by an approving smile? *Incredible.*

It was interesting to note the seat Iliana had occupied at

their table remained empty. Had the model left the event? Somehow Alesha didn't think so.

A fact that was confirmed half an hour later as the focus of the evening featured a fashion parade by three of Athens' top designers with models showing a selection ranging from casual chic to evening wear.

It came as no surprise Iliana formed part of the group of models hired for the evening.

Alesha had to concede the model's professionalism, for her figure bore the perfect lines to showcase the garments to maximum effect.

The personal touches, however, were a deliberate payback as Iliana tossed her long mane of gloriously wavy hair and pouted a little too prettily as she gazed overlong at Loukas.

An effort to show him what he was missing?

Maintaining an interested expression took some effort, and Alesha shot Loukas a startled look as he took hold of her hand and soothed the rapidly beating pulse at the base of her wrist.

This was meant to be reassurance? *Please.*

She endeavoured to tell herself it didn't matter…but it did.

To a degree she felt exposed, even vulnerable, knowing there had to be a number of guests present who were aware Loukas and Iliana were once an item. Given how gossip travelled, it was now common knowledge Loukas had taken a wife. Cue in Iliana's public display on the catwalk, and it wasn't difficult to do the maths.

She'd ridden out worse with the fallout from her experience with Seth. What was a model's wrath in comparison?

So she continued to smile and converse, and generally project the image of someone enjoying the event. Her demeanour earned a surprisingly gentle smile from Daria, as if she knew and saw all…which she probably did.

The charity chairperson thanked the assembled guests for their generosity, and gave a closing speech.

Filtered music provided a muted background and there was a general shift as businessmen converged, while women took the opportunity to catch up with friends seated elsewhere.

An elderly man sought Loukas and Constantine's attention, and both men excused themselves from the table to converge into a group of three a short distance away.

'I'll be at my studio on Monday, if you'd like to call in,' Lexi offered, and Alesha responded with enthusiasm.

'Love to. Give me a time and I'll be there.'

'Eleven? Then we can do lunch.'

'Done.'

Loukas returned to her side, and when she attempted to extricate her hand from his, he made the exercise more difficult by threading her fingers through his own.

Eventually the evening came to a close and the guests rose to leave…a lengthy process as the ballroom slowly emptied and guests spilled into the foyer to mingle as the concierge directed cars be brought to the entrance.

'Tuesday will be splendid,' Daria declared as she bestowed a light kiss to Alesha's cheek. 'Have faith, my dear.'

This was the same Daria, she of the acerbic tongue? Perhaps it was a rite of passage, from which she'd emerged having gained Daria's approval.

Constantine's driver appeared with their limousine, followed immediately by Cristos, ensuring farewells were exchanged and both limousines moved quickly away from the hotel entrance.

CHAPTER TEN

LOUKAS turned towards her as the large car eased into traffic. 'Now would be a good time to tell me what went down with Iliana.'

Alesha didn't pretend to misunderstand. 'The powder-room incident?'

'That's the one.'

'You could ask Lexi.'

'I'm asking you.'

'Do you need me to draw a verbal picture?'

'Iliana is a diva, with the temper to match.'

'Like I didn't get the drift of both?' Or her obsession with *you*? she added silently. 'Okay, words were said, and Iliana took umbrage.'

'That's it?'

'Not exactly.'

'There's more?'

'I—used preventive measures to avoid being slapped.'

There was a few seconds' pause, and his voice assumed a musing drawl. 'And how, precisely, did you manage that?'

She looked at him carefully and could detect little from his expression in the dim light. 'Precisely?'

'Please.'

'Nerve pressure.'

'I'm almost afraid to ask.'

Alesha told him.

He lifted her hand and brushed his lips across her knuckles. 'You want me to say there were few women before you?'

'Not according to the media.'

'Would it help if I assured you that I ended a relationship before beginning another, and practised fidelity with each lover?'

'You want marks for integrity?'

It was late when they bade Cristos goodnight and entered the house. Loukas reset the security alarm and followed her upstairs to their bedroom.

The catch fastening on her pendant proved elusive again, and she gave a frustrated sigh as she tussled with it.

Then he was there, freeing the catch with ease, and she felt his fingers move to the zip fastener on her gown, felt the faint slide, followed by the slither of fabric as it slipped to the floor.

She turned to face him and eased off his jacket, then undid his tie and reached for the shirt buttons, freeing each one with deliberate slowness before releasing the fasteners holding his trousers in place.

He dispensed with his shoes, socks, and stepped out of his trousers.

'I want you naked.'

When he complied, she led him to the bed, then pushed him down onto the mattress.

'Stay.'

He lifted his arms, cupped his head and met her determined gaze with quizzical amusement. 'You want to play?'

Alesha merely smiled as she placed one knee on the mattress and straddled him. In one glorious movement she arched her body, then she lowered her head to brush the length of her hair across his chest, trailing it down until it rested on his arousal, tracing the sensitive skin back and forth as she heard his breath hiss through his teeth.

A satisfactory murmur of appreciation escaped her lips as she tossed her hair back before shaping him with gentle fingers…light, teasing strokes that caused his stomach muscles to tauten, then clench as she replaced her fingers with her mouth and stroked him with her tongue, bestowing feathery kisses until he hauled her close and took her mouth with his own.

'Uh-huh,' she cautioned. 'I'm not done yet.'

It became a leisurely exploration as she stirred his senses to fever pitch, teasing with gentle nips of her teeth, only to soothe with the tip of her tongue.

His male nipples earned her fascination, and he groaned as she circled him with her mouth, taunted with the edge of her teeth…then it was she who cried out as he clasped her hips and surged into her. Again and again, with a ravaging hunger that blew her away, and then some.

Cataclysmic sex. Passion at its most wild and wanton.

Primal.

Gradually their breathing slowed, and he pulled her down and held her close to nuzzle the sensitive curve at the base of her neck.

Her body trembled as he trailed a hand down the length of her spine and gently pressed its base, heard her soft sigh, then he slid a hand beneath her nape and kissed her so gently it made her want to cry.

She didn't want to move…didn't think she was capable as he feathered light fingers over the curve at her waist, shaped her buttocks, and simply held her.

There were no words for what they'd just shared, and she didn't even try to voice them.

At some stage she must have drifted into a dreamless sleep,

for she came awake slowly to the sound of gushing water and an awareness she was alone in the bed.

The scent of gardenia teased her nostrils and she lifted her head as Loukas appeared from the en suite and scooped her into his arms.

There was no sense of time as he stepped into the bath and lowered her down to sit in front of him. With care he applied the soap to her skin as she caught her hair and pinned it high so it wouldn't get wet.

Her eyes searched his, and her heart melted beneath the warmth of his smile.

He was a gorgeous man, and he was hers.

There were words she wanted to say, but they remained locked in her throat.

He'd taught her to trust again, helped to restore her faith in men...one man, she corrected silently. The pieces of her heart were fusing together, almost making that life-force whole and complete so that it beat for him.

Only him.

To be with him like this was heaven. Everything she could ask for...

The soporific effect of warm scented water combined with his ministrations lulled her almost to the edge of sleep, and she smiled as he lifted her out, then enveloped her in a large bath towel, dried her, then he blotted the excess water from his body, released the bath plug...and carried her back to bed.

He gathered her close, touched his lips to her temple, and felt her mouth part with pleasure as she snuggled in against him.

Lexi's studio was situated in a trendy part of the city, where small shops competed with cafés and bars, boho chic wear, hand-tooled leather goods and stores selling organic foods.

'I'll call when I'm done,' Alesha assured Cristos as she alighted from the limousine and crossed the street to where Lexi stood waiting.

'Hi,' she greeted and shared a quick hug. 'I'm really looking forward to today.'

Lexi indicated a set of stairs. 'Let's go on up.' She led the way, and Alesha followed. 'The studio is only small. Cosy,' she elaborated over her shoulder.

But so interesting, Alesha accorded as she saw the various shaped casting moulds, metals, tools of trade, and a glass case with finished pieces on display.

A young girl and a guy in his mid-twenties worked with intricate pieces of metal, using specialized tools with an expertise she could only admire.

Enamelled flower brooches and pins, exquisite pendants, ear-studs, bracelets, dress rings, each individually designed and crafted.

'You have tremendous talent,' she complimented with sincere admiration. An enamelled bracelet set in gold caught her attention... It was utterly beautiful, the teal and blue melded perfectly.

It was fascinating to learn the varying stages between design and completion, marketing and distribution.

There was little awareness of the passage of time, until Lexi glanced at her watch and declared they'd break for lunch.

'A delightful café not far from here does wonderful food. Their baklava is to die for.'

'Sounds good.'

It was everything Lexi said, authentic, family owned and well patronized.

'You'll adore the island,' Lexi relayed as they sipped coffee. 'It's a private sanctuary reached only by boat and helicopter.'

'Hey, Lexi.'

Alesha glanced towards two young men who pulled up two chairs to share their table. Mid to late twenties, she estimated, attired in jeans and tee shirts, and attractive.

Lexi introduced them as friends from her university days who ran a graphic art studio not far from her own.

They ordered coffee and food, and proved to be good company as they chatted, laughed, and exchanged anecdotes.

'So you are the lady who managed to snare Loukas with a love net,' came the teasing observation.

The jury was still out on that one. Affection, great sex...but she doubted she had his heart.

'Mention his name, and the man himself appears.'

Lexi raised a hand in greeting as Loukas moved towards their table. 'I told Loukas we would be lunching here. He said he might join us.'

Alesha felt her pulse kick into a faster beat as he drew close, and her eyes widened a little when he lowered his head and brushed his lips to her cheek.

She met his dark gleaming gaze and offered a warm smile as he pulled up a chair, ordered, then curved an arm over the back of her chair.

Staking a claim?

Perhaps, Loukas mused, tussling a little with his reaction to seeing his wife enjoying the company of Lexi's two male friends.

He didn't like another man sitting close to his woman—*his* by marriage, by circumstance. But it was more than that. Affection, the need to protect.

Desire—*his*—for her. She'd crept beneath his skin, invaded his senses...dammit, with each passing day she came closer to capturing his heart.

Something no other woman had achieved.

Last night...*Theos*...even thinking about her deliberately

tactile teasing with her hands, her mouth…and it took all his control to rein in his arousal.

It made him want to take hold of her hand and lead her to the nearest room, somewhere private, preferably with a bed.

He couldn't remember being so in need of a woman. Alesha, only *Alesha*, for no one else came close.

His body clenched tight and he barely masked the glitter of expectation and anticipation, threatening to reveal his desire to anyone who happened to look closely enough.

Did she know?

Possibly not. She had yet to reach the place where she could read him. Or could it be she subconsciously resisted allowing herself to do so?

Slowly, surely, he was earning her trust. She felt comfortable with him…except he wanted more than that. He wanted it all. Everything.

To see her face light up when he entered the room. For her to come to him and gift herself with joy and no reservation.

He'd rescheduled an appointment…something he almost never did, except in extenuating circumstances, and had been quietly surprised at the ease with which he'd done so.

To join his wife for lunch, for heaven's sake. He, who always put business matters before anything or anyone else.

An hour later he rose to his feet, paid the bill, then contented himself with framing his wife's face as he kissed her thoroughly…and derived a certain satisfaction in seeing her cheeks colour a soft pink when he released her.

Minutes later Loukas walked from the café and had Cristos drive him to the city block where Andreou owned a building.

Whereupon Lexi's two friends indicated a need to return to their studio, and Lexi regretfully said she should do the same

Alesha opted to browse some of the shops lining the Pláka before calling Cristos to collect and drive her to Kifissia.

Dinner was a leisurely meal, after which Alesha checked emails and touched base with her Sydney PA, while Loukas secluded himself in his home office.

Constantine and Angelina generously opened their magnificent home to host the renewal of vows ceremony presided over by an official and attended by family and numerous guests.

It was held late afternoon on a luxury terrace setting overlooking beautiful gardens. Alesha walked with Constantine behind Lexi along a rich carpet strewn with rose petals towards an arbour where Loukas stood waiting for her.

The ankle-length gown of cream slipper satin skimmed her slender curves, and Angelina's lace veil added the perfect touch.

The ceremony seemed almost surreal, conducted in Greek, and concluded with a special blessing as Loukas slid a stunning diamond solitaire ring onto her finger.

Alesha lifted her face as he drew her close and bestowed a gentle kiss to the accompanying sound of clapping from the assembled guests.

It was incredibly special, and so different from the civil ceremony in Sydney weeks ago when she'd felt filled with doubt and resentment.

Now there was a sense of hope their future together would bring happiness and contentment. Possibly *love*…although maybe that was expecting too much.

It was easy to accept congratulations from the guests, to smile and sip champagne, and enjoy the splendid dinner Angelina and Daria had organized exclusive caterers to serve.

Coloured lanterns provided illumination as dusk became

night, and there was music and dancing, conviviality and laughter.

Loukas rarely moved from her side, and she became supremely conscious of the light touch of his hand at the edge of her waist…the gentle brush of his fingers as they traced the length of her spine.

He made her feel special, as if he cared. And she began to long for that elusive something that seemed just beyond her reach.

There were words she wanted to say, except she felt tentative in voicing them in case he failed to reciprocate in kind. How humiliating would that be?

Perhaps actions were enough. The way she kissed him, made love with him…*to* him. Wasn't that a language in itself?

If so, how could he not know?

Yet there was a part of her that wanted the words…his, wherein she'd *know* she held his heart as she'd gifted him her own.

To release every last vestige of doubt so joy could invade every cell in her body, every throbbing pulse-point…and fill her heart.

Maybe while they holidayed on the island, alone except for a housekeeper and caretaker. Warm sunshine to bask beneath, crystal-clear waters in which to swim, and soft balmy nights.

Just the two of them.

The guests stayed late and partied, and when the hour reached midnight Loukas caught hold of her hand, family and guests formed a loose circle, and together they personally thanked and bade every guest goodnight.

Cristos, whom Loukas had insisted join the guests, brought the limousine out front as everyone assembled outside the main entrance to provide a cheering send-off as Loukas handed Alesha into the rear seat before moving round the rear of the car to join her.

The drive to Kifissia held a certain magic as Loukas took hold of her hand and linked his fingers through her own.

It had been a beautiful day…a glorious evening, and she said as much.

'Thank you.' She turned to search his features and saw his smile.

'For what, specifically?'

'Agreeing to indulge your parents and Daria to arrange a second wedding on Greek soil.'

'It meant a lot to them to do so.'

'I know.' And she did know. To bring happiness into the lives of loved ones was a special gift.

'My ring is beautiful,' Alesha offered as she touched the exquisite solitaire resting above her wedding band. 'I didn't think about a gift. I have nothing for you in return.'

'Yes, you do. *You.*'

Did hearts melt? She was sure hers did. Together with every bone in her body.

'That's a…' she paused to gather the right words together, and faltered '…lovely compliment.' If only you mean it, she added silently.

For the first time she felt as if she knew where *home* was.

Not bricks and mortar in any country in the world. For it mattered little whether it was Sydney, Athens or other cities elsewhere.

It was Loukas. Knowing she'd follow him wherever he chose to lead. For without him she was nothing.

Love?

Wouldn't that be the ultimate irony?

She, who had wanted a paper marriage with no emotional

involvement. Who had fought so hard to gain emotional independence after a disastrous first marriage...and who had vowed never to love again.

Alesha became aware the limousine had drawn to a halt, and she cast a surprised glance at the front entrance of Loukas' Kifissia mansion. She'd been so lost in contemplative reflection she hadn't noticed the passage of time.

Minutes later she entered the foyer and gasped as Loukas placed an arm beneath her thighs and swept her into his arms.

'What is this?' she demanded in laughing query.

'I believe it's referred to as carrying one's new wife over the threshold,' he drawled with amusement as she wrapped her arms around his neck.

'And?'

He began ascending the stairs. 'An indication the night is far from over.'

'Really?'

Loukas touched his lips to her temple. 'Indeed.'

'Sounds promising.'

They reached the landing and he took the wide hallway leading to their bedroom.

'It's my intention to drive you wild.'

Sensation spiralled through her body, and she brushed her fingers over his beautiful mouth. 'Oh.'

He entered the bedroom and kicked the door shut, then released her in a slow slide down his body to stand on the floor.

'Just...*oh, agape*?' he teased as he carefully removed the veil from her hair.

'I'm lost for words.' She urged his suit jacket over his shoulders and tossed it onto a nearby chair as he reached for the zip fastening of her gown.

'I doubt *words* will form part of your vocabulary.'

She dealt with the buttons on his shirt, pulled it free and reached for the waistband of his trousers.

'Payback for last night?'

Her gown slithered to the floor, and she stepped from the puddle of slipper satin.

He buried his mouth into the soft scented hollow at the base of her throat. 'I promise to deliver.'

He did.

With such consummate skill, she didn't have any breath left in her body to do more than subside against him, totally spent…aware he'd brought every sensory cell achingly alive with a pleasure so intense it had been almost more than she could bear.

It was mid-morning when Cristos deposited them outside the main entrance to the Andreou building where a helicopter waited on the helipad at roof level to transport them to the island.

Within minutes of their boarding and being secured in their seats the rotors kicked in to a higher speed, then the helicopter lifted effortlessly into the air and began its flight over city buildings to the deep blue sparkling waters of the Aegean sea.

The scenery was magic as several islands, both large and small came into view. Some bore small towns, hillside homes, hosting a populated community and geared to the tourist trade. While others bore small villages and olive groves. Then there were those tiny uninhabited islands covered in overgrown shrubbery.

Loukas pointed out a few privately owned islands and relayed their fascinating history, then he indicated another that had been owned by one of Greece's famed shipping magnates and used as a holiday home where his moored luxury cruiser hosted parties for the rich and famous.

The Andreou-owned island was small, with only thirty-odd

acres of land, five of which had been levelled to hold a beautiful double-storeyed home whose stark white-painted stucco and brilliant blue-tiled roof epitomized Greek island architecture.

As the helicopter began to lose height Alesha saw luscious green lawn surrounding the house, garden borders, the dappled waters of a swimming pool and a tennis court. There was a designated helipad, and a separate cottage where, Loukas explained, the manager and his wife resided.

A middle-aged couple came forward as the helicopter rotors slowed, and Loukas introduced Spiros and Sofia, who offered an affectionate greeting before Spiros moved to take their bags from the helicopter.

'Magical,' Alesha accorded as she viewed the grounds. An idyllic haven, she added silently, far away from the hectic pace of a bustling city, and absent from any tourist trade.

The interior of the house bore tiled floors with patterned rugs of varying sizes, ivory-painted walls, solid furniture and modern amenities powered by a generator.

A comfortable home designed to promote relaxation with its spacious covered terraces and airy rooms.

The perfect private sanctuary, Alesha commended as she viewed the large bedroom offering splendid views over a small cove and beyond.

'I have prepared lunch,' Sofia informed. 'An evening meal is in the refrigerator to be heated in the microwave when you are ready to eat.'

'Thank you,' Alesha said with polite sincerity, and Sofia's smile widened.

'It is a pleasure.'

Minutes later she heard the faint click as the front door closed, followed by Sofia's footsteps as she trod the path to her cottage.

'Come here,' Loukas beckoned quietly, and she cast him a faintly wicked grin.

'You can't possibly be considering sex before lunch.'

'No?'

He was deliberately teasing her, and she poked a cheeky tongue in his direction. 'I have plans.'

One eyebrow slanted and his dark eyes gleamed with amusement. 'You do?'

'Uh-huh.'

'Do I get to hear about them, or do you intend to surprise me?'

'We play during the day. Swim, play tennis, sunbathe, maybe take that small boat out I saw moored to the jetty and catch fish.'

'You want to catch fish?'

'It's therapeutic,' she managed solemnly, and heard his quiet laughter.

'And the night?'

'Oh, I don't think you'll have anything to complain about there.'

'And now?'

'We explore, maybe swim before lunch.'

'Tennis in the afternoon?' he posed, and she inclined her head.

'It's called "keeping active",' she managed with a straight face.

'I can think of an infinitely more pleasurable activity.'

'Imagine the anticipation,' she offered with a wicked smile. 'And focus on the mutual reward.'

She was something else.

She'd been a tense young woman who held a fear of intimacy, and he'd taught her to trust again and gradually the barriers she'd erected in self-protection had diminished until they no longer existed.

'You're proposing we change into casual clothes, pull on trainers and explore?'

Her eyes lost their teasing gleam and became serious.

'Do you mind?'

He caught hold of her hand and drew her into the circle of his arms. 'For you…anything,' he said quietly as he lowered his head and kissed her.

So very thoroughly she gave serious thought to discarding any plan that took them away from this room.

'That *almost* worked,' she offered with a tremulous smile when Loukas lifted his head.

'I could always put more effort into it.'

'Do that, and we'll never get out of here.'

The corners of his mouth lifted as he released her.

'Explore, I think you said?'

It became a light fun-filled day, followed by a night of slow loving that took them to a place where passion flared and ignited every sensory cell in her body. Followed by an aftermath of such piercing sweetness she prayed it would never end.

On the edge of sleep she had to wonder if it was the same for him.

Each day brought them even closer together, and Alesha adored the light teasing quality they exhibited with each other. The shared laughter as they swam laps in the pool, walked along the sandy foreshore, and played tennis.

There was the occasional hour spent in the electronically equipped office, as they checked emailed reports from Athens and Sydney and despatched emails in response.

Lacey wrote every few days relaying amusing anecdotes on life and love from her own perspective…and queried when Alesha and Loukas intended returning to Sydney.

All too soon the island idyll would end, Alesha recognized

with regret. Yet the real world awaited, and perhaps in another year they'd return to enjoy another relaxing sojourn.

It was early Friday morning when a call came through from Constantine citing a problem requiring Loukas' urgent attention. One involving an emergency meeting in the Athens' office. The helicopter was on its way to collect him.

'I have—'

'To be there,' Alesha said at once. 'I know.'

In a short space of time a business suit replaced casual gear, and she accompanied him outside as the sound of the helicopter rotors drew close.

'I'll call you.' Loukas covered her mouth briefly with his own, then he climbed into the cabin, belted the harness and attached a headset as the pilot increased the rotor speed...then they were in the air.

Alesha re-entered the house, poured herself a second cup of coffee and contemplated the day ahead without him. So she'd go for a walk along the beach, then persuade Sofia to reveal recipes for some of the delicious meals she'd served them. She could spend time on her laptop, slot in a DVD...and wait for Loukas to call.

Which he did as she ate lunch.

'There's a complication,' he relayed. 'I'm about to head into another meeting. I could be late.'

Resolve it and hurry back, I miss you... Words she refrained from voicing. 'Take care.'

'I'll call as I board the helicopter.' Then he cut the connection.

CHAPTER ELEVEN

THE phone rang late afternoon, and Alesha picked up on the third peal.

'Loukas?'

'Alesha?' Not Loukas' voice, but that of a woman, and she answered cautiously.

'Yes?'

'Eleni Petrakis, Loukas' PA.'

Her heart sank a little. Something had come up and Loukas wouldn't be back until tomorrow. So much for planning a special meal.

'Eleni,' she acknowledged.

'I'm so sorry to have to tell you Loukas was involved in a street accident and has been taken by ambulance to hospital with a gunshot wound. He's currently undergoing emergency surgery. The company's helicopter is on its way to collect you. I'll meet you at the helipad, a car will be waiting at the front entrance and I'll accompany you to the hospital.'

Alesha felt cold, so icily cold it felt as if her body were in shutdown mode, numb, totally without feeling.

'How bad is it?' She knew she breathed, knew she had a heartbeat…because she could feel its thud, loud in the sudden stillness.

'The full extent of damage won't be known until the bullet is removed. The Andreou family have been informed.'

Oh, dear God…what if…? The words banked up and stalled as the horror of what might be filled her vision.

Loukas, injured, bleeding and broken, in surgery attached to numerous machines…

It was almost impossible to believe. The man was invincible.

'I suggest you pack a bag.' Eleni's voice softened a little as she gave the pilot's estimated time of arrival.

'*Kyria?*' Sofia glanced up with a smile as Alesha entered the kitchen…only to have her face sober with concern. 'Something is wrong?'

'I need to go to Athens. It's Loukas.' She managed a brief summation, witnessed the housekeeper's wordless prayer before she turned and moved quickly to the main bedroom.

She banished the overwhelming urge to cry as she thrust a few necessities into a carry-bag. Tears wouldn't achieve a thing, and she had to be strong.

She was unaware of worrying her lip with her teeth, or the faint element of pain.

All she could think of was Loukas. Diminished, filled with painkilling drugs, unconscious, maybe even close to… Dear God, *no*, a silent voice screamed.

He couldn't die. She wouldn't let him.

The agony of never saying she loved him struck her body like a physical pain, and for a moment she couldn't breathe, couldn't move.

What if she didn't have the chance to tell him? What if she was too late?

It seemed an age before she heard the increasing whap-whap sound of incoming rotors, and she watched from the house as the helicopter hovered then lowered down to land.

She was out there in a matter of seconds, climbing up into the cabin, then shutting the door and securing the harness as the pilot increased rotor speed.

The ride seemed to take for ever, and Alesha alighted the instant it was deemed safe to do so, barely remembering to thank the pilot before she moved quickly towards the woman waiting for her.

Presumably she voiced a greeting, but she retained no memory of having done so as they took the lift down to ground level to where a limousine stood stationary at the entrance.

Traffic snarls lent impatience of a kind she rarely experienced, and if sheer will power aided speed they would have reached the hospital in record time.

Eleni's cellphone beeped and she took the call, speaking rapidly in Greek before cutting the connection.

Alesha demanded, 'That was the hospital?'

'The injury isn't as severe as first thought. The bullet entered his upper left arm and fractured the bone. The surgeon successfully removed the bone fragments and has inserted titanium plates. Loukas is on a drip with pain relief, and he has been transferred to a private suite.'

Alesha was barely aware she traversed a maze of corridors as she demanded details of how, when and why.

'I understand Loukas emerged from the building where he'd attended a meeting and was unable to avoid being caught up in a street demonstration. Police barricaded the area, shots were fired, people arrested. Loukas just happened to be in the wrong place at the wrong time, and one of a few who caught a stray bullet.'

She felt numb as vivid images flashed through her brain, and she automatically followed Eleni as they checked in at a nurses' station before being directed to Loukas' suite.

For a minuscule second she caught an overview of the medical set-up, but it was the man himself who garnered her total attention as her eyes moved hungrily over him, searching his chiselled features, noting a paleness beneath his natural skin colour, his ruffled hair...the sling securing his arm.

Dear heaven.

Another few inches...

Dark eyes held her own, and she felt her body sway beneath the naked emotion evident.

For a moment she couldn't move. She wanted to rush to his side, take his mouth with her own, and say the words she'd held back from gifting him.

'Eleni,' Loukas directed in a quietly voiced drawl. 'You will allow us some privacy, if you please. Stand guard outside the door, and allow no one—' his eyes bore the strength of his command '—I repeat *no one*, to enter this suite until my wife appears in the corridor.'

Within seconds they were alone, and Alesha was powerless to prevent the tears welling in her eyes. Blinking hard did nothing to dispel them, and they spilled over to roll ignominiously down each cheek.

'Come here.'

His voice held a gentleness that almost undid her, and she moved to the side of his bed.

A faint smile curved his lips. 'Closer.'

He lifted a hand and brushed each cheek with the soft pad of his thumb, dispersing the warm moisture that continued to flow unchecked.

'Tears, *agape mou*?' His voice seemed deeper than usual and the slight accent it bore on occasion had become more pronounced.

'I love you.' Saying it seemed more important than anything else.

Just getting the words out released some of the pent-up fear she'd harboured from the moment of Eleni's call. For it had acted as a catalyst, flinging her into the darkness where she was forced to think of her life without him.

Something that acted like a spear through her heart…impossibly painful, unconscionable, *impossible*.

For in that moment, she knew she'd surely die, too.

His gorgeous mouth curved, and her own trembled as he shaped her head and urged it down to within touching distance of his own.

'You think I don't know?' His lips touched her own, sensed the faint quiver and savoured the sweetness.

'*Theos.*' The sound was a soft groan against her mouth. 'I want more of you than this.'

'Not going to happen,' she murmured a trifle shakily an instant before his tongue swept her mouth, seeking the sensitive tissues, staking a claim.

Evocative and incredibly sensual, she became temporarily lost in the magical chemistry they shared.

For several heart-stopping seconds she had little recognition of time or place…there was just the heat, the solid *live* feel of his mouth on hers, his hands cradling her head.

Soon, much too soon he trailed gentle fingers down her cheek, pressed a thumb-pad to the soft centre of her lower lip, then he released her.

'You're my life,' he vowed gently. 'Everything.'

Her lips trembled at the wealth of emotion flooding her body, and the moisture she'd so recently conquered welled in her eyes.

'Don't cry,' Loukas groaned, and she shook her head.

'I'm not.'

'No?' There was a tinge of humour in his voice as she brushed shaky fingers over each cheek.

'When Eleni rang,' she began, unable to control the way her body trembled, 'it killed me to think you could die without me saying you mean more to me than life itself.' Her eyes held his, beseeching him to understand. 'That without you—' She faltered, and held up a hand, palm outwards, when he sought to pull her close. 'Don't—please. I need to say this.'

Mere words didn't seem to cover what she wanted, *needed* to convey.

'My experience with Seth destroyed any faith I had in men,' she owned with a watery smile. 'Karsouli became my life. Every waking hour was devoted to the family firm. When Dimitri brought up the question of a suitable heir for the next generation, I offered to have a child via a sperm donor and artificial insemination…which he refused to countenance at any cost.'

Her eyes held his, steady, unblinking. 'When I was acquainted with the marriage clause in his will, I wanted to run, but I *lived* for Karsouli, and I refused to give it up, even if it meant I had to marry you.'

She swallowed the sudden lump that rose in her throat.

'I tried to convince myself I could set the terms…to maintain control. Except it didn't work.' She used her teeth to worry her lower lip. 'You were *there*, a constant I steadily accepted. *Wanted* on a level I had difficulty attempting to comprehend.' Her eyes clouded a little. 'I thought I could sleep…have sex with you,' she amended. 'Only to baulk at the last moment.'

Loukas reached out and tucked her hand within his own.

'You were patient, understanding,' Alesha expounded softly. Her fingers threaded through his own. 'And what I imagined was merely sexual chemistry became more. Something so much deeper, I was reluctant to give it the name it deserved.'

'Do you have any idea of my anger when I discovered what your ex had subjected you to?' Loukas queried with dangerous quietness. 'If I could have put my hands on him…' His eyes darkened with barely controlled rage.

She lifted their linked hands and lightly brushed her lips to his knuckles.

'It annihilated me at the time,' she admitted with painful honesty. 'But I survived.' She managed a winsome smile. 'The experience eventually led me to *you*…and the kind of happiness I never thought I would ever find.'

He tugged her in and cupped her nape, brought her head down to his own and took possession of her mouth in a kiss that sent the blood fizzing through her veins.

When at last he released her, she could only look at him with her heart, her love there for him to see.

'*Agape mou*,' he began in a voice husky with emotion. 'You crept beneath my skin, affected me as no other woman did, or ever will, and you invaded my heart, my soul. Until you became the very air I breathe. *You*. Only you.'

Her mouth shook a little, and she struggled to contain the ache of emotional tears. 'You complete me…in every way there is.' She took a moment to find her voice. 'Losing you would be more than I could bear.' She closed her eyes in an effort to still the well of tears threatening to spill…and lost as two overflowed to roll slowly down each cheek. Somehow it no longer mattered if he witnessed her emotional meltdown and she lifted her eyelids without any sense of shame. 'Today I had to face how close it came to being a reality.'

A sound emerged from Loukas' throat as he traced each rivulet and gently dispensed the moisture.

A distinct double-knock sounded, and the door was

pushed open to reveal a stern-faced nursing sister who barrelled into the suite.

Alesha failed to comprehend the rapid flow of Greek, but the severe tone was sufficient to convey the nurse's disapproval!

Loukas' silky response did little to appease as the woman checked the saline drip, and took note of his vital signs, then she directed Alesha a stern look before exiting the suite.

'You need to rest,' Alesha said quietly, noting the faint weariness etching his features. He had to be feeling the after-effects of anaesthetic, combined with pain. 'I'll go get some coffee and check back in an hour.'

Loukas' dark eyes seared her own. 'Soon.'

A slight smile curved her lips. 'Rest.' The admonishment held humour, then she turned and walked from the suite, discovered Eleni waiting in the corridor, and by mutual consent they shared coffee.

'The driver is on call and will take you to Loukas' home in Kifissia whenever you're ready to leave the hospital,' Loukas' PA informed her as she handed over a card. 'Just ring this number and he'll wait for you outside the main entrance. I've also added my own number in case you need help of any kind.'

'Thanks.' Alesha's gratitude was genuine as she bade Eleni goodnight.

It wasn't difficult to elicit details regarding Loukas' ongoing treatment, his stay in hospital and the expected length of his recovery.

There was a need to alert the Sydney office the sojourn in Greece would necessarily be extended by at least a week or two...and why.

Loukas was asleep when she re-entered his suite, and she slid quietly into a chair facing his bed, exulting in the opportunity to examine his beloved features unobserved.

Strong facial bone structure, the fine lines bracketing each cheek, more deeply etched in repose. The shaped fullness of his mouth stirred emotions deep inside in memory of how it felt to have him possess her own. A firm jaw, denoting a strength of purpose and a certain ruthlessness.

Integrity, honesty…qualities he possessed in spades.

He was her saviour, her warrior, her protector, her love…everything.

As she was *his*. Mind, body and soul.

No more misgivings or doubts. No more pretending to hide beneath a veil of indifference or pretence.

The important factor, the major one…he *cared*.

The world suddenly became a brighter place as she hugged the knowledge close.

'Alesha,' a soft masculine voice drawled with amusement, and she sent him a stunningly sweet smile.

'Hi.'

'Where were you? Sydney?' Loukas teased. 'The island?'

'Here,' she said simply. 'Just looking at you.'

He patted the bed. 'You're too far away.'

'And incur the nurse's wrath again?'

Her eyes held a wicked gleam that did little to still the heat flooding his groin. 'Minx.' The edges of his mouth formed a wry smile. 'Enjoy your feeling of power, hmm?'

A soft laugh emerged from her lips. 'I am, believe me.'

'Not for long.' The promise was there, vibrantly alive and tantalising. He watched her eyes coalesce and become dark with a sense of satisfaction. 'Count on it,' he added gently.

'I doubt you'll be…' she paused delicately '…able to manage the kind of physical activity you have in mind for a while.'

One eyebrow rose in quizzical disbelief. 'You think not?'

'Feasible,' she allowed. 'If I do all the work.'

'*Agape mou*,' Loukas drawled, 'that's the plan.'

She pretended to give it consideration. 'I don't think the hospital staff would be impressed.'

'You realize I can discharge myself and employ the services of a nurse?'

Alesha deliberately widened her eyes. 'Why, when you have excellent medical attention here twenty-four/seven?'

He waited a beat. 'I need to hold you through the night.' His voice held a gentleness that almost undid her. 'Be there when you wake.'

Her heart yearned to be there with him, cradled close to his side…safe, secure, *loved* as she'd given up hope of being loved, for herself, not as Alesha Karsouli, the favoured daughter of Dimitri Karsouli.

The door swung open to admit a nurse bearing medication. Loukas took it without argument and bore the routine of recorded notations, and accepted the stern dictum that visiting hours were over.

Any privacy was limited, and Alesha crossed to his side, brushed his mouth with her own…or at least that was her intention, except he curved a hand round her nape and held her there for countless seconds as he deepened the kiss before reluctantly releasing her.

He noted the pink colouring her cheeks and smiled. 'Sleep well, *yineka mou*.'

The driver was waiting for her in the entry lounge, and he escorted her to the car, saw her seated, then he negotiated traffic as he headed to Loukas' Kifissia mansion where Hera greeted her and made anxious enquiries about Loukas' injuries.

'You have eaten, *kyria*?'

She hadn't, at least not in quite a while, and she gratefully accepted the offer of a light meal before heading upstairs to shower and change.

It was late when she retired for the night, and she read for a while before extinguishing the light.

Sleep should have come easily, except she lay awake addressing events of the day…visualizing in her mind the street demonstration and how a bullet had almost cost her the man she'd learnt to love more than life itself.

Imagining how it went down, the ambulance with its medical team attempting to stem the blood flow, assessing Loukas' injuries, the emergency dash to hospital, the surgery…and the relief on learning he was going to be fine, when she'd feared the worst.

Somehow the scenario slid into her subconscious mind and emerged in a nightmare so dark, so vivid, she woke with tears streaming down her cheeks and his name on her lips.

There was a pressing need to replace that image with another, and she retreated to the en suite to press a cool flannel to her face before collecting an electronic reader from her bag. Then she slid into bed, bunched a few pillows behind her back and settled in to read.

Alesha ate a light breakfast and planned the day around hospital visits…with emphasis on the need to keep busy. A shopping expedition, perhaps, with a view to purchasing a few items to gift friends on her return to Sydney? The gorgeous pendant she'd seen displayed in a shop window would be perfect for Lacey…if only she could remember *which* shop and *where* in the city.

She'd ask Cristos to accompany her, and with luck they'd be able to locate it.

Athens held a tremendous sense of history, with aged buildings that held an aura of ancient times and warriors of old. Open-air food and craft markets blended with modern department stores, galleries, and individual stores.

'Monastiráki and Pláka,' Cristos informed as he sought parking prior to midday.

While strolling the Pláka she visited Lexi's studio and purchased the bracelet she'd admired and matching ear-studs with a view to gifting it to Lacey for Christmas.

Thirty minutes in, Alesha recognized the window display with its dazzling items, and Cristos' mention of the name Andreou resulted in the manager insisting on a private showing.

'Apparently you possess a certain reputation for purchasing expensive gifts,' she teased Loukas later in the day, and saw the edges of his mouth lift with cynical amusement.

'It bothers you?'

He had a past that included any number of women. She'd seen the tabloids over the years…slender beautiful women captured by camera clinging to his arm at one function or another.

'Should it?'

Loukas' eyes darkened as he took in her carefully composed features, her steady gaze, and sensed the faint indecision beneath her query.

'No.' She had to know there could never be any other woman for him…only her. She was the light of his life. *Theos.* All of it, the very air he breathed. Without her, he'd lose the will to live.

For a brief moment he silently damned being confined.

He wanted out of here, away from hospital routine and its restrictions. Most of all, he wanted *her*…

When it came time for her to leave he kissed her so deeply her eyes widened with momentary surprise.

Intense passion, leashed…and primitive beneath the surface.

Just to look at him made her toes curl…not to mention other parts of her body.

She lifted a hand and placed the palm over his cheek as her mouth formed a tremulous smile. 'Take care.'

Then she turned and walked from the suite, paused at Reception to text Cristos she was ready to leave the hospital.

'Where would you like to go, *kyria*?'

She'd done the shopping thing, and didn't feel inclined to wander the boutiques without a purpose.

Loukas' palatial home beckoned. She'd visit the kitchen, make a cup of tea and filch a snack from the refrigerator.

'Kifissia, Cristos.'

The beautiful mansion seemed large with its high ceilings, marble floors and solid furniture. Alesha's footsteps echoed as she crossed the foyer and ascended the curved staircase to the upper level.

On reaching the master suite, she toed off her stilettos, then she discarded her outer clothes and pulled on comfortable leggings and a loose-knit top whose hemline rested low on her thighs.

Tea, she decided, and chose to forgo the snack. The last day or two had wrought a change in her desire for food, and she sipped her tea, then checked her watch, calculated the time in Sydney and reached for her cellphone, hit Lacey's number on speed dial and heard her friend pick up.

'Alesha! How are you? *Where* are you? What's happening?'

It was easy to laugh, wonderful to talk, and great to catch up as they exchanged mutual news.

Ten minutes, fifteen…Alesha wasn't sure when a slight sound alerted her attention, and she paused mid-sentence as Loukas entered the room.

Startled disbelief widened her eyes as the words fell from her lips without thought. 'What are you doing here?'

'Alesha?' Lacey demanded over the phone. 'Is everything okay?'

'I— Yes.' Distracted didn't begin to describe it. 'You should be in hospital.'

'Loukas is home?'

Conducting a three-way conversation when attempting to collect one's wits was bound to be...disjointed, to say the least.

'Lacey?' Loukas queried, and when she nodded he took the phone from her hand. 'Alesha will call you tomorrow. And, yes, thank you. I'm fine. Take care.'

With that he disconnected the call, tossed the phone onto the sofa, then he caught hold of her hand and drew her to her feet.

'You shouldn't—'

'Later,' he said gently.

She opened her mouth, and closed it again as he slid a hand beneath the weight of her hair to cup her nape, then he lowered his head and kissed her with a thoroughness that left her faintly breathless.

'And that was...because?'

'You need to ask?'

A delicious smile curved her lips. 'Uh-huh.'

'Minx.'

He felt so good. To think—

A hand caught her chin and tilted it. 'Don't.'

So many emotions...an entire gamut ranging from fear to relief.

And joy. True happiness.

Loukas had gifted her both.

Love. The most precious gift of all.

Alesha wanted to cry…and laugh…but most of all she needed to offer her touch and savour his own.

To celebrate *life*. Theirs, together…for all time.

The words would come later.

But first, she determined to tease him a little.

'Discharging yourself against medical advice isn't a wise decision. And don't think you're going to discard that arm sling any time soon,' she admonished.

His eyes gleamed, dark, liquid, and incredibly sensual. 'No? I'm sure with care we can work around it.'

She tried for stern remonstrance, and failed miserably. 'You should rest.'

'I plan to. In bed. With you.'

'The emphasis will be *rest*.'

A warm smile curved his generous mouth. 'Eventually.'

'Have you eaten?'

'You want to talk *food*?'

'I'm thinking of your stamina level,' she managed with a straight face, and felt her nerve-ends curl at the sound of his husky laughter.

His hand slid beneath her top and sought the warm skin, murmuring his appreciation at her lack of a bra, and her body arched into his as he palmed each breast in turn, creating a delicate friction on each tender peak.

A sigh of pleasure escaped from her lips seconds before his mouth closed over hers, and she became lost in the emotional tide he created.

Together they moved upstairs to their suite, undressed each other slowly, she helping him with such gentle care it brought him undone.

Together they savoured each lingering touch…the slide of

a hand, the trail of gentle fingers. Lips seeking and caressing sensitive pulse-points, vulnerable hollows.

Lovemaking in its most sensual form, Alesha accorded as Loukas lay down on the bed, and she moved over him, taking her time to explore him gently with her mouth…finessing each light touch until he groaned and urged possession.

She slid down onto him with care, and her eyes didn't leave his as she began to move with captivating sensuality, exulting in the control, the power as she set the pace.

He growled deep in his throat when she lowered her head and brushed the length of her hair back and forth across his chest, then began tormenting him with her lips as she leaned in and inched her way up to the hollow at the base of his throat, traced it with the tip of her tongue before seeking his mouth in an erotic kiss.

Afterwards she lay curled close against him, her head pillowed into the curve of his shoulder as his hand drifted a soothing pattern over her hip, lingered there, then travelled to settle at her nape.

It was late when they rose, showered together as Alesha encased his injured arm in waterproof plastic, towelled him dry, then helped him into a robe before tending to herself as he re-entered the bedroom.

When she emerged, he handed her a slim jeweller's box. 'I have something for you.' The warmth of his smile melted her heart. 'Open it.'

An exquisite diamond necklace lay nestled against a bed of black velvet. Brilliant pink Argyle stones alternated with blue fire in a delicate setting that showcased a beautiful pear-drop pendant. A matching bracelet and ear-studs completed the set.

'It's beautiful.'

It was the one she'd admired displayed in a jeweller's

window. Cristos must have mentioned her interest…coincidence didn't stretch so far.

'Thank you.' She swallowed the sudden lump that rose in her throat as she became lost in the gleaming darkness of his eyes. 'But you've already given me the most precious gift of all.' Her eyes misted, and she blinked hard to dispense the moisture. 'You. Just you.' Her breath hitched as she sought control of her emotions. 'Nothing else compares.'

With one exception, Loukas added silently. The fitting conclusion of measures he'd put in place to deprive her ex of every last cent he'd gained from Alesha's ill-fated short-lived marriage. To date, the bank had foreclosed on Seth's home. The Porsche he revered had been sold. It was only a matter of time before he'd be forced to walk away from his business.

Several days later the helicopter flew them to the island where the gentle ebb and flow of the water against the sandy cove lent an air of tranquillity.

The days were pleasant with cool temperatures and rain overnight, but they didn't care. For it was there they spent an idyllic few days, made leisurely love, taking time when the rain cleared to wander the beach, pausing every now and then to examine a piece of driftwood, a smooth pebble, to the sound of a keening gull, the excited bark of the golden retriever who called the island home.

Soon, they'd return to the mainland, and within days board a flight to Sydney, where life would settle into its former routine.

With possibly one exception, and she hugged the knowledge close, not wanting to share until the tiny life she was instinctively sure she nurtured could be confirmed.

On the final day they pulled on boots, donned jackets, and took the dog for a late afternoon walk. A breeze caught the length of Alesha's hair and tossed it into a tumbled mess, and after attempting to confine it she simply laughed and gave up, pausing to look out over the choppy sea.

Loukas stepped behind her and wrapped an arm around her slender waist, then he rested his chin against the top of her head.

Only that morning he'd received the confirmation his strategy with Alesha's ex had reached its completion.

Seth Armitage's investments had diminished to almost nil; he'd been forced to sell all his assets at rock-bottom prices, and his reputation was in tatters. A fitting end for an unscrupulous and cruel man.

It had taken considerable effort to achieve such an outcome, and all the relevant strings were tied…with one exception.

With care he turned her round to face him and extracted a sealed envelope from the pocket of his jacket. 'For you.'

Alesha's eyes widened as she searched his features…and gleaned little other than the deep passion evident, together with something indefinable. Resolve?

'I have everything I need,' Alesha assured quietly.

'Open it.'

She did, releasing the flap with care, and extracting a slim piece of paper. Her lips parted in startled surprise as she identified a certified bank cheque for five million dollars.

Her eyes flew to his. 'What is this?'

'The settlement your father paid your ex for an uncontested divorce on the condition he got out of your life.'

Ohmigod. Her breathing became ragged as shock encompassed her body. *That much?*

'I won't accept it from you,' she refused in a voice husky with emotion.

'It represents the sale of Seth Armitage's business, his home and everything he owned.'

Blood money.

The realization hit her, and she simply looked at him, her eyes locked with his own.

'You ruined him.'

'You doubt I could?'

There was only one answer. 'No.'

He had the power, the ruthlessness to tear Seth limb from figurative limb in a manner that would hurt more than anything else…stripping her ex of everything he'd gained out of their marriage and the divorce.

Loukas captured her chin and tilted it. 'I wanted to kill him for what he did to you.' He traced gentle fingers over her trembling mouth.

'Instead you devised a fitting revenge.'

'One he deserved.'

She was silent for several long minutes as she mustered the courage to reveal details she hadn't told a living soul.

'It began a few days after the wedding,' she began quietly. 'The belittlement when I failed to satisfy him. The cruel taunts when I refused to comply with his demand for kinky sex. I was too uptight, too straight-laced and needed to be taught a lesson.' Her eyes didn't leave his, and she glimpsed his pain, the darkness of his anger…and she placed a soothing hand on his rigid jaw. 'I ended up in hospital with a few fractured ribs, a fractured arm, and bruising.'

She'd started this…she needed to finish it.

'I called a lawyer, and hired security to stand guard in shifts outside my room.'

'Dimitri—'

'Was in Melbourne on business, and was only apprised of my injuries on his return.'

A muscle tensed at the edge of his jaw as he recalled her fear, the nightmares, the evidence of broken and fractured bones.

'Yet you didn't press charges.'

'My decision. I didn't want the episode to become fodder for the media or dragged through the court.' She drew a deep breath. 'It was done...over. Seth took a financial settlement.' Her eyes hardened at the amount her father had added to ensure Seth never made any further demand on her again. 'And I moved on with my life.'

'Alesha—'

Anything else he might have said remained stilled as she placed light fingers over his mouth.

'Don't...please.' Her expression softened, her incredible eyes became luminous with emotion. 'We have the future together, *love*...the once-in-a-lifetime kind. Infinitely special,' she added gently. 'Everything I ever wanted...and more, so much more. With you. I can't keep this money, Loukas. I don't want it—it's tainted. But I can put it to some use and help others who might be in the same position as I was—do you agree?'

Loukas lowered his head down to hers and brushed his lips to her forehead.

'I thought the marriage clause in Dimitri's will a cruel and heartless act.' She moved her head to look at him. 'Instead ultimately it became a unique gift.'

'Without question.'

'It would be wonderful if somehow he knows,' she pondered a trifle pensively.

'Perhaps he does.'

She turned slightly and looked out over the bay whose surface rippled beneath the stiffening breeze.

'This is an incredible place,' Alesha voiced wistfully.

His arm tightened a little and she felt his lips nuzzle the

sensitive pulse beneath an ear lobe. 'A private haven with no tourists, no marina housing a host of boats.'

Just us…heaven.

'I want to thank you,' she began quietly.

'For what, in particular?'

He sounded mildly amused, and Alesha smiled a little.

'Believing in me,' she said simply. 'Being there. You're my life. My love. Everything.'

Loukas turned her to face him, and she became lost in the wealth of emotion evident in his dark eyes.

He brushed his lips across her own, parted them, then lingered to savour a little. 'I imagined a contented union, a compliant wife, cementing a successful business merger.'

'Instead you gained a neurotic divorcee with emotional baggage.'

He drew her lower lip between his teeth and nipped the fullness. 'A beautiful young woman,' he corrected, 'who crept beneath my skin and captured my heart.' He eased the tip of his tongue over her lip, soothing it.

'You taught me to believe in love,' Alesha added gently.

'*Agape mou.* I exist only for you.'

She wanted to cry…and almost did. He was a very special man. She intended to show him just how special every day for the rest of her life.

Her eyes acquired a wicked sparkle as she tilted her head to one side and regarded him with musing humour. 'The sex helped. You're rather good at it.'

A husky laugh emerged from his throat as he caught hold of her hand and threaded his fingers through her own. 'Let's go back to the house.'

The air held a chill as they trod the path and traversed the slight incline. The house was warm, and she turned towards the kitchen.

'It's Sofia's night off. I'll fix dinner.'

'Later.' He pulled her close and took her mouth in a deep slow kiss, then he captured her hand and led her upstairs to the bedroom.

EPILOGUE

A YEAR later a number of invited guests, including Constantine, Angelina, Daria and Lexi who flew in from Athens, attended a party at Loukas and Alesha's Point Piper mansion to celebrate the christening of their twins...Sebastian Loukas and his sister Sienna Lucille.

Two beautiful children whose birth via Caesarean section saw Sienna emerge seconds ahead of her brother, and whose cry...*howl*, her father amended...was loud in protest. Not to be outdone, Sebastian surpassed her in pitch, and only subsided when he was placed into his mother's arms.

Now three months of age, they slept in their nursery in adjacent cribs, in the care of a nanny.

'You have gifted us the joy of beautiful grandchildren,' Constantine declared as he and Angelina prepared to leave the party at evening's end.

'Beautiful,' Daria echoed, and brushed her lips to Alesha's cheek, before she turned to Loukas. 'You're a fortunate man.' She assumed a stern expression, which was totally contrived. 'Take good care of your family.'

'With my life, *Thia*,' he assured gently.

It was late when Loukas set the security system after the

last guest departed, and he curved an arm around Alesha's waist as they crossed the foyer.

Together they ascended the stairs and crossed to the nursery. A dimmed night light revealed two dark-haired babes, their chubby faces serene in sleep.

'Special,' Loukas said softly. 'So very special, *agape mou*.'

They moved quietly from the room and entered their bedroom suite.

'Have I told you how much I adore you?' Loukas turned her into his arms and took possession of her mouth in a kiss that stole the breath from her throat.

Only every night. 'A wife can't hear too much of a good thing,' she responded with teasing lightness, knowing every word came from the heart.

Her pregnancy had delighted him, for he'd been there for her every step of the way, loving the changes to her body, amazed at the discovery the babe she carried was in fact *two*. He'd gowned up and witnessed their birth, marvelled at the miracle, and become as much of a hands-on father as time would allow.

'I've been thinking.'

'Why do I suddenly have the feeling that could be dangerous?'

Her mouth curved into a winsome smile. 'This is a very large home with several bedrooms.'

His eyes darkened measurably. 'You say this...because?'

'Perhaps we should consider providing Sebastian and Sienna with a brother or sister.'

'Are you sure you're ready for another pregnancy so soon?'

'How does May sound to you?'

'A year from now?'

'Ah, my husband is good at maths.'

'Witch.'

'It will give you time to get used to the idea,' Alesha said with a wicked gleam as she linked her hands at his nape.

'My concern is only for you.'

'I know.'

And she did, aware she'd come full circle in a marriage to a man she hadn't expected to love more than life itself.

HIS PRISONER
IN PARADISE

Trish
MOREY

Trish Morey is an Australian who's also spent time living and working in New Zealand and England. Now she's settled with her husband and four young daughters in a special part of South Australia, surrounded by orchards and bushland, and visited by the occasional koala and kangaroo. With a life-long love of reading, she penned her first book at the age of eleven, after which life, career, and a growing family kept her busy until once again she could indulge her desire to create characters and stories—this time in romance. Having her work published is a dream come true. Visit Trish at her website, www.trishmorey.com.

To editor extraordinaire, Jo Grant.
Thank you for your patience, your insight and your
wisdom, along with your wonderful advice and
support through these last eleven books!
Long may it continue.

With thanks, too, to the generous and gracious
Helen Bianchin. A class act, an awesome writer,
and an inspiration in every way.

Thank you both!

CHAPTER ONE

'OVER my dead body!' Daniel Caruana hadn't made it past the first paragraph of his sister's email before he crumpled the printout in his fist and hurled it in fury at the closest wall. Monica marrying Jake Fletcher? No way in the world!

Not if he had anything to do with it!

Too wound up to sit, too agitated to stand still, he gave in to the need to pace, his long strides eating up length after length of his sprawling office's floor, while his restless hands took turns clawing though his hair. By his side, full-height windows took full advantage of the view of a white, sandy palm-lined beach and the azure sea that glinted under the tropical Far North Queensland sun.

Daniel saw nothing of it.

Daniel saw only red.

Whatever had possessed him to allow Monica to study in Brisbane? So far from Cairns, so far away from his influence. *And clearly nowhere near far enough away from the grasping hands of Jake Fletcher.*

He stopped pacing, his mind making connections that sent ice floes careening down his spine. Fletcher had called twice this week out of the blue, leaving messages for Daniel to call back, messages Daniel had brushed aside like he was swiping at an annoying insect needling at his skin. For he had no desire to speak to Fletcher ever again. Had no purpose.

But now it appeared Fletcher had purpose—if only to gloat…

Bile rose in his throat, its bitter taste the perfect accompaniment to his mindset. Please God, not Fletcher.

Please God, not his sister.

Especially after what had happened before.

Daniel leaned his forehead against the glass and closed his eyes, a vision remaining of a girl with laughing blue eyes and a sweet, sweet smile.

Emma.

As long as he drew breath, he would not forget Emma.

Nor what Jake Fletcher had done to her!

He opened his eyes and gazed far out to where the cerulean sea met the sky, searching for answers and solutions. Ordinarily the picture-postcard view was a sight that inspired him. Cheered him. Even, on occasion, soothed his fractured nerves.

Today all that sun-drenched perfection only served to mock the storm-tossed contents of his mind.

He slammed one palm against the glass. Damn—not Monica! He'd barely seen off Monica's last so-called boyfriend, an effort that had left him twenty-thousand dollars poorer on the deal. Small change, given what the jerk might have held out for if he'd done his homework a little more thoroughly and found out what his girlfriend was really worth.

Fletcher, on the other hand, probably knew how much the Caruana fortune was worth down to every last cent. Twenty-thousand dollars would be nowhere near enough to deter his kind, especially not now he probably imagined he was practically family.

No way. His fingers pressed hard against the glass, as rigid as his resolve. As long as Daniel had any say in it, Jake Fletcher would *never* be family.

Fletcher wouldn't come cheap—there was no doubt of that—but everyone had their price, and whatever it took to free Monica of his poison influence would be worth it.

The phone on his desk buzzed behind him. Daniel scowled at the interruption—surely his empire could cope for just ten minutes without him? Then he reached for it. After all, he hadn't taken the Caruana name from the brink of financial disaster to its dizzy heights by ignoring his businesses, whatever the reason.

He would deal with Fletcher—nothing was surer—but he would not lower his game in the process. His hand snatched up the receiver. 'What?'

A moment's hesitation met his retort, a moment in which he remembered it was a temp sitting outside and not his usual indestructible PA.

'Mr Caruana?' she squeaked. 'There's a Miss—a Miss Turner here to see you.'

His scowl deepened and for a second the problem of Fletcher took a back seat. He couldn't remember anything about any Miss Turner. 'Who?'

'Sophie Turner: from *One Perfect Day*.'

The name made no sense to him but he was used to people trying to talk their way into his office, looking for favours, or more frequently cash contributions towards shaky business-plans the banks had already turned down. This Miss Sophie Turner was no doubt another of their ilk. 'Never heard of her. Get rid of her.' He slammed the phone back down, annoyed again with the unnecessary interruption when he had important things on his mind.

Even more annoyed when the phone buzzed a second time not thirty seconds later. 'What is it this time?' he growled into the mouthpiece, unforgiving at the interruption, even if the girl didn't know better.

Her voice sounded even more timid. 'Miss Turner says it should have been in the email your sister sent you. All the details about her visit were apparently there.'

'What email?'

'You did read it?' the temp continued apologetically, a crack in her voice; she sounded as if any moment she would burst into tears. 'It was on your desk. I printed it out especially.'

That email? His eyes crossed to the crumpled ball of paper that had come to rest in a corner of the room. He hadn't got past the casual bombshell Moni had dropped that she intended to marry the one man he had reason to hate with a passion. How the hell was he expected to absorb anything more?

'Hold on,' he said, dropping the phone down on the desk and crossing the office floor in long, purposeful strides. He swept up the ball of paper and unscrewed it, flattening it against his broad palm. The paragraph stared out at him, the same one that had turned his vision red scant minutes before:

Daniel, please be excited for me. I thought I was sworn off men for ever, especially after being dumped for the third time in quick succession, but then I met Jake Fletcher and the last few weeks couldn't have been more perfect. He treats me like an absolute princess and he's asked me to be his wife, and I've said yes.

No; his mind revolted. *Never!* He closed his eyes, the same rush of anger winning supremacy over his veins, the same flood of revulsion as the first time. Little wonder he'd been unable to bring himself to read the rest. His fingers ached to crumple the page into a tight ball once more, but this time he took a deep breath, willed his eyes open and read on.

I know you two never used to get on in the past, and
maybe that's why you didn't return Jake's calls last
week, but I'm hoping you can put the past behind you
when you see how much we love each other.

Put the past behind you? A thousand snapshots of a young
woman's bright smile formed a moving slide-show through
his consciousness. How was he ever supposed to put the past
behind him when she would never get to see another day?

I know it's sudden but I want you to be among the first to
know our happy news and just how much we love each
other. It's the real thing this time, I know.

Daniel snorted his contempt. The real thing? He had no
doubt Fletcher thought it the real thing, but if he was in love
with anything it was the Caruana fortune. When would his
sister ever learn that that was all men wanted? *Especially* men
like Fletcher.

But she'd soon see the light, just as she had before, just
as soon as he'd dispensed with this latest in a long line of
gold-diggers whose so-called love didn't extend past her trust
fund.

I wish I could give you this news personally, but you
were in transit, and now Jake is whisking me off to
Honolulu for two weeks for a surprise engagement present and there simply wasn't time to get a connection
through Cairns to meet up before we left.

He growled, the fingers of his free hand curling and uncurling into a fist; bile wasn't the only bitter taste that filled

his mouth. The thought of his little sister with *him* made him want to catch the next flight to Honolulu and drag her back before the bastard got her pregnant.

Or was that his intention— To make this marriage a done deal before the ceremony?

Daniel shook his head. It would take more than a baby before this marriage went ahead. The fires of hell would freeze over before he let someone like Fletcher marry his sister.

Monica was twenty-one now, so physically dragging her back was hardly an option, but there was no way he was going to stand by and let her get cornered into this marriage. Not by a long shot. He glanced down at the last few lines.

So instead I've arranged for our wedding planner to visit you. Her name is Sophie Turner and she's already much more than a friend. Will fill you in on the details later.
Meanwhile, be nice to her!

His sister had signed off with a promise to send a postcard from Waikiki Beach, but that wasn't what held his attention. It was the 'be nice to her'.

What did his sister take him for—some kind of monster?

He wasn't a monster. He was a businessman and a brother: a brother who had his eye out to protect his little sister from those who sought to take advantage of both her and the family fortune.

He was careful. Cautious. Protective of his own.

Did that make him such a monster?

Of course he'd see this Sophie Turner. And he'd be nice, just as his sister had requested. He'd invite her in, listen to her spiel and then he'd set her straight.

Because her services would not be required. As long as he drew breath, there would be no wedding between his sister and the likes of Jake Fletcher.

He picked up the receiver that lay abandoned on his office desk.

'Send Miss Turner in.'

CHAPTER TWO

SOPHIE perched uneasily on the edge of the waiting-room chair, the leather portfolio that contained all the details of Monica and Jake's wedding resting on her knees. She couldn't help but notice the bloom of pink spread over the young PA's cheeks as reluctantly she placed the second call to her boss in less than a minute. Clearly what she'd read on the Internet about Daniel Caruana's take-no-prisoners reputation extended beyond his business rivals and his girlfriends to his staff; the girl looked petrified.

Sophie might have felt guilty at insisting the girl call again and explain, but she wasn't about to waste an entire day travelling from Brisbane to Cairns and back again for no good reason—not when Monica had told her today's meeting had been all arranged and how much they were both relying on her.

'Oil on the waters', Jake had labelled her role, not exactly imbuing her with confidence. Apparently Daniel was superprotective of his little sister, having practically raised her since their parents had died, so of course he'd take the news of Monica's plans with less than enthusiasm. Especially given Jake and Daniel hadn't exactly hit if off back in high school, which Jake had admitted when attempting to explain why Daniel might not have bothered to answer his calls.

Something seriously wrong had gone on between them, Sophie mused, if Daniel wouldn't even speak to him. Her suggestion had been for Jake and Monica to visit Daniel themselves, given he could hardly refuse to see Jake if Monica was with him, but Monica had come up with what she thought was a more diplomatic solution.

She'd break the news to her brother in an email and then the to-be-weds would disappear for two weeks while Sophie ran through the wedding arrangements with Daniel. By the time the happy couple returned from Hawaii, Sophie would have everything arranged and Daniel would have come to terms with the idea that his little sister was a grown woman, old enough to make her own decisions about getting married and to whom.

It was simple, Monica had told her.

Failsafe.

Monica had hugged her tight and thanked her. She'd looked so hopeful, if not half-desperate, this bride-to-be who wanted everything to be absolutely perfect, Sophie had swallowed back all her arguments that it should be them visiting Daniel and ironing out any problems face to face, and had nodded her agreement instead.

Now it seemed a crazy idea. Conscious of time spinning away while the PA waited for a response, she clamped down on the bubble of nervousness that had her suddenly fidgeting with the folder perched on her knees.

Failsafe? She wished she could be so sure. Anyone who could put the fear of God into his receptionist with just a word or two was hardly likely to be the pushover Monica imagined her brother to be. But she supposed she had to meet the man some time, especially given they were practically related.

How ironic. She'd always wanted family; reconnecting with Jake after all their years apart had been amazing, even if it had taken their mother's death to get the siblings back together. Now it looked like her tiny family was set to expand. Monica was a sweetheart. The two of them had hit it off from the first time they'd met, and she couldn't imagine a nicer sister-in-law.

But somehow the prospect of being Daniel's sister-in-law didn't come with quite the same thrill. That was the down side of families, she supposed: you didn't always get to choose your relatives.

What was taking the man so long? Impatiently she crossed and uncrossed her ankles, unclipping the portfolio to check its contents were all present and correct before snapping it shut without having registered a thing. Damn the man and his arrogance! If he'd just bothered to talk to her brother, she wouldn't have to be here at all.

The girl shrugged apologetically at Sophie's questioning glance, and Sophie sighed and turned her attention out of the full-length windows to where the palm-fringed, sandy shore met the Coral Sea. Some PA's office, she thought. It was a million times better than her own office in Brisbane which boasted not even a sniff of river view between the multi-storey office blocks. Maybe there were compensations for working for the boss from hell. At least his PA had a decent view between the no-doubt frequent ear-bashings.

'Mr Caruana will see you now.'

Sophie jumped, her insides lurching at the announcement, and not entirely with relief. Sure, she'd got what she'd come here for—admittance to the hallowed inner sanctum for an audience with Mr High and Mighty—but there was no sudden burst of enthusiasm at the prospect. The time he'd taken to make up his mind was hardly welcoming, and if it was up to her she'd like nothing better than to turn and snub one Daniel Caruana's churlish and clearly reluctant agreement.

But this wasn't about her. She was here to champion Jake and Monica, and telling the man where to get off was hardly going to help. So instead she took a deep breath and smoothed the silk of her skirt as she rose, doing a last-minute check of her sheer stockings for ladders, and putting a hand to the sleek coil behind her head for any escaping tendrils.

Cool, poised and professional was the look and manner she was aiming for. The Daniel Caruana she'd researched demanded first-class presentation and she intended to deliver. Later, in the afterglow of a successful wedding between their respective siblings, and when they knew each other better, there would be time to relax in each other's company.

Because, while the prospect seemed unlikely at the moment, it would be nice if she could at least like the man who was soon to be her brother-in-law.

Though given what she'd experienced so far of Daniel Caruana, she wasn't too confident.

She smiled her thanks to the PA, whose colour had returned and who managed to smile back, clearly relieved she wasn't going to have to ring her boss a third time. Sophie rapped her knuckles lightly on the door and let herself into the largest office she'd ever seen.

She stopped dead, stunned by the sheer dimensions of the room. All this space for one man? *Maybe he needed it to accommodate his ego.* She shoved her scorn back where it belonged. He *had* agreed to see her, even if it had taken an eternity; maybe the man wasn't completely beyond redemption.

She worked up a smile, remembering the old adage that to think positive was to be positive. 'Mr Caruana,' she offered with an enthusiasm she didn't feel and that barely cloaked her nerves. 'It's a pleasure to meet you at last.'

He was standing with his back to her against the wall of windows that brought the best of the far-north Queensland beach views into the office, his arms crossed and feet planted wide apart. Maybe it was because she'd already witnessed

the view that five storeys could offer over the coast line that
Sophie found herself assailed with impressions that had nothing to do with the view outside and had no place on today's
agenda.

Broad shoulders.

Narrow hips.

Long, lean legs.

Then he turned and the view outside faded to grey. She
blinked, wondering what it was exactly that the pictures on
the Internet had missed. Sure, they might have captured the
short, tousled black hair, the steel-like gaze and the wide, generous lips. They might have contained a hint of the aura that
surrounded him of power and success and raw masculinity.
Yet they'd been unable to capture that grace of moment, that
animal-like quality that turned even his slightest movement
predatory.

His head tilted and his narrowed gaze assessed her, as
if he had stripped through all her professional-development
bluff and seen her for the nervous sister of the groom anxious to make a good impression that she really was. 'Is it a
pleasure?'

Maybe not. Not that he was waiting for her answer. She got
the distinct impression Daniel Caruana wasn't used to waiting
for anything, even before he continued, 'You wanted to see
me?'

'Ah.' She swallowed, his prompt reminding her why she
was here, and that it wasn't to ogle the brother of the bride
or lose herself in her thoughts. 'Of course.' She forced her
frozen legs into motion and crossed the space between them,
holding out her hand. 'Sophie Turner, from One Perfect Day.
One Perfect Day makes perfect memories to last a lifetime.'
The business's advertising blurb rattled off her tongue before
she could stop herself. She was proud of her business and all
she'd achieved. She believed that she offered her clients as

perfect a wedding day possible, but right now in this office, faced with this man and battling her own rattled thought-processes, her words sounded trite and hackneyed.

He surveyed her hand for what felt like an eternity before his eyes once again lifted to snag on hers. This close she could see the dark shadow of a beard accentuating the strong line of his jaw. This close his dark eyes seemed to swirl with un-plumbed depths, the hint of a smile in those ever-so-slightly-upturned lips.

Then he finally took her hand in his and sent a jolt to her internal thermostat. She dragged in much-needed oxygen, only to find it fuelled with the warm, spiced tang of male. She pressed on, trying to ignore the feel of her hand in his, trying to discount the skin-on-skin contact and the scramble it was making of her senses. 'Monica has told me a lot about you. She wishes she could have visited you herself, to tell you about her plans, but—'

'But she was suddenly whisked away to Hawaii?' His voice was deep and rich and with the merest trace of an accent. It rolled over her senses much like the way his thumb seemed to be skimming the back of her hand. 'By the latest man she's apparently fallen head over heels in love with?'

The tension hummed through his words, an obvious cyni-cism shining in the gleam of his dark-as-night eyes, despite the easy smile that revealed a line of perfect white teeth.

That man, she wanted to say, *is my brother, and he loves Monica as much as she loves him.* But right now all her thoughts and senses were centred on the hand that somehow still remained firmly lodged within his.

Power, she felt in his touch, and a heat that radiated up her arm to fan out to her extremities in a delicious wave.

She tugged her hand free, sensing a slight reluctance on his part to let her go, and then wondered if she'd just imagined it.

Wished it were so.

Now she really was losing it.

Her eyes scanned the spacious office and fell on a nearby suite, three leather settees arranged in a U formation around a glass-topped coffee table. She sensed an opportunity to escape his close proximity and gather her scattered thoughts to the deal. 'Perhaps we could sit there?' she suggested with wash-day brightness laid on thick. 'And I can fill you in on Monica and Jake's plans.'

She was already seated, her briefcase beside her on the floor and unclipping her portfolio, when she realised he was still standing there, his lips curled again, a facsimile of a smile fading before reaching his eyes.

Then he seemed to shrug, making even that slight gesture look elegant and full of animal grace. 'Perhaps we could,' he agreed, before surprising her completely by ignoring the other sofas and sitting down alongside her, as if determined to turn her escape into purgatory.

He liked the way she seemed to shrink back against her armrest after that initial look of shock, especially after he'd angled himself sideways, snaking one arm along the back of the chair. Now she squeezed herself into the corner of the sofa and focused on sorting through the contents of the folder on her knees like it was some kind of lifeline. 'I have some brochures,' she mumbled, her long fingers fumbling.

She was flustered.

He liked a woman flustered. It kept her on the defensive, right where he wanted her. Unless she was in bed, of course, and there he welcomed the occasional tigress.

Would prim-looking Miss Turner be a tigress in bed?

He took his time to look at the woman alongside him up and down. The button-through blue silk dress with modest neckline hid more than it revealed, but first impressions had told him she had a reasonable body hidden beneath: nicely balanced in the hip and bust departments, slim-waisted and long-legged, with her facial features arranged just as acceptably as her body parts.

Second impressions only confirmed the first. Even in profile—the real test—her features were engaging. High cheekbones, a classic nose, that lush mouth...

He frowned. He couldn't remember the name, but something about her looked almost familiar. The thought was discarded the very next instant. He met a lot of women, and if he had met this one before he was sure he wouldn't have let her get away without knowing her better.

Unless she'd been out of bounds. Some people didn't share the same scruples, he knew from experience, but if there was one thing he wouldn't touch it was someone else's woman. 'Are you married, Miss Turner, or engaged?'

Her head snapped around, a couple of brochures sliding unnoticed from her fingers into her lap. 'Why do you ask?'

He smiled, scooping the pamphlets up, noticing with satisfaction the tremor as the back of his fingers skimmed the top of her legs; it was no more than a featherlight contact through the silk of her skirt, but enough to elicit the kind of reaction he was used to. The kind of reaction he welcomed when he himself was attracted. 'You work in the wedding business—wouldn't someone who has been married themselves understand what a bride really wants to make her day perfect? How else would you know?'

'Oh, I see, I...' Colour invaded her cheeks, and this time he kept his smile to himself. *Most definitely flustered.* Did she imagine he had ulterior motives in determining her marital status? Did she hope?

'It doesn't work that way,' she continued, accepting the brochures back and sweeping an imaginary strand of hair behind her ear, fiddling with an already perfectly aligned pearl earring. 'I've arranged more than one hundred weddings now. I can assure you, I've had plenty of experience to ensure Monica's wedding goes off without a hitch. Now—'

'So you're not married, then?'

She blinked, the shutters coming down over deep violet-coloured eyes, a movement that only drew attention to the long sweep of her dark lashes over the biggest surprise— cheeks flushed with sudden colour—before she once again opened them. Did she have any idea how innocent yet sexy she looked when she did that? He sighed. *What a waste.* In other circumstances he might have been able to pursue this attraction to its logical conclusion—in other circumstances he most likely would have. But she'd hardly be in the mood for sex once he'd given her the bad news.

'Did I say I wasn't married?'

'You intimated it, I'm certain.'

Her teeth pestered her bottom lip as she frowned, and he could tell she was rewinding her words, working out which of them had given her away. Then she shook her head. 'And is it actually relevant?'

'Not really.' He smiled, knowing he had her right where he wanted her. 'I'm just a curious kind of guy.'

The fog of indecision cleared in her narrowing eyes. 'In which case, you're no doubt curious to hear about Monica and Jake's plans.'

Touché, he thought, awarding her a mental tick of approval for steering the conversation back to the wedding. Except that it was the one place he didn't particularly want to go. 'Actually, no. I'd rather talk about you.'

Even with her mouth open he couldn't fault her looks. A shame the game had to end here. 'Mr Caruana,' she recovered enough to say, 'I don't think—'

A knock at the door had them both turning to where the young PA stood, looking uncertain. 'I'm sorry to interrupt, Mr Caruana. Would you like me to bring in any tea or coffee?'

'No, thank you. Miss Turner was just leaving. Let my driver know to have the car out front.'

He stood as the girl nodded, withdrew and pulled the door closed behind her—unnecessarily, given his guest would soon be leaving, but something he could easily remedy. Meanwhile his visitor was looking more flustered than ever. 'But Mr Caruana, we've hardly begun. We haven't even discussed the date for the wedding.'

'Ah, there would be a reason for that.' He was already reaching for the handle, ready to swing open the door in preparation for her departure. If she was about to storm out, as he predicted, he'd hate her to have to break her stride on the way. 'That's actually because we don't need to.' He swung the door open and waited. 'It would simply be a waste of time. And in my business—as in yours, I expect—time is money.'

She shook her head where she stood, a slash of colour accenting each high cheekbone. 'This is your own sister's wedding we're talking about. Surely you want to support her on the most important day of her life?'

'Whatever do you take me for? Of course I would never be so callous. My sister, and her happiness, are of the utmost concern to me.'

'Then why are you not prepared to even talk about the arrangements for her wedding?'

'There's a very simple explanation for that, Miss Turner, an explanation that seems to have escaped your notice: you see, there's actually not going to *be* a wedding.'

CHAPTER THREE

No WEDDING? She'd learned through her research that Daniel Caruana was regarded as one of Far North Queensland's most ruthless business tycoons, known equally for his ability to create millions as for his ability to blow any opposition away. Likewise she'd been warned by Jake that Daniel Caruana was super-protective of his little sister and that her suddenly getting married mightn't sit easily with him.

Still, the sheer force of his reaction shocked her. It was one thing to want the best for his sister—who wouldn't want that?—but to deny this wedding would happen, to pretend that it would go away if he so decreed, just beggared belief.

'Is that so?' she managed, determination stiffening her spine as slowly she rose to her feet, swallowing back on a more personal, more biting, retort. 'I suspect Monica and Jake might have something to say about that.'

'And I suspect my sister will soon see sense, and this mar- riage rubbish will be nothing more than a distant memory. In which case, I'm sorry to say, it appears your services will no longer be required.'

From somewhere deep inside her she summoned a smile. She hadn't wasted a day to come and not see him. Likewise she hadn't wasted a day to come and be summarily dis- missed—not without him hearing her out. 'Mr Caruana,' she said, knowing instinctively that if she took a step towards the open door she would be giving in to his heavy-handed tactics. Instead she stood right where she was, clutching the portfolio and the wedding arrangements it contained to her chest as if protecting her own child.

Right this minute the wedding of Jake and Monica *felt* like her baby. She'd put so much time and effort into making sure Monica had everything she wished for—palm trees, a romantic beach setting and, hopefully, a glorious sunset to accompany the reception. Finding a venue that could provide all that and could take a wedding at short notice had consumed one hundred per cent of her time lately, and if it hadn't been for a cancellation she wouldn't have a booking at all. If she didn't confirm tomorrow morning like she'd planned, she'd lose it; she'd be blowed if she'd do that because His Nibs didn't like the idea of his little sister getting married. 'If I might be so bold, I don't think Monica and Jake consider it "rubbish". They would no doubt both be offended you felt that way, as am I.'

He glanced at his watch, managing to look both impatient and bored in the same instant. 'Is that all you have to say before you leave?'

'No, as a matter of fact, it's not. For as much as you might be able to dismiss me from your office and continue living in your precious little world of denial, you're going to have to face the fact some time that your sister is all grown up now and she and Jake will soon be married, with or without your seal of approval—which I'm sure you appreciate, given Monica's age, she doesn't actually need.

'Naturally, I don't need to tell you that she'd be happier if you could dredge up some semblance of support for her at this, one of the most important times of her life, but the marriage is going to go ahead whether you like it or not. In which case, it might be better and easier for all concerned if you just accepted that fact now rather than fighting it, wouldn't you say?'

She wanted to sag with relief after completing her impromptu speech, but there was no respite, not from the steel-like glare that held her pinned to the spot, nor from the fury drawing his features into a tight mask.

Beyond the glass walls of the office the sun continued to blaze in an azure sky. The diamond-flecked waves along the shore were studded with swimmers taking advantage of the warm winter sun, while inside the temperature had dropped below freezing.

Suddenly the door slammed shut with a crash that made the walls shudder and Sophie jump with them as Daniel stormed away along the length of the windows. Just as suddenly he stopped and turned, his hand slashing through the air. 'I don't have to accept anything! Not when there will *be* no wedding!'

'You really think you can stop them?' She dragged in a breath, shaking her head, realising that arguing was futile and that she would do better to try and persuade. 'Look, Mr Caruana,' she said, taking a tentative and what she hoped was a conciliatory step forward, 'Monica and Jake are crazy about each other. You should see them together—this is a true love-match.'

His left palm cracked down so hard on his timber desk that she flinched. 'She does *not* love that man!'

'You don't know that.'

'Don't you think I know my sister? Monica likes to think she's in love. She always has. She's been in love with fairy tales for ever, in love with the *idea* of being in love, always waiting for a knight in shining armour to come riding over the hill and rescue her. But if there's one thing my sister doesn't need it's rescuing. Not by anyone.'

No? With a brother like him, rescuing by a knight in shining armour sounded like a perfectly reasonable idea, if not a necessity. 'I'm not actually talking fairy tales, Mr Caruana. I'm talking about love—deep, abiding love.' She hesitated, wondering how far she could go before overstepping the mark from 'cool and professional' to tripping into 'foot in mouth' territory. Then she figured that, with all that had gone before, she was already there. 'I gather from your reaction that you're unfamiliar with the concept.'

The sudden tightness of flesh against cheek and jaw was his first response. 'I'm talking reality!' was his second, before he took to pacing again, eating up the floor in long, fluid strides. She would have liked to ignore him, but she was compelled to watch. Compelled to admire the big-cat-like grace and economy of his movements, even when anger seemed to be the prime motivator behind his motion.

Whoever his tailor was, he was a genius, she thought guiltily; there was no way he'd bought those trousers off the rack. The fabric moved over the tight musculature of his behind and thighs like it was part of his very flesh.

'How much do you think my sister is worth?' He wheeled around so suddenly she had to drag her eyes north, and her wayward thoughts with them. 'How many millions?'

Sophie shrugged, struggling for nonchalance as she reined in thoughts that had no place in this confrontation. 'And that's relevant because?' It seemed a fair question to her—she'd never given two thoughts to Monica's wealth or otherwise— but it only appeared to make him madder.

'Are you really that naïve, Miss Turner?' Three long steps brought him closer—perilously closer. Now there was only a pace between them, and even that seemed shrunken and almost vibrating with tension, a tension that inexplicably made her breasts ache and her nipples harden. 'Do you have any idea how many men have come sniffing after my sister, hoping to find a way to the Caruana fortune?'

She forced herself to concentrate on his words instead of the shimmering sensations of the flesh, kicking up her chin in a futile effort to appear taller, even though he had at least six inches on her five-foot-eight frame. 'And you'd know that was their motive, because…?'

'Because as soon as they got a sniff of a cheque they conceded defeat and cleared off.'

Shimmer turned to shock, rendering her momentarily speechless. When she could finally put voice to thoughts again, out spilled the disbelief in words. 'You paid them?'

She put a hand over her mouth, swaying a little on her feet at the revelation. Monica had mentioned in passing the fact that she'd never been able to hang on to a boyfriend for long, how she'd been left cold on more than one occasion and how she felt Jake was different. Sophie had imagined it had merely been to do with not finding the right guy yet, and had never once imagined there was a more sinister reason. 'You actually *paid* your sister's boyfriends to back off?'

'Which they did. Which proves my point, wouldn't you say, that they only wanted her for the money?'

She was still reeling, amazed that he was so unabashed about his interference on the one hand, and imagining the pressure he must have exerted on his sister's hapless suitors on the other. Confronted by one of his henchmen, or worse still Daniel himself, they'd probably been terrified of what might have happened if they didn't take the money and run.

She searched his eyes for some hint of remorse but their dark depths were cold and unapologetic. She shivered, the earlier shimmering heat she'd felt suddenly vanquished with his cold-as-ice revelation.

She had no doubt he thought he was doing good in protecting the family fortune, but in doing so he'd left his sister thinking there was something fundamentally wrong with her and that she would never find a partner who would stick by her in the process.

It was sheer luck that Monica had found Jake—not that there was any way she was going to convince Daniel of that. Just as clearly she could tell she'd wasted her time coming here today. Daniel didn't just want his sister to remain unmarried, what he really wanted was to lock her in a gilded cage and throw away the key.

'You should be pleased your sister has found someone who appreciates how special she is.'

'Oh, Fletcher knows she's special, all right. Special to the tune of an eight-figure sum. Why else would he have zeroed in on her?'

'Because he loves her.'

'So why the desperate rush to marry if he *loves* her so much? Is he afraid she'll change her mind and he'll lose his entrée to a fortune? Or is it that he can't wait to get his hands on her assets—those assets he hasn't already availed himself of, that is?'

'You're disgusting,' she managed, already turning her thoughts to getting to the airport, maybe catching an earlier flight back to Brisbane. 'You're not a brother. You're some kind of monster.'

'Am I more a monster than the men who would take advantage of Monica's fortune in pretence of love?'

She bowed her head, disbelieving, already turning away. 'You don't know they were after her money. They were probably just too terrified to argue. I'm sorry, I've wasted—'

An iron grip on her forearm put a stop to her escape before it had begun. When she turned back, his eyes were narrowed, their darkness intensified, his head at an angle as he moved closer. 'Yet you're not too terrified to argue, are you, Miss Turner? Why is that? Are you afraid of missing out on your big, fat fee?'

Resistance sparked once more in her veins. 'Is that all everything comes down to with you, Mr Caruana? Money? Do you really believe everyone is motivated by the same almighty quest for the dollar? Well, maybe you should think again. And then maybe you might stop judging everyone by your own low standards.'

She jerked her elbow out of his grip, wanting to get away, needing to get away. Failure weighing heavily on her shoulders.

Oil on the waters. What a laugh. She might as well have thrown petrol on the flames of his familial discontent. She'd blown her role as peacemaker completely. 'I have to go.'

'Why? So you can warn Fletcher I'll be making him an offer? To advise him he should hang out for more? You mark my words,' Daniel continued, 'Fletcher will have his price, just like the rest.'

'Oh no.' She shook her head. There was no way Daniel was slotting her brother into the likes of his damned fortune-hunters. 'Jake isn't like that—even if those others were, and you've given me no proof of that. Jake isn't interested in her money. He loves Monica.'

'Of course he does,' he sneered. 'How long exactly have they known each other? A fortnight? A month?'

'Some people don't need that long to know the person they're with is the one they want to spend the rest of their lives with.'

'Is that so? Next you'll be telling me you believe in love at first sight.'

'It happens.'

'But of course you would have to say that, in your line of work. You want people to get married; you don't actually care if they *stay* married.'

Sophie turned for the door. 'Look, I'm leaving. I don't have to put up with this.'

But he was already there in front of her, blocking her exit, and again she was struck by the way he moved with such effortless grace for such a powerfully built man. But it was what he was doing to her internal thermostat that concerned her more. Again he'd tripped some switch that sent her body from frigid to simmering in an instant. Her skin prickled with heat, her nerve endings tingled with awareness and it was only the portfolio clutched in her folded arms that concealed her rock-hard nipples.

It was in his eyes, she realised as he stared down at her. In his dark, challenging eyes that could suddenly turn from cold and flat to molten pools that radiated their heat to hers and then downwards to her very extremities. Eyes that were telling her things that made no sense, yet still her toes curled in her shoes.

Then he smiled and reached out a hand, running the backs of his fingers down her cheek so gently that she trembled under his electric touch. It was like being in a bubble where the room had shrunk to a tiny space around them, where even her peripheral vision had shrunk to fit no more than his broad shoulders. 'If I said to you right now "marry me", would you say yes?'

His voice seemed to come from a long, long way away, while his thumb stroked her chin; her lips parted on a sigh. 'Mr Caruana...' She swallowed, her thoughts scrambled. She was supposed to be leaving. She was sure she'd been about to leave. They'd been arguing. But what about?

'Daniel,' he said, his voice like the darkest chocolate, smooth, rich and forbidden. 'Enough with the "Mr Caruana". Call me Daniel. And I shall call you Sophie.'

'Mr Caruana,' she attempted again. 'Daniel.' She licked her lips. The name felt way too informal, tasted almost intimate, or was that just the way his eyes seemed to spark and flare as he watched her mouth his name? As he watched her lips taste the sound as hungrily as she'd watched his lips utter her name?

He was closer, his hand at her neck, drawing her towards him, towards his mouth. 'What would your answer be?'

There was a point to all this, she recognised that much, if only she could tell what it was. But in air spiced with his musky, masculine scent she couldn't make sense of what he was asking, only on some fundamental level that it shouldn't be happening. She held onto the thread of logic, clung to it, even when his lips brushed over hers and then returned for another pass just as feather-light as the first. Just as earth shattering.

She trembled under the silken assault, her knees almost buckling beneath her as he drew her closer until her folded arms met his chest, the folded arms protecting the folder she clung to like a shield, reminding her why she was here.

And it wasn't to allow herself to be seduced by the man who opposed his sister's marriage! She freed one hand and pushed against the hard wall of his chest, trying not to think about how good his hard flesh felt under her fingers even as the fingers deep in her hair attempted to steer her still closer.

Sophie turned her head aside, felt the brush of his warm breath on her cheek this time. 'Mr Caruana,' she pleaded, needing the formality to put distance between them. 'This is ridiculous. We barely know each other.'

His hands were gone from her as he wheeled away and cold air rushed to fill the places he'd been. 'Exactly my point,' he said, sounding angry, his back to her as he gazed out at the view, raking the fingers of both hands through his hair. 'We hardly know each other. And yet you seem to think it's perfectly reasonable for my sister to marry someone she's known barely a month.'

'So maybe Jake didn't maul her the first time they met.'

His shoulders stiffened before he turned and already she regretted her hasty words, even before she'd seen the potent depths of his eyes. 'Believe me, if I'd have mauled you I would have left the marks to prove it.'

A quake shuddered through her bones and she had to muster every last crumb of control she could to hide it. He'd touched her with a caress as soft as silk, and that had been enough to leave its mark, so how much more delicious would it be to feel the full brunt of his passion?

Oh yes, she believed him. Which was why now, more than ever, she had to get out of here. She was supposed to be a professional wedding planner, and professionals didn't get involved with family members of people whose weddings they were arranging, even when the groom was your brother. *Especially* when the groom was your brother. 'Like I said, I have to go.'

Yes; the sooner she went, the better. Her colour was high, her hair was mussed where he'd pushed his fingers in the thick coil and her eyes were wide and watchful, like she was afraid he'd kiss her again. The chances were, if she kept looking at him that way, he just might.

Why had he done that? He'd wanted to prove a point, to make her see how ridiculous it was for anyone to make the momentous step of getting married when they barely knew each other. Instead he'd got lost somewhere along the line, somewhere between the sensual curve of her cheek and the warm scent of woman.

'The car's waiting downstairs to take you to the airport.'

She nodded, leaning to gather her portfolio and briefcase without taking her eyes from him, as if to check he wasn't about to ambush her again. Then she straightened and headed for the door.

Halfway there, she stopped and turned. 'I feel sorry for you—I really do. But I feel sorrier for Monica, who thinks the sun shines out of her big brother. Who believes you love her and that you'll come round to her plans for marriage, when all you're really interested in is keeping her locked away from the world in some kind of gilded cage.'

'I want what's best for her.'

'No, you don't. You want what's best for *you*. What's easiest. You actually don't care about Monica's happiness at all. Well, all I can say is it's lucky she found someone like Jake at last, someone with a bit of backbone who can stand up to her overbearing, bullying brother. God knows, he'll need it.'

Her words rubbed him raw, her arguments playing on his mind. Once again she was defending the indefensible. Once again she was acting as if Fletcher were the injured party in all this. Fletcher was supposed to be her client but, the way she came out fighting every time he mentioned his name, anyone would think she was in love with him herself.

She was already reaching for the door handle when he found the words to respond. 'You don't know the first thing about Fletcher. Why do you insist on defending him the way you do?'

Her hand stilled on the handle. He saw her shoulders rise and fall on a sigh before she glanced over at him even as she pulled open the door. 'Why wouldn't I defend Jake? After all, he is my brother.'

CHAPTER FOUR

FLETCHER was her brother? She'd pulled the door closed behind her and disappeared before he could react, but it was shock that kept him rooted to the spot. Fletcher didn't have any sister, not that he could recall. He'd certainly never mentioned one in all their years at college, not that they'd ever spent any time in idle chit-chat. Daniel had always been too busy facing up to the brash challenger who'd insisted he was as good, if not better, than him, Fletcher trying to prove it at every opportunity. Besides, she'd said her name was Turner—or was that just part of the ruse?

Nothing made sense.

Nothing but knowing that he should have handled the meeting with her a whole lot better. He would have, if he hadn't been thrown off balance completely this morning by his sister's email.

And now the mess he'd made of the meeting had grown a hundred times worse. Because Sophie Turner wasn't simply a wedding planner, as he'd believed. She was Fletcher's sister.

She should have told him. He glanced out of the windows in the direction of the street, caught a glimpse of the car as it pulled into the traffic before it was lost from view and swore under his breath.

But of course she hadn't told him. She was probably in on the deal, no wedding planner at all but rather a convenient intermediary, no doubt expecting a cut for her part in playing a role and making the marriage plans look real. She'd probably be calling Fletcher already, telling him to expect an offer, advising him to hang out for a better one.

Or would Monica and Fletcher still be on their flight?

Maybe there was still time.

He snatched up the phone on his desk and punched in a number that would connect him with his head of security. It answered on the second ring, as he knew it would. 'Jo? Caruana here. I want you to find out all you can about a wedding-planning business called One Perfect Day, and a Miss Sophie Turner who supposedly works there. I want financials, personal contacts and history, as well as details of family members of every employee, as fast as you can.'

'Will do,' came the rapid-fire response. Then a pause. 'Do I take it congratulations are in order?'

From anyone else the question would not have been tolerated, but Jo had been with him almost from the beginning, their association going back to their high-school days together.

'I'm not. But Jake Fletcher's apparently got his hooks into Monica. They're talking weddings, and Sophie Turner claims to be their wedding planner.'

'Fletcher's back?' Daniel heard the squeak of his security head's chair as he sat to attention. 'You want me to sort him out, boss?'

Daniel had anticipated just such a reaction. Jo hated Fletcher almost as much as Daniel himself did. But then Jo was the one who'd been waiting at the airport when Daniel had returned from Italy in time for Emma's funeral. He was the one who'd kept him together when they'd learned the results of the autopsy. And he was the one who'd stopped him marching into Fletcher's hospital ward and pulling him off his life support.

He appreciated the loyalty, but while once upon a time he'd have settled contests with his fists, those days were gone. These days he preferred to use subtler, even if more expensive, means. Not that he couldn't afford it.

'He's already flown the coop and taken Monica to Hawaii— and left the wedding planner to convince me the wedding's kosher, no doubt to secure a higher settlement.'

'Like hell it's kosher! Okay, boss, I'm onto it.'

'And Jo—something else you should know.'

'What's that?'

'The wedding planner, Sophie Turner, she's claiming to be Fletcher's sister.'

Jo whistled through his teeth. 'I never knew Fletcher had a sister.'

'Neither did I. That's one of the things I want you to check. If she's not his sister, she's probably in on some kind of percentage from a settlement to make him disappear. And if she is his sister…'

'Given her scum dog of a brother, she'd be even less trustworthy.'

'Exactly what I was thinking,' Daniel agreed before he hung up, still leaning over his desk, hauling air into his lungs as his brain made the connections. Fletcher had to have taken Monica to Hawaii for two reasons—first, to ensure nobody could arrive in Brisbane while Fletcher wasn't around and bundle her on the next flight back to Cairns to talk her out of making the biggest mistake of her life, and secondly to suck her further and further into his web.

Meanwhile the sweet Miss Turner had the job of playing the supporting role at home to make it look like the wedding was real, no doubt in the hope it would crank up any pay-off offered to Fletcher.

He growled. If she'd been speaking the truth, then he'd had Fletcher's sister right here in his office and he'd let her walk away. God, he'd even held her in his arms and all but kissed her. Fletcher's damned sister. What had he been thinking?

But he hadn't been thinking then, not beyond the silky-smooth perfection of her skin, the unusual blue of her eyes, and the tantalising scent of woman.

So much for wanting to make a point about the irrationality of things happening too quickly. If she hadn't stopped him, if she hadn't pushed him away, he doubted he could have stopped himself.

Not the point he'd been trying to make at all. But Monica's news had thrown him for six. No wonder he hadn't been thinking straight.

But he was thinking straight now.

The old and familiar competitiveness cranked back into life. Fletcher would soon be sitting in his five-star hotel suite waiting to hear from his sister about Daniel's reaction, rubbing his hands together in glee while he waited for a nice plump offer for him to disappear to drop into his lap.

The last thing he'd be expecting would be for Daniel to join in the game. If Fletcher wanted to play 'whisk away the sister', why couldn't Daniel do likewise?

Maybe he should just *whisk away* one Miss Sophie Turner for however long it took.

And he sure as hell wouldn't let her go again until he knew Moni was safe.

He glanced at his watch. They should be nearing the airport by now. Miss Turner would be thinking she was just about home free.

He picked up the telephone again, punching in another number and smiling for what felt like the first time today, already anticipating her confusion. 'Cedric, there's been a change of plans…'

Sophie pushed back into the butter-soft upholstery, willing herself to relax. She'd almost turned her back on the car waiting for her when she'd emerged from the lobby. She'd had enough of Daniel Caruana for one day, and she'd wanted nothing more to do with him and his. But the driver had greeted her with a friendly smile and, much as she resented his boss, she'd had no reason to be rude to an innocent driver—especially one who was probably smiling in relief because it wasn't Mr Arrogance himself that he was picking up. Besides, she'd had no idea how long it would take to wait for a taxi this far north of Cairns, and the sooner she made it to the airport, the better chance she would have of catching an earlier flight back to Brisbane.

So she'd allowed herself to be handed into the spacious interior of the luxury sedan, satisfied at least that every minute took her another kilometre from Daniel Caruana.

She sighed and dropped her head back against the head rest, closing her eyes and wondering what she was going to tell Jake and Monica. They'd expected resistance to the wedding news, certainly, but Daniel hadn't even given her a chance to explain the wedding arrangements and the fact that nobody was expecting him to pay for anything. Not that he would have believed her, given he'd already made his mind up on that point.

Apparently nobody went out with his sister unless they were gold-digging fortune-hunters looking for nothing more than a juicy pay-out. And of course he wouldn't care who was supposed to stump up for the wedding bills. Hadn't he already made it plain that there was to *be* no wedding?

Sophie put a hand to her forehead, her fingers trying to stroke away her tension as the car continued down the palm-lined highway towards the city of Cairns and the airport that promised escape. How on earth had Jake ever thought she'd be able to convince someone like Daniel Caruana that this wedding was a good idea? And how was she going to tell him that she'd blown her peace-keeping role big time?

She opened her eyes in time to see the sign signalling the turn off for James Cook Airport. She sighed in relief. At least she'd soon be away from here. Away from Daniel Caruana, the man who could be her brother-in-law.

The man who had almost kissed her...

She jammed her eyes shut, trying to blot away the memories, but she could still feel the brush of his lips, could still smell his intoxicating, masculine scent weaving its way into her senses as his fingers worked their way into her hair and directed her face towards his.

When he'd told her that if he had mauled her she'd have the marks to prove it... Oh my. Sophie dragged in a lungful of air, hot and breathless, the car's air conditioning was suddenly found wanting. Thank goodness she'd found the sense to turn away before she made more of a fool of herself than she already had.

What was his point? Had he been trying to convince her he was the red-hot lover the tabloids hinted at? Or had he just been toying with her, like some random plaything, before throwing her out?

Either way, the man clearly had no conscience. She was glad she'd have nothing more to do with him. At least not until the wedding—if he even bothered to show up.

Then she smiled. If there had been one glimmer of satisfaction she could take from this morning's meeting, it had been the moment before she'd left, when she'd finally had the opportunity to tell him she was Jake's sister. In the scant seconds after her revelation, and before she'd pulled the door closed behind her, she'd seen his look of smug dismissal give way to shock and a kind of numb disbelief.

So maybe she hadn't managed to convince Mr Hot Shot Caruana to give his blessing to his sister's upcoming wedding—and maybe she'd blown her role as peace maker—but at least she'd managed to get the last word in. How fortunate it was that he hadn't allowed her to get a word in edgeways so she could save that little gem until last. That part of the meeting, at least, had been infinitely satisfying.

Sophie looked up, thinking for a moment that the driver had said something to her, only to find him talking into his hands-free phone. She looked around. They were in the departure lane, slowing as they neared the drop-off zone with the maze of vehicles pulling in and out along the kerb before them. She strung her briefcase strap over her shoulder, her hand ready on the door release so that she could quickly alight. Except the driver didn't pull in to stop like she'd expected but kept on driving.

'There's a spot just there,' she called, pointing to her left, wondering what was wrong with the last two spaces he'd driven past.

'Sorry, miss,' the driver said, glancing at her in his rear-view mirror. 'Change of plans.'

'No, I have a flight to catch.' She looked over her shoulder as the airport buildings and her escape plans disappeared behind, the first frisson of fear slipping down her spine and taking root in her gut.

She turned back in time to catch the driver's shrug as he accelerated back along the airport exit-road. 'Didn't Mr Caruana tell you? Apparently now you're going by chopper.'

'What? No.' Fear turned to anger as she reached for her PDA and found his number. 'No, Mr Caruana didn't tell me that.'

Mr Caruana still wasn't telling her anything. The young PA told her he was unavailable and couldn't be reached—perhaps she'd like to leave a message?

No, Sophie decided, breaking the connection. What she had to say to Mr Caruana was best said face to face. No matter what stunt he was pulling now, she'd make sure there'd be ample opportunity for that sometime.

She called her office in Brisbane, something she'd been intending to do once she'd confirmed her flight.

'Meg,' she said as soon as her assistant answered. 'It's Sophie.'

'How did the meeting go?'

Sophie pulled a face. 'Not as well as it could have. I think Monica might be walking down the aisle by herself.'

'Oh, I'm sorry to hear that. But at least you tried. What time will you be back?'

Good question, Sophie thought, biting her lip as she watched the passing parade of palm trees lining the wide highway, heading the wrong way, wondering if she should let Meg know what was happening. But what *was* happening? It wasn't like she was being kidnapped. Not exactly. She still had her phone, after all. It wasn't as if she couldn't call for help if she thought she needed it. But that still didn't mean she was happy about her plans being turned upside down for no good reason and without explanation. 'I'm not sure,' she said, and at least that much was true. 'It looks like I might be delayed. I'll let you know as soon as I can.'

'Okay. I'll hold the fort until you get back. Oh, and don't forget, you have that meeting at the Tropical Palms first thing tomorrow to finalise the arrangements.'

'Don't worry, Meg.' Whatever surprises Daniel Caruana had planned, she'd be back in Brisbane long before then. 'There's no way I'd miss that. See you soon.'

She snapped her phone shut and looked around. Here the rainforest covered mountains rose sharply from the narrowing coastal plain, and she realised she was almost back at the Palm Cove turn off and the office she'd left barely forty minutes ago. What the hell was he playing at? Surely he didn't feel so bad about the way he'd behaved during their meeting that he was going to make up for it by having her flown all the way to Brisbane in his private helicopter? She swallowed. As much as she wanted to get back to the office, she wasn't sure she was too crazy at the idea of spending two hours or so in one of those tiny buzz boxes.

But no, she decided, a man like Daniel Caruana wouldn't do remorse. It wouldn't be in his vocabulary. So what was he trying to prove?

Anxiety warred with anger inside her. Her stomach felt like it was already taking flight. The thought of going into battle with the man again set her nerves jangling, and her senses to high alert, but if he wanted a battle that was exactly what he would get.

Because, whoever Daniel Caruana thought he was, however much money he had, he had no right to ride roughshod over other people's wishes and plans. Not his sister's. Not her brother's. And least of all hers. She was just in the mood to explain that to him.

They turned off the highway, the car pulling into a clearing not far from the office block where a sleek red helicopter sat amidst a circle of white markers, its rotors lazily circling. But it was the tall, dark haired figure standing alongside a black coupe that was even sexier looking than the chopper that Sophie focused on. He was holding a phone to his ear, the other hand in his trouser pocket as he leaned against the low sports car, his long legs crossed casually at the ankle, his white open-necked shirt rippling softly in the breeze. He looked relaxed, urbane and totally without a hint of apology, which only made Sophie even more angry.

She was out of her door and on her way across to him before the car had barely stopped. He saw her coming, and even behind his sunglasses she could feel his dark eyes following her every step. But she was damned if she was going to let that slow sizzle under her skin bother her, not when it gave her yet another reason to resent him.

She stopped directly in front of him, although that still left her more than a metre away, courtesy of the long legs so idly stretched out in front of him. 'Do you mind telling me what this is about? I've got a flight back to Brisbane to catch, and the last thing I need is to be brought back here without one word of explanation.'

He uttered something into his phone and slid it shut, deposited it in the top pocket of his shirt and slipped that hand into his free trouser pocket. He looked so brutally good-looking and so frustratingly unmoved that she felt like tearing him limb from limb, if only to get a reaction. 'Miss Turner,' he said with a smile a crocodile would have been proud of, a smile that irritated her all the way down to her bones. 'I'm so pleased you could join me.'

'You've got a nerve. You know I had no choice.'

'Did Cedric tie you up and throw you in the boot?' His eyebrows rose. 'I must speak to him about his technique. I've warned him about treating my guests that way.' He gave a nod to someone over her shoulder, and she turned to see the driver give an answering wave as he drove off. She swung back, her indignation turning to fury.

'You think this is funny?'

'I think your reaction is slightly amusing, yes.'

The blood in her veins simmered and spat. 'Because I object to having my plans to return to Brisbane thrown into disarray by a man who made it plain my presence wasn't welcome here? You have a strange sense of humour, Mr Caruana.' She threw a glance at the chopper. 'Is that thing waiting to take me to Brisbane?'

'That's not exactly what I had in mind, no.'

'Then you can just forget whatever you had in mind. I'll do what I should have done before and call myself a taxi.' She wheeled away, pulling her phone from her bag, but she'd barely slid it open when it was extracted smoothly from her hands.

Something inside her snapped. She spun around, lunging for his hand. 'You bastard! Give that back.'

'Such language. I should have picked you for Fletcher's sister from the start.'

Her open palm cracked against his cheek so hard that her hand stung with fire at the impact, and she fervently hoped his cheek hurt at least half as bad. 'Did you bring me back merely so you could further insult my family?'

Open-jawed, he rubbed one side of his face where the darkening bloom was already spreading under his olive skin. 'Miss Turner,' he said, looking down at her, crowding her with an almost feral gleam in his eyes. It was with some satisfaction that she saw that any hint of a smile had been wiped from his face. 'You continue to surprise me.'

'I'm sorry I can't return the compliment. I was warned to expect an arrogant bastard used to throwing his weight around. Seems like I heard right. And now—' she held her hand out to him '—may I have my phone back? I have a plane to catch.'

His fingers only seemed to curl tighter around the device. 'What time is your flight?'

'What's it to you?'

'Because where I want to take you is only ten minutes away.'

'Why should I agree to go anywhere with you?'

'Would it help if I said I didn't give you a fair hearing during our meeting today?'

She was more suspicious than ever now. 'I think we both know that's true, but you didn't have to drag me back here to admit it. You could have called. I do have a phone…' She stared pointedly at the fingers still curled around her mobile. 'Or, at least, I did.'

He chose to ignore her reminder. 'It occurred to me after you left that I can't stop my sister getting married if that's what she really wants.'

'That's not what you said before.'

'Hear me out. I take it Monica would actually like me to be at her wedding?'

Sophie bristled. She'd been thinking that a wedding without a certain Daniel Caruana in attendance held a considerable appeal. But he was Monica's brother, and getting Daniel's cooperation was the reason she'd been sent up here. So she nodded reluctantly, little more than a tiny dip of her head in acknowledgement. 'Monica was hoping you might walk her down the aisle. When I left your office, that prospect didn't look too likely.'

'You haven't told her?'

She shook her head. 'Not yet. They'll still be *en route*.'

He looked skywards, exhaling as if relieved, one hand raking through his thick black hair. Sophie's eyes were involuntarily drawn to the broad expanse of chest, the uninterrupted view of his strong neck and the deep-olive skin revealed by his open-necked shirt. Monica was tiny when compared to her brother. Her skin was almost a honey gold whereas Daniel's was burnished bronze, as if he spent as much time as he could with his shirt off, soaking up the rays. She swallowed. She really didn't need to think about Daniel Caruana undressed. *Not one bit.*

She blinked, mentally chasing the unwanted thoughts away, only to find him watching her, a glimmer of something predatory in his dark eyes that disappeared even before she'd turned her eyes away, feigning interest in the fringe of palms bordering the lot. Heat flooded to her face. God, he'd seen her ogling him like some drooling teenager—a man she couldn't even stand. She'd clearly been in the Far North Queensland sun far too long.

'I'm sorry,' he said beside her.

Not as sorry as I am, she thought before his words sank in and she realised he was talking about something else entirely.

'You are?' It was the last thing she'd expected from him.

Her reaction brought a smile to his face. 'I'm not in the habit of apologising,' he told her. 'It does not come easily to me.' He sighed and looked over at the waiting helicopter and held up his hand to the pilot, his fingers splayed. The pilot nodded and turned away.

'Walk with me a while,' Daniel said beside her, strolling off towards the trees and a flower bed bursting with colour. 'Let me explain. You see, my sister's—Monica's—email took me by surprise. I hadn't had time to assimilate her news before you arrived on my doorstep. But you were right. She has never seemed so serious about any man, but she is twenty-one and I can't stop her getting married, if that's what she really wants.'

'It is what she wants.'

He paused, looking as though he was searching for acceptance, although the tic in his jaw looked anything but accepting. 'And if that is indeed so, then I should at least give you a fair hearing, if only for my sister's sake.'

They wandered closer to the flower bed where it seemed colour was king. Every colour seemed vivid here, she mused, the reds more vibrant, the greens more intense, oranges looking like flames from the fires of hell. Nothing, it seemed, was pastel, least of all the man walking alongside her right now. He was large and powerful and darker in impression than any man had a right to be, and it wasn't just the flowers that looked like they'd stepped straight from hell. With his chiselled dark beauty and the power he wore like a cloak, he could be the ruler of the underworld.

She stopped and shivered slightly, not liking the direction of her thoughts, turning instead towards the waiting chopper, the pilot sitting patiently at the controls. 'So why the chopper?'

'Where is the wedding to be held?'

She groaned inwardly. Couldn't he just answer a simple question? The man was jumping around so much it was impossible to get a handle on him. He'd gone from arrogant to abusive to underhand to reconciliatory in the time most people could have lingered over a lazy Sunday brunch. But, then again, what did his character faults really matter as long as he did right by his sister and her brother? It wasn't as though Sophie had to like him. Not that there was any chance of that.

'I've booked the Tropical Palms golf club on the Gold Coast. I'm confirming it tomorrow, first thing.'

He scowled, and if his PA had been here, Sophie could imagine the girl running for cover. 'A *golf club* is going to play host to my sister's wedding?'

She wasn't his PA and yet still she bristled, feeling defensive, knowing she shouldn't give a damn about his reaction but unable to help it. She'd wanted something more exclusive, sure, but given the timing… 'It was all I could get at short notice. We were lucky as it was to score a cancellation. And Monica's happy with the venue.' She stole a breath, paused for thought and wondered why it mattered. Damn the man! Why should she have to justify the choice of venue? 'Monica's more than happy, actually, because when all's said and done she just wants to marry Jake as soon as possible.'

She caught the flicker in his eyes, that tell-tale tic in his jaw even while he tried to put an appearance of civility over his hard, chiselled features, and she wondered again what the hell this was all about. Why his sudden interest in the arrangements? Why the sudden change of heart that meant he could even contemplate his sister's wedding?

Especially when it was crystal clear that he found the idea of his sister marrying Jake repugnant.

Sure, he'd been taken by surprise by his sister's news—but to go from being vehemently opposed to the match to suddenly being so interested in the details of the wedding seemed too good to be true. It *had* to be too good to be true.

She crossed her arms over her slim briefcase in front of her. 'What is this all about, Mr Caruana? And this time I'd appreciate a straight answer.'

He smiled, if you could call it that. 'I want to show you something—a place better befitting any marriage of my sister.'

'I just told you, we have a venue. Monica—'

'You have a golf club.'

'It's a reception centre.'

'It's old, overrated and it's not good enough, not for Monica. It's too public, it's too cheap.'

'Monica and Jake are working to a budget on this.'

'As head of Monica's family, I should be paying for my sister's wedding. People will expect it. You will make me look cheap.'

'I'm sorry.' She turned away, unable to listen any longer; she'd heard enough. Did Mr Impossible care about nothing but himself and the impression he made? 'It may surprise you to know that this wedding isn't actually about you.'

'Maybe not, but everyone will assume that I am paying. The press will have a field day, claiming that Daniel Caruana spends less on his sister's wedding than on his latest mistress.'

She closed her eyes, trying not to think too hard about what it would be like to be Daniel Caruana's mistress—and not because of the money he must throw at them. He would be an uncompromising lover, she imagined, hard, demanding and as ruthless in the bedroom as in the boardroom. What would it be like to be that close to him, to be the one to rake her nails across that broad, sculpted chest?

Not that she cared.

Liar.

If she didn't care, a menacing voice inside her questioned, then why had she even thought of it? Unless she was still remembering that whisper of a kiss and how it had made her tremble all the way to her toes…

'I wouldn't have thought,' she said, battling a mouth that suddenly felt too dry to extract the words she needed, 'that you were the type of man who worried about what anyone said, let alone the press.'

'There are some things,' he started, leaning towards her, his dark eyes like a promise and his voice like a glove that stroked velvet down her spine, 'that are so private they have no place in the press.'

Under an indigo sky and a sun so warm that her skin felt kissed by the very air, still she shivered with the force of his words. Or was it their content? Whatever it was, it was threatening to scramble her brain.

'Let me show you an alternative,' he suggested. 'A mere ten minute flight away,' he said, jerking her back to the present, reminding her of what they were doing here. 'No more.'

'Look, Mr Caruana.' She shook her head, trying to clear her thoughts, wishing she could rid herself of this infernal

instability that seemed to beleaguer her while he was anywhere near, 'I told you, we have a booking. I hardly see the
point.'

'Indulge me.' His voice performed that velvet glove stroke
down her spine again. She fought against a melting spine and
glanced at her watch, because she had to look somewhere and
if she looked into his eyes and saw that he'd meant his words
to have that reaction, she would be lost. She didn't want to
think about indulging Daniel Caruana in any way, shape or
form.

'The longer you argue,' he pressed, 'the longer it will be
before you get back to the airport for your return flight. You
do want to make that return flight, don't you?'

She snapped her head up. 'I don't have to come with
you.'

He appeared totally nonplussed by her outburst. 'I can
assure you, when you do come, your time won't be wasted.
On the way you can fill me in on all the details I didn't give
you a chance to tell me in our earlier meeting.'

She looked at her watch before realising she'd just done
that and taken no notice of the time, before looking back up
at the man she suspected of playing games with her without
bothering to fill her in on the rules. But she had come to
Cairns to try to reconcile him to the notion of Monica and
Jake's marrying; if he was even now contemplating that the
wedding might happen, then maybe he wasn't entirely a lost
cause. And maybe her day hadn't been a complete waste of
effort.

If she left now without getting his agreement to walk his
sister down the aisle, what would she tell Jake and Monica
when they called later tonight—that she had failed them because she was scared of Monica's brother?

She had no choice when it all came down to it. There were
still a couple of hours before she had to be back at the airport

for her scheduled flight. What did it matter if she didn't get an earlier one when Monica and Jake were relying on her to make this wedding happen? She couldn't let them down.

She kicked up her chin. 'And maybe I might even get my phone back?'

'But of course,' he said, handing it over with a smile that spoke of victory and made her wonder if whatever she was conceding was worth much more than the price of a mere mobile phone. 'You only had to ask.'

CHAPTER FIVE

SOPHIE wasted no time calling the airline to confirm her flight time, ensuring Daniel was within earshot when she repeated the time by which she had to check in so he could not pretend later that he hadn't known. There was no way she intended to miss her flight, especially when she wasn't at all convinced at the necessity for this side trip.

Daniel merely smiled and excused himself, walking a little distance away as he made his own brief call before they both climbed into the waiting helicopter.

The ground fell away below along with Sophie's stomach as the helicopter rose effortlessly above the palm trees and set out towards the nearby coast. Beneath them the land slipped behind, houses and buildings giving way to a border of palm-studded sand and a sea that lapped at its shores in various shades from pale blue to aqua to turquoise. Once again she was struck with the sheer force of colour; the sand was bleached to a startling white, the waters so bright and beautiful, while the densely tangled, forested mountains behind were a bold contrast of green.

It was breathtaking, almost as breathtaking as the man alongside her and his unexpected about-face and subsequent apology.

Never in a million years would she have expected an apology from someone like Daniel Caruana. The man had appeared a complete Neanderthal just this morning. Surely evolution was meant to take longer?

Maybe, like he said, he'd been taken unawares with the news of his little sister's wedding? That at least made some kind of sense. She had to admit, she'd been taken aback too with the suddenness of the announcement. In some ways she'd been frightened she was losing the brother she'd only recently found. It was only when Monica had made it plain that she'd never be excluded from Jake's life again, and she realised that the other woman meant it, that she'd really come to embrace the news herself.

Had Daniel similarly been afraid of losing Monica?

Is that why he'd ultimately changed his mind—because he was genuinely worried he'd put his own relationship with his sister at risk by refusing her right to decide who to marry?

Who could tell how Daniel Caruana's mind worked? After all, this was the man who paid off his sister's prospective suitors. Did he really care anything about her happiness?

Besides, she hadn't missed his reaction when she'd mentioned Jake's name before boarding the helicopter. It was clear that what he felt for her brother bordered on hatred. So, while on the surface he seemed more amenable to this wedding, nothing had changed there.

And nothing explained why he had all but kissed her. Her lips tingled at the memory, at the remembered heat of his proximity.

It had been little more than a brush of lips, as brief as it was unexpected, and then he'd wheeled away and turned his back on her as if it had been the biggest mistake of his life. What had that been about, if not a blatant, testosterone-driven attempt to try to scuttle her thoughts and arguments and show her who was boss?

And it had so very nearly worked.

She felt a tap on her arm and jumped, as if she'd summoned his attention with her thoughts, and she was thankful beyond measure that he couldn't read them.

He pointed now, and yelled something at her she couldn't quite catch over her headphones, but she followed where he was pointing and understood.

Just a smudge of bluish green appeared on the horizon, with a zig-zag line jutting into the sky. But she recognised the shape immediately. So that was Kallista. She remembered seeing pictures of it years ago in an article about the private playgrounds of Australia's rich and famous. She'd never thought for a moment that one day she'd be setting foot on it herself.

The island sat like a jewel just off the coast, plump green hillsides and jagged peaks sliding to blindingly white sand beaches thickly fringed with palms, and ringed with the coral reef that made the sea around the island appear a thousand different shades of blue.

As they circled the mountains, even more treasure was revealed. A lagoon on one side, the water so clear she could see fish darting to and fro in the shallows.

Sophie's heart sank.

It was tropical perfection.

It made the Tropical Palms golf course look like a shabby try-hard.

What bride wouldn't prefer to get married in such a picture-postcard setting?

But they had a booking and Monica was happy, she reminded herself. And it would be perfect on the day. It was Sophie's job to ensure it would be so.

'So what do you think?' Daniel asked, after landing, as they strolled along the short jetty towards a waiting golf buggy.

His eyes were hidden behind his sunglasses, his white-teeth smile wide, the smile of a man who assumed he'd already won the battle, if not the war.

She looked anywhere but at him as they reached the buggy. 'It's nice,' she said with a nod, probably making the understatement of the year, but she wasn't about to gush, not when he would take any encouragement she offered as support for his plans to shift the venue from Brisbane to the island.

'Nice?' he repeated, rolling the word around his mouth like it had left a bad taste. 'You don't think you could be just a little more enthusiastic?'

She looked around. 'Well, it's got a lovely beach and loads of palm trees.'

'Monica loves this island,' he insisted. 'She always said that one day she wanted to get married here.'

Sophie didn't doubt it; no wonder Monica had specified palm trees and sunsets on her must-have list. She imagined the sunsets here must be something to behold. But what she did doubt was Daniel's conviction about wanting there to be a wedding at all, let alone playing host to it. For someone who had seemed so vehemently opposed to the idea just a few short hours ago, now it seemed he wanted control of the entire event.

And why? Because he was so happy he wanted his sister's wedding to be perfect? She seriously doubted it. His turnaround had been too quick, too contrived.

Too convenient.

Something was going on, if only she could work out what it was.

But one thing was clear—there was no way she'd agree to Kallista being the venue for the wedding. Jake had made it clear he'd prefer the wedding to be on neutral ground. She'd thought it a strange thing to specify at first, but having met

Daniel and witnessed his animosity towards her brother she could see where Jake was coming from. Daniel was the sort of man you had to stand up to, or get railroaded in the process.

She turned back to him, determined not to be railroaded herself. 'Okay, you're right, it is a beautiful island—perfect, I guess, if you want to plan on getting married barefoot on the sand. But in terms of infrastructure for a wedding?' She shrugged. 'For a start you'd have to have catering and accommodation facilities. Unless you'd be happy to boat everything in and lug everyone back and forth to the mainland on either a launch or—' she nodded towards the helicopter '—that thing.'

She could swear she could see the glint in his eyes even through the dark glasses. 'That won't be necessary.' He banged his hand on the top of the buggy. 'Climb in. I will let you judge if Kallista has the necessary *infrastructure*.'

Sophie did as he asked, climbing into the front seat beside him without bothering to tell him about the article she'd read all those years ago citing a house set high above the sea nestled amongst the vines and palms. Just one house. Sprawling around the hillside, perhaps, but barely enough to cater for an entire wedding party and guests.

Neither did she bother to repeat that there was no point to this entire trip anyway. Tomorrow morning she would pay the deposit that would secure the Tropical Palms golf club, as Monica and Jake had agreed, and Daniel Caruana could go to hell. What did he know about what was needed to organise a wedding? The Tropical Palms might be in need of refurbishment, but if he thought his sister was going to be happy to put up with marquees and sand flies on her special day he could think again.

The buggy took off along the track carved through the sands, heading for the shade of the palms. Somewhere along the line he'd undone the cuffs of his shirt and turned them up, exposing his forearms, his bronzed olive skin making his white shirt look more dramatic as the soft material billowed softly in the breeze. Suddenly she was transported back to her childhood and B-movie matinees featuring swashbuckling pirates with tight breeches, white shirts and gold rings in one ear.

He could almost be a pirate, she thought, with his midnight-black hair, his strong features and his arrogant, 'it's my way or the plank way' attitude.

The buggy's tiny tyres bumped over a fallen palm frond, the vehicle swaying as he immediately rounded a bend, a bubble of laughter erupted unbidden from her throat.

Almost a pirate—but for the fact she'd never thought of a pirate driving a golf buggy before.

'Is something funny?'

She pressed her lips together, looked at the track in front of them and avoided his gaze, even when she sensed it burning holes in her. 'It's just I saw your car—the black one you were leaning on where we met the helicopter.'

'And?'

'And it looked exactly like what I'd imagined you'd drive.'

'Oh, and what's that?'

The tiny vehicle rattled along the track. 'You know, something sleek and black and…' *Dangerous.* She stopped herself just in time 'And fast.'

'And that's funny?'

'Well, no, not really, it's just that—' She faltered, suddenly wondering why she'd ever been crazy enough to open her mouth. Next she'd be admitting she could imagine him as a pirate with a cutlass in one hand, a rope from the rigging in the other and a dagger shoved in his belt. And wouldn't that do her cause a power of good? She looked up at him, thankful for the shade from the canopy above them so he wouldn't be able to see the colour flooding her cheeks as she dreaded how he might react to the words she was game to put voice to. 'It's just that I guess I never imagined a man like you driving a golf buggy.'

He didn't get angry like she'd expected. Instead his lips curved upwards before he turned to her. 'I bet there are a lot of things you never imagined a man like me doing.'

He held her eyes for a fraction too long, an unnecessary fraction, before he turned his attention back to the weaving track.

She was so glad in that moment that he couldn't possibly read her thoughts, because then he might know that already she'd imagined him doing plenty.

He wondered what she'd been going to say when she faltered, wondered what she was thinking now; if he didn't know better, he'd think she was blushing. 'As it happens,' he admitted, 'I do have a thing for sleek, black and—' he threw her a glance '—fast cars. But here on the island this is how we get around. I'm sorry if it's not sleek and black and fast enough for you.'

His smile widened. She was blushing—even under the dappled light her face was flooded with colour—but this time she wasn't angry, he was sure of it, by the way her eyes wanted to avoid him rather than impale him. In fact, if he didn't know better, he'd even have thought Miss 'Prim'n'Proper' Turner had caught herself out. What had she been thinking? The way she was sitting up now, so stiff backed and strait-laced, she could have been a Victorian spinster school teacher on her way to meet her new school in a village full of head hunters.

But she wasn't as strait-laced and spinsterish as she liked to make out, he knew that first hand. She'd been no unbendable block of concrete in his hands. Instead, she'd felt all woman, a combination of tantalising dips and sweet curves, her feminine scent beguiling, her lips a silken caress.

He almost growled at the memory. And she was here now, on his island, *in his territory.* How would Fletcher react to that news? An eye for an eye, a sister for a sister.

Which reminded him...

'How is it your name is Turner?'

'Excuse me?' She swung her head round but not before he'd noticed how the breeze shook tendrils of her hair loose to curl around her face and sculpt the soft fabric of her dress so it clung to her breasts and playfully teased around her knees. Then she noticed the direction of his eyes and tucked the wayward material under her legs. He didn't mind that either, because now it only highlighted the elegant tapering of thigh to knees.

Long, shapely legs. Nice breasts. He could only imagine what other treats the surprising Miss Turner had in store. A pity, really...

'You're name's Turner,' he said, pulling his thoughts back into line. 'Not Fletcher. But you weren't married, you said, or at least you're not now. Fletcher never mentioned having a sister.'

She hesitated, and he sensed the cogs in her brain working out his angle. She didn't trust him, that much was obvious, although she was beginning to lose a little of that abrasive defensiveness. All that talk about what kind of car he drove—she'd been thinking about him, and he'd lay odds she hadn't been thinking about automobiles. Finally, when he'd almost given up on a response, he picked up her shrug in his peripheral vision.

'It's no big secret,' she began on a sigh, almost as if resigned to the fact he'd find out eventually anyway. 'Our parents separated when I was barely a year old, splitting everything in two, including the kids. Dad kept Jake, Mum took me. She changed my name to hers, I guess so she didn't have a constant reminder of her ex. I didn't know about any of it for years.'

The gears in Daniel's mind crunched. So she was Fletcher's sister, as she'd claimed. Jo's digging would confirm it, but he had no doubt she was telling the truth. Which meant that she probably was in on whatever her brother had planned to make this so-called marriage look as legitimate as possible in order to extract the best settlement. 'So, how did you two find each other again?'

The buggy sped along the narrow track. Glimpses of brilliant sunshine and a sapphire sea appeared only to be swallowed up again by the foliage.

'Mum died two years ago. Some lawyer told me then that I had a brother. I'd had no idea. I was too young to remember anything. We met for the first time at her funeral. And that's when I learned that our father had died ten years before. My mother never…'

Her voice broke. He glanced over, but she wasn't looking at him, her eyes appeared fixed on some point ahead of them as she took a deep breath, her breasts rising under the slip of silk.

'Anyway, that's the whole gruesome story.'

She sounded so lost and alone in that instant that it was his turn to take a deep breath. Next thing he knew, he'd be feeling sorry for her—Fletcher's sister, of all people! Besides, he remembered seeing Jake's old man once, sitting on the veranda of their timber house. The place had been practically falling down around him while he'd sucked his beer dry, the empties scattered around him like toppled ninepins. It was no surprise to hear that he'd gone.

Maybe it was better she'd never met him. She might have ended up more like her brother. A brother she defended like a tiger would defend her cubs. Would she be so quick to defend him if she knew more of his past? He doubted it.

'So, you haven't actually known Fletcher that long?'

Her jawline hardened, her mouth tightening. 'I've known him long enough.'

'Maybe you don't know him as well as you think.'

'Look, Mr Caruana, I think we've established how you feel about my brother.'

'Daniel.'

'What?'

'Didn't we agree you'd call me Daniel? And that I would call you by your first name?'

'I—'

'After all, Sophie,' he argued softly, slowing the vehicle for a bend, 'We *are* almost related.'

She sat upright in her seat, even stiffer and more tight-lipped than before, and he got the distinct impression she considered the idea of him being her brother-in-law with even less appeal than he contemplated her becoming his sister-in-law, though why that notion should grate he wasn't entirely sure.

They rounded the last curve and he heard her small gasp of surprise beside him as the first timber and palm bungalow came into view with the hint of more hidden in the dense palm forest beyond. 'What's this?'

He jerked on the handbrake and jumped out, offering her his hand. 'You said you wanted *infrastructure*,' he mocked. 'And I always give a lady what she wants.'

She'd just bet he did. Although her cynicism would have been far more effective if his words had not just sent a burst of heat all the way down her spine.

'Don't worry about your things,' he said as she reached for her briefcase. 'The only people on the island are my employees. They know if they do anything wrong, they'll be FBO'd.'

'"FBO'd"?' she asked, keeping the rising panic from her voice as reluctantly she put her hand in his, feeling his warm fingers wrap around her hand, feeling his strength, his heat and his sheer masculine power as he helped her out of the buggy. It didn't help that he was smiling. It didn't help that she could feel that smile all the way down to her toes.

Surely it shouldn't feel so good to touch someone who was so arrogant and unlikeable, someone who made clear his feelings that her brother was in no way good enough to marry his sister? Then he let her hand go to indicate she precede him up the steps to the timber deck, and she had to clamp down on a bizarre sense of disappointment. 'What does FBO mean, exactly?' she asked with false brightness, wishing she had either her briefcase or portfolio to cling onto, anything to make her hands feel less awkward and empty as she climbed the short flight of steps up to the deck, skirted a table and two chairs and stood by the railing, looking out at the view.

He came alongside her where the bungalow looked out through the thinning spread of trees towards the sandy beach and the promise of oceanic perfection.

'It means they'll be on the first boat off.'

'You mean like on those reality shows where someone gets voted off the island?'

'There's no voting involved,' he said unapologetically, crossing the deck to slide big glass doors that opened to billowing curtains, standing back to let her pass. 'You mess up, you pay the price.'

She almost laughed. Almost. Until she caught his deadpan expression and realised he was completely and utterly serious. 'Sounds like a mantra to live by,' she murmured.

'It works for me,' he said simply, swiping off his sun-glasses. As she moved past him she wondered if he was only talking about his employees.

This was Daniel's island and he was in charge. King of his island castle. Thank heavens Monica had agreed to hold the wedding in Brisbane. She couldn't imagine trying to organise a wedding here with Daniel watching, waiting for every mistake. Not that there was any chance of that happening, no matter what he thought of his 'infrastructure'.

Sophie entered the bure, removed her sunglasses and felt her heart sink as her eyes adjusted. The sight of the bungalows hidden in the rainforest had been a surprise in itself; the article she'd read had mentioned nothing of scattered bungalows. But, while the decking had been thoughtfully designed, the simple exterior had given no indication of the luxury contained within. The timber-framed glass doors opened straight into a spacious sitting-room decorated not in the usual and unimaginative palm-tree prints but in tasteful russet, cream and coffee shades. The prints on fabrics and walls were minimal, the furnishings inviting, and Sophie applauded every decorating choice.

In a wall opposite the entry, bi-fold doors beckoned, hinging back to reveal a bedroom even larger than the living area with a pillow-laden bed so wide and inviting that the child in her was tempted to dive straight onto it. Sophie would have too, until her adult brain reminded her that Daniel was just behind her. Any sign of enthusiasm now was only going to make it more difficult for herself later on when she had to argue that this venue wouldn't work.

She still believed it, even with the glimpse of more bures tucked between the trees. A few cabins, after all, did not make a resort. The catering facilities would have to be first rate too, though a niggle in the back of her brain told her that bures of this standard would require more than a simple barbeque on

the beach every night. But whatever they were like, she told
herself, the inspection was pointless. They had a venue. End
of story.

'Very nice,' she conceded with a terse nod, schooling her
face to bland, knowing Daniel was waiting for her reaction.
Another door led to the adjoining bathroom with spa bath and
rainforest shower head which she eyed with as much detachment and as little envy as she could manage.

But there was no denying the sudden stab of guilt. It was
gorgeous, seriously gorgeous, and she couldn't have blamed
Monica in the least if she'd wanted to get married here on
the island. She didn't know what else was in store for this
inspection, but a bit of dressing up could turn a bure like this
into every girl's fantasy honeymoon suite.

Her teeth scraped her bottom lip as she recalled the rooms at
the Tropical Palms. Outdated. Bordering on shabby. Seriously
in need of refurbishment. Whereas here...

Jake had wanted the wedding to take place in Brisbane
and Monica had agreed to the Tropical Palms because she'd
thought Daniel would never agree to her marriage, that he
would never tolerate it, let alone offer to pay for it. And also,
she had to admit, because it was the only place going at short
notice that could offer a taste of the tropical paradise that
Kallista was.

What if Daniel was right and Monica had always wanted
to be married here? Right now she only had Daniel's word
on that, but looking around it didn't take too much stretch of
the imagination to believe it.

Had Monica suppressed her heart's desire to be married
here on Kallista because she had thought it would present the
path of least resistance and accommodate both her brother's
and her fiancé's wishes?

Which left her—as a wedding planner who promised a
perfect day—where, exactly?

'So, what do you think?'

She wheeled around so quickly that her head spun. Was it just the sight of him reclining on the side of the bed behind her and not waiting in the doorway like she'd expected? Her mouth went dry. His eyes were level with her breasts. She knew that because he was looking right at them. And once again she cursed the absence of anything she could hold up against her chest as a shield to hide her suddenly achingly hard nipples.

'About what?'

He glanced up at her eyes, looking for all the world like a predator at ease, propped up on one elbow against the pillow-decked headrest, all long-limbed elegance sprawled ever so casually and yet with a barely suppressed energy just waiting to be unleashed.

'About whatever you've been thinking about this last five minutes you've been staring into space.'

She swallowed, attempted a smile and was sure it came off as too contrived, but she was still too thrown by the picture of him lounging ever so casually against the wide bed to know how to compensate. If he looked that good dressed, lying on a big, wide bed, how much better would he look undressed? *Oh, no!*

She knew in that moment that there was no way—*no way*—she wanted this wedding to take place here on Kallista. Her thoughts would be forever distracted by pictures of Daniel sprawled back against the bedding, or with the fine cotton of his shirt rippling against his bronzed olive skin as the warm wind tugged at the fabric, or with him just being there.

So she made a show of checking her watch and flashing her brightest, most meaningless smile. 'I think we better get on with the inspection if I'm going to make my flight.'

It was as bad as she expected. There were twenty such bures, all just as superbly appointed. They were tucked between the palms around the lagoon with enough distance between them to make you think you were the only inhabitants on the island, plus there was a central long house that served as lounge-bar and restaurant.

It was worse than bad, she decided, sipping on a mango cocktail and overlooking a crystal clear pool set amidst the palms.

It was an absolute disaster.

It was perfect.

Or it could be, if not for the man sitting opposite her right now.

Daniel Caruana leaned smugly back in his chair like he thought he had the whole world and not just his sister's wedding stitched up.

Sophie was more and more fearful that he did—at least, when it came to the wedding. After all, this was a man used to fighting and winning corporate battles every day, used to manoeuvring against major players in the boardroom and beating them at their own game. How was she supposed to hold her own against the likes of him?

'I guess we should be heading to the helicopter soon,' she suggested, 'if I'm going to make my flight.'

'I guess we should,' he said, leaning back and crossing his arms behind his head as if he had no intention of going anywhere. 'Except...' He smiled. 'You haven't told me what you think of my *infrastructure* yet.'

She sipped her drink, gazing as inconspicuously as possible over the rim of her glass at the broad expanse of chest under the snug-fitting shirt. There was nothing at all wrong with his infrastructure from where she was sitting; the man was a perfect specimen, fit, strong and sexy as sin, and that was putting it mildly. Not that she was about to admit it. 'I didn't expect to find the island so developed. I was under the impression there was just the one dwelling.'

He dropped his hands to his front, lacing his fingers over an impossibly flat stomach. Did the man not have an ounce of fat anywhere? 'It seemed selfish to keep all this to myself.'

'But there's nobody here but us and a handful of staff, and you don't operate as a resort. What's it all for?'

He shrugged. 'Caruana Corporation has many employees who require the usual training and professional development. Sometimes they come for team-building exercises, sometimes as incentives. One group of managers has just left this morning. Another team will arrive next week. A skeleton staff keeps the place ticking over in between.'

'But it looks like a five-star complex. You must have spent a fortune on this place.'

He leaned forwards, his elbow on the table, his fingers out wide to support his point. 'And why pay a fortune for them to go somewhere else when I have my own island just off the coast? But what I have spent is not your concern. What I am more interested in is whether you now agree that this is the perfect place to host Monica's wedding.'

It *was* a perfect venue. There was enough accommodation for plenty of the nearest and dearest with the best accommodation that Far North Queensland had to offer just a short helicopter flight or launch ride away. Absolutely perfect, except for one not quite so small fly in the ointment.

Daniel Caruana.

'Mr Caruana?' she began.

'Why do you have so much trouble calling me Daniel?'

She sucked in air. Did he mean apart from the fact it seemed so informal? Too personal? 'Okay—Daniel. You're right, it is a fabulous venue. And I'm sure it would be perfect in the right circumstances. But maybe not this time. I've already told you, we have a venue, and one which Monica and Jake have both agreed on.'

'So cancel it.'

'Excuse me?'

'Cancel the venue and save the money. You said Monica and Fletcher were working to a budget—this venue won't cost them a cent.'

She breathed deep. She had to in order to give herself time to think. Everything he said made perfect sense. The venue was divine, the accommodation superb and she had no doubt the food would be exquisite. All that, and Jake and Monica could save themselves a bundle into the deal. She must be mad to be so desperate to find a reason to say no. But Daniel was so adamant—disturbingly so—and there was no way she was being railroaded into saying yes, certainly not before she'd had a chance to speak to her clients.

Monica might well be in love with the idea of getting married on the island, but Sophie only had Daniel's word for that. Meanwhile her own brother, she knew, had other ideas about what constituted a perfect venue. Daniel Caruana's private island was hardly likely to fit the bill on that score.

'Look,' she ventured, glad she'd never shared the fact that the deposit on the Tropical Palms hadn't yet been paid. 'It's very short notice and there may be penalties for cancellation that reduce any potential savings. But I'll certainly speak to both Monica and Jake regarding your generous offer.' She glanced at her watch, shocked to see how time had slipped away, and stood, collecting up her things. 'I have to go. I have an early morning meeting tomorrow and I'm not prepared to miss that flight.' And then, because she knew she had to offer him something, 'How about I call you tomorrow? Let you know what Monica and Jake are thinking?'

A hand on her arm stopped her flight and she jumped. 'And how about we discuss it now?'

She looked up at him, his brow was brooding over dark narrowed eyes and a jaw set like concrete. She tested his grip with just one tiny tug on her arm and found no give, no weakness. 'I can't afford to miss my flight.'

'Why are you so opposed to holding the wedding here?'

She swallowed. 'Can you blame me for being a little reluctant to agree to your every whim? May I remind you that you were the one who said there would *be* no wedding?'

He made a sound like a growl. 'We've been through that. Getting married here is what Moni really wants.'

'And we have a booking Monica agreed to. Somewhere else.'

'This is my sister we're talking about.'

'And Monica is my client. I've acted in accordance with her wishes. Thank you for your advice and your tour, Mr Caruana; I will pass on your thoughts to my client, but I'm afraid I must leave. I have a plane to catch.' She looked pointedly down at the hand that still maintained an iron grip on her arm. 'If you wouldn't mind?'

He said nothing, but she sensed his anger in his heated breath, in the flare of his nostrils as his chest expanded with every intake of air and in the red-hot brand of his fingers pressing into her arm.

It was only her arm he was holding, she had to remind herself, so why did her skin prickle from her scalp to her toes? And why did heat ribbon and curl in dark and secret places until she was sure she would ignite?

Then something sparked in his eyes and he let her go so suddenly she almost lost her balance. 'As you wish. I will take you to the helicopter.'

Breath whooshed into her lungs as she regained her balance. 'Thank you.' But she doubted he heard her. He was already striding away when her phone rang.

She pulled her mobile from her bag and checked the number, breathing a sigh of relief that it was Meg at the office calling and not a new client looking for the perfect day—the only perfect daze she was qualified to talk about right now was the one she was currently in.

'Meg, what's up? I'm on my way to the airport right now.'

Her assistant took her own sweet time answering—long enough for Daniel to have come looking for her, no doubt wondering why someone so desperate to leave was now dragging her feet. She turned away from his storm-cloud presence. 'Meg? What's wrong?'

'That all depends,' came the tentative response. 'Do you want the good news or the bad news?'

CHAPTER SIX

SOPHIE swallowed. Things went pear-shaped in the wedding planner business all the time—wedding cakes missing a layer, string quartets going their own separate ways and citing irreconcilable differences, limousines breaking down. There wasn't much they hadn't seen and there wasn't much they couldn't deal with. So why Meg sounded so shell shocked...

'So, what's the good news?'

'You don't have an eight a.m. meeting tomorrow morning at the Gold Coast any more.'

'What? Okay, what time is it scheduled for then?'

She could almost hear Meg's anguish in the silent prelude to her reply. 'Well, that's kind of the bad news. You don't need another time. They've cancelled the booking.'

'*Cancelled*? But they can't do that!'

'I'm sorry, Sophie, I really am. But a girl—Annaliese, I think she said her name was—just called and said they had someone who could book out the entire function centre, not just the gazebo and reception room, and they paid up front in full so they had no choice but to take it.'

'But they can't do that,' she repeated. *Surely they couldn't do that?* 'I'll call them. Annaliese is only new there. She probably got her dates mixed up.'

'Good luck,' came Meg's voice down the line. 'Only she sounded so certain. I hope you're right.'

'Problem?' Daniel's voice intruding into her thoughts was the last thing she needed right now. Daniel's presence was the last thing she needed, point blank.

'Excuse me a moment,' she said, drawing away, needing distance. 'I have to make an urgent call.'

He made an exaggerated play of checking the gold watch at his wrist, a small frown creasing his brow. 'You did say you had a plane to catch.'

'I'm sorry,' she hissed, wheeling away. 'Please, this won't take long.'

Her mind was racing, her heart thumping loud in her chest as she retrieved the number. Her teeth gnawed at her bottom lip as she waited in turn for the connection, then the pick-up, and then the seemingly interminable wait for the transfer to the functions manager. She registered the metallic taste of blood, realised her lip was stinging, and willed herself to take a deep breath to relax. At this rate she could chew her way right down to her jaw.

The Tropical Palms had to be available. Someone had merely made a mistake. Otherwise…

Forget otherwise.

'Philipe!' she cried with relief when finally the connection was made, hope reborn. 'I just heard the craziest thing. I thought I should double check.'

A bare minute later she severed the connection, Philipe's rapid-fire excuses buzzing in her head.

'Sincere apologies.' 'If only you'd already paid the deposit.' 'Our hands are tied'…

Numbly she turned. Sure, she'd understood that her booking wouldn't be solid until the deposit was paid, but they'd given no hint of any other interest in the date, and it had been Philipe who'd told her not to worry—that paying when she came for the meeting would be early enough. They could at least have called and warned her someone wanted to book out the entire complex. They could at least have let her know.

'Trouble in paradise?'

She gritted her teeth, wishing she was back in the office right now. Somewhere she could throw things. Instead she had to put up with a smiling inquisitor while trying to ignore the prick of tears. What the hell was she supposed to tell Monica and Jake? 'Nothing I can't handle,' she sniffed as she headed past him towards where he'd left the buggy.

'No?' he said, already catching up and way, way too close for comfort. 'I couldn't help but overhear. I got the impression it was more serious than that.'

'It'll be fine.' It had to be fine. It *would* be fine, just as soon as she could get away from Daniel Caruana and think.

'It was about Monica's wedding, wasn't it? I take it that was the venue you just called?'

She shook her head, breathing deep as a day filled with frustration after frustration forced a renegade tear from her eye. Damn it, but she would not cry. Not here, not in front of him. 'It's between me and my clients. It's got nothing to do with you.'

'It has if it concerns my sister!' She felt a hand on her shoulder, felt herself hauled around to face him. 'What's going on?' He paused, lifted the hand from her shoulder and touched the pad of his thumb to her cheek even as she turned her face away. But nothing could stop the jolt of electricity that sparked through her at his touch. 'You're crying. Was it such bad news?'

She jerked her head away, swiping at the dampness on her cheek. 'I am not crying.' But her voice was shaky, her breath was choppy, and she knew that he would have had to be blind, deaf and dumb not to notice. Besides, it wasn't as if she could keep the news some kind of secret. She sucked in a deep breath. 'The Tropical Palms apparently got a better offer. We've lost the venue.'

He took less a second to assimilate the information before nodding decisively. 'Then the matter is settled. You will arrange the wedding here.'

She blinked away her tears. 'Now, just hold on. It's not actually up to you.'

'And you have a better idea? Other options?'

'I haven't explored the other options yet.'

'I've just saved you the trouble.'

'We could still get a cancellation.' But she knew she was clutching at straws.

'Is that what you're planning on telling Monica? That you're waiting for a cancellation when she could be married here, on Kallista?'

She looked up at him, just for a second wondering—was it just coincidence that on the very day she met with Daniel Caruana her plans for his sister's wedding had gone pear-shaped? He'd been determined the wedding should take place here. Was it possible that he was somehow behind the sudden booking? 'I told you where the wedding was to be held before we took off.'

'And?'

'And isn't it a coincidence that suddenly I find someone's come along and booked out the entire function centre at the exact same time you're arguing for the wedding to be held here?'

He leaned an arm up on the roof of the buggy, so close to her shoulder that she wanted to shrink away. 'You think I did it?' His tone made her sound completely paranoid. Maybe she was. It was too easy to believe Daniel would go to whatever lengths it took to get his way. Then again, maybe she wasn't so paranoid. How could she trust him after the massive about-face he'd made today? It was clear that if this wedding was to go ahead he expected it to be on his terms.

She cocked her chin. 'Didn't you?'

'And when exactly was I supposed to have made this booking when I have been with you the entire time?'

It was the question she'd been battling with herself. 'I don't know. But you did make a phone call, just before we left the mainland.'

Something skated across his eyes. 'And there would be no other possible reason for me to make a phone call, not even to inform the island to have a buggy waiting for us by the helipad?'

She wanted the ground to open up and swallow her. She sounded worse than paranoid; now she was practically blaming him for losing the booking. 'I'm sorry. But what else was I supposed to think? You've been determined to have this wedding here ever since you accepted that there was nothing you could do to prevent it.'

'I just want what's best for Monica. I suspect you do too. Which is why maybe we should be working on this together.'

'What do you mean?'

'I think when Monica calls from Honolulu we should both be there to talk to her—find out what she really wants to do. And maybe put her mind at rest that I'm serious about having the wedding on Kallista.'

She shook her head. 'I don't see how. It could be a while before she calls, given even after they land they'll have to clear customs before their hotel transfer. I'll probably be back in Brisbane by then.'

'Then don't leave. Stay here, on Kallista.'

Sophie blinked, his seemingly simple words performing cartwheels over and over in her head, her thoughts in turmoil.

How could she stay when she wanted nothing more than to be out of this man's company as soon as possible? Already once today that escape had been denied her, pulled from beneath her feet as effectively as the proverbial rug.

But she wanted Monica and Jake happy and, now her morning meeting with the Tropical Palms had been cancelled, it wasn't as if she had to be back in time for the commute to the Gold Coast first thing tomorrow.

It was the last thing she wanted, but maybe she should delay her departure a little longer. There was a lot to be said for Monica knowing her brother was more supportive of the marriage than she'd anticipated, and perhaps Jake might benefit from hearing it too. Perhaps this was actually what everyone needed, a chance to talk things through and get over whatever it was in the past that was potentially such a barrier. After all, if they were going to be family, they'd all have to learn to communicate with each other some time.

And after the call maybe there might be a red-eye that would still get her back to Brisbane tonight.

Please God she could get back home tonight. It could be hours that she was forced to hang around waiting for Monica's call. And the longer she was in Daniel Caruana's company the more his presence messed with her head, muddled her brain and her thought processes along with it, even while setting her other senses alight. It wasn't a state she was used to. It wasn't a state she particularly enjoyed.

She was used to being in control, cool, detached and unaffected. Her mother had taught her that a woman didn't need a man to validate her, in fact that sometimes she would be better off without one. While she knew her mother's view had stemmed from a failed marriage, and a couple of aborted relationships since, her own experiences with men had only lent weight to her mother's advice.

Which had proved a positive boon to her job. She could stand back unemotionally and deliver the best, most romantic wedding in the world without getting all misty-eyed herself. She was the practical one, the unemotional one. The rational one.

Until now.

Until Daniel Caruana.

Oh no; it would be better—*safer*—to be gone.

Daniel watched the indecision swirl in her violet eyes. She was gnawing her bottom lip again, a gesture that took years off her. She looked young and vulnerable. Her hair was loosened by the breeze so that tendrils had escaped, wisping around her face, and he had the insane desire to kiss her again, if only to soothe her besieged lip.

He liked the way she tasted. He liked the way she battled with her conscience as she gnawed on that lip, and he couldn't help but wonder how it would feel if she turned those nibbling teeth on him.

He almost growled. There was no way she was leaving the island before he found out.

'What are you so afraid of?' he asked, moving closer, dropping his other arm to the vehicle behind. 'Why is it so hard to make a decision?'

She looked up at him, surprise at his sudden move turning her eyes wide, shock at finding herself trapped neatly against the vehicle when she tried shuffling backwards filling them with alarm. 'Oh, nothing. I'd have to call Meg at the office, get her to take care of a few things. And change my flight booking, of course, although I don't know what time I'll be able to get away.'

She was babbling, flustered again, and delightfully so. 'Is that all you're worried about?'

Her eyes darted from one side to the other, checking the positioning of his arms as if assessing her chances of escape.

Didn't she realise? *It was much too late for escape.*

'Or perhaps you're you worried I might kiss you?' He wanted her to be. If she hadn't been worried before, he wanted her thinking about his lips on hers right now. 'Is that what you're afraid of? Is that why you seem so desperate to rush off now, because you're afraid of a repeat performance?'

'What? No, why would I be worried about that? It never crossed my mind.'

'Never?' he murmured as he moved inexorably closer, the circle around her drawing tighter. 'You wound me, Miss Turner. You never once entertained the prospect of finishing what we started?'

'I never…' She shook her head but there was no point trying to deny it. Her eyes were on his lips; her chest was rising fast and her lips were slightly parted, waiting. *Anticipating.* 'You wouldn't—'

She didn't get a chance to finish. His mouth met hers, his lips relieving her of the word she'd been about to utter, her lips soft and warm and wondering. He sensed her doubts in her hesitation. But beyond that he also sensed her desire and her need.

It amazed him to think that any sister of Fletcher could taste as good. He expected there to be some trace of corruption, some hint of decay, and yet instead the taste of fruit was on her lips, plump and sweet as they moved under his, warm as their breath mingled. And wrapped seductively around it all he sensed the evocative scent of woman.

He made no attempt to hold her; they touched nowhere but at their mouths, and yet the connection was electric. He could feel the glow from her as if he'd flicked a switch that set her body humming with need, matching the music of his own. And yet it wasn't a kiss of passion, of unrequited lust. Instead it was tender and sweet and utterly, utterly necessary.

'Wh...why did you do that?' she whispered, her lashes lowered as if too scared to look at him when finally, reluctantly, he raised his head.

'It seemed a good idea to get it out of the way.'

'Oh.' It satisfied him no end that she sounded confused and halfway disappointed.

'Because now I know that first time wasn't a mistake.'

She gasped as her lashes flickered open, her pupils tiny in the bright sun; her irises seemed appropriately named given their suddenly dark, velvet colour. He laughed, because he knew that if he didn't he wouldn't be able to stop from pulling her back into his kiss and finishing what he'd begun. This wasn't the time, and definitely not the place. The sun beat down hot and heavy on his back, reinforcing his need for a cold beer and a cold shower—not necessarily in that order. 'Look, it's been a long day. Monica's probably not going to call for an hour or two. How about a swim to cool off while we wait? I know I could do with one.'

Her brow creased into a slight frown. 'Did I say I was staying?'

'Aren't you?'

She looked away then in the direction of the helipad, even though there was nothing to see from here but the thick tropical plantings of palms and bamboo bordering the parking area, before slowly she turned back. 'I guess I can stay, just for the call. But I haven't brought anything with me. I wasn't expecting to swim.'

'Not a problem,' he said, tossing the buggy key up in his hand. 'I'm sure we can find you something half decent.'

The house was halfway around the island and perched up high, all timber and glass, with decking and sails nestled amongst the forest and wrapped around the hillside. But despite the stunning beauty of the house it was the view to which the eye was drawn—on one side to the ocean, studded with island jewels, and on the other to the spectacular line of mainland coast that ran as far as the eye could see. Beyond the shore-line rose the steep mountains, the spectacular gateway to the hinterland.

'It's beautiful,' Sophie said as he helped her from the car. 'I don't know how you could ever bear to leave.'

He smiled that lazy crocodile smile once more, the smile aimed right at her, and that scored a direct hit. 'I'm glad you think so.' Breathless, not seeing or understanding the message she was sure lay behind the words, she moved away, pretending to be more interested in the view. It was magnificent, it was true, but right now she had more pressing things on her mind.

Like why she'd let him kiss her. She was planning his sister's wedding, after all. She was supposed to be a professional. She was supposed to be detached.

Letting him kiss her had hardly been detached.

But supposition was one thing. Knowing what she should do when he was looking at her that way, when her skin was tingling, her heart trembling and her thoughts as scattered as the winds was another thing entirely. How was she expected to think when all she knew was that she hungered for his kiss, that every cell in her body had been primed for his touch?

Was it only this morning they had met? It hardly seemed possible to reconcile the man who'd kissed her so tenderly with the man she'd encountered in his office—the man who'd turned arrogance into an art form and bundled her out without a decent hearing. Although he'd almost kissed her then too, practically reducing her to a puddle on the floor before she'd managed to find the will to push him away.

But had she pushed him away when he'd come back a second time? Oh no. Her body had been strung tight as a wire, not from dread or revulsion, but from the anticipation thrumming in her veins as she'd watched his mouth descend.

And the only thought in her mind was that there was no way she was going to stop him.

Far below them the azure sea lapped half-heartedly at a tiny cove of diamond-tipped water and a beach of brilliant white sand protected at either end by a rocky point jutting into the sea. Totally private and utterly inviting. It would be a long climb down the wooden steps she could see, but already she could feel the cool water sliding over her heated body.

Except would it really cool her down? Her teeth gnawed on her bottom lip as her mind churned over the implications. Was it really wise to strip down to a borrowed swimsuit and share the water with a man who was distracting enough with his clothes on, let alone wearing nothing more than bathers? She squeezed her eyes shut, desperate to extinguish the pictures that thought conjured up, of a body naked but for a band of black lycra. Oh no! A swim was a really bad idea.

'I think I might actually pass on the swimming after all,' she decided, searching for an excuse that didn't scream 'coward', and trying to pretend she wasn't more hot and bothered than ever. 'My heels would never last the climb down those steps. But you go right ahead.' When she looked up it was to find him not looking down at the cove, like she'd hoped, but still watching her. Heat flared in her cheeks, his unrelenting gaze unnerving, even while shrouded by sunglasses.

'I'd hate to risk your heels,' he said, half-smiling, as if he found her discomfiture amusing. 'So why not use the pool, like I intend to? I gather your heels are good for a few more metres.'

As if realising he'd won the point, he turned and led the way through the tangle of bougainvillea that spilled a riot of colour over the entrance to the courtyard, while Sophie followed meekly behind, feeling more of a fool than ever. Of course a house like this would have a pool tucked away somewhere, so what excuse was she going to dream up next without looking like she was afraid of getting into the water with him—that she was afraid of crocodiles?

Not that that would work, she decided, abandoning the idea as useless. Daniel was exactly the kind of man who would probably be flattered by such a comparison.

The timber entry door swung open before they reached it, and a middle-aged woman beamed at them under her apron. Sophie took to her warm and welcoming eyes on sight. 'Mr Caruana! You should have told me you were bringing back a guest,' she chided as they entered the spacious room, clearly with no qualms about castigating her boss over his lack of forward notice. 'I would have prepared something more special for dinner.'

'I'm sure whatever you have planned, Millie, will be superb as usual. And I have no doubt Miss Turner here will soon likewise be a fan of your cooking.' He turned to Sophie. 'Millie used to run a café in Cairns, until I happened in for lunch one day and made her an offer she couldn't refuse.'

His phone beeped then and Millie took his jacket as he excused himself and checked the caller ID. 'He did too,' Millie agreed conspiratorially, her smile growing dimples and her clear green eyes sparkling. 'And the next thing I knew, I'd upped sticks and was living on a tropical island paradise. Mind you, this one could talk the leg off a chair. So you watch out, Miss Turner, if you know what's good for you.'

'Now, Millie,' Daniel cautioned, sliding his phone away. 'Don't go giving away all my trade secrets.'

'Thanks for the advice,' Sophie told Millie, seeing a different side to Daniel and enjoying the unexpected banter between employer and employee. 'I'm not actually sure I'll be staying for dinner, but I'll definitely take all the tips I can get.'

Millie looked genuinely disappointed until Daniel intervened. 'Of course Miss Turner is staying for dinner,' he announced. 'And, in the meantime, I wonder if you might show her to the guest room and rustle up a swimsuit? I'll catch up in a while. I have a couple of calls to make.' And then he smiled. 'Just don't be too hard on her heels.'

'Of course. I know just the suit for you. Come this way.' Millie bustled up a short flight of timber stairs to another level and a long passageway. 'What was that about heels?' she asked, glancing over her shoulder.

'He was having a joke at my expense,' Sophie admitted. 'I thought I had to walk down to the beach for a swim and I used my shoes as an excuse. I didn't realise there was a pool.' She didn't admit she was trying to avoid swimming with Daniel full-stop, but if he was busy with calls maybe she could get in a quick dip now. She could surely do with a cool down to dispel some of this heat.

Millie chuckled. 'He has a way with him, that one. There is a path down, and the beach is just beautiful. Get Daniel to show you. But, yes, preferably when you're wearing flat shoes.'

Sophie smiled her thanks. As much as the beach looked special, she was sure she wouldn't be around long enough for a personal inspection.

But that didn't stop her appreciating the house itself with its high-ceilinged rooms, cool timber floors and a wall of windows that brought the magnificent view inside. 'It's always nice when Mr Caruana brings a friend home,' Millie offered as she led the way. 'I tell him it's not natural for one man to rattle around a big house like this all by himself. I keep telling him he has to settle down one day.'

The house was indeed enormous, wrapped around a hillside so you couldn't see from one end to the other—although why would you want to look anywhere but at the view, which changed with every angle, a view now complemented by the crystal-clear infinity pool that bordered the decking. An aqua plunge-pool lay at one point that a casual living-area wrapped around.

But Millie's words settled heavily on Sophie as she followed her into a bedroom that looked out over treetops to aquamarine waters and the mainland coast beyond. *Friend.* The housekeeper assumed she was Daniel's latest girlfriend. 'We're not actually friends. Not like that, I mean. I'm just waiting for Monica to call from Honolulu. I'm organising her wedding.'

'Monica's getting married?' The housekeeper abandoned her rummaging in the fitted wardrobe and turned around, delighted. 'Well, I never! That is exciting news. Who's the lucky man?'

'My brother, Jake, actually.'

Millie smiled broadly. 'Then you're much better than a friend. You're practically family.' She returned to the surprisingly well-stocked closet. 'Now, let's see, there's a colour in here that would suit you perfectly. Where is it?'

'Who owns all these clothes?' she said, looking around, wondering about the guest room with its high bed, snowy-white comforter and cupboard brimming with clothes.

'They're just spares, really. Handy in case Monica drops by with friends.'

Sophie could see Monica used the room sometimes. There were pictures of her on a dressing table. One of her in bathers at the beach. Another in school uniform, grinning self-consciously, trying not to show her braces. She smiled at that one. She remembered the ignominy of braces herself. Only for two years, but at the time it had seemed like an eternity of humiliation. And she'd resented it so much she'd never really thanked her mother for doing all those hours of overtime so she could afford to pay for them.

She put the photo down, lip stuck firmly between now perfectly aligned teeth. God, she missed her mum. Thank heavens Jake had found her after her death. It was one thing to be independent, rational and aloof, but it could be lonely.

There was another photo, but Sophie didn't recognise who it was. She picked up the silver frame. A pretty girl with laughing eyes looked out at her, her long blonde hair whipping around her face as she blew a kiss to the camera.

'Ah, here we are,' said Millie from behind her. 'Try this one for size, and there's a matching sarong. I'll fetch you a towel.'

Sophie turned, caught the gleam of sapphire-and-gold coloured fabric on the bed and smiled appreciatively. It was a rich, sumptuous pattern, and with a sarong to cover her she wouldn't feel quite so undressed. 'Thank you, Millie, it's lovely. By the way, who's this—do you know? One of Monica's friends? I don't think I've met her, although I've met the girls she's asked to be bridesmaids.'

Millie drew close and took the picture from her, giving the glass a gentle dust with a cloth she pulled from a pocket in her apron, her smile now sad. 'A good friend of Daniel, apparently. Died in tragic circumstances. Daniel can't bear to have the photograph where he can see it, but he can't bear to put it away, so it hides in here where he's unlikely to come across it. Pretty little thing, wasn't she? I sometimes wonder if...'

The woman trailed off to silence and Sophie wondered if it was because her thumping heart had drowned out the other woman's words. Why did it matter so much? She didn't know, but she had to ask. 'What do you wonder?'

Millie sighed. 'Oh, just whether whatever happened back then turned Daniel off the idea of ever getting attached to anyone else. Apparently it was quite serious.' Then she flicked her cloth over the shelf before she replaced the photo. 'Ah well; I best be getting you that towel.'

Sophie sat down on the side of the bed, idly picking up the richly coloured wrap the woman had left. The fabric slipped through her fingers, smooth and shimmering, a faint gold thread catching the light. Exquisite.

But then her eyes were drawn again to the picture of the smiling girl—so special to Daniel that he couldn't bear to look at her photograph, so special that he couldn't bear to part with it.

Had it been Daniel holding the camera all those years ago? Had the love shining in her eyes and that kiss been meant for him?

He must have loved her very much.

For some inexplicable reason she didn't want to linger too long on that thought. It was hard imagining Daniel loving anyone; he seemed so driven and angry and unrelenting, and if he'd ever had a heart it was so deeply buried it had probably atrophied by now. Even his love for his sister seemed more of a guard-dog mentality than brotherly love.

She scooped up the bikini and headed for the *en suite*. A swim was definitely what she needed right now. Given Daniel was busy with his calls, she'd have the pool to herself for a while. And when he did arrive she could plead she'd had enough and cover herself with the sarong.

Besides, Millie was here. What on earth could she have to worry about?

CHAPTER SEVEN

'WHAT have you got?'

'She's Fletcher's sister all right.' Jo's voice sounded like gravel rattling down the line. 'Seems her parents broke up and split the kids.'

Daniel leaned back and put his feet up on his desk. So it was as she'd said. He wasn't sure whether he was relieved she hadn't been lying, or disappointed she really was related to that Fletcher scum. 'And the business?'

'It exists. Small to middling. Seems to have a good reputation, although business has been a bit thin on the ground lately.' There was a weighted pause. 'Could definitely do with an injection of funds.'

Daniel's gut churned and he dropped his feet to the floor. 'You think she's after a cut?'

'What else would she be doing here? Monica's old enough now to take herself off and get married without your permission. This Miss Turner, or whatever she calls herself, is here to make the wedding look legit—nothing surer—so you'll panic and offer more for Fletcher to clear off.'

A growl rose in his throat. Yet she'd acted as if her brother's affair with Moni was the romance story of the decade. But Jo's discoveries had only confirmed what he'd first suspected as soon as she'd finally revealed who she was: she was in it for the money. Nothing more.

Which made her a superlative actress. But then, con men—and con women—usually were.

'We're talking to Monica tonight. Once I find out where they're staying, I want you to get an offer to him.'

Jo was well rehearsed in the drill, all except for the one variable. 'How much?'

Daniel had been mulling over the same thing himself. It wasn't going to be cheap, so there was no point starting low and extending the process with bid and counterbid. 'Let's cut to the chase. Offer him a million. The usual deal: clear off and never get in touch with Monica again.'

'A million? Jeez, boss, offer me a million and I'll never talk to Monica again myself.'

'Quit it, Jo!' he said, not in the mood for jokes. Besides, it wasn't as if he didn't pay his security manager a better than decent salary. He massaged his forehead with his fingers. 'This is serious.'

'I am serious,' the man protested, although this time the laughter was noticeably absent from his voice. 'You'd offer that bastard a million dollars when you know he's only going to ask for more? You know he's not worth it.'

'It's worth whatever it takes to get him away from Moni! You understand that?'

'Yeah. Of course, boss,' he said grudgingly. 'I was there, remember?'

Daniel remembered. Jo had been there through those years of high school to witness Fletcher's futile efforts to prove himself Daniel's equal over and over. The scholarship kid with a chip the size of a log on his shoulder versus the kid with money—not that his family had hung onto that long enough to enjoy it. But all those challenges, brawls and endless niggling irritations to prove he was as good as, if not better than, Daniel—Jo had been there. Jo had seen it all.

Fletcher had been a poster boy for persistence, and the ironic thing was that by the time the final year was over, Daniel had almost developed a grudging admiration for him. He'd felt the kid with the deadbeat father might actually make something of himself.

Or so he'd thought.

Until he got the phone call that changed his life.

The phone call telling him Emma was dead.

He'd realised then that Fletcher hadn't just wanted to be as good as Daniel Caruana. He'd wanted to *be* him, lock, stock and fiancée.

It was Jo who had scraped Daniel off the floor and stood by him while they'd buried the girl he'd loved. Jo who had fed him beer after beer while he spilled his guts about all the ways he was going to kill Fletcher. Jo who had convinced him Fletcher wasn't worth it and had stopped him when drunken bravado had convinced Daniel it was the only option he had.

Yeah, Jo had been there, and his loyalty deserved better. 'I know he'll ask for more,' Daniel continued, his tone less aggressive. 'He knows more than anyone what Moni's worth—but I bet Miss Turner will soon get him to agree, simply so she can get off the island and collect her cut.'

There was another pause. 'She's still there, then?'

'The fastest way to prove she's in on it is to force her to organise a wedding she knows isn't going to happen. She won't be able to keep up the pretence twenty-four hours a day.'

'You reckon she'll stay put, then?'

'She's not leaving the island. Not while Fletcher's got my sister.'

He severed the connection with an assurance he'd call with Moni's location as soon as he'd heard from Honolulu. Then he dropped his feet to the floor and swung his chair around to gaze out through the wall of windows, grateful that there was someone who understood, someone who knew the history, who didn't have to ask too many questions.

What would he do without Jo? His old high-school friend had also been there when one of Moni's first boyfriends had decided that she was worth more in cold hard cash than for herself. Barely eighteen, Monica had fallen head over heels, never realising that at the same time the guy was pretending to be the man of her dreams he was threatening to publish secret images of them on the Internet. Daniel's sister, immortalised on film, at what should be one of the most intimate and special times of her life. Unless her brother paid—big time.

Jo had arranged the payment to send him on his way and the bastard had disappeared, the files destroyed. But it seemed there was always someone else lining up to take his place, someone ready to accept an offer before they had time to do any damage.

Given they'd taken the money, didn't that prove that it was the dollars they'd really cared about?

Fletcher would be just the same—worse, really, given his history.

The sapphire perfection of sea and sky suddenly came into focus, filling his vision as he dragged in air, restoring him.

Jo wouldn't fail him. The trap would soon be set and Fletcher would soon be gone. And meanwhile...

A movement low down in the window snagged his attention, a ripple at the end of the pool.

He growled.

Meanwhile he had other things to attend to.

She might be a good actress, but she wasn't the only one who could play at make believe. Only, the way he played, she'd soon be wishing she'd never gone along with that dead-beat brother of hers.

He made another quick phone call, anxious now to join her in the pool, eager to take the game to the next level but first needing to make sure that she had no argument for a sudden departure.

Because Miss Turner wasn't going anywhere, any time soon.

Sophie rested her chin on her crossed arms on the edge of the pool and floated as she gazed out at the expanse of sea and sky. The warm air was sweet here, any hint of salt or beach concealed under the scent of the tropical flowers that clambered rampant over walls and gateways. It was paradise.

But she was here to do a job. She had to keep reminding herself of that, because instead of focusing on Jake and Monica's needs she found her thoughts more and more hijacked by the bride's brother.

How could she trust him, both after the way he'd treated her and had spoken of Jake this morning? How could she believe he was now so keen for this wedding to go ahead here, a wedding that he'd been so vehemently opposed to and probably still was, if truth be known?

And how could she trust herself if, knowing what she did, she still practically swooned every time his lips drew close? Was it wrong to be so aware of and so attracted to your potential brother-in-law?

Tiny birds darted through the whispering treetops, unconcerned by her presence, while brightly coloured butterflies negotiated a zig-zag course through the air, so close at times that she could almost reach out a hand and scoop them into her palm.

It had just been a kiss, she reminded herself for what must have been the hundredth time. Nothing more. And nothing would come of it, she knew. A man like Daniel would have a little black book the size of the phone book; given the unsurprised look on Millie's face when she'd been introduced, half of them had no doubt turned up here for a swim and who knew what else? A kiss would mean nothing to a man like him.

A few moments with the water lapping at her breasts gave rise to a new thought: maybe it did mean something? He was a businessman, used to tactics in the boardroom and no doubt in the bedroom. Was that latest kiss designed to throw her, to make her think he was interested, all in the hope of disarming her defences? Maybe he thought that if he seduced her he might drive a wedge between her and Jake? Divide and conquer—was that his ploy?

But if he seriously thought she could be seduced by a few kisses into doing his bidding he could think again. She kicked lazily at the water while she mulled over the thought, wondering if she could turn it to her advantage. She wasn't sure she knew enough to play the attraction game; she hadn't had near enough experience with men. But maybe, if he got to know her a little better, he might be more willing to listen to her, and maybe he might see that Jake wasn't all bad.

The sun felt warm on her shoulders and she slipped back to duck them under the water to cool them down. She'd get out soon, before Daniel finished with whatever business was keeping him. But it was too delicious not to enjoy just a minute longer.

Her feet swirled the water behind her, not enough to break the surface, just moving the water enough so that it swirled and eddied around her in a blissful water-massage, soaking away the tensions of the day. She sighed and closed her eyes. A person could get used to this. Just a minute more…

Something cold hit her back and she came to with a start. 'You'll burn if you're not careful.'

She would have jumped to her feet, but her arms were tangled, her thoughts already in havoc. Already he was there beside her, his feet planted in the water alongside and his hands on her shoulders, long fingers rubbing lotion into her skin, the press of his hand not allowing her up. 'You were asleep,' he said, clearly delighted with the discovery.

'I must have dozed off,' she said breathlessly. 'It was so relaxing.'

'You don't feel relaxed,' he bothered to note. 'You feel as stiff as a board.'

There was good reason for that, she thought wryly as his hand sought to work the lotion into her back with long, languorous strokes. Long strokes that transmitted their languid caress all the way down to her core and made her even tenser. She squeezed her eyes shut, wishing she could so easily block out the sensations assailing her. This was no casual application of sun block. This was a caress. Every one of his fingertips was like a probe that sought and found exactly the right pressure points to make her gasp with pleasure.

When he kneeled down in the water alongside her, his second hand joined the first, one hand at each shoulder, his fingertips brushing perilously close to her breasts as he circled to her underarms. She couldn't take any more.

She pushed up, turning her head to roll over. 'I should get out.' She almost wished she'd stayed right where she was, for now she could see him. Her mouth went dry. She was surrounded by water, had probably been soaking long enough to turn into a prune, but right at that moment her throat was drier than the Sahara in a sandstorm.

Because somehow she'd known he'd wear black, had known he'd wear it better than most against his sun-bronzed skin. But nowhere in her wild imaginings had she'd estimated he'd bypass simply being devastating and head into the realm of the gods of ancient mythology. He was way beyond dangerous. He was positively lethal.

'There's no rush, is there?'

Against her better judgement, his words made some kind of sense as she drank in the olive-skinned perfection of his torso, the whirls of dark hair dusting his naked chest, only to arrow down to his naval and disappear in a line in his trunks. Maybe he was right—there was no rush. So why her desperate rush to get away?

Oh yes…

'Monica might call,' she managed at last, levering the tongue from the roof of her mouth and peeling her eyes away to locate her sarong in the same action, mentally estimating the seconds before she could hide herself beneath it. 'I want to be ready.'

'She already called.'

Her eyes flicked back to his, sure she'd misheard. 'She what?'

'I just spoke to her. She couldn't raise you on your mobile so she checked with your office and they told her you might still be up here.'

Now he had her full attention, and not just because he had a body that shorted her senses. She rolled over until she was sitting up on the submerged ledge of the pool, thoughts of imminent escape momentarily forgotten. 'Monica called and you didn't bother to let me know? When you know I've been waiting for her call?'

'She did try to call you,' he reminded her. 'Is it my fault you didn't pick up? But does it really matter who she spoke to? The important thing is, she said she's delighted to have the wedding here on Kallista.'

'Oh, I'll just bet she did.' Sophie rose up like the proverbial phoenix, water sloughing from her limbs. For the first time she was uncaring at being clad in only a bikini, if only because she was so angry. 'Because you no doubt told her the Tropical Palms was now unavailable.' She swiped up the sarong from the chair where she'd left it and knotted it around herself before searching for her phone, wondering how she could have missed a call. Even if she'd dozed off, it would have woken her.

'It is unavailable. I didn't realise it was a secret. You should have said.'

'And you should have called me!' she said, lifting her towel, knowing the phone had to be here somewhere. 'Monica might be your sister, but I'm supposed to be the one who's organising this wedding for her and Jake.' She turned back, temporarily giving up on the phone. 'Or did Jake jump up and down with excitement at the prospect of holding the wedding here too? Somehow I doubt it, given how much you two seem to get on.'

His lips were a grim line. 'He was down at Reception. I didn't speak to him.'

'So you thought you'd take advantage before I had a chance to discuss the options with them first.' And then she remembered—she'd been so busy thinking about that picture in the guest room, and so desperate to have her swim before Daniel emerged from his calls, that she'd completely forgotten to grab her phone from her bag. *Damn.*

'What options?' he challenged from the pool, leaning back on the edge, looking way too relaxed and reminding her again of how a crocodile looked before it launched its attack on unsuspecting prey. 'You haven't one other option and you know it.'

But it was Sophie who snapped, angry with him for being so high-handed, angry with herself for being so distracted by thinking about him that she would make such a stupid mistake. 'Did I even get a chance to look? No, because the great Daniel Caruana has decided his is the only option. End of argument. Tell me, does it ever get boring riding roughshod over people or do you get some kind of kick out of it?'

'What are you so angry about?' The once-calm pool exploded, the water bubbling as Daniel erupted from the pool. Water sluiced from his body, running in rivulets down his long, powerful legs, and for the first time she got the full visual impact of the man under the clothes. He could have been a marble statue come to life, some mythical god from the ancient world with his proportional perfection of tautly packed body, long limbs and beating, savage heart. Her own heart thumped loud as he strode purposefully towards her, but it was the potent look in his eyes that turned that thudding beat to fear.

'You are lucky you have a venue at all,' he snarled. 'But, rather than thank me for bailing you out of your problem, you prefer to rail against me as if I have done you some kind of injustice.'

She turned to go, unwilling to hear any more, knowing that his words were at least partly true. Kallista did offer a solution to her problem of a lack of venue, even if it did offer up a host of other problems into the deal.

But she just couldn't take any more. She'd felt the balance of power shifting, and control of this wedding slipping through her fingers, ever since she'd first arrived in Daniel Caruana's offices this morning with what should have been the upper hand. And she'd felt control over her own emotions slipping away just as completely, until she felt raw, bruised and ill-prepared for yet another confrontation.

Yet another defeat?

Or would it end in yet another kiss? But even that would be no victory. 'I don't have to listen to this.' But his hand stayed her forearm, his powerful flick wheeling her right back so that she crashed bodily against him, the shock momentarily winding her.

Another kind of shock had her gasping then, for nothing more than damp fabric—once warmed by sunshine, now warmed by body heat—lay between them where their bodies met from chest to knee.

He might just as well have flicked a switch inside her. Like a power surge she felt the burst of sensation, the contact of flesh against flesh generating a warmth that swelled her breasts and turned her nipples hard. At the same time it pooled and she felt aching heat low in her belly. When she breathed, even that tiny movement created a friction that ramped up the sensations tenfold. She couldn't even take a breath without breathing him in with it.

'What are you afraid of?' he demanded, his eyes searching her face. 'Why are you always so desperate to run away from me?'

'Who says I'm afraid?' But she belied her own defence with breathless words that sounded like she'd been turned upside down and shaken till they'd rattled from her.

He frowned, her trembling arm still held prisoner in his own. 'Am I really that terrifying?'

'I'm not…' Her teeth snagged her bottom lip. There was no point pretending she wasn't afraid, but she didn't have to admit it, either. She kicked up her chin. 'I'm not running now.'

The look in his eyes turned distinctly primal even as he smiled. 'Just as well, because there would be no point. When I want something, I usually get it, whether or not it's a moving target.'

In her fractured mind, his words made no sense at all. 'What are you talking about?'

'I want you, Sophie. I wanted you when you showed up in my office in a buttoned-up dress and with a buttoned-up attitude to match. I want you even more now I've seen you out of both of them.'

The shudder caught her unawares, like his words and she trembled openly against him. 'Daniel, I…'

He stroked her hair, catching a stray tendril and winding it around her ear, his touch tender, sensual and tingle-inducing. 'You feel it too,' he said, even as his gaze remained focused on the hand stroking her hair. 'You feel this attraction between us.'

She tried to tell herself it was all part of the plan. Tried to convince herself that this was what she had wanted, to get Daniel on side and ensure that he might be more receptive to ensuring the wedding between his sister and her brother would be a success.

But how could she pretend it was all part of a plan when she didn't have to pretend to sway into his touch? How could she make herself or anyone else believe it was otherwise? Then she felt his lips press against her hair, his warm breath against her scalp, and she was very nearly undone.

She swallowed against a need to lift her face and meet his lips with her own. Fought against it with all the power she could summon. But there was hardly any resistance left in her.

When he acted arrogantly and made all the decisions, when he was overbearing and unbearable with it, she could summon a resistance and fight him. But when he was like this—tender, gentle and with a touch that melted her bones and defused her resistance—how could she fight?

She couldn't.

Not when she knew he was right. Not when she knew she wanted him too. Damn it.

Sophie heard a knock and the sound of a door sliding behind her and she jerked away, but not as far as she'd have liked to because Daniel still kept hold of her arm. 'Excuse me for interrupting,' she heard Millie say, 'But Monica's on the phone again asking to speak to Miss Turner.'

It took a second for her brain to shift gears and to make sense of Millie's words. 'To me?' Daniel nodded.

'I didn't get a chance to tell you, but Moni said she'd call again once she'd had a chance to talk to Jake.'

Sophie didn't have to ask why he hadn't had a chance to say it—because she hadn't let him. She'd jumped straight down his throat and practically accused him of hijacking the wedding arrangements.

'I'm sorry,' she managed. 'I got the impression you were taking over.'

'So I gather.' He managed a tight smile. 'Maybe you'd better go take that call.' He nodded towards the door. 'Millie will show you to the office.'

'You're not coming?'

'Moni asked to speak to you. I thought you might appreciate doing it alone.' He watched her watching him for a second and then he said, 'Are you going to take the call or not?'

She nodded and disappeared into the house.

It was only a small lie, he told himself as he headed for his suite. He would normally go out of his way to be there, overseeing the call, ensuring it went in the right direction. But he'd planted the seed in Monica's mind and got her excited, and he was sure not even Fletcher could change her mind. She had no other option now. It was Kallista or nothing.

Besides, there was no way he was going to speak to Fletcher. He couldn't even bring himself to hear the man's voice.

If all went to plan, he would never have to. Once Jo contacted him and made him an offer, he'd be all too willing to escape a wedding planned slap-bang in the centre of the enemy camp. It shouldn't be long now, and they wouldn't see Fletcher for dust.

He snapped on his shower and waited for the steam to rise as he reefed off his swimming trunks, a niggling concern in the back of his mind.

Because there was another reason that had kept him from being there for that call. It was the smile he'd heard in Moni's voice when she'd talked about Fletcher, the admiration, the adoration.

Almost as if…

Almost as if she really was in love with him.

The thought nearly turned his stomach. No way, he thought, discarding the notion as he stepped under the cloudburst spray. She only thought she loved him. She was infatuated, like she always was, and probably on the rebound.

But if she did love him?

He breathed deeply, turning his face under the torrent. Then she would take the break-up harder than ever. He hated his own part in it, hated that he had to be the one to save her and yet maybe hurt her in the process. But who else could do it? Who else knew what Fletcher was capable of?

No, it was better to suffer now than for her to discover later that Fletcher had only ever been interested in her money.

And one day she would thank him, he was sure.

Monica was every bit as excited as Daniel had maintained. Getting married on Kallista was, in her words, a dream come true and she couldn't be happier. Then she handed the phone over to Jake so he could have a few words with his sister.

'What do you think, Jake?' Sophie asked. 'Are you happy about the change in venue?'

'Sounds like we haven't a choice, given the Tropical Palms has cancelled. But Monica's over-the-moon happy. And if Daniel can see his way clear to offer his island I don't see how I can say no.'

Which meant *she* couldn't say no. She dragged in air, suddenly hot, those places in her body that had so recently been pressed up against Daniel's hard, packed torso throbbing all over again. For Jake's agreement had sealed her fate—the island of Kallista would host the wedding and there was no getting out of it now, no escape from dealing with Daniel Caruana. But when had that concept secretly thrilled rather than repulsed her? And when had she started looking forward to seeing more of him, rather than less?

When he had set her body alight with just one look, just one touch? Or when he had told her that he wanted her?

'What does surprise me,' her brother continued, forcing her thoughts back to the phone call, 'is that he's being so supportive. I didn't expect that.'

He wasn't the only one. In one day she'd been witness to Daniel acting as if Jake was the devil incarnate who would never in a million years marry his sister, then offering his idyllic island as the venue for them to seal their vows. And here was Jake, more resigned than enthusiastic about the change; she knew he was going along with it because it was what his bride wanted.

'What happened between you two?' she asked. 'I'm beginning to hope Daniel might be coming around to the idea of his sister getting married, but something more than high-school competitiveness must have happened. His reaction this morning to the news was nothing less than extreme.'

There was a weary sigh at the end of the line and she suspected it wasn't all about jet lag. 'Look, Sophie, it's not something I really want to talk about over the phone. I'm not even sure I know the whole story myself. I was hoping I could clear the air with Daniel before we left but he wouldn't return my calls.'

'Maybe you should come back via Cairns, then, and sort it out before the wedding. Daniel might be more comfortable with the whole idea by then. It could be a good time to mend some bridges.'

'Maybe you're right. Hey, we've gotta go. We've got a surfing lesson booked.'

She was just saying her goodbyes when he said, 'Oh, hang on—Monica just wants to say something.'

There was a brief hesitation and then, 'Sophie? I just wanted to thank you so much for being there,' Monica said breathlessly, as if she'd made a sudden dive for the phone. 'Daniel told me you'd be staying on Kallista now until the wedding, to make sure everything is absolutely perfect. It means so much that you're prepared to do that. Thank you so much. See you when we get back!'

Monica was gone by the time Sophie could manage a numb reply and she replaced the receiver with more questions than answers. She was staying on Kallista?—Daniel had told Monica that? So when had he decided that was going to happen? And when had he been planning to fill her in on the details?

Her earlier apology for wrongly accusing him of taking control suddenly seemed premature. Daniel Caruana didn't just like things to go his way, he liked to be in the driver's seat to ensure he got where and what he wanted. It was like playing chess with someone who was always two moves ahead. There was no way she was going to be told what she was doing by him.

In the very next breath she remembered that it was Monica who had told her, Monica who had thanked her for staying. Sure, Daniel was clearly behind the idea, but Monica's effusive thanks for staying proved she was right behind the concept. Sophie was trapped somewhere between Daniel's heavy-handed tactics and her responsibility to Monica and Jake. Her very own rock and a hard place.

Infuriating man! But he was Monica's brother. He had to know his sister better than she did. After all, he'd been right about her wanting to get married on Kallista, hadn't he?

Maybe he really did just want his sister to be happy.

And then she almost laughed out loud. This was the man who'd made no apology for disposing of his sister's previous boyfriends by paying them to disappear. Instead he'd practically boasted about it! Was this a man who really cared about his sister's happiness? Not likely. Which brought her back to earth with a crash.

So why was he going along with these wedding plans?

Did he really believe his sister was in love this time? Given his mistrust of her previous suitors, and his intense dislike of her brother, the idea seemed incomprehensible. But what other reason was there for his suddenly being so compliant?

She didn't know. But what she did know was that this wedding would be everything that Monica and Jake wanted it to be, and that she would do her utmost to make it so—no matter what Daniel Caruana had planned.

CHAPTER EIGHT

DANIEL had been called away on an important call, Millie advised when Sophie emerged, but she was to show her to her new office and to make sure she had everything she needed in the guest room for her stay.

Sophie nodded numbly. Slowly she was coming to terms with the concept she might have to spend most, if not all, of the next few weeks here on Kallista if this wedding was to get off the ground. What was more disconcerting was that everyone else seemed to accept it as a given. It was just lucky Monica had warned her.

Clearly she could forget about getting back to Brisbane tonight, or any time soon.

'I didn't bring any clothes,' she offered by way of a half-hearted protest. Daniel had already taken care of that minor inconvenience, Millie informed her; a selection of items was arriving tomorrow to supplement whatever was already in the guest-room wardrobe.

Sophie suppressed her irritation. How typical of Mr Bossy Boots Caruana that now he assumed he could dress her. Did he think that just because he owned or employed everything and everyone on the island he now owned her too? Not a chance. She'd have Meg sort some stuff out and courier it up tomorrow. She might have to live here, but that didn't mean she'd have to wear his clothes.

The guest office sat at the far end of the house, just beyond her room, boasting a view that could never improve productivity, she was sure. The windows here were angled towards the mainland, the ribbon of white coast and lush green mountains the perfect foil for the cerulean perfection of sea and sky.

But, if you could manage to drag your eyes away from the view, the office had everything that opened and shut—computer, printer, wireless broadband along with a phone and fax.

Sophie looked around her, wondering at the calibre of person Daniel entertained here that he would have an entire guest office laid on, as well as a guest suite. Clearly not your average aunt and uncle. Not that she knew the first thing about his family, really, beyond the guest list Monica had provided her with.

In the space of a few short weeks she'd get to meet them herself, assuming she ever got the invitations out. Monica and Jake had decided on the stationery, but the printing had to wait until the venue was confirmed. That would be one of her first tasks, to get the invitations out; then, given the extremely short notice, she'd have to follow up each and every one by phone or email to ensure those who could make it would attend. Plus she'd have to add transfers to the arrangements too, she noted, for those arriving via Cairns airport. She'd ask Daniel about making available his helicopter, and maybe the launch he'd mentioned too.

The string quartet she'd organised could fly up, though she'd have to arrange flights and accommodation; then she had to find a cake, originally part of the Tropical Palms package. And Monica wanted doves.

She felt a rush of adrenaline as what seemed like a million thoughts vied for priority. This was what she loved about her job, the building blocks falling into place, the wedding becoming more real with every concrete decision.

This was only the tip of the iceberg. There was so little time and so much to do.

Game on.

Sophie surveyed the office around her and nodded approvingly. She'd need a space like this and it was good she'd be on the spot to iron out any difficulties as they arose. It made sense.

This wedding would be as perfect as she could make it and Daniel would see he'd done the right thing by his sister and that he'd done the right thing by her. She was determined it would happen.

She looked up to see Millie waiting expectantly at the door. 'It's perfect,' she said with a smile, feeling good for the first time today. For she realised she was thinking about the wedding again, planning what had to happen. Doing her job instead of fantasising about the brother of the bride.

And didn't that make for a welcome change?

An hour later she'd showered and changed back into her own clothes and was in the new office, getting the computer set up with files from her USB drive, when Daniel knocked on the door. The look on his face was unreadable. 'Making yourself at home?'

In a cool linen shirt and lightweight trousers, he should have looked safer than the last time she'd seen him. Yet still his appearance sent a jolt to her senses and jagged her pulse a notch higher. Casual had never looked so sexy. Maybe it was the late o'clock shadow that graced his jaw that turned property magnate into pirate, but whatever it was it was a potent force that threatened to destabilise her and make her forget what she was doing here all over again.

'There's a lot to do, to get this wedding off the ground,' she managed. 'Especially given there's not much time.'

He cocked one eyebrow and tucked his hands into his pockets. 'I can imagine. Exactly why I knew it would be wise to base your operations here. I'm so glad you agree.'

She stood up straight. 'It's not about agreeing, though, is it? It's about making the best of it.'

But he just laughed off her thinly veiled objections and moved with that panther-like grace across the tiled floor to the wall of windows that lined one whole side of the room, gazing out over the beautiful view before he turned. 'I have to go to Townsville for a meeting early tomorrow and I'll probably be late back. Will you be all right by yourself?'

She was tempted to tell him that she'd get more done with him absent than with the distraction of him being around. But instead she said, 'I've got heaps to do. I doubt I'll even know you're gone.'

She could swear she saw a tic in his jaw as he looked her over; maybe he was just unimpressed she'd put her own dress back on rather than having chosen something from the wardrobe.

'I've arranged for a boutique to send clothes.'

She waved his offer away, his words confirming her suspicions. 'Thanks, but my assistant's sorting some clothes.'

'There's no need.'

'On the contrary,' she said firmly, 'There's *every* need, so long as they'll find a way over to the island. I'm having them couriered to your office.'

He nodded. 'They'll come over on the launch, then. I'll have the chopper in Townsville.'

'I need to talk to you about that,' she said, remembering one of the points on her to-do list. 'I'll have to arrange for transfers of guests from Cairns to the island. Will your helicopter be available for those? Or maybe the launch? Otherwise I'll have to try to secure another vessel.'

He pulled his hands from his pockets, looking suddenly uncomfortable, his eyes hooded as he checked his watch. 'Sure, make whatever arrangements you like. I forgot, Millie asked me to let you know dinner is ready. We're eating out on the deck. This way.'

She blinked in his wake, following him when it was clear he wasn't about to wait. So, now he'd guaranteed the wedding would be held here, she could do whatever she liked? She really didn't understand Daniel Caruana at all.

Late the next day Sophie put the phone down and rubbed the back of her neck, ready for a break, surprised to find it was already five o'clock. It had been a full-on day of organising, and she'd been on the phone since breakfast. It was amazing, she mused, just how much you could get done without distractions. Away from her own office, where the phone seemed to ring every ten minutes, and with Daniel away, she'd made amazing progress. Maybe this arrangement would work better than she'd expected. Millie popped her head around the door to tell her that dinner would be ready in an hour, which suddenly seemed an eternity away. Already the smells wafting their way from the kitchen had her stomach rumbling in anticipation. But then she had skipped lunch while she'd been on a roll.

What she needed first, though, was some exercise. A walk down those steps and a swim in the tiny cove would be perfect.

She changed into the blue bikini and dug out a pair of sandals from the bottom of the wardrobe that were more or less the right size. With a quick word to Millie to let her know where she'd be, she set off for the path. The steps down to the shore were longer and steeper than they looked and it took some time to wend her way down the short flight of steps that zig-zagged down the hillside. But she did keep stopping to enjoy the way the view changed from different angles. It was quiet here, peaceful; the rustle of lizards scurrying through the leaf litter, the call of birds and the gentle shush of sea meeting sand at the beach below was the music that accompanied her steps. The canopy sheltered the steps from the worst of the sun, but it was warm and still, and by the time she reached the white sand beach she did no more than kick off her borrowed sandals and untie her sarong before heading straight for the water.

Bliss. She sank down, letting the current play out her hair, letting the water refresh her. It was magic. Nobody could see her, nobody could bother her. It was like having her own private beach.

Oh yes. There were definitely compensations for having to stay on Kallista for a few weeks. The climb back was definitely the exercise she needed, and Sophie arrived breathless, hot but definitely more relaxed for the exercise. She patted her forehead with her towel as she slid open the door to her room, only to find someone already there.

'Well well, look what the cat dragged in.'

The man was on the other side of her bed, the side where she knew she'd left her handbag. He straightened and she got the impression of bulk and power; his arms were muscled, his hands curling and uncurling at his sides. A thief, here on Kallista? Daniel had said there were none. But it was the look in his eyes, the long, leery stare from top to toe, that made her shiver and suddenly feel fearful for Millie. Where was she? How had he got past her? 'Who are you?'

'So you're Fletcher's sister?'

She bristled, pulling the knot in her sarong tighter, the scent of stale cigarette-smoke hitting her nostrils. She didn't appreciate being so clearly at a disadvantage, and had no intention of answering his question if he wouldn't answer hers. 'What are you doing in my room?'

'I have to admit, I didn't expect you to be such a good looker.'

Sophie tried to look past him—surely Millie was around somewhere?—but his shoulders were so broad he blocked her vision of the door. 'I wish I could return the compliment, but as I didn't expect you at all, Mr…?'

'Call me Jo. I'm Caruana's security manager. Just checking to make sure everything's all right for the little lady.'

Snooping, more like it. At Daniel's behest? Then he smiled and took a step closer, holding out his hand, a big, beefy paw with a brassy gold watch at his wrist, a thick, gold chain that matched the one at his neck. Two gold bands glistened on nicotine-stained fingers. Reluctantly she put her own hand out, felt it practically absorbed into his and had to stop herself from pulling away.

'A pleasure to meet you.' She wondered if she'd misjudged him. He was large framed, but it was all muscle, like you'd expect on someone who worked in security, and when he smiled he didn't look quite so frightening. But then his eyes shot a glance down her body, lingering where she knew the two sides of the sarong parted near her bikini bottoms. 'All of you, that is.' She decided she didn't like the man after all.

'Is that you back, then?' Millie's voice sounded down the hallway and Jo dropped her hand and turned.

'Hello, Millie. Just getting acquainted with our new guest.'

'Oh, Jo,' she said, wiping her hands on her pinny as she looked uncertainly from one to the other. 'I didn't know you were here.'

'I didn't want to disturb you, Millie. I let myself in.'

The older woman sniffed, as if he should know better than go skulking around the house by himself, but she said nothing more to him. 'Dinner's almost ready, lovey,' she told Sophie. 'If you want to get out of your wet things.'

'Sounds good, Millie,' Jo said. 'I've missed your cooking at the café.'

'Won't your wife be expecting you?'

'Not tonight. She's staying at her sister's. And I did go to all the trouble of bringing this…' He reached down and picked something from the floor then placed it on the bed. A parcel. Sophie could see by the return address that it had come from Meg.

'My clothes?'

'I thought you might be needing this sooner rather than later.'

'Thank you.' So he hadn't been snooping. Or had he just taken the opportunity for a little digging while he was making the trip?

Jo sucked in air and gave another self-satisfied grin. 'I reckon I might have earned myself a dinner. What do you reckon?'

She looked searchingly at Millie. She didn't relish the idea of sharing a meal with someone who made her feel so ill at ease, but would it be churlish to refuse, given he'd brought her clothes? Was it her decision to make?

'Where is everyone?' Daniel's voice boomed down the hallway and she wanted to sag with relief. He was back earlier than expected and she wanted to hug him. If Jo stayed to share dinner, she'd feel much better if Daniel was that too—even though Daniel was as dangerous as hell and made her feel at times as skittery as a cat on a hot tin roof. Much safer.

He entered the room and took in the scene, smiling at Millie. He scowled, she realised, when his gaze fell on her, still damp from her swim. 'Jo,' he said, jerking his eyes to the big man. 'I didn't expect to see you here.'

His security chief crossed to his boss. 'I just dropped off that package you said might turn up.' He hesitated a fraction or two. 'You were going to be longer in Townsville, I thought.'

One half of Daniel's mouth turned up. 'We finished up early. Thanks for delivering the package. Did you have anything else for me?' The big man shook his head.

'I'm waiting. I'll text you.'

Daniel nodded. 'Then if that's all?'

'Well, all except for Friday night's poker game—we still on for that?'

Daniel looked at Sophie, a frown tugging his brows. 'Not this week. Maybe next.'

Jo followed his gaze and smirked. Sophie wanted to protest that it was nothing to do with her, but he was already leaving. 'Later,' he said.

Millie gave a matter-of-fact harrumph and excused herself for the kitchen with the news that dinner was now only ten minutes away.

Daniel leaned one hand against the wall and sighed. Sophie sure was a sight for sore eyes. Her hair was wild and stiff around her face, her damp sarong clinging to every curve, and he applauded the disarray. She looked so much better like this than in that buttoned-up dress he'd seen her in yesterday. She looked more real. More woman. Oh yes; coming home early was the best decision he'd made in a long while.

She looked in the direction where Jo had exited. 'I don't think I like that man.'

'Jo? Why? What did he do?'

'He was just...' She crossed her arms over her chest and shivered. 'I don't know. Creepy—the way he looked at me.'

'Jo's ex-army. He's tough, but he's a good operator. One of my most loyal employees, in fact.' Still he noticed the tremor that moved through her, and he wondered if there was more to it than she was letting on. Then again, no man in his right mind wouldn't want to stare at Sophie, given the way she looked right now, still damp from the sea, her cheeks flushed, her hair like he imagined it would look after a long, hot session making love.

Damn. Come to think of it, he wasn't sure he liked the idea of anyone else wanting to stare, not if their thoughts ended up along the same path...

He had to change the subject. 'How was your day?'

She blinked, and once again he got to appreciate that sweep of impressive lashes against her cheek. Strange, how something so innocent could be so sexy.

'I got a lot done.'

He smiled. He'd just bet she had; probably lazed around the pool all day. 'Because I wasn't here?'

'It helped.'

Her honest reply made his smile grow wider. He'd been right to ditch that meeting early. Debate had been going round and round for hours; ordinarily he would have stopped it long before. Whereas she maintained she'd found his absence productive, he'd been distracted all day by thoughts of her, what she was doing in his house, and whether she was wearing that blue bikini again.

How much more enjoyable to be here, at home, and see that she was.

'Are you hungry?'

He could swear he saw something in her eyes flare. Desire? He wanted to think so. For he was hungry for more than just food now and it would suit him fine if she felt the same way. There would not be that many opportunities, not once the offer process got under way and Fletcher's plan started to unravel. It would be foolish to waste the few nights they had.

'Famished,' came her softly spoken response through lips plump and pink—tastier than anything Millie might serve up, he knew. For a moment, he was tempted to dip his head and taste her once again and forget all about dinner. But instead he merely took her hand, ignoring her protest that she needed to shower when she looked ready to serve up on a platter herself.

'Then we should eat.'

He liked watching her eat, he decided through the meal as twilight moved to dark within minutes. He liked watching her, full-stop. Even when she was talking incessantly about the wedding and the arrangements she'd apparently made, as if he was actually interested, he liked watching her. Her face was animated, her eyes bright, whether gilded by the lowering sun's rays or, like now, kissed by the soft pearlescence of the moon; that was all that mattered.

She was beautiful.

She was here.

And tonight he would have her.

Millie was serving up dessert when Sophie finally worked up the courage to ask; he'd glossed over her questions about the guest list earlier. In fact, he'd glossed over anything to do with the wedding, with glib responses that had given her nothing. But if she was going to get these invitations out this week it would help to understand something of Monica's family. Besides, she was curious. And, given Daniel seemed to be in a good mood tonight, there was no time like the present.

'Your family name is Italian,' she said, 'But you were born here, weren't you? I know Monica was. Was it your parents who came from Italy?'

He took a sip of his coffee before leaning back in his chair and lacing his fingers in his lap. A delaying tactic, she knew, because the coffee was still way too hot to drink. For a while she wondered if he was going to answer her question at all.

'No,' he said at last. 'It was my grandfather who came out. He was barely out of his twenties, and desperate to work anywhere. He landed a job on a tobacco farm up at Mareeba.' He pointed to the dark shadow of mountains that loomed above the line of lights along the coast, marking the start of the hinterland. 'It's an hour or so up from Cairns on the Atherton Tablelands. He worked hard, and in a few years he'd earned enough to buy his own place. Married the daughter of another tobacco-farming family and was probably planning on starting a dynasty. Didn't work out that way. My father happened along late, and they never had any more kids.'

She nodded. So he'd grown up without uncles, aunts and cousins, with the extended family back in Italy? That kind of explained why the guest list was short on family.

'Did your father take over the farm?'

'For a while, until he decided that sugar was the way to go and made the switch. He did all right, too, until the bottom dropped out of the sugar market. He made a few bad decisions and was wiped out.'

'Oh, but I assumed…'

He smiled. 'That I was born with a silver spoon in my mouth? I was. Only to have it wrenched out when I was barely out of high school. My dad never got over the loss. He felt like he'd betrayed his father's trust and let my mother down. He was never the same after that.'

He was staring at his hands and she knew he was thinking about his parents; Sophie didn't have to ask. Monica had spoken of the car being swept from the road into a swollen creek in the midst of near-cyclonic conditions. She'd told her about the police arriving at the house to give them the grim

news that their parents were never coming home. She'd told
her how Daniel had held her while she'd cried that night, and
every night for a week, and told her he'd never let anything
bad happen to her.

No wonder he was so protective of his little sister.

She was the only family he had.

Strange, how she'd divorced that story from her first
impressions of Daniel. It didn't fit the picture she'd had in
her mind of the arrogant businessman who got his own way
whichever way he could. But it was this man, sitting beside
her, who'd cradled his grieving sister in his arms and tried
to soothe away her tears. It was this man who'd practically
raised her.

'Your parents would be proud of you with all you've
achieved.'

He scoffed. 'Well, when you've lived in luxury, you know
what you're missing when you've not got it. It's a powerful
motivator.'

'I'm sure there's more to it than that. You did it the
hard way. You had to drop out of university to look after
Monica.'

He shrugged. 'Maybe. I got lucky, too. I stumbled into
a job in a property-management business and it was a good
fit. The property market was just starting to take off when I
started dabbling. It paid off.'

Coming from one of Queensland's richest men, it was a
massive understatement.

He downed his cooling coffee in one long gulp and stood.
'This is boring.'

She pushed back her own chair, her cheeks burning with
embarrassment. 'I'm sorry. Dinner was wonderful, thank you.
But I should leave you now.'

He was at her side in a heartbeat, his hand curled around her neck. 'I don't want you to leave me. I just don't want to talk about me.'

'What would you rather talk about?'

'Who said anything about talking?'

CHAPTER NINE

SHE would have laughed. She wanted to laugh, to dispel the tension that had suddenly weighted down the air until it was heavy and thick with anticipation. But the look in his eyes told her it was no accident.

'All night,' he whispered, his eyes on her mouth, his other hand joining the first behind her neck. 'All that time we were sitting here, this is really what I wanted to taste.'

He dipped his head, his mouth brushing hers, his tongue flicking over her lips. 'Mmm, salt,' he said, licking her taste from his lips.

'I was swimming,' she said. 'At the beach.'

'I like it,' he said, already making another pass. 'And coffee, and something sweet.'

His kisses grew deeper, his lips coaxing hers apart, his tongue tasting her, exploring, inviting her into the dance.

The breeze whispered through the leaves, a bird called out its final goodnight and the moon hung low and turned the sea into a silver ribbon. But none of it mattered. Not now, not with his lips upon hers, his taste in her mouth and the feel of his hard body pressed up against her.

He was unrelenting; his kisses intensified. He ravaged her mouth, plundered its depths with his tongue and tipped her head back so he could turn his hot mouth to her throat until she was gasping with the heat, the pleasure and the need.

And when he took one breast in one hand her knees went weak.

'Make love to me,' he said as he nuzzled her ear. A wave of pleasure rolled through her, so intense and so huge that she thought it might carry her away. Instead it passed, leaving her skin alive and tingling and with a heavy pooling heat between her thighs.

'We barely know each other,' she whispered, amazed and impressed that with a body screaming 'yes' she'd managed to find at least some kind of defence. *Not that she'd actually said no.*

She didn't do casual sex; she didn't do one-night stands. She didn't need any man. And yet 'we barely know each other' was the best she could do?

'We know that we want each other.'

Unfair! Then she gasped, her protest forgotten as his thumb stroked a nipple, sending arrows of exquisite pleasure straight to her core. 'You want me.' It was true, but surely that wasn't the only point?

'I can't,' she said, shaking her head, finding him harder to shake. 'This is crazy. Jake and Monica...'

'Are in Hawaii.' His lips found hers again. Coaxing. Persuading.

She pulled away. 'But I'm supposed to be here planning their wedding.'

His hand kept her head close to his mouth even while she voiced her argument, returning to her lips as soon as she'd uttered her words. 'And meanwhile,' he asked, 'you should live like a nun?'

'But it doesn't mean anything.'

'It means we want each other.'

'I don't do this sort of thing.'

'Have you ever wanted to before?'

She shook her head, her teeth troubling lips already exquisitely sensitised as he took her head between his hands and looked at her. 'Then maybe it's time you did.'

She was drowning in his eyes, falling hopelessly and helplessly in the direction she knew she should not go. And there was nothing, no will or thought or crumb of hope to save her.

Except for…

'Millie!' she whispered, looking around, stiffening in his arms as she suddenly remembered where they were.

'Has taken herself off to her apartment for the night. We're alone, Sophie. Just you, me and the moon.' His hands skimmed down her back, collecting up the hem of her sarong and easing it upwards, his hands curving around her behind, skimming over the small of her back as his mouth continued to weave magic on hers. Grit rolled under his fingertips, and she flinched as she remembered the forgotten shower.

'This is crazy. I'm covered in sand.'

His face drew back, just enough so he could rest his forehead on hers and look into her eyes. 'Something that is easily remedied.' And she felt herself swept from her feet and into his arms as if she weighed nothing.

He moved with the certainty of a man who knew what he wanted, but beyond that with the certainty of a man who knew what she wanted too. She *did* want this. It might be crazy; it might be a type of madness. He eased open a sliding door with a foot, kissing her until she felt faint, breathless and giddy with desire.

It *had* to be madness, she told herself. One short day ago she couldn't wait to get away from this man, had sought to flee from his dangerous acquaintance, and yet now she was trembling at the prospect of making love with him.

No wonder she'd felt compelled to run. For even then, underlying the hostile emotions and bitter words of yesterday's torrid meeting, she'd sensed he'd connected with her on some deep, elemental level. A level she'd shied away from. A level she'd feared to explore.

It was too late for fear now, as he pushed open a door and kicked it shut with his foot. His room, she figured. It was wide and high and with a bed the size of a minor principality. He didn't bother with the lights. The silvery glow from the moon slanting through the windows was enough to light his way past the bed, where he lingered only long enough to kick off his sandals and rid himself of his phone, before heading to the generous *en suite* turned magical by the same warm lunar glow.

Still he kept her in his arms, even when he entered the spacious shower cubicle, even as he turned the taps on full.

She gasped as the first burst of water hit, the torrent from a showerhead the size of a dinner plate cool against her super-heated flesh. Then her vision and her senses cleared enough for her to realise the insanity of what he'd done. 'You're drenched!' But he only laughed and, keeping her so close to him that she could not miss the press of his arousal, lowered her slowly to the floor.

'Does it matter if they're wet when they're coming off anyway?'

His kiss was deep and filled with longing, filled with need, and she drank him in as the water poured around them, as he untied the knot of the sarong at her chest. The sodden fabric fell to the floor with a smack and she trembled, feeling exposed in just her bikini. 'You're beautiful,' he said as he looked at her, his eyes dark with desire, his hands skimming her sides, drinking in her curves. She trembled again because being exposed when someone she wanted wanted her suddenly felt good.

But not half as good as he felt.

The wet shirt clung to his skin, moulded to his shape, but it wasn't damp cotton she wanted under her fingertips right now, it was the skin he'd worn last night in the pool. The skin he'd held next to her when she'd tried to run away. She wasn't trying to run away now. This time all bets were off. She wanted that skin under her fingers. She wanted it next to her own.

She fumbled with a button as his mouth fused once more with hers, but her hands were trembling with need, the buttonhole was waterlogged and resistant, and fine motor-skills eluded her. The next button proved equally uncooperative, and with a burst of frustration she wrenched the sides of his shirt apart and his glorious chest was hers to explore. Her nails raked over his skin, her fingers relishing the feel of his hard, packed flesh and the tight nub of nipple.

He growled with approval into her mouth and let her go long enough to peel the shredded garment from his shoulders. Then he was back, his fingers busy at her back until she felt the strap of her bikini-top go.

He paused then, his hands at her sides, his brow upon hers, almost as if he was catching his breath. Then his hands scooped around and pushed the bikini top up from below, his hands capturing her breasts, his thumbs rolling her nipples so that she arched into his hands. Then he peeled the top over her head and kissed a hot path to her breast, and she wanted to sag when he drew her nipple in deep.

Something shorted inside her. She was sure she must have blacked out in that instant, in that moment of utter pleasure that had consumed her world. But then she was back, to find him performing equivalent magic on her other breast.

Oh God. Suddenly his shoulders and chest were not enough for her hands. She fought with his belt, wanting to release the bucking power she felt straining beneath, the power she ached to feel. The power she knew was intended for her.

Desperation ruled her actions as the water rained down, beating against her sensitised skin, pulsing down in time with her heartbeat—washing away the salt of her swim but, more than that, washing away the last of her inhibitions.

When had she become a woman who initiated anything sexually? she pondered vaguely as his mouth left her breasts long enough for her to wonder. When had she decided for once to embrace the dangerous, instead of the safe and solid path? His mouth moved south down her belly, his tongue circling her naval before darting inside, hot, hard and insistent, his fingers tugging at her bikini bottoms; she forgot how to think, only how to feel.

He pressed her against the tiled wall, one hand at her breast, the other at her thigh. His mouth—oh God!—his mouth was there, hot, wet and urgent, parting her and finding that slick, sweet spot that ached with primal need.

Her hands tangled in his hair as his tongue flicked a fiery trail around that tight nub of nerve endings; his fingers circled her very core and the sweet, perfect agony of expectation was almost so much that she cried out with the injustice of it all. Then he sensed her need and sucked her tight into his mouth, his fingers plunging deep inside her.

She came in an explosion of sensation and a rainbow of colours, vivid colours, she recognised vaguely as they splashed around her. Colours bright and beautiful, the colours of the tropics. Vivid, potent and alive.

The colour of Daniel.

He scooped what was left of her into his arms before she sagged to the floor, then he snapped off the tap and snatched up a towel in his fingers, splaying it out on the bed next door before he put her down on it.

'Wow,' she said, her senses still humming. 'Amazing.'

Her words were enough to make his erection buck under the sodden trousers she'd never quite managed to get off. The sight of her on his bed with the moonlight turning her skin pearlescent was another thing altogether.

God, he wanted her! She'd come apart so spectacularly it had been all he could do to resist lunging into her to share the moment.

But there would be other moments—as many other moments as he could manage before she discovered the truth.

He finished the job she'd started and unzipped his trousers, letting the weight of the water drag them to the floor, stepping out of them as he freed his aching self from the band of his underwear.

'*You're* amazing,' she said, her eyes wide, her voice a blend of awe and wonder.

He knelt on one knee beside her, coiling one finger through her damp hair, taking a corner of the plush towel and gently blotting away the droplets of water that beaded on her satin skin. 'It's you who are amazing,' he said, leaning over, his lips unable to resist the kiss-plumped allure of hers. 'And I want to be inside you next time you come.'

She looked up at him, her dark lashes blinking against her cheeks, and smiled. 'I want you inside me.'

He groaned, her words ratcheting up his desire and his need. He'd been at the razor's edge of release before, gratified beyond anything he'd known before at the power of the orgasm he'd driven her to with his mouth. But nothing would beat the heady sensation of being, and coming, inside her.

Their eyes caught, their mouths meshed and their bodies tangled on the bed, mouth to mouth, mouth to nipple, hand to naked flesh.

He groaned with pleasure as her fingers coaxed him, teased him, led him to her entrance.

Then she gasped as he found that place, and bucked involuntarily beneath him as he settled himself between her legs.

His body pulsed at her core; her body was already willing him deeper, but as much as he wanted her, somehow he still had the sense to drag a foil from the bedside table.

'Let me,' she said, her eyes shy, her long lashes sweeping her cheek as if she was too embarrassed to look at him. He realised what courage she possessed to ask that even as he handed it over. For this was not a woman who moved with practised ease. This was a woman out of her depth, caught in deep water and eager to learn how to swim. He groaned through teeth clenched tight as she rolled protection down his length; even while her look of concentration at doing the job right was almost endearing, he knew that her innocent handling might just be his undoing.

All of it was his undoing: the touch of her fingers. The invitation of her parted legs as she lowered herself back down. The heady scent of desire from a woman whose skin turned to pearl in the silvery lunar glow.

He held himself poised over her, a moment of calm before the storm, a moment to savour, a brief moment to wonder what he had done to deserve such a feast for the senses.

'Please!' she said, desperate now, driven, and prepared to beg as her body once again screamed for release that only he could give. 'Now, please!'

And he lunged inside her in one fluid stroke that buried him to the hilt. Her head dug deep into the bed, her eyes wide with wonder, her gasp strangled before it was given birth.

He could stay there, he decided, held hostage by those exquisite, tight walls for ever, and it would not be long enough.

But he could no more stay still than hold the moon captive to glow on her skin for ever. He eased himself back, felt rather than heard her tiny whimper of loss, and made up for it one-thousand-fold as he lunged home again. This time she did cry out and he captured her ecstasy in his mouth, tasting her pleasure as he built the rhythm of their joining.

She matched him, tilting her hips to change the angle, using her muscles to hold him just a moment longer even as the pace turned frenetic and uncontrolled.

Skin slick with sweat, she glowed in the moonlight as she writhed under him, her breathing erratic, her increasingly desperate cries torn from her as he plunged again and again into her depths.

'Daniel!' she cried, reaching for him blindly, teetering on the edge of the precipice they both shared. He drew one perfect breast into his mouth and sucked on it hard, ramming himself home and exploding inside her with what felt like fireworks.

She came all around him, a vivid starburst of colour and passion, a wild release that blew his mind and took him shuddering over the edge with her.

Later, when the silvery moon had tracked higher in the night sky and Sophie lay sleeping, he stood outside on the deck in a pair of shorts, his hands palm-down on the railing, his restless thoughts a dark hole in a world of such moonlit perfection.

Electric—it was the only way he could describe how she'd felt, like a switch had been thrown and she'd turned from woman into electrical storm, sparking, pulsing with energy, crashing like lightning about him.

But how many nights would they have? How many opportunities to sink himself into her exquisite depths and feel her body come apart around him?

He turned and looked through the windows of his room to where he could make out her shape on his bed, her face urned away, one arm hanging over the side of the bed and a glorious curve of flesh from waist to hip illuminated by the pale moonlight.

How many nights?

Or was this thing to end before it began?

He walked barefoot along the deck, the rustle of leaves and the occasional rustle in the undergrowth the only sounds as he put off the inevitable, refusing to open the phone he'd heard beep—the reason he'd come outside.

Damn. He wanted Fletcher gone. He wanted this farce of a wedding to be proved the lie it was. But once it was, once Fletcher had his money, she'd be gone too, eager for her cut.

And by now Jo would already have made him an offer. Fletcher might already have said yes and be on his way back to collect it, setting Monica free.

He wanted Monica free.

But then Sophie would leave.

He rubbed the back of his neck and sighed. There was only one way to find out. He slid the phone open and clicked through to 'messages'.

It was from Jo.

With a tight gut he clicked it open, read the words—*Fletcher said no*—and released a lungful of air he hadn't realised he'd been holding.

He slid the phone shut and turned back to the shadowed view of diamond-crusted velvet sea and the clusters of lights along the coast. Jo would be waiting for his instruction to up the offer, but for the moment Jo could wait. Which meant that, for the moment, Sophie was his to enjoy.

Besides, she seemed to enjoy making her wedding plans— in fact, she'd seemed so full of it tonight that anyone would think *she* believed it was real.

Who was he to deprive her of her fun?

'Daniel?' She was standing half-behind the sliding door wearing only the moonlight and a tumble of golden hair. Instantly he stirred to life. 'Is something wrong?'

He held out a hand to her. 'I couldn't sleep.' And sheepishly, like a shy virgin instead of a woman with the body and responsiveness of a goddess, she moved silently to join him, the sway of her breasts like a call to action.

She took his hand and allowed herself to be drawn into the circle of his arms at the railing. 'Is there anything I can do?' she asked as he nuzzled her neck from behind, breathing in woman spiced with the heady scent of their love-making; his hands traversed from breast to thigh in one delicious, sensual exploration that had her arching her back on a sigh.

Was there anything she could do?

Oh, sweet Jesus, yes.

She moaned as he parted her, sliding his fingers between her slick folds while he patted his pockets with his other hand; he wanted to howl at the moon when he found what he needed. 'Maybe there is something,' he groaned as he ripped open the packet with his teeth. He dropped his shorts and kicked them away as he donned protection, thankful when he had two hands free again to stroke her, two hands to both give and find pleasure.

'Daniel!' she cried, already panting, her nipples tight and hard between his fingers. The curve of her behind fitted his hand perfectly as he soothed her legs apart, entering her in one delicious thrust that had them both gasping.

The lights of the coastal towns winked on the distant shore, the sea glittered where kissed by the moon, and the warm breeze carried the perfume of a thousand exotic flowers. When they came, the lights, sea and moon stayed the same, but the warm, perfumed breeze carried with it the cry of both their names.

CHAPTER TEN

'No rush,' Daniel said from behind his office desk. 'Let him sweat a little. We don't have to look too eager.'

Jo squirmed noticeably in his chair. 'I thought you were in a hurry.'

Daniel picked up a paperweight from his desk, testing its weight in his hands, thinking abstractly that Sophie's breasts must weigh about the same—only they filled his hands so much more satisfactorily.

'You *were* in a hurry, you said.'

'I hear patience is a virtue.'

Jo wiped his brow with a handkerchief. 'I think you should make him another offer. Ramp up the pressure. It's obviously what he's waiting for.'

'And I think you should listen when I say I'm happy to sit tight.'

'So you're not worried about your sister—with him—any more, then? After what happened to that other girl?'

Daniel dropped the paperweight back on the desk, swiveling his chair around to directly face the big man down. 'That *other girl's* name was Emma.'

'Yeah. Her. You wouldn't want the same thing to happen to Monica.'

Daniel was caught between a bloodlust for retribution for what had happened so many years ago, and an anger for what he stood to lose now. Who did Jo think he was, telling Daniel what was important?

But Monica was his sister.

And if anything happened to her, he would never forgive himself.

Whereas Sophie was a passing lust—entertaining; sexually satisfying; mind-blowing, even. But ultimately disposable.

They all were.

Unlike Monica. What right did he have to indulge his own primal urges before ensuring the safety of his own sister? 'All right,' he said through gritted teeth, seeing the sense in Jo's argument, glad he had someone who knew enough history to keep him honest. 'Double the offer. Make it two million.'

If Millie noticed or disapproved of the change in sleeping arrangements, she didn't say anything. And she must have noticed. Sophie's bed had been untouched whereas Daniel's bed was a total shambles with wet clothes trailing from the shower to the bed, even though she'd tried to minimise the damage. There was no way Daniel's housekeeper could miss the carnage or fail to extrapolate from it the facts.

Yet Millie's smile appeared genuine when she brought Sophie a cup of lemon-scented tea halfway through the morning. 'How's it going, lovey?' she asked, peering over Sophie's shoulder at pictures of wedding cakes she had pulled from the Internet. 'Ooh, aren't they lovely? I used to dabble with wedding cakes—nothing like these modern ones, of course— before I got work in the café.'

Sophie nodded absently. It was the full and pitiful extent of her work this morning, she reflected, this thin pile of pictures. She'd convinced herself it was work, even though she'd found nothing that nearly approximated the traditional and simple tiered cake Monica had hinted at—like the cake her parents had had at their wedding—even though her mind had been miles away.

Or, rather, hours ago.

If last night had blown away her every inhibition, this morning's efforts had blown her mind. Daniel was the kind of lover you only read about in books. Nobody could make love that many times in one night, she'd been convinced. Nobody.

But Daniel had. And every time had been different, every time better, in some undefined way.

No wonder she hadn't been able to focus on her work. She was still trying to count up the different ways he'd made love to her, the number of orgasms he'd brought her to in just one night.

'Hmm?' she murmured vaguely; some hint of a message had been in Millie's words that was struggling to strike a chord.

'I could never do these fancy mudcake or cream-puff things,' Millie continued, pointing to a picture of a *croquembouche*. 'Mine were more the old-fashioned type. But these are pretty.'

Finally her words worked their way through the fog that had been Sophie's morning. She swung her chair around. 'You make wedding cakes?'

Millie looked abashed. 'Well, I used to. I once won a bake-off competition with my fruit-cake recipe. I'm not so good at learning fancy new stuff—like all this Vietnamese and Thai cuisine I know Mr Caruana would like, for instance—but I do a pretty mean classic wedding cake.'

Sophie couldn't believe what she was hearing. 'Monica wants a traditional cake. Something like—' She scrabbled through the papers on her desk for a copy of the old photograph, diving on it when she found it. 'Something like this.'

'Oh!' Millie took the copy and gave a wistful sigh. 'S⟨
that's her parents, then. I never met them, you know. Bu⟨
doesn't Monica resemble her mother so?'

Sophie agreed. The likeness was uncanny, whereas Danie⟨
seemed more of a blend, the strength of his father's nose an⟨
jawline coupled with the high cheek-bones and generosity o⟨
his mother's lips.

'Oh, and that cake,' Millie continued. 'I made one just lik⟨
it for Sybil Martin's wedding, only we had fresh roses rathe⟨
than orchids.' She shook her head and clucked. 'Hard work
keeping those roses fresh-looking in this climate, I tell you
We had them in the cooler until the last moment.'

'You made a cake like this?'

'A piece of cake!' the older woman said before laughin⟨
at her own joke.

'Millie, do you think you could you make one for Monic⟨
and Jake? In return, maybe I could teach you how to coo⟨
Thai. It's dead easy, really. Much easier than producing ⟨
wedding cake.'

The woman's smile vanished, though there was just th⟨
tiniest glimmer of interest mixed with the disbelief in her eyes
'You really want me to have a go at a wedding cake, then?'

'I'm serious. I'd pay you, of course. I wouldn't expec⟨
you to do all that work for nothing. And we'll have a Tha⟨
cooking-class first chance we get.'

Daniel let himself into the house, weary, hot and disgrun⟨
tled. His day had been a waste. The fallout from the aborte⟨
Townsville conference had consumed most of the day's over
efforts, while secretly he'd been waiting for his phone to beep
waiting for the message that would spell the end to his affai⟨
with Sophie. Because there was no way Fletcher would tur⟨
down two million in cold, hard cash, surely?

Something good wafted from the direction of the kitchen, spicy, aromatic and flavoured with garlic, ginger and fresh herbs; his stomach growled so appreciatively he had to investigate for himself, if only to grab a beer and find out how long it would be before he could eat.

The last thing he expected to find was both his women in the kitchen, Millie and Sophie wearing matching pinnies and engrossed in cooking up a storm. Millie noticed him first.

'Mr Caruana, I didn't hear you come in.'

He wasn't surprised, there were so many pans and woks simmering on the hotplates the extractor could hardly keep up. But it was Sophie's reaction he was more taken by. She looked up from whatever she was chopping, her eyes shadowed by her long lashes, and he could swear she was doing that blushing thing again.

Millie pressed a cold beer into his hands. 'Sophie's giving me a lesson on how to cook Thai. I hope you're hungry. We've got a veritable feast in store for you.'

He levered the cap off his beer and pulled out one of the bar stools along the wide kitchen bench, uncharacteristically plonking himself down; usually he'd head straight to his office. 'You didn't tell me you could cook, Sophie.'

She looked sideways at him, the knife in her hands suddenly stilled. 'I can do lots of things.'

Oh, now that he *did* know. Already he was looking forward to finding out more. He raised the open bottle to her. 'Here's to discovering your other hidden talents.' And he smiled when her blush deepened. How could she be so shy on the one hand, when she was so explosive in bed? But then he remembered the woman last night standing half-hidden by the doors, as if embarrassed by her nakedness, and he wondered again at how inexperienced she seemed. She hadn't been a virgin, but she couldn't have had too many men, that was for certain. One of them would surely have whisked her off the market by now.

He was pondering the significance of that thought when the phone in his pocket beeped, souring both the taste of his beer and his lighter mood-change since walking in the door.

Sophie, on the other hand, seemed suddenly brighter. 'Oh, but you'll never guess what—Millie used to make wedding cakes. She's agreed to make Monica and Jake's. Isn't that great?'

Suddenly his beer wasn't just sour; now it tasted like crap.

He pushed himself from the chair, leaving the half-empty bottle on the bench. 'I have a call to make.'

'Don't take too long,' Millie called behind him. 'Dinner will be ready in twenty minutes.'

He slammed his office door with unnecessary force, making the windows rattle. How could Sophie do that? How could she pretend the wedding was going ahead when she knew damned well it wasn't? He paced the wall of his office, end to end and back again, finding no answers, no reason.

And how could she drag Millie into it, getting her hopes up about making some bloody wedding cake for a wedding that was destined to be a non-event from the start?

Why did she persist with this whole wedding-planner fantasy, anyway? Was she so desperate to convince him that it was real that she needed to involve his personal staff? Did she really believe Millie's involvement would sway him? Now she was only going to let Millie down when it all came unstuck.

None of it made sense, least of all whatever it was gnawing at the recesses of his mind. She was a good actress. She had to be, to pretend the wedding was real and to suck everyone into her plan.

Yet what kind of actress could blush on demand? What kind of actress could turn shyness into an art?

Was Jo wrong about her motives? Did Sophie actually believe the wedding was real? Nothing he'd witnessed so far gave any hint that her efforts to get this wedding underway were half-hearted.

And nothing she'd done gave any hint that she'd got wind of his million-dollar offer to her brother. Sure, it would pay her to keep quiet until the deal was done if she was getting the cut Jo suggested, but wouldn't he have noticed just a glimmer of interest once the game was on?

Was she cleverer than that, too clever and too interested in a hefty-dollar payout to give herself away?

Or was her brother playing her for a fool, using her as his blind while he sucked the bride's brother dry?

The idea appealed, made a sick kind of sense. Fletcher had no loyalty to his sister; they'd only known each other a few short years, after all. She and her wedding-planner business was just a cover, her business's need for capital a mere coincidence. He refused to believe she was part of Fletcher's plan.

He sat down on the edge of his desk, the pieces reassembling themselves in his mind. Sophie's brother was playing her for a fool. She and her wedding-planning business validated his story, that was all.

And, once Fletcher had the money, he'd run, leaving both Monica and Sophie high and dry, and leaving Daniel to pick up the pieces.

Someone like Fletcher would do that.

The phone in his pocket beeped again, reminding him he had messages waiting—reminding him that whatever he thought or hoped probably wasn't the issue. He had to deal in facts.

So he checked his messages, found the one from Jo he'd been expecting and opened it: *Fletcher and Co on three day cruise. Offer made. Awaiting response on return.*

He snorted, letting go some of the angst he'd felt building from the first time his phone had beeped. So Fletcher was making the most of Hawaii's attractions while he was there and no doubt Monica too. He knew he should feel angrier. He knew his gut should be rebelling at the prospect of his sister with that man.

Only it didn't, and it wasn't, and it was all because of one thing: *he had Fletcher's sister.*

No news was definitely good news. Three days would be more than enough. Fletcher would have to accept defeat this time and more than likely Daniel would have had his fill of Sophie. They all paled after a while, no matter how tempting they'd been in the beginning. Sophie was good, he granted her that, but three days surely had to be enough for this crazy fire to burn out?

More than enough.

There was a tap at the door and it slowly opened. 'Daniel?' the subject of his thoughts said tentatively. 'Dinner's ready if you are.'

He was at her side in a heartbeat, determined to make the most of the next three days. He curled his hand around her neck and hauled her into his kiss. 'Oh,' he said after she'd been thoroughly and deeply kissed so that her taste and scent filled his senses, stoking the flames of that fire once more. 'Believe me, I'm ready.'

They made love in the plunge-pool afterwards, a slow, delicious tangling of bodies, tongues and limbs, an exquisite pleasure-filled torture where delay heightened desire and where postponing the inevitable increased the need. Unti finally, their eyes driven dark with desperation, they came together in a writhing, heaving conflagration that churned the water until it was white with foam.

Later, when both the water and their heartbeats had calmed and she lay like a sleepy cat against his body, he wondered about those three days being enough. He'd just had the best sex of his life; the way this woman felt under his hand, the way his body reacted to that touch, there was plenty more to come.

She stirred in his arms and stretched deliciously against him, her eyes fluttering to wakefulness—but it was the smile she gave him, a heady mix of innocence and temptation that made him feel that the bottom had just dropped out of the pool. 'Thank you,' she said, her hand lazily stroking his chest.

He picked it up, took it to his mouth and kissed it before softly dropping it down again. 'For what?'

'Lots of things. For sex in the pool. And sex on the deck. And sex in the shower. I don't think I'll forget that for a while.'

He found himself grinning along with her. Was it only last night they'd first come together? They'd made love so many times already, it felt like it must be longer.

'My pleasure,' he growled, meaning it, liking the way her fingers had found his nipple, how her nails raked tiny circles around its peak.

'I never knew it could be so good—the sex, I mean. Not that I've had that much experience, of course. Not like you, I imagine. You've probably had loads and loads of women.'

That many? He couldn't recall. 'Does it matter? You're the best so far.' She blushed, the way she did, but this time she seemed to blush all over.

'Yeah, sure.'

He didn't know why he'd admitted it, but it was out there now, and he wasn't about to argue the point. 'So, how many lovers have you had?'

She screwed up her nose. 'It's a bit embarrassing really. Only the one. Two, really, if you count the first time, but really just one.'

'So who was he?'

'A guy I met. I did a volunteer programme for a year doing English as a second language in a small village in Thailand.'

'That's where you learned to cook so well?'

'You really liked it?' Her head lifted from his shoulder, her eyes bright with pleasure.

'I loved it,' he said, kissing her on the tip of her nose. 'Thank you.'

She snuggled her head back down, the water lapping at their joined skin. 'I'm glad. Anyway, Craig was another volunteer from New Zealand. We were the only foreigners, and it was pretty isolated. I was homesick, and Mum had just got sick—not too bad, at that stage, but I was worried about her because I had six months left on my contract, and…'

'And Craig was there.'

Her fingers made whirls in his chest hair. 'And Craig was there. He was a nice enough guy, but we knew it was temporary. Kind of like sticking on a plaster: it helped cover the wound when I was a bit sad and lonely.'

He nodded. 'So who was the other one?'

She screwed up her nose again.

'That was a bit more embarrassing. I had a bit of a crush on this guy at school. Anyway, someone laced the punch with alco-pop at the end-of-school party and Simon and I got a bit carried away—maybe more than a bit, if you know what I mean. It was awful. We were both so horrified, we never spoke to each other again.'

He knew what she meant. He'd done his own fair share of experimenting when he was in high school. *Until he and Emma had become an item.*

God, he didn't want to think about Emma now. Not here, not while he was screwing Fletcher's sister.

He pushed away, letting go of her as he sat up, his head in his hands, waiting for the explosion of pain he knew would come. The guilt at his betrayal that he should be sleeping with this woman.

That he would be *enjoying* it, after what Fletcher had done!

And the pain came, though nowhere near as intense as he had expected. Dulled through too much sex, he assumed. It was a wonder he had feelings left at all.

'What's wrong?'

He looked skyward, to the blanket of stars and moon overhead, and sighed. 'It's late and I've got an early start. Let's go to bed.'

Whatever had been bothering him that night—first in disappearing so abruptly into his office before dinner, and then his all-too-rapid change of mood in the pool—it hadn't hung around. Sophie looked dreamily out of the window of her office, wondering if she'd ever regain the ability to focus for longer than two minutes at a time. The last few days and nights had been amazing and it was hard to imagine a time when sex or memories of their love-making hadn't figured so prominently in her life.

But how could she—as someone who had never hungered for the touch of a man, who had never missed it from her neatly ordered life—suddenly be so obsessed by the sensations stirred within her?

And how could Daniel make her feel the way he did with just one look, one caress? How could he reduce her to nothing more than a mass of screaming nerve endings again and again?

Those nerve endings made themselves known to her now. She looked at the clock; he would be home soon. He'd been coming home earlier and earlier every day. When Millie had commented on it, he'd said there wasn't much on, but he'd winked at her while he said it and had given her *that* look and whisked her off to the bedroom before dinner. And last night he'd had Millie prepare a picnic basket and they'd had dinner on the private beach in the cove below, taking turns at swimming, making love and feeding each other with treats from the basket.

If he kept this up, a girl could almost think she was special. *Almost.*

If he hadn't told her that she was his best lover so far, she might already believe she was. For, even if he'd been telling her the truth that night, his words had been a stark reminder that she was one of many and that Daniel was used to moving on.

As he would no doubt do again.

With a sigh she forced her thoughts back to the reason why she was here—to organise a wedding, not fall head over heels with Daniel Caruana. There was no future in it, no point to their relationship. Because even if their affair lasted that long once Monica and Daniel were married there was no reason for her to stay on the island, no reason not to return to Brisbane.

She refused to look at the clock again, to see how much or how little the minute hand had moved since she'd last looked. She had to keep her head, not lose her heart.

If only he didn't make it so difficult.

The computer on the desk behind pinged with incoming mail: hopefully confirmation at the last of the printing job's completion. She turned to her desk, happy to have an excuse to think about work, and clicked on her email programme. She smiled when she saw it was from Jake instead. She opened it, thinking they must be back from their cruise, wondering how it had gone even as her smile turned to a frown.

I need to talk to you. Urgently. Are you alone?
J

She stared vacantly at the message, hit reply with trembling fingers and sent off a brief message.

Bare seconds later, her phone buzzed. 'Jake,' she said, 'what's wrong? Is Monica okay?'

'She's fine. She's at the hairdresser. We're both fine.' But he sounded anything but, his words tight and clipped and angry as hell. 'I need to give you a message for Caruana.'

'Sure, what is it?'

'Tell him I don't want his money. Tell him to call off his dogs.'

Her blood ran cold. 'What money?' But somehow she knew before he'd uttered another word.

'The money he offered me to dump Monica. We hadn't been here ten minutes and his thug was on the phone, offering me half a million to leave her cold.'

'He offered you that?' Sophie dropped into her chair. It was an obscene amount of money, but what she'd been doing with Daniel while he'd been plotting to rid himself of her brother and this marriage was more obscene.

She'd slept with him, practically offered herself to him.

And, all the while he'd been pretending to go along with the plans she'd been making, he was busy planning to ensure the wedding never happened.

'That was just the opening gambit,' her brother continued. 'I told him to get lost and he's upped the offer to a cool million now.'

Something squeezed tight in her chest. This couldn't be happening. Why would Daniel want her here, organising a wedding he was busy trying to ensure would never happen? She'd actually believed he was coming round to the idea.

Yet hadn't Daniel practically boasted how he'd got rid of Monica's previous boyfriends?

Despite everything, despite all she knew and suspected, she still had to ask the question. 'You're sure it's Daniel?'

'Oh, yeah. It's him. And this thug who calls himself security—Jo Dimitriou—I know him, but I didn't know he was working for Caruana now. I've got this really bad feeling about him. Watch out for him. He's dangerous.'

And Daniel wasn't? Jo gave her the creeps, she was the first to agree, but who was the more dangerous—the man who offered you money at someone else's behest, or the man who made you believe in one thing when he was busy destroying everything you were trying to build up while you were looking the other way? 'I should have warned you, Jake. He's done this before—offered money, I mean—to get rid of Monica's boyfriends.'

'Bastard! Monica told me she was beginning to think if there was something wrong with her, not being able to hold onto a man.'

'What are you going to do?'

'Stay here for now. I figure Monica's better off out of it. I haven't told her yet. She thinks the sun shines out of her darling brother.'

'I understand.'

'Listen, Sophie, I've told this Jo guy no. There's clearly no way Caruana's going to listen to me, but if he hears it from you he might actually believe it. Can you tell him? Tell him to save his efforts? It doesn't matter what he offers me, the answer's still no. Tell him I'm marrying his sister, whether he likes it or not.'

Sophie put the phone down, her mind numb, her body in shock, and a great, gaping hole where her heart should have been. She'd thought she'd been wrong about him. She'd thought it had been the shock of the wedding announcement that had turned him into a raging monster that first day, and that he was coming round—*had* come round—to accepting that the wedding would go ahead. Bit by bit, he'd seemed to soften.

Or was that her? Falling into his bed and wanting to believe he was different, so that her first impressions had been wrong. Seduced by sex until she'd believed the monster was the lie, that the man was better than that.

When clearly he'd been a monster all along.

She looked around the office: at the pictures she'd stuck up on the walls; at the various lists that seemed to cover every horizontal surface; at the samples of stationery and swatches of fabrics she had for colour matching.

Daniel had no intention of this wedding going ahead. So what was she even doing here?

From down the hallway came the sound of voices and she had to fight the sudden urge to retch.

Daniel was home.

It had been the day from hell. A bank in one of his shopping centres had been host to a hold up, there'd been another blow-up with the Townsville negotiations, which meant he'd have to head back up there first thing tomorrow, and Jo had been giving him grief about upping Fletcher's offer again in the wake of this latest rejection. And the worst thing about that was the random thought he'd had that maybe Fletcher's reluctance to accept an offer meant Fletcher really did love his sister. He'd shoved the idea away as quickly as it had arisen, but the sick feeling had lingered all afternoon.

If he hadn't had Sophie to come home to, there would have been nothing to make the day worth living.

Millie handed him a beer and he chugged half of it down before drawing breath. 'Thanks, I needed that,' he said, looking around, surprised Sophie wasn't hanging around the kitchen where he usually found her this time of day. 'Where is she?' he asked.

'Still working in that office of hers, I imagine. Probably didn't hear you come in. Why don't you go and pry her away from that computer? She's been in there all day.'

It would be his pleasure. The second half of the beer met the same fate as the first, and he put the empty bottle down. He was feeling better already.

He'd already kicked off his shoes and unbuttoned his shirt by the time he was halfway to her office. If he had to pry her away from her computer, he didn't want to waste any time on the basics.

Already he could feel her cool hands on his skin, feel the flick of her tongue over his straining tip, feel her trembling with need beneath him in that hitched moment of anticipation before he lunged into her.

Oh yeah; already he was feeling a *lot* better.

The door was open and he found her standing by the windows, her back to the door. Just one glance and already he'd worked out how he was going to get her out of the little strappy number she wore in the minimum time. 'Knock knock,' he said.

Then she turned, and a foul day turned belly up.

She looked like the eye of a storm, he thought, the brief moment of respite after one onslaught and before all hell broke loose. She stood as straight as a pillar, her features drawn tight.

her eyes ice-cold and malevolent, the storm building within; he wondered what the hell had happened to bring this on. Just this morning she'd been telling him she couldn't wait for him to come home. And now this?

Maybe he'd been right. Maybe three days had been long enough for whatever it was to burn out. A pity, in that case, given Fletcher had said no to this latest offer, that potentially they had more time together before it must inevitably end.

But the thought that she might have lost interest first irked him. He'd assumed he'd be the one to know when it was over.

'How was your day?' he asked, determined not to be swept into her foul mood. If she wanted to tell him whatever was bugging her, that was fine, but he was no masochist. He wasn't about to go poking about, looking. Better to turn to something he knew she could talk about ad infinitum. 'Get lots of wedding things organised?'

Her head jerked up, her eyes flashing fire. 'And you really care because…?'

He'd provoked a response, that was something, not that she'd given him any clues with it. 'I'll admit, talking weddings doesn't hold the same appeal for me as it does for you. But don't let that stop you. There's nothing I adore more at the end of a long day than being regaled with tales of the latest decision about flowers or decorations or the advantages of two tiers versus three.'

'You bastard!'

The words didn't stick. He'd been called much worse in his time, no doubt would be again. But it didn't help that he hadn't spoken the complete truth. He had no interest in her pointless wedding arrangements, that was true, but at the end of his work day he'd liked nothing more than hearing her talk. He didn't care about what, he'd just loved her enthusiasm and energy and hearing the laughter in her voice.

But there was no laughter now.

'I don't know what's bothering you, but clearly you're in no mood for company. If you'll excuse me?'

He'd barely made it to the door when he heard the words. 'Did you offer Jake money to break off with Monica?'

So she wasn't in on it. That was his first thought. He'd suspected Fletcher was taking advantage of her all along and he was right. *So why would he have told her now?*

But that didn't matter. What mattered right now was that she knew and that was why she was so angry. *Damn.* He spun around. 'Did he tell you that?'

'Answer the question! Did you, or that henchman you call a security boss, offer Jake money to break off with Monica? Seems to me it's got your *modus operandi* written all over it.'

He stiffened and dragged in a breath. So the truth was out. There was no point denying it, even if he wished she didn't know. Even if he wished for that other Sophie back, the warm, sensual woman who responded to his touch as if she was made for it. But that Sophie was gone, probably for ever, and even though part of him ached inexplicably at the thought he'd always known it would happen some time.

And now he could only defend his actions. His record might damn him in her eyes, but history was on his side, after all. 'He'll say yes. They all do.'

He watched her almost crumple in a heap. Her fisted hands came up over her face as her knees buckled beneath her. But she didn't fall. She pushed herself up straight, thrust her arms away and glared at him, her eyes like polished stone. 'For God's sake, Daniel. Can't you see? Jake *loves* Monica.'

'So he *says*.'

'Because it's the truth! And he asked me to tell you he doesn't want your money, whether it's five-hundred thousand, or a million, or whatever else you decide to throw at him. He doesn't want it because he's marrying Monica, whatever you want to believe in your tortured, twisted mind.'

He frowned. She had the numbers wrong, but then she was hysterical and there was no point correcting her.

'I thought you'd changed,' she continued, her voice softer, resigned, with a hint of melancholy. 'I thought the fact you insisted the wedding would be held here, the way you insisted I should stay to make all the arrangements on site...' She shook her head, her eyes uncomfortably direct as they searched his out. 'I know you're desperate to protect your sister because she's all you have, and you've been looking after her ever since your parents died, but I thought for once that you might be more interested in her happiness than shutting her off from the world. I thought that over the last few days you were at least coming to terms with this wedding, even if you couldn't openly embrace it.'

She drew breath, kicked up her chin. 'I thought there might actually be hope for you. I'm sorry. I was wrong.'

Her last few words were the kick that set his blood pressure rocketing. She didn't know him. She didn't know the first thing about him. And yet she stood there and made out that he was some kind of disappointment?

'You don't know the first thing about it!'

'I know you can't bear the thought of anyone else loving your sister, so much so that you pay anyone who gets close to get rid of them.'

His spun round, needing to hit something, his open palm slamming against the wall before he turned back. 'And you don't think I have reason?'

'Sure you have reason—you're jealous they'll steal her away from you—and you use the excuse of them being nothing more than fortune-hunters to drive them away.'

'No!' With a few purposeful strides he was before her. 'Did Monica tell you about her first boyfriend, the charming Cal, her first *true love*?'

Sophie backed away, her eyes wide, but there was strength in them too, he could see, and a determination not to be cowed. In the very next moment her chin cocked up. 'Not specifically. She said she'd had a few boyfriends but none of them had stuck around long. And we all know why that is, don't we?'

'Do we? Let me tell you about Cal. He was ambitious and determined to make a million dollars before he was twenty-one.'

'And this was a reason to resent him? Didn't you do something similar yourself?'

'Not that way. Not by blackmailing the brother of the girl you're supposed to be in love with. Not with a movie of them having sex.'

Her eyes widened and he awarded himself a mental victory. At last she might begin to understand where he was coming from. 'He did what?'

'Either I paid up or he'd plaster the images all over the Internet. My sister. Her first time. Do you know what that does to a brother when you're supposed to be looking out for her? Of course I paid him out.'

'Daniel, I had no idea.'

'No, you didn't. You were too happy to judge from a distance. But maybe now you can understand why I never hesitated to get in first with an offer, before any damage was done, before they found a way to extract it by other means. And they took it. Which proves something, wouldn't you say?'

'It proves that this Cal was a monster. It proves that maybe they weren't deeply involved with Monica and taking the money was easier. But it doesn't mean that every man is like that. And it doesn't mean that Monica should be punished for ever. Don't you think she deserves a chance at happiness?

Or do you intend dispensing with every man she ever shows an interest in, ensuring she leads a long, lonely life thinking there is something wrong with her. Is that what you want?'

He looked skywards. Of course he didn't want that. He wanted his sister happy, with a man who would put her on the pedestal she deserved, not some fortune-hunter. 'She'll find someone worthy of her one day.'

'What about Jake? Doesn't it occur to you that the reason he's saying no to your offers is because it's not the money he wants? He loves Monica. Can't you see that?'

'He's not marrying my sister!'

'What is your problem? What have you got against my brother, other than the fact he grew up poor and you grew up rich. Maybe he gave you some schoolboy grief at high school? What else did he ever do to you?'

'What did he do to me?' He laughed as blood fired the furnace of his eyes, painting her outline red. 'Your sweet and innocent Jake did nothing, nothing at all, apparently. Clearly I should welcome him into the bosom of my family.'

The tone of his voice put chills down her spine. 'Tell me,' she said, simultaneously too afraid to hear, too frightened not to find out what it was that had driven this man to such bitterness and to take the measures he had. 'Why is it that you hate Jake so much?'

'Why wouldn't I hate him?' He looked at her then, his eyes suddenly empty shells, lost, lonely and soulless. 'Because your brother killed my fiancée.'

CHAPTER ELEVEN

His fiancée? *Oh God.* She remembered the photo in the guest room, the smiling girl Millie had said had died in tragic circumstances, and whose picture Daniel couldn't bear either to part with or to see. But what could her brother possibly have had to do with her death?

Nothing.

'No.' Sophie wasn't even sure why she'd believed that, but she did and it was out there; now the word hung between them, a one-word rebuttal to an accusation of nightmarish proportions. 'You're wrong.'

'You don't even know him. You don't know what he was like back then. You have no idea what he was capable of!'

'Maybe not, but I still don't believe my brother is the type of man that could have done what you said and be lining up to marry your sister. What kind of man could do such a thing? I'm telling you now, Jake's not that man.'

'Then you don't know your brother at all.'

She shook her head. 'No. I don't know you.' She moved to go past and he caught her arm, his fingers like claws in her flesh, although she felt no pain, her fury consuming her ability to feel anything else.

'Don't you want to hear what he did? Or are you too scared to learn the truth about your precious brother?'

He was wound tight as a drum, his skin like a mask over the bones of his face, his eyes deep pits as he challenged her, continuing unbidden, his voice empty and flat. 'It was our final year at high school. We'd just finished exams and my family all went to Italy for three months, to visit the extended family my parents hadn't seen for years. Emma and I were to be officially engaged the week after we came back.'

He seemed to realise he was still holding her then, and let her go, turning his head away. 'Emma wanted to come with us, but she'd just scored a job and we thought it was better to start saving up. Three months away from her seemed an eternity—stupid, really, when I had no idea then what eternity even meant.'

He paused, his head dipped on sagging shoulders. 'I couldn't wait to get on that plane home. Except just before we left for the airport we got a phone call. Emma had been thrown from a car when it careened off the road. She wasn't wearing a seat belt. Maybe she might have survived the crash if she was, maybe she might have survived anyway, but the car rolled on top of her. She didn't have a chance.'

Sophie shivered, the chill of his words going bone-deep. He'd lost his fiancée in tragic circumstances, then he'd lost his parents in a similar way not long after. No wonder the trauma had cut so deep.

'I'm truly sorry,' she said, meaning it. 'But I still don't understand what that had to do with my brother.'

His eyes turned to black holes. 'She was in your brother's car!'

Sophie swallowed. She knew Jake sometimes had headaches, a legacy of a crash he'd once been in, but she'd had no idea of the details. Was Daniel right? Did she really not know her brother that well? Could he be responsible for such a tragedy?

'And you blame him?'

'Who else am I supposed to blame? He always resented that I had money and he had none. He was jealous of my success at sport and my academic results. And he hated the fact the most beautiful girl at school wasn't interested in him, despite his efforts. So, the moment my back was turned and I was away, he went after her.'

'You can't know that, surely? Just because they happened to be in the same car together.'

'Oh, I know it.' His lips turned into a thin line. 'Because there's more—the autopsy discovered she was pregnant.' He tilted his head and directed eyes of bleak, black ice at her. 'The baby wasn't mine.'

'You're sure?'

'How could it be, when we'd never had sex? We were waiting for the engagement, which was half the reason I couldn't wait to get back.'

'And you think it was Jake's child?'

'She was six weeks' pregnant. I'd been gone three months. She was with him when she died. You work it out.'

She swallowed. The horror of the past was so vast, ugly and heinous right here in this room, wound tight inside this man, that she wanted to flee from it and from the island for ever. Because now that horror belonged to her too, courtesy of her brother's involvement, courtesy of Daniel's callous seduction of her. And still she couldn't believe it could be true; she wished she could find the words to console Daniel for his loss, wished she could find the words to defend her brother before she could talk to him and determine the truth herself.

But another thought intruded, another gut-churning question demanding to be answered: 'Why am I here, then, organising a wedding that you never had any intention of holding? Were you just trying to pretend to Monica that you actually cared about her happiness? Or did you somehow think, in your twisted mind, that sleeping with me was how you intended getting even with my brother?'

He flinched and growled out his response. 'Does it actually matter?'

She decided it didn't. But she'd be damned if she'd give him the satisfaction of running away. 'I hate you for what you've done to your sister. I hate you for the way you've treated Jake. Most of all I hate you for what you've done to me.

'But, mark my words, this wedding is going to happen,' she said with a resolve tapped from a well she didn't know she possessed. 'Something awful happened all those years ago, yes, but I don't believe that Jake could have done what you say he did—and I'm going to prove it. And then that wedding is going to go ahead right here, right under your nose. And you're going to suck it up!'

She wasn't leaving. Somehow as Daniel stared blindly out at the pristine view of sea and sky, that one piece of information filtered through the morass of his mind and settled like a feather in the foreground. In a day when everything that could possibly have gone wrong had gone wrong, at least he'd salvaged that.

She wasn't leaving.

He wasn't even sure why it was so important. She'd been going to leave some time anyway; it had been inevitable from day one. But it was strange how the concept of her departure had gone from something he'd treated as a cold inevitability to something he'd been happy to avoid every time Fletcher had turned down the latest offer. Because the sex was so good?

Must be.

Although it might take some doing, getting her back in his bed after today. Damn. What a waste.

He turned and sighed. Did she really believe this wedding could go ahead after what he'd told her about her brother? She was either blindly loyal or blindly stupid, yet in a way he could almost admire her devotion to her brother. Wasn't it how he felt about Monica? He'd do anything for her.

Except stand by when she married Jake Fletcher.

The call came when he was back in his room, and because it came from Jo he picked up. If something was happening in Hawaii, he needed to know. 'What's up?'

'I doubled the offer. Thought you should know.'

'What the hell for? I told you to wait.'

'Because you've got to get rid of him! He's scum, Dan, you know that. You don't want him marrying your sister. Isn't it bad enough that right this minute he's probably screwing her?'

'Shut up, Jo!' He didn't need to hear the words. He didn't need those pictures in his head.

'She'll be banged up, just like that other one, if you don't get rid of him. I'm just trying to do my job.'

Are you? Daniel wondered, one hand massaging his pounding temple. If he didn't know better, he'd think Jo was more interested in railroading this wedding than he was, when it was he who had the issue with Fletcher.

Then again, it was probably just Jo's overactive loyalty kicking in again. After all, he'd seen the damage Fletcher had inflicted upon him before. No doubt he didn't want to have to scrape him off the floor again.

'Okay, Jo. The four million is offered now. Let it go at that. But don't make any more offers without my okay. Got that?'

'What happened?' Sophie cried when her brother picked up the phone, 'He thinks you killed his fiancée; he thinks you got her pregnant. What happened that day?'

'Sophie, hold on. I have to change phones.' She heard the rush of movement, the echo of a second connection before the first clicked off, and the sound of a door being shut before her brother picked up again, his voice low. 'Sophie's dozing. I don't want her to hear.'

'Maybe you should tell her. Maybe you should tell all of us. I told Daniel I didn't believe him, but it's too awful. I can't fight this battle for you, Jake. I thought I could smooth the waters between you, but he hates you, and the way he tells it I can't see a way through. Please tell me it's all a lie.'

'Sophie, I'm sorry. I should have told you. Believe me, I wanted to, but how can I when I don't know the whole picture myself?'

'What do you mean?'

'I should have said something, but it's hard for me. Even now…' Down the line she heard the rasp of his breath, as though it physically pained him to have to remember. 'I survived the accident but I was in a coma for two months. I still get flashbacks and nightmares, but I still can't remember clearly what happened just before the crash.'

'You can't? But you have to, Jake. It's the only way.'

'Listen, Sophie, the doctors think my memories of those minutes may never be recovered. All I have is fragments and impressions, but they may mean nothing, the doctors think, or they may be scenarios I've come up with since to explain in my mind what happened.'

She swallowed and wiped away moisture she hadn't realised she'd shed from her cheek. 'What do you think happened?'

There was a long sigh at the end of the line and a sound like he had slid down the wall to the floor. 'I have this impression—this feeling—that Emma came to me for help that night. We weren't really good friends but we'd talked sometimes at school—when Caruana wasn't around, that was. I'd heard they were getting married and I didn't see her all summer. Until that night.'

Sophie heard his ragged breaths as he paused, willing him silently to continue so that she could make sense of the horror of that night, make sense of everything that had happened since.

'It was raining heavily, and I have this impression of her standing on the doorstep, soaked through, her eyes swollen with tears. I can't remember the words, but it was all mixed up with the baby and Jo and Daniel coming home. She was scared, desperate to get away. *But I can't remember why!*'

'It's okay, Jake,' she said, wishing he wasn't locked alone in a bathroom half a world away, wishing she could be there to hold him. 'Take your time.'

'I'm okay.' He sighed. 'And then I have this picture, like a photo in my mind, of Emma behind the steering wheel, with me beside her yelling at her to stop. But she didn't stop. We were both thrown from the car. The police didn't believe I wasn't driving.'

'And the baby? Was it yours?'

'I swear to God I never slept with her, Sophie. I didn't see her all summer before that night.'

She let go a breath that carried much more than just air. 'But everyone assumed you were.'

'I didn't wake up for two months, and by that time everyone believed it. Emma was dead and buried and people were starting to come to terms with it. What point would there have been in digging it all up again?'

'So you let them go on thinking it?'

'It never mattered, Sophie, because I could live with myself. I knew I hadn't done the wrong thing and that was good enough. But it mattered when I fell in love with Monica and found out who her brother was. I tried to talk to him; I knew we had to sort it out some time. But he wouldn't return my calls. And what could I really tell him that he'd believe anyway?'

'I understand.'

He sighed. 'I'm sorry. I know it was asking too much of you, but I was really hoping that if I disappeared with Monica he might get used to the idea. I thought he'd have to. I see now I was running away when I should have stayed and dealt with it myself. I'm sorry to drop you in it like that, Soph. It must have been a nightmare for you, putting up with him all this time.'

'It had its moments,' she said quietly. 'But I'm glad you told me at last. You know you have to tell Daniel. He has to know the truth.'

'Even though I don't know it all? Why would he ever believe it wasn't my baby?'

'You have to try.'

'Yeah, I guess you're right. Maybe we'll come back early. At least then it might put an end to these offers I've been getting.'

Sophie's ears pricked up. 'You've had more?'

'It's up to one and half million. Nice work, if you can get it.'

Fury welled up inside her. What would it take to make Daniel believe it? 'I told him, Jake. I told him you weren't interested.'

'It's okay. It means I need to come back, in that case, so I can tell him where to shove his money myself. There's no way we're going to sort this out with text messages.'

She heard the muffled sound of a woman's voice and a knocking. 'Soph, I've got to go. Talk to you tomorrow.'

'I'm moving to one of the cabins,' she said matter-of-factly over an untouched plate of mushroom risotto. She'd only come to the dinner table to tell him what she was intending to do, not to eat. 'I'll continue my work from there, which makes sense, given we'll be having the reception at the long-house pavilion.'

Across the table from her, he put down his fork. 'You're still persisting with this farce of a wedding, then?'

'I spoke to Jake. He's coming back to talk to you. He's got things you need to know—need to hear. Like the fact Emma wasn't carrying his child.'

Daniel leaned back in his chair, arms sprawled lazily over the sides, but she knew there was nothing lazy about him, nothing relaxed. It hurt her to realise how much she missed those arms around her already. 'You need to talk to Jake about that. He can't remember the details, but—'

'How convenient.'

'Talk to him, Daniel, and hear it for yourself. You made your mind up all those years ago when my brother was lying in a coma and couldn't defend himself. Was that fair?'

'It was obvious!'

'Was it? Or was it easy when you needed someone to blame? Why not pick on the man who wasn't even conscious? That's what I call convenient.' She stood. 'Oh, and as for your latest offer, do I need to tell you where my brother suggested you shove your one and half million?'

He steepled his fingers. 'One and a half million?'

'That's the figure Jake quoted.'

He leaned forward, an uncomfortable sensation crawling its way down his back. 'Sophie, let me ask you a question. How is your business doing? I mean, cash wise. Everything all right?'

She shrugged, thrown off-balance, eyebrows pulled into a frown. 'Fine. We had such a great year last year, we're look-ing to either expand our operation, or invest in case things get tight.'

'I see.' Whatever had been crawling over his back found its way to his stomach and turned solid. He picked up his napkin from his lap and placed it on the table. Suddenly he wasn't hungry any more. 'And Sophie?'

'Yes?'

'I've got something to chase up now, and I have to be in Townsville tomorrow, but I'd like to talk to you when I get back. You meant that about staying in one of the cabins?'

She nodded uncertainly.

'Then I'll see you when I get back. All right?'

She nodded and he gave a thin smile, 'I'm glad you're not leaving.'

She walked blindly back to pack her things, feeling even more confused. The monster had retreated, a hint of the Daniel she loved back again.

She stopped dead.

Oh God.

Where the hell had that come from? No way could she love him. No way. Not after all the things he'd done and said, and after the way he'd done everything in his power to break up Jake and Monica. No way could anyone love a monster like that.

Even if she did love his body and loved the way he made her feel when he made love to her. *Had sex,* she corrected.

Although it had felt like more.

All her own misguided emotions, she knew. Because Daniel Caruana was still in love with a girl who'd died years ago. A girl he'd put up on some kind of pedestal of perfection. A girl he was still fighting for.

He wasn't capable of loving anyone else.

And yet, if she wasn't in love with him, why had she found it so impossible to leave? Why had she been so secretly thrilled when he'd told her he was glad she was staying? If she'd really been serious about leaving him, wouldn't she have moved back to Brisbane, or even to somewhere in Cairns where she'd be close enough to arrange things?

But no. She'd decided to stay on the island. Why?

Because she couldn't bear the thought of being too far away from him.

Even though he could never love her. Even though anything between then was doomed from the start on so many levels.

She'd known it was a kind of madness that first night they'd made love. She'd known it and still she'd persisted, refusing to pay heed to logic. And now she had the proof of her madness: she loved him. She blundered into the room she used as an office and dropped into a chair, her face in her hands.

What a mess.

Sophie didn't see him again that night and he was gone early in the morning, the sound of the chopper stirring her from a restless night's slumber in the guest room. The picture of Emma smiled out at her from the bureau and Sophie had found herself staring back at her long into the night.

How must it have felt to be loved by Daniel? And how special must Emma have been to earn that love? And why did she hurt so much because that would never be her?

With sleep-deprived eyes and a head thick with too many pointless ramblings, she packed up the last of her things onto a golf buggy and waved goodbye to Millie, who was waiting with a basket of lunch and other treats to stock her cabin. 'I'm so sorry things haven't worked out for you here, lovey. I've so enjoyed having another woman for company.'

'Me too,' she said, giving the older woman a squeeze. 'But I'll come and visit.'

Millie sniffed. 'Make sure you do.'

The cabin was dark and cool inside; whoever had prepared it for her arrival had thoughtfully turned on the air conditioner. Without turning on the light, she sank gratefully to the bed and closed her eyes.

What the hell was she supposed to do? Daniel was coming to talk tonight—about what? Hopefully tomorrow Jake and Monica might be back. She'd sent Jake an email so he'd know to call her on her mobile, although she hadn't bothered to fill him in on why. But she had to admit, it would be easier with Monica and Jake here if she wasn't living in Daniel's house and sleeping in his bed. Things were bound to be complicated and ugly enough without that, if they were to find a way through the next few weeks.

Was she even kidding herself to think there *was* a way through?

She forced herself from the bed. She had no choice but to think that way, which meant she better get herself up and organised.

The meeting had gone better than expected. The arguments the lawyers had voiced that had held things up the other day seemed to dissolve into nothingness, compared to the massive stumbling block they had been. Thank God. At least something was going right.

He loosened his tie, looking out of the windscreen for the familiar landmarks that would mean he was getting close. He wasn't going back to the office. They didn't expect him, and he had more important things on his mind—like working out how wrong he'd been.

Why had Jo betrayed him that way? He didn't know; it wasn't as if he didn't pay him enough as it was. But maybe he should have seen the writing on the wall when he'd insisted

Daniel pay more to get rid of Jake. The tone of his voice had had greed written all over it. Was that when he'd hatched his plan to steal half the funds for himself?

But it wasn't only the money. It was his lies that Sophie's business needed a cash injection, implying from the start she was involved with the scam. So Daniel had a reason to hate Fletcher. Why had *Jo* been so ready to crucify Sophie into the deal? What was in it for him?

Damn the man. And so much for his pleas to forgive him. Forgive him, nothing; loyalty only went so far. And Jo had shown him he had none at all.

He should have got rid of him years ago.

They rounded a point and the familiar shape of Kallista appeared before them, lush and beautiful, like the woman he couldn't wait to see. He wasn't entirely sure what he was going to say to her, but he was hoping that by the time he got there something would have occurred to him that would make sense to them both.

He was so glad she hadn't left. He'd spoken the truth when he'd said that. The idea of her leaving was anathema to him. And it wasn't because he wanted to get even with her brother—not any more.

Because Sophie belonged there. With him. He just had to make her see it.

After all that had happened, the call had still taken her by surprise. The tears that had followed were almost impossible to staunch, the knowledge that it had all been for nothing almost too much to bear. Sophie held the cool facecloth to her swollen eyes, glad at least she hadn't got far with her unpacking. It would save time.

She took a deep breath and pushed herself away from the bathroom cabinet on legs finally strong enough to support her, blinking away the last of the moisture that blurred her vision, trying to work out what to do next. A warm draught stirred her skirt and she looked around, surprised to find the screen door open. Strange; she was sure she'd shut it. But maybe someone had dropped by with the milk she'd requested and forgotten to shut it. Not that she'd need any supplies now.

She reached for the handle and caught a whiff of stale sweat and nicotine. Fear speared down her spine, clearing her vision quicker than anything, but not fast enough to dodge the hand that snaked out from behind the curtains and grabbed her wrist.

CHAPTER TWELVE

SHE screamed, sensing it was Jo before the glint of gold at his wrist and fingers confirmed it, even before a thick gravel voice told her to shut up. He shoved her back and let go and she stumbled against the coffee table, before collapsing against a bucket chair as the big man slid closed the doors and locked them, pulling the curtains shut so nobody could see inside. Fear seized her at the calm and purposeful way he went about his business, as if he had all the time in the world, almost as if it was a well-rehearsed drill. She shivered. Without taking her eyes from him, she pushed herself out of the chair, putting as many pieces of furniture between them as possible, 'What are you doing here?'

He sneered, his eyes bloodshot and evil as he turned. 'You little bitch. You cost me my job.'

'How?'

He moved towards her and she moved back slowly until she hit up against the kitchenette bench. 'What did you tell Daniel?'

'What are you talking about? I don't know. Nothing that concerns you.'

He moved closer, his eyes wild, and she edged sideways. The last thing she needed was to be stuck in a corner. 'You told him how much I offered your stupid brother.'

'I only told him what Jake told me! Why is that such a problem?'

'You think I was going to waste all Caruana's money on that scum?'

The penny dropped. 'You were planning on stealing it! You were going to take your cut, and you're mad at me because you got your filthy, fat fingers caught in the till. Don't try to pin it on me.'

He growled. 'I would have got away with it, too, if you hadn't shot your mouth off. You owe me!'

She rubbed the wrist that still stung from his grip, trying to work out distance and angles, knowing she had to keep him talking if she was to have any hope of getting out of here before...

Oh no. She wasn't going there.

He took a step closer and she knew she'd have to move soon. She wondered how long the bathroom door would last if she locked herself in, wondered if she'd be courting disaster to search for a decent knife in the kitchen drawer before she bolted. 'You should have got away, little lady, while you could. When Millie finally told me you were down here in the cabins, it was almost too good to be true. She didn't want to tell me, either. Dunno why.'

Fear snaked down her spine. 'What did you do to her?'

'She'll live,' he said with a leery grin as he rubbed his groin. 'And don't worry. I saved the best for you.'

She dragged in air, trying not to retch, looking for reason or an argument that might sway him. 'Daniel's going to be here any minute. We've got a meeting.'

He laughed. 'Nice try. He's in Townsville all day. Besides, he's obviously finished with you if you're down here by yourself. Did he decide he'd had enough and threw you out like yesterday's leftovers?'

Her hands guided her as she edged along the bench top, fingers chancing upon something cane—the basket Millie had given her. 'You don't know anything.'

'I know he only wanted you here because Fletcher was screwing his sister. An eye for an eye, a root for a root.'

His words hit some place she didn't want to go, and she shoved them aside before they could do any damage. 'You're disgusting!'

'And you're a slut, but I'm not choosy.' And then he smiled. 'Didn't he tell you he was the one who booked the Tropical Palms? Paid them a million in cold, hard cash to get you here?'

'You're lying.'

'Ask him yourself, at this *meeting*.' He laughed at his own joke and took another step closer but there was still a small dining setting between them and Sophie knew it was now or never. She grabbed the handle of the basket with one hand and flung her arm in an arc, letting the basket fly directly at him while she ran around the other way.

She saw a big, beefy arm go up to ward it off, and it bounced away, but not before raining down its contents on him. 'Bitch!'

But she was already at the door, her fingers working at the lock, sliding the glass doors open. He slammed into her from behind and she crashed against the glass with a scream, her fingers losing the handle, clutching at the curtains, pulling them from their tracks with a crash as he dragged her back. 'You'll pay for that!'

'Let me go!' She struggled against his more powerful frame, caught a handful of his face and raked her nails down, drawing blood. The back of his hand smashed across her cheek, cracking her head back and momentarily stunning her.

He bundled her in his arms and carried her to the bedroom, throwing her sprawling on the bed. She landed with a whump.

rolling over, scooting up to the headboard as far as she could and folding herself into a ball, her hand rubbing her aching jaw. 'Jake said you were a bully.'

He snorted as he unhitched his belt, and she pulled her feet in tighter. 'Did he, now? What the hell would he know? He was unconscious for months. Nobody knows nothin'.'

Fear sliced through her like the blow from a scythe, fear and a strange kind of horrific understanding. 'What are you talking about?'

'Shut up.' He moved around the bed and she scooted to the other side.

'I'll scream.'

'Scream all you like, honey. Caruana's other bitch did too, and it only made it all the better for me. Almost as satisfying as when your brother got lumbered with the blame.'

Realisation hit her with lightning-bolt force. 'It was your baby! She went to my brother's that night because she was pregnant with your baby and she didn't know what to do.' And, like a second lightning-hit, a more sickening truth hit home. 'You raped her. The minute Daniel's back was turned, you raped her, and all the years you let my brother take the blame.'

'Do you ever shut up? C'mere bitch.' He leaned over and lunged with surprising speed for such a big man. She screamed as his big fist snared an ankle, screamed louder as he tugged her back down the bed until she was flat on her back.

'Let me show you what a real man can do.'

Panic made her lash out with her other foot. She felt a crack as she made contact with something that felt like a brick, a sudden rush of pain spearing up her leg so intense that she almost thought the yowl she heard had come from her, until blood spurted from his nose. 'Bitch!' he cried, before reaching for her again.

'Get off her, you bastard!'

And then the bed beside her seemed to explode with flailing limbs and flying fists and she rolled away, falling to the floor, wondering if she were caught in some cruel dream. Because Daniel wasn't due back for hours, yet somehow he was here.

Someone rushed to her aid, pulling her away from the mess of tangled, writhing bodies while others swarmed over the bed, finishing the job of subduing Jo that Daniel had started until he was led away, bleeding and unrepentant.

Daniel rushed to her side and held her close, making out that she was something precious. Like she meant something. She wanted to be grateful to him. She wanted to with all her heart.

Except it was too late.

Cairns Base Hospital was cool and clinical and with just the right amount of detachment Sophie needed. She breathed in the sterile atmosphere, steeling herself, knowing she'd need it for the next visitor. Especially when her heart felt like a bleeding mess.

If only her doctor had been by to discharge her already, she would have been gone before the nurse called to ask if she was up to having a visitor.

There was a knock at the door as she stuffed things into her bag and she turned to see him already filling the space. Damn. She turned away almost as quickly.

Damn. Damn. Damn. Why did he always have to look so good no matter what he was wearing? He looked like he'd just walked out of an article on 'Saturday-unshaven, designer-casual' from the pages of *GQ* magazine: the alpha-male edition.

'You're leaving?'

'The doctor's on his way. I'm expecting to be discharged. All observations in the range of normal, apparently. No residual trace of concussion.'

'I can take you home.'

She sighed, her hands stilling over the bag. Home. Now there was a concept. 'I've organised transport, thanks.'

'Sophie.' And when she turned back it was to find him right there, so close to her that she flinched. The terror of yesterday's events was much too recent, the fear that she might throw herself into his arms much too real. 'I'm sorry,' he said, dropping his lifted hand as he gave her space. 'But your cheek...'

'The swelling will fade, along with the bruises.' Besides, it was the bruises he couldn't see that hurt more. 'I guess it could have been worse.'

'I'm sorry.'

'What are you sorry for?' She managed a tremulous laugh as she shifted away. 'You're the one who saved me, aren't you?'

'You were doing a pretty good job of saving yourself when I saw you. Did they tell you you'd broken Jo's nose with your foot? Remind me never to get in your way in bed.'

She smiled a wan smile of resignation. 'I think we both know there's not much chance of that happening.'

A pause followed her words; she wasn't sure what she was expecting to come, and she wasn't sure whether she was more relieved or surprised when he did speak. 'It's my fault. I should have suspected how dangerous Jo was when we discovered he was stealing. I should have known he'd come after you.'

So he wasn't mourning her loss from his bed? That was good, wasn't it? Sophie's teeth found her lip, bit down on the pain of swollen tissue and suddenly realised the old habit was something she hadn't done for what seemed like ages.

She nodded numbly, wondering more about the lip than anything else. Maybe because that seemed easier to deal with.

'I want to explain about Jo.'

'There's no need.'

'Believe me, there's every need. Will you hear me?'

She sat down on the bed. What choice did she have? Until the doctor came, it wasn't as though she was going anywhere. And it wasn't as though it was going to change anything. 'Okay, I'm listening.'

He took a deep breath and blew it out in a rush. 'After Emma's death I got home from Italy as soon as I could. I couldn't believe it. I blamed myself for not insisting she come with us, like we'd originally wanted. I was a mess. I wanted to break something—someone—Jake. He was lying critically injured in a coma and I wanted to go finish the job.'

Sophie lowered her lashes, aching inside for her brother, lying in hospital so close to death, and for the tortured man who'd just lost his fiancée.

'Jo stopped me. At least, I thought he stopped me. I credited him with saving me in those dark days, of saving me from myself. When we met a few years later, after he'd been in the army and was looking for a job, I wanted to repay him. My business was just taking off. I gave him work, thinking I was repaying his friendship. His *loyalty*.'

He ground the word out between his teeth, his voice growing bitter. 'But all the time he was living a lie. I thought it bad enough when I discovered he was planning on pocketing half the pay-off money, but he'd already betrayed me in the worst possible way and I'd been too blind to see any of it. He told me that Jake had taken advantage of Emma while I was away and that he was probably taking her off for a back-street abortion to hide the evidence when they crashed. He fed me all this at the same time he was holding me back from wanting to tear your brother limb from limb.

'And to think I'd thanked him all these years for holding me back…' He shook his head. 'But then I learned of Monica's plans to marry Jake, and what had happened before all came rushing back. It wasn't just Jo feeding my hatred—I know I had more than plenty to go round myself—but it was almost as if Jo wanted your brother gone more. He told me your business was in trouble and needed cash. It all fitted with the idea your brother was in it for the money, and that you were too.'

He looked at her, his eyes dark with regret, underlined with shadows she hadn't noticed before. 'I was wrong, Sophie. So wrong.' He looked broken, shattered, and it was all she could do not to go to him, put her arms around him and tell him it didn't matter.

But it did matter. So many people's lives had been ruined back then; the shock waves continued to wreak devastation, even now, so she stayed where she was.

'It was Jo who got Emma pregnant,' she whispered. 'Not Jake. He… He raped her.'

And he closed his eyes, his chest expanding on a breath. 'I know. Which is why he didn't want Jake around.'

'But Jake couldn't remember.'

'Jo didn't know what he knew. He couldn't take the risk of the marriage going ahead and the truth coming out. He didn't want your brother anywhere near me. He was going to take the money and run. And he would have, if you hadn't tipped me off with numbers that didn't make sense. I have a lot to thank you for, Sophie. Even more to apologise for.'

It was something, at least.

'Jake seems to think Emma had come to him out of desperation. But I keep wondering why she didn't go straight to the police.'

'I don't know. Except her parents were very strict. Maybe she thought they wouldn't believe her. After all, he was supposed to be my friend. I'd asked him to look after her while I was away…'

She squeezed her eyes shut, wishing she could turn off his pain when she had so much of her own to bear. Because, if he'd blamed himself for her death before, now he had more reason than ever. Damn. She would not feel sorry for him! Not when he was hardly the victim in all this. She swallowed back on a sob.

'It was you who gazumped us at the Tropical Palms, wasn't it? So you could get me to the island. Have us all thinking the wedding was going ahead. All while you hatched your plan to pay off Jake in the background.'

His hands curled into fists at his sides. Then he nodded, his eyes the bleakest black.

'You made the phone call before the helicopter like I said, didn't you? And then you made out you'd been calling up the island, to let them know we were coming. You lied to me.'

'By omission—I tried to justify it to myself. But, yes, you're right. I lied to you.'

'And you were going to keep me, weren't you, as long as Jake had Monica? "An eye for an eye, a root for a root". That's how Jo put it. That's why you slept with me, wasn't it, Daniel? To get even at the basest level with someone you decided long ago you'd hate for ever.'

'Those were not my words!'

'But that was your intent! I was to be your prisoner in paradise, and you thought you might as well take advantage while I was here.'

'Sophie, it wasn't always like that, you have to believe me. Yes, I thought there was justice in having you with me while he had Monica. And, yes, to make that happen I made sure the Tropical Palms got an offer it couldn't refuse. I know that nobody can understand, but I had to do whatever I could to ensure I had complete control over this wedding. It was the only way. Only then, when you got here, I found more reason than ever for you to stay.'

'Because you had sex on tap?'

He blinked slowly and when he opened his eyes their deep sincerity almost made her look away. 'I told you you were the best, and it's true.'

She heard the rattle of a tea trolley and looked hopefully towards the door. Any interruption would be preferable right now to hearing these pointless words. She was good at sex, and he was in love with a dead woman.

It was never going to be a fair contest.

She stood up and started fussing with the recalcitrant zip on her bag, realised her toiletries were still in the bathroom and got frustrated with the slow progress. Where the hell was that doctor, anyway? Not that any doctor could help her now, because no doctor could help what was hurting inside her.

She took a calming breath. 'Look, Daniel, thanks for being there yesterday. Thanks for stopping by and explaining all that. Please give my regards to Millie. Please let her know I was relieved to hear she hadn't been hurt.'

He frowned. 'Where are you going?'

'Back to Brisbane. I have a flight booked. Meg's going to meet me at the airport.' She injected a dose of enthusiasm she didn't feel into her voice. 'I can't wait to catch up with all the news.'

'Sophie, I want you to come home.'

'I am going home, Daniel. My home.'

'But the wedding? What about the wedding?'

'Didn't you hear the news? I'm not needed here any more.'

He looked at her, dumbfounded. 'What are you talking about?'

'Why so shocked, Daniel? I thought you'd be pleased. It's what you wanted, after all: the wedding's off.'

His mind and senses reeled. He'd assumed he'd pick her up from the hospital and take her back to the island where he could soothe away her bruises, gentle her pain. He'd thought if he explained everything she might eventually understand, might forgive him.

She had to forgive him.

And he'd thought there was time, because there was a wedding to plan and she'd never walk away from that.

But if there was no wedding...

'What happened?'

She put a hand to her hip and tilted her head with the falsest smile she could muster. 'You know, it was the strangest thing. Apparently Monica overheard Jake talking to me on the phone and insisted he tell her what all the secrecy was about. When he told her that you were offering him money to break off the engagement, and had been responsible for dispensing with her last few boyfriends, she refused to believe you were capable of such a thing. You. The perfect brother.' She laughed a little. 'Imagine that.'

His hands fisted in his hair. What the hell had he done?

'So you'll no doubt be delighted to hear that they had a huge argument and it all got too hard—she couldn't marry anyone who didn't think the sun shone out of her brother, like she did, and he couldn't marry anyone who didn't believe him.'

She sucked in air.

'So you finally got what you wanted. I hope you're satisfied.'

She turned back toward her bags and made another effort at zipping up the zip, trying to make this chapter in her life final, all her efforts concentrated on the task in hand.

'Sophie—'

She spun back round. 'You're still here?'

'I'll speak to them. I'll fix it.'

'Good luck. It didn't sound too fixable when I heard the news.'

'You can't go. I said you were the best, Sophie. I meant it.'

Her sore lip suffered another ill-timed bite. 'You played me for a fool—making love to me and flattering me like you actually cared. When all the time you just wanted to keep me held hostage in paradise, so I'd fall for your charms and believe you took this wedding seriously. Why the hell shouldn't I go?'

'Because I love you.'

He wasn't sure who was the most shocked. She stood stock-still, her face drained of colour on one side, the garish blue bruises on the other standing out all the more.

While he reeled inside from the thunderclap discovery. *He loved her.* That was why he'd rejoiced when he'd discovered she wasn't after his money. That was why he'd rejoiced every time Jake had turned his offers down, and why he didn't rejoice when he'd heard the news the wedding was off. And that was why he'd never wanted to let her go.

'I didn't realise it myself. I didn't know until now. But why else would I spend hours in meetings thinking about you rather than what's on the agenda? Why would I rush home every day? Because I couldn't get you out of my head. I wanted to be with you, Sophie, because I love you.'

'No. You're in love with Emma. Always have been. Always will be.'

'I *loved* Emma. I know she'll always be special in my heart. But you're the one I love.'

She dipped her head in her hand and breathed deep. 'There are too many people hurting, Daniel. So much damage done. How can you expect me to embrace your love? How can you expect me to return it? Even… Even if I wanted to.'

She looked up to see hope in his eyes for the first time in days. 'Daniel, you have to let me walk away. You have to give me time.'

The door burst open, the doctor bustling in and swiping up the charts at the end of her bed near her packed bag. 'Someone anxious to go home, then?' He looked up at her, switched his glance to Daniel and turned his gaze down to the chart. 'Hope I didn't just interrupt something important.'

She gave a wan smile and shook her head. 'Not at all. Mr Caruana was just leaving.'

EPILOGUE

IT WAS the kind of day you wished you could bottle—not a cloud in the azure sky, the cerulean sea dotted with pleasure craft and a tempering sea breeze to keep the temperature from climbing too high.

It would have been perfect if her heart hadn't been permanently lodged in her mouth since she'd arrived.

Kallista had turned on its best and Meg had done a brilliant job bringing it all together while Sophie had held the fort in Brisbane these past couple of weeks. A white pavilion had been installed on a grassy patch near the shore and festooned with colourful bougainvillea over fluttering white chiffon, the perfect, romantic setting for the perfect wedding.

And it was. She'd slipped in, arriving on the very last launch when everyone was busy with last-minute details. She'd planned it that way. Even a couple of weeks away hadn't been enough to make her forget or stop her longing. But it seemed it had been long enough for Daniel. He hadn't contacted her in all that time. Clearly his profession of love hadn't meant a thing. She'd done the right thing by walking away.

What she hadn't planned was how highly strung she felt. She almost cried when she saw Jake up front with the celebrant, pulling at his collar, looking nervous and excited, like every proper groom should. She did cry when she saw

Monica, the most beautiful bride she'd ever seen, her smile joyous, her face radiant, as she walked down the aisle on the arm of her proud and equally beautiful brother to the man she loved.

The tears continued when she saw the men shake hands as one man handed the bride over to the other, and then when bride and groom exchanged vows and kissed she cried again.

She dabbed at her eyes as the congregation cheered the newly married couple and filtered behind them along the shore. At this rate she'd be a complete puddle by the time they made it to the speeches.

'It's good to see you again.'

She blinked and he was there, gloriously there before her, all magnificent male, dressed in a suit fit for a god. Appropriate, really, given what lay beneath. 'How have you been?'

Lonely.

'Busy. How about you?'

'The same.' He was looking at her with those hungry eyes, warm and sensual, his mouth turned into the beginnings of a smile although there were lines of strain there too. 'You look beautiful.'

She smiled. She had red eyes and a heavy heart, but she'd take the words in the spirit they were given.

'Sit with me at the reception,' he said. 'I got Meg to save you a seat.'

'Of course.' Sitting with him meant nothing. As sister of the groom, she'd expected not to be able to fade entirely into the woodwork. She could last a few hours in his company; she'd almost convinced herself.

They got corralled into wedding photos of family and friends and it seemed like ages before the party moved to the long-house pavilion. In pride of place was the cake Millie had made for them spilling with orchids in soft pinks and whites. 'It's beautiful, Millie,' she told the woman as they embraced. 'You've done a wonderful job.'

Millie wiped a tear from her own eye. 'We've missed you, Sophie. Him more than anyone. He's been like a bear with a sore head. Worse these last few days, waiting for you to turn up. You'd think he was the one getting married. Will you be staying a while?'

She smiled, not sure how she should feel about Millie's revelations. Excited? Hopeful? Or had he merely been dreading her presence. 'Just overnight. I have to be back in Brisbane.'

The older woman's face dropped momentarily. Then she sighed and nodded. 'I understand.'

Did she? Sophie wasn't sure she understood herself.

Finally everyone filed in and took their seats for the reception. Daniel held out her chair for her. He leaned down as she lowered herself, his warm breath like a living thing stroking her ear. 'I've missed you, Sophie.' And she felt his words all the way to her toes. 'I've missed you bad.'

'You didn't call.' She tried to keep the hurt from her voice, and failed miserably.

'I thought you needed space.'

'Oh.' What did that mean? But she nodded and picked up her wine, taking a sip, her eyes on the bride and groom. They were so happy and so much in love it almost hurt to look at them. 'How did you do it?' she asked. 'How did you get them back together again?'

He followed her gaze. 'I had a lot of bridges to mend before that happened. Luckily you'd shown me how.'

'I did? How?'

He looked around at the appetiser that had just been placed in front of them. 'Are you hungry?'

She shook her head. She knew what was on the menu; she'd put the courses together that week she'd spent on the island. She knew it would be fabulous without tasting a thing. Besides, there was something she needed more than food right now.

He took her hand and they headed for the beach, where the sun was just beginning to set, lighting the warm, tropical world with its soft glow.

'I spent too long in a world of hatred,' he said as they kicked off their shoes and set off along the sand. 'It consumed me. Powered me. Drove me to think I was doing right, when I was doing wrong. I hurt Monica. I thought I was protecting her and I hurt her.'

He stopped and looked at the sun and she saw the glint of moisture in the corner of his eyes. 'You taught me that the bonds of love were stronger than the chains of hate. You taught me that love wasn't about control. Love was being able to let something go, and trust you would keep it for ever.'

He looked down at her, taking her chin so softly in his fingers that her skin tingled at the contact. 'You taught me that, Sophie.

'And, even though I didn't want to let you walk away from me that day in the hospital, even though I knew it would break me and that however long it took would be hell, I knew in my heart that if I was ever to truly have you I would have to let you go and hope above hope that you would return to me.' He rested his forehead against hers and she put a hand to his cheek, relishing the touch of the face she had dreamed about every night since she'd left.

'Oh, Daniel.'

'So now... So now I need to know. Is there any chance for us, do you think? Is there any chance—after all the wrongs I've committed, after the nightmare I've put everyone through— that you might return to me and return my love?'

Her heart was singing so loud it was a wonder he couldn't hear its song of joy himself. 'I thought…I feared…'

'You thought what?'

'That you'd changed your mind. Realised that you'd made a mistake. I don't know. I just worried, when I hadn't heard from you, that I'd imagined you ever telling me.'

He put his arms around her. 'Not a chance. I haven't thought of anything else these last few weeks but how much I do love you. Marry me, Sophie. Marry me and make me the happiest man on earth.'

And suddenly there were more tears to contend with. Tears of joy, tears of relief, tears that welled up from a heart that swelled with love for him and washed away all the pain. 'Daniel, I love you so much!'

He pulled her, spinning, into his embrace and kissed her until she was dazed and drugged with the taste of him. Then he stopped spinning and dropped her feet to the sand. 'So you'll marry me?'

She smiled up at him, loving him, knowing she would love him for ever, knowing this tiny thing was not too much to ask. She pulled his head down and whispered in his ear and he smiled before pulling her back into another kiss.

It was late by the time they made it back to the reception; the cake had already been cut. They hung around the back of the pavilion so as not to interrupt, but Millie saw them entering, Sophie's hand encased in Daniel's, the sprig of bougainvillea he'd picked and woven into her hair, and she beamed and skirted around the tables towards them.

'It's the most magical wedding,' she said, taking in their knotted hands and the flush to their skin, her generous eyes both curious and hopeful. 'Just magical.'

'It's what Sophie's business promises,' Daniel grinned. 'One Perfect Day, to make perfect memories to last a lifetime,' and Sophie laughed.

'You memorised our advertising slogan!'

'I thought I might need it one day, if I ever needed a wedding planner.' He curled his arm around her and pulled her in tight. 'Turns out I might.'

Millie clapped her hands over her mouth. 'Oh lord, is it true?'

Sophie hugged the older woman. 'Daniel's asked me to marry him.'

Millie whooped with joy. 'And you said yes?'

'I told him I'd like to, but I want to make sure someone else gives their blessing too.' And she looked around, to find Daniel already threading his way through the crowd until he found his target. She watched him slap her brother on the back, she watched her brother frown as Daniel leaned close and then she saw his look of surprise as he sought her out, his frown transformed into a broad smile the second he saw her face and realised it was what she wanted.

She squeezed the older woman's hand. 'I think you better not hang those cake pans up in a hurry, Millie.'

Millie whooped again and hurried off to share the good news, not that Sophie was alone for long. Daniel was back and he picked her up and spun her around in his arms until she was dizzy. 'Thank you,' he said. 'How did you know that would feel so good? I feel like it's over. It's finally over.'

She laughed as he lowered her feet to the floor, dizzy with happiness as she cupped his face with her hands and held his gaze. 'No, Daniel. The way I prefer to think of it, it's only just beginning.'

His smile widened, his eyes radiating love. 'I like the way you think, Sophie Turner.'

And she feigned disappointment. 'Oh, and there was me thinking you liked the way I did something else.'

He growled his appreciation. 'Oh yes. I like that too. I like that a lot.' He looked around, suddenly agitated, that look back in his eyes. 'Is it too early to leave the party, do you think? It is my sister and your brother getting married, after all.'

She smiled up at him on a shrug and tugged on his hand. 'Sometimes you just have to be prepared to let go. Are you prepared to let go, Daniel?'

'Every night of my life.'

And she smiled and pulled him into the night. 'Then I'll keep coming back. For ever.'

'For ever,' he echoed as he swept her up into his kiss.

WEDDING NIGHT
WITH A STRANGER

Anna
CLEARY

As a child, **Anna Cleary** loved reading so much that during the midnight hours she was forced to read with a flashlight under the bedcovers, to lull the suspicions of her sleep-obsessed parents. From an early age she dreamed of writing her own books. She saw herself in a stone cottage by the sea, wearing a velvet smoking jacket and sipping sherry, like Somerset Maugham.

In real life she became a schoolteacher and her greatest pleasure was teaching children to write beautiful stories.

A little while ago she and one of her friends made a pact to each write the first chapter of a romance novel in their holidays. From writing her very first line Anna was hooked, and she gave up teaching to become a full-time writer. She now lives in Queensland, with a deeply sensitive and intelligent cat. She prefers champagne to sherry and loves music, books, four-legged people, trees, movies and restaurants.

CHAPTER ONE

ARIADNE leaned over the balcony rail and contemplated plunging into the sea. Serve Sebastian Nikosto right if she was found floating face down. He'd have to look elsewhere for a bride. But though summer heat shimmered on the afternoon air, Sydney Harbour looked deep and chill, and she edged back. Knowing her parents had died in those restless waters didn't make them any more appealing. She could be eaten by sharks!

The view was spectacular, she supposed, even after the heart-stopping beauty of Naxos, but it all felt remote to her. Her joy in coming back to Australia had withered. She felt as alien as she ever had in any foreign place. Incredible to think she was born here.

She turned back into her hotel suite and sank onto the bed's luxurious coverlet, reaching listlessly for the tour brochure that had sucked her in. The Katherine Gorge. Uluru. How thrilled she'd been, how excited. The sad joke was there never had been any such pleasures intended for her. She was here to be chained to the bed of a stranger.

Unless she ran. The minuscule hope reared again in her heart. This Sebastian Nikosto had failed to meet her plane. Maybe he'd changed his mind?

The phone rang and she nearly jumped out of her skin. Thea, ringing to apologise for the trick and tell her to come home? Explain about the mistake with the hotel booking?

It was Reception. 'Good afternoon, Miss Giorgias, you have a visitor. A Mr Nikosto. Do you wish to meet him in the lobby, or shall I give him your room number?'

'*No.*' Her heart had jolted out of its niche but she gasped, 'I'll come down.'

With a shaking hand she replaced the phone. She would just have to tell Nikosto she was Ariadne Giorgias, an Australian citizen, not a commodity to be traded in some deal.

She struggled on with her jacket. Her face was paler than her blonde hair, her eyes the dark blue they looked when she was angry, or afraid.

Her legs felt numb. On the way down in the lift she tried to quell her nerves with some positive thinking. Courage was all that was needed. Australia was a civilised country. Women couldn't be forced here. In fact, she was curious to see what sort of man would sink so low as to barter for a wife in the twenty-first century. Was he so old he was locked in the traditions of the past? So repulsive as to have no other choice?

Anyway, she was brave. She would refuse. After all, she was the notorious bride who'd left the heir to one of the richest fortunes in Greece standing at the altar. That had taken courage, though her uncle and aunt's world had judged it differently.

Still, when she stepped out of the lift on the ground floor and saw the obese elderly man in baggy clothes standing near the reception desk, she felt the blood drain from her heart. How could they? How *could* they? Then, even as the opulent lobby with its long low lounges and glass-walled views of the city swayed sickeningly in her sight, the man hailed some people across the room and walked to join them.

Oh. So not him. That small relief, at least. For the moment.

Her anxious gaze roved the groups of travellers, busy hotel staff, people queuing at the desks, and lighted on another unaccompanied man, this one tall and lean, dressed in a dark suit. He was standing by the entrance with his back to her, phone to his ear, jacket switched back at one side while his free hand rested on his hip. He was pacing backwards and forwards with a lithe, coiled energy, occasionally gesticulating with apparent impatience.

He turned suddenly in her direction, then checked. Her nerves jumped. She could tell he'd caught sight of her because the lines of his tall frame tensed, and even from this distance she could see him frown. He said something into his phone, then snapped it shut and slipped it inside his jacket.

Despite her moment of bravado, her stomach clenched.

He hesitated a moment, then walked across the wide lobby towards her, his frown smoothing away. Too late though, because she'd already seen it. As he drew nearer she saw, with a growing sense of unreality, that he was good-looking. A sleek, beautiful male in the matchless Greek style, though he had that indefinable, characteristic bearing of an Australian man. Athletically built, even in a suit. Why would he ever need to order in a woman?

He wasn't so old. Thirty-three or -four, nothing more than that. He might just be a nephew, or cousin. Perhaps she was mistaken, and he wasn't the one.

He halted at a couple of metres distance.

'You're Ariadne Giorgias?'

His voice was deep and beautiful, but it was his eyes that held her. They were mesmerising, a dark glinting chocolate fringed by thick black lashes. They swept over her in a cool assessment, made cooler by the stern set of his mouth, but she could guess what they sought. Her breasts, her legs, her child-bearing hips. Would she be a sufficient trophy?

She felt the proud colour rise to her cheeks. Anger and humiliation made her voice scrape in her throat. 'Yes. I'm Ariadne Giorgias. And you are…?'

Sebastian heard the stiff tone and his expectations received instant confirmation. So, Miss Ariadne Giorgias, child of the

Giorgias shipbuilding dynasty and his potential wife, was as spoiled as she was rich. Despite his fury at the trap he found himself in, he felt a curious edge of anticipation as he examined her face for the first time. Whatever transpired, this might be the woman he married.

Her face was nothing like the one he'd once thought the ultimate in feminine beauty, but he could concede it had a symmetry. He could imagine how his sisters would have described it. Heart-shaped, with those cheekbones.

She had creamy skin with an almost satin translucence, and quite astonishing deep blue eyes, glittering now with some sort of emotion. Her full mouth was especially sensuous, somewhere between sweet and sulky. An alluring blend of sultriness and innocence, if he could believe that. A siren's mouth.

She could have been worse. If a man was blackmailed into marriage, whatever the failings that had brought the woman to this point, she should at least look presentable.

He swept the rest of her with a judgemental gaze.

Her hair was a pale ash, paler than it had been in the photo the magnate had posted, though her dusky eyebrows and lashes gave away its true colour. He supposed she was beautiful, if a man happened to admire that particular style of beauty.

She was slightly smaller than he'd expected, though in her designer jeans and jacket her body appeared slim and, he had to admit, graceful, with pretty breasts, a waist so slender a man could span it with his hands, and sweetly flaring hips.

As far as he knew anything about women's apparel she was dressed well, nothing flamboyant. Limited jewellery, though what she had was no doubt the finest money could buy.

He realised his pulse was pumping a little faster than the average. All right, so she was attractive with those eyes. She could afford to be. She seemed pale, perhaps she was nervous, but he cut any softer emotions that might have evoked.

She should be nervous. She'd be even more nervous when she

understood the sort of man she'd had the gall to attempt to add to her acquisitions.

As the full picture sank in he found his eyes needing to return to her face.

His lungs tightened. Yes, certainly, it could have been worse.

'Sebastian Nikosto,' he said finally, making a belated move to extend his hand.

Ariadne kept hers at her side. Never to touch him, she resolved fiercely. Not if she could help it.

His brows twitched, and she knew he'd taken note of her small rebuff. But he stayed as smooth as glass. 'Your uncle arranged that I should meet you and show you around Sydney.'

'Oh,' she said softly. 'So it was you who was to meet me at the airport?'

His eyes glinted, then were almost immediately screened by his thick black lashes. 'I apologise for not managing to be there. Tuesdays are always demanding for my office and I'm afraid I got caught up. Still…' He smiled, though it didn't reach his eyes. 'I guessed you would be quite experienced in these matters.' Somehow his voice was the more cutting for being so gentle. He spread his hands. 'And here you are. Safe and sound, after all.'

What 'matters'? With a pang she wondered what he'd heard about her. Would news of the wedding debacle have reached this distant shore? 'Experienced' was no innocuous word. Or did he assume she must be easy? Traded like a piece of livestock on a regular basis?

'No harm done,' he added.

Offhand, to say the least.

She thought of the morning she'd spent waiting for someone—*any* friendly face—at the airport, her agony of fear and indecision after the long trip and being tricked onto the plane. Praying that somehow, against all the odds, she'd misunderstood, and there *would* be a representative of the Nikosto family waiting with open arms to invite her into their warm family home. Worrying if she should take herself to the hotel, or run like the wind to some safe haven. Only what safe haven, when she was a stranger here?

The only vague knowledge she had of Australia, apart from her memories of her parents' home, remote flashes of that first little primary school, was the beach house her parents had taken her to for a visit with some distant relative of her mother's. She had no idea where it even was.

As an apology this didn't even rate. Had he been so reluctant to interrupt designing his satellites, or whatever he did? These days, did men expect their mail-order brides to deliver themselves to the door?

'I'm sorry you are dragged away from your work now,' she said, equally gentle. 'Perhaps you would prefer to postpone *this* meeting.'

One thick black brow elevated. 'Not at all, Miss Giorgias. I am charmed to meet you now.'

The words were smooth, but uttered in a silky tone that conveyed a wall of ice inside that elegant dark navy suit and pale blue shirt, colours that perfectly enhanced the bronzed tones in his skin and his blue-black hair.

Then, paradoxically, as if her coldness had somehow stirred the male in him, his dark eyes made an involuntary flicker to her mouth, hooked there an instant too long.

She angled a little away, her blood pulsing, indignation struggling with her body's involuntary response to the disturbance in the atmosphere surrounding his big masculine body. Testosterone, no doubt. It was only natural he'd be thinking about her in terms of sex.

She pulled the edges of her jacket a little closer. 'I'm not sure what my uncle told you, Mr Nikosto, but I came out here for a holiday. Nothing more than that.'

He considered her with an unreadable expression, then blasted any pretensions of innocence she might try to place on the situation.

'I'd have thought Pericles Giorgias would have been in a position to buy his niece a bridegroom from any of the grand houses in Europe, Ms Giorgias.' His eyes swept over her again in a smouldering acknowledgement of her desirability. 'I'm surprised to have been so—honoured. And flattered, of course.'

The words blistered her sensibilities. She saw his eyes flare with a dark, dangerous emotion that wasn't anything like feeling flattered, or honoured, and shock jolted through her. The man was angry. Was she such a disappointment? She didn't want him to want her, but the insult sank deep, just the same.

But she mustn't let him see her as some toothless lioness. He'd better learn she could defend herself.

'I'm surprised you *could* be bought, a man like you,' she mocked, though her voice trembled.

His eyes flashed. 'You'd better be sure you know what you've bargained for, Ms Giorgias. Tell me, once you have me shackled to your side, what do you hope to do with me then?'

She met his smouldering dark gaze, and tried to repress visions of lying naked beside him on some wide bed. Of being held in his arms, pressed against his lean, hard body, his dark eyes... But, she wouldn't... And he couldn't want to... She'd never...

She quickly thrust the images away. What could her uncle have promised on her behalf? With a helpless sense of shame, she scrambled to find some gloss to minimise the outrage Thio Peri had committed against her autonomy.

'My uncle arranged this holiday simply so we could meet. That was all. Just so we could—*meet*. To see if we... To see if there would be any...' She felt the hot tide of embarrassment rise through her chest and neck and all the way to her ears, and, furious at her weakness, added hoarsely, 'There is no requirement for—for anything further. I'm a free woman. This is the modern world.'

His chiselled, sexy mouth made a faint disbelieving curl, then he said very politely, 'Oh, right. Sure it is. But try to understand this, Miss Giorgias, I'm a serious guy. I'm not some racing-car celebrity or a prince with time on his hands between yacht races. I have a company to run. Some people choose to work, in case you haven't heard. I won't be able to devote myself to your entertainment twenty-four seven.'

He was so cold and unfriendly, all her hurt and tension, the fear and helplessness of the plane trip, the shock of the betrayal, wound her up to an emotional explosion. The fiery blood rushed to her head and she snapped, 'I'd rather you didn't devote yourself to me at all, Mr Nikosto.'

She felt the shock impact of her words, then all at once had a burning consciousness of his gaze on her clasped, trembling hands, and tried to shift them from view. Her loss of control had generated something, though, because she sensed a change in the air.

Sebastian stared, for the first time seeing the shadows under her fierce blue eyes, the rapid, vulnerable pulse in her tender throat. With a sudden lurch in his chest he had a flash of himself as a brute holding some delicate, threatened creature at bay.

A creature with sensitivities, nerves and anxieties. With soft silky breasts under her stiff little jacket. He couldn't control the overpowering thought. A creature—a *woman* who might soon be his to undress.

If he signed that contract.

Her sulky mouth made a tremor, and against his will, against all the odds, his blood stirred. Hell, but she had a kissable mouth. An intensely kissable mouth.

Poised on an emotional tightrope, her defensive instincts up in arms, Ariadne sensed the tension emanating from him rock into a different sort of beat.

He drew in closer, bringing her the faintest trace of some pleasant masculine cologne, and her sexual receptors suddenly roared into awareness of his big, vibrant body. Behind that blue shirt there was a beating heart, flesh, blood and raw, muscled power.

'Sebastian,' he stated. 'Look, er, Ariadne… It's all right if I call you Ariadne?'

She gave a jerky shrug.

'Whatever you choose to call your presence here, I've agreed to play my part in it. Unless you'd rather pass on the whole thing?' His expression was suddenly grim, his eyes hard and challenging.

It was an ultimatum. Her heart skipped an alarmed beat. What if he phoned her uncle and told him she was being uncooperative? After the plane trick, she wouldn't put it past Thio to refuse to help sort out the accommodation mix-up. It occurred to her then that the bungled hotel booking mightn't even be a mistake.

With limited money, and no way of paying for thirty nights at Sydney prices, she might very well be forced to beg for this man's generosity.

With a sinking heart she realised this could be exactly what they'd planned. Her uncle's words came back to her with a chilling significance.

'The Nikostos are good people,' Peri Giorgios had asserted before she'd woken up to his ploy. 'They'll look after you. I'm guessing they'll have you out of that hotel and into the Nikosto family villa in no time.'

The Nikosto family villa. Except it wasn't the Nikosto *family*. It was one member of it. One angry, ice-cold member.

Until she could talk to her uncle and aunt again, get a clearer idea of where she stood money-wise, perhaps her best option was to pretend to play along.

She met Sebastian Nikosto's dark eyes and crushed down her pride. 'No. No, look.' The words were as ashes on her tongue. 'I'm—really very grateful for your kindness.' Her voice cracked on the last one.

His heavy black lashes lowered. The faintest flush tinged his cheek as he said brusquely, 'All right, then. So—dinner this evening? I'll pick you up here at seven.' His eyes flickered to her mouth. 'Might as well—make a start.

CHAPTER TWO

ARIADNE walked fast, up and down the hotel suite's sitting room until she'd nearly worn a furrow in the carpet. Then she strode furiously around straightening the pictures, shifting lamps to more pleasing positions, realigning the chairs.

Her uncle's scheme had placed her in an impossible situation with that icy, smouldering man. What had he been offered to marry her? No wonder he had such a low opinion of her, but why, oh, why had he agreed if it enraged him so much?

Maybe, if she could have despised *him* more, she wouldn't feel so ashamed. Ashamed of her uncle. Ashamed of herself and the mess she'd fallen into by thinking she was in love with that smooth-talking liar, Demetri Spiros.

Imagine if Sebastian Nikosto heard about the wedding scandal. Her uncle's words on the subject had rung in her ears all the way to Sydney. 'There isn't a man in Greece who would touch you now with a very long pole.'

Surely her uncle must know that if she did ever marry someone, even someone 'bought'—she flushed again in memory of Sebastian's stinging words—the man would have to be told about the scandal.

Other things Sebastian had said returned to her now with scathing significance. *Some people choose to work, in case you haven't heard.* As if he'd assumed she had no professional qualifications of her own. Did she look as if she'd spent her life as a useless ornament?

She kept rephrasing the things she'd said to him and turning them into what she should have said. Next time she saw him… Tonight, if she could bear to face him tonight, she'd set him straight about what sort of woman she was. And if he thought for a second, for an instant, that she would ever be available to him…

When the storm had calmed a little, she sat on the bed and forced herself to reason. In Athens it would be morning. Her uncle would be on his way to his office, her aunt engaged in either her beauty routine or instructing the housekeeper. Thea Leni was always affectionate and easy to deal with, though her compliance in the subterfuge to trick Ariadne onto the plane had been a painful shock. The hurt felt more savage every time she thought of it. Her loving aunt must have believed in her husband's solution to the 'Ariadne problem', at least a bit.

She put her head in her hands, still unable to believe all that had happened. Had they intended it as a punishment? She'd believed in their kindness absolutely, ever since, after the accident, they'd brought her as a seven-year-old to her uncle's house on Naxos. Though quite a lot older than her parents, they'd done all they could to replace them. In their old-fashioned way they'd loved her, protected her, even to the point of making her feel quite suffocated by the time she reached eighteen.

Why hadn't she woken up sooner to this holiday idea? When had Thio Peri ever wanted her to leave Greece without them in the past? Everything she'd done, every step she'd taken from the time she was seven, had been done under his care and protection, as if she were the most precious individual on the planet.

Even when they'd sent her to boarding school in England, either Thea Leni or Thio Pericles himself had come personally at every half-day and holiday to collect her. Long after she'd returned to Athens to attend university, she'd been told that one of the gardeners employed at the school had in reality been her own personal security guard. Thio Peri had never stopped worrying that she might be kidnapped and held to ransom.

How ironic. Once she'd been their jewel, but since she'd let them down and caused the scandal she must have lost her lustre. In their traditional way of thinking they still believed a large part of family honour depended on the marriages their sons and daughters made, the grandchildren they could boast of.

It wasn't too hard to understand. They'd never stopped grieving over their own childless state. They'd pinned all their hopes on her, their 'adopted' daughter, to provide the nearest thing to grandchildren they could ever achieve.

'You'll *like* the Nikostos,' Thio Peri had enthused on another occasion, determined to lure her into the trap. 'They're good people. They'll look after you. My father and old Sebastian talked in the taverna every night for fifty years. They were the best of good friends. You will be taken care of there every step of the way.'

Thea Leni had hugged her so tightly. She should have seen then that it all felt like goodbye. 'It will do you so much good, *toula*. It's time you visited your own country.'

'I thought Greece was my country now,' Ariadne had put in, grateful they were at last moving on after the months of recriminations. And, face it, a little nervous to be venturing so far on her own at long last.

'And so it is. But it's important to see the land of your birth. Admit it. You've lost your job, you've lost your flat, people are whispering about you… You need the break.'

They needed the break. She could see that now. From her. From the embarrassment she'd brought them.

It wasn't until she was on the plane buckling her seat belt that she'd woken up.

'Sebastian will meet you at the airport and show you around Sydney,' her aunt had said at the very last.

Her uncle's hearty laugh had followed her down the embarkation corridor. 'Don't come back without a ring on your finger and a man in your suitcase.'

She should certainly have known then. Sebastian's name had hardly been mentioned until that moment. Still, it wasn't until the hostess was preparing to embark on the safety rigmarole that a shattering possibility had dawned. In a sudden panic, Ariadne had whipped out her mobile and dialled.

'Thio. Oh, oh, Thio.' Her voice shaking with a fearful certainty. 'This isn't some sort of matchmaking thing, is it? I mean, you haven't set something up with this Sebastian Nikosto, have you?'

Guilt always made her uncle bluster. 'You should be grateful your aunt and I have taken matters into our hands for you, Ariadne.'

'What? How do you mean?'

His voice crackled down the phone. 'Sebastian Nikosto is a good person. A fine man.'

'*What?* No, no, Thio, no. You must be joking. You can't do this. This isn't my choice…'

'*Choice.*' His voice rose in her ear. 'You've had choices, and look what you did with them. *Look* at yourself. You're nearly twenty-four years old. There isn't a man in Greece—*Europe*—who will touch you. Now try to be a good girl and do the right thing. Be nice to Sebastian.'

'But I don't *know* him. And he's old. You said he was old. This is a *holiday.* You promised—you said—'

Her tearful protests were interrupted.

'Miss, miss.' The flight attendant was hovering over her, something about turning off her mobile phone.

'I can't,' she told the man. *She,* who had always hated a fuss and had turned herself inside out at times to avoid making trouble. 'Sorry,' she tried to explain to the anxious little guy. 'I have to…' She made a hurried gesture and turned back to the phone, her voice spiralling into a screech. '*Thio Peri,* this isn't *right.* You can't *do* this. This is against the *law.*' Her uncle hung up on her and she tried furiously to redial.

'Miss, please…' The attendant held out his hand for the phone, insistence in his tone. Her neighbours were staring with avid interest. All heads were turned her way.

'But this is an emergency,' she said. Glancing around, she realised the plane was already taxiing. She panicked. 'Oh, no, no. I have to get off.'

She dropped the phone, unbuckled her seat belt and tried to rise. Someone across the aisle dived for her phone.

The urgent voices. 'Miss, sit down. Miss. Sit, please. You are endangering the passengers.'

People around her stared as she half stood, clinging to the seat in front of her, craning their necks to see the distressed woman. Then the plane accelerated for lift-off, and she plumped down involuntarily. She felt the wheels leave the ground, the air under the wings, and was flooded with despair. They would have to turn back. The pilot would have to be told.

When the white rooftops of Athens were falling away below two more attendants had arrived, concerned and more authoritative. 'Is anything wrong, Miss Giorgias? Are you ill?'

'It's my—my uncle. He…' Already they were out over the sea and heading up through clouds. 'We have to go back. There's been a mistake. Can you please tell the pilot?'

She took in their bemused expressions, the quick exchange of glances, and lurid images of the headlines flashed through her head. *Ariadne Giorgias provokes airbus incident. Ariadne of Naxos in more trouble.*

More scandal, more shame. More mockery of her name, using the coincidence of the ancient myth. She cringed from the thought of any further notoriety.

In the end she fastened her seat belt and apologised.

But she couldn't just acquiesce. She might be stranded in a

hotel room, in a strange city on the other side of the world with no one to turn to except a man who despised her, but she mustn't give into panic. She had to keep her wits about her and find a solution.

First, though, she needed to be practical. She had expected many of her meals and all of her accommodation to have been paid in advance for the coming weeks, and her bank account was virtually empty except for the holiday money. Money for a little shopping, taxis, tips, day trips here and there. Holiday money. What a cruel laugh that was.

She took a deep, bracing breath and dialled Thea Leni's private line at the Athens town house. This time she mustn't lose control, as she had with the call from the plane.

'Eleni Giorgias?'

Her aunt's voice brought Ariadne a rush of emotion, but she controlled it. Thea sounded wary. Expecting the call, Ariadne guessed.

'Thea. It's me.'

'Oh, *toula*, don't… Don't… Your uncle has arranged everything and it will be good. You will see. Are you…all right?'

Ariadne's heart panged at the note of concern but she made herself ignore it. This wasn't the time for tears. 'There's been a mistake in the hotel booking,' she said in a low, rapid voice. 'I find that I'm only booked for one night, and it hasn't been paid for. The travel agent must have made an error. And when I met the tour director in the lobby my name wasn't on his list. I thought Thio had paid in advance. And he was supposed to have paid the hotel for four weeks.'

There was a shocked silence. Then her aunt said, 'Not paid for? But—but how…?' Then her voice brightened. 'Oh, I know what he's thinking. Consider, *toula*, you won't *need* to be in that hotel for long.'

The ruthlessness of the trick stabbed at Ariadne. Whatever had happened to chastity before marriage? 'Oh, Thea, what are you asking me to *do*?' This time there was no controlling her wail of anguish. 'Are you expecting me to go straight into that man's bed?'

Guilt, or perhaps shame, made her aunt's voice shrill. 'I'm not asking you to do anything except to give Sebastian a chance. He is a good man. He will marry you. He is rich, he has brains… Your uncle says he is a genius at what he does with the satellites.'

'He doesn't *want* to, Aunt. He doesn't want to marry me.' She wound up to a higher pitch. 'I'm not even cut out to be a wife.'

A gasp came down the line loud and clear, all the way from Athens. 'Never *say* that, Ariadne.' Her aunt was shocked to the foundations. 'Where is your gratitude?' she wailed. 'You had a bridegroom who *was* willing and you stood him up at the altar rails and dishonoured the entire Giorgias and Spiros families. Your uncle's oldest *friends*.'

Emotion welled up in Ariadne's throat. She understood. After they'd taken so much care to keep her pure for her husband, in the eyes of their traditional world she'd been deflowered, dishonoured, and still had no husband to show for it. And what else was a woman for, in her aunt's old-fashioned view, except to be a wife and mother?

'I told you, Thea. He was unfaithful. You know it. He had a lover.'

Even from a hemisphere away she could hear her aunt's world-weary sigh. 'Oh, grow up, Ariadne. If you want to bear children you have to compromise, and put up with—things. Anyway, there is no use in all this arguing. Your uncle won't change his mind.'

'He has made a mistake, Aunt. This man won't take an unwilling wife. If you met him you'd know. He's not… He's an Australian. He will walk away. Could you please…please, Thea, transfer enough money into my account for the hotel bill?'

She could hear tears in her aunt's voice. '*Toula,* if it were up to me…of course I would. Listen, when you're married all your money will be settled on you. Your uncle loves you. He thinks this is right. He only wants the best for you.'

'He always thinks he knows best, and this *isn't* best,' she said fiercely. 'And I won't do it. Tell him there's no way anyone will force Sebastian Nikosto to go through with marrying an unwilling woman.'

Her aunt was silent for a second. Then she said in a dry voice, 'Oh, yes, he will. He certainly will go through with it. As I understand it, there's nothing he wants more.'

'What are you saying?' Ariadne said, seized by an icy foreboding. 'Why do you think that?'

'Oh…' Her aunt's voice sounded weary, more distant somehow. 'You know I don't know about business, Ariadne. Your uncle says Sebastian knows he has everything to gain from this marriage, and everything to lose if he doesn't choose it. His company will fail if he doesn't marry you. Celestrial. Isn't that what it's called?'

Sebastian rang the bell of his parents' house, then strode straight in. He should have been back in his office, combing through the departments for more ways to cut costs to avoid cutting people, but events had wrenched his unwilling attention in another direction.

Before he took another false step, he needed to do some research. There had to be some explanation of why he of all the eligible Greeks on the planet had been chosen as bridegroom to the niece of Peri Giorgias.

When Giorgias had thrown in that extra clause at the time the contract was all but finalised, the completed designs on the table, at first it had seemed nothing more than a bizarre joke. The cunning old fox had chosen his moment well. With Celestrial suddenly adrift in the recession, the market dwindling, the sly operator must have known if he pulled out then, Celestrial would make a significant loss in terms of the precious resources already used to develop the bid.

In the gut-wrenching moment when Sebastian had understood that the eccentric old magnate's demand was deadly serious, he was faced with a grim choice. Accept the woman and save his company, guarantee the livelihoods of his workforce, or walk away and face the possible ruin of all he'd built.

But why him? Why not some rich lothario back in Hellas?

Angelika, his mother, and Danae, his married sister, were ensconced in the kitchen, arguing with the cook over the best method of preparing some delicacy. Angelika interrupted her tirade with hugs, and a multitude of solicitous enquiries concerning his diet and sleep patterns. Danae listened to all of it with an amused expression and an occasional solemn nod.

Sebastian shot his sister a glance. She might have been amused, but he was willing to bet she was soaking up the technique so she'd know how to suffocate her own sons when the time came for them to escape from her control.

'Look at how *thin* you are,' his mother wailed like a Greek mother. 'What you need is a really good dinner. Maria, set him a place. I have a moussaka in the fridge I was saving for tomorrow's lunch, but this is the bigger emergency. Danae, put it in a box and he can take it home with him. Show that woman how to feed a man.'

He held up his hand. 'No, thanks, Maria.' A really good dinner was his mother's inevitable cure for any disorder from flu to insomnia. 'I'm not staying.' He waved away the proffered dish. 'Put it back. I do have a full-time housekeeper, you know. And Agnes is very touchy about her cooking.'

His mother snorted her contempt. 'Cooking? *What* cooking? The trouble with you, my son, you are too wrapped up in your satellites to see what's in front of your nose.'

His nephews caught sight of him then and came running with a thousand urgent things they needed to tell him at once.

Sebastian listened as patiently as time would allow to all the recent details of their exuberant young lives, while Danae looked on, beaming with maternal pride.

Eventually, he detached himself with a laugh. 'That's enough,' he said, ruffling the two four-year-old heads. He waited for a brief respite in the voluble trio of voices, then jumped in with a query of his own. 'Is Yiayia here?'

His mother tilted her head in the direction of the hall. 'In the orangery.'

Sebastian approached quietly, in case his grandmother was having a late afternoon nap. He needn't have been concerned.

Dressed in her gardening smock, her hair coiled loosely into a bun, the small, frail woman was up and active, struggling to lift a terracotta pot onto a bench.

'None of that,' Sebastian said, striding forward and removing it from her worn hands. 'You know what the doctor said, Yiayia.'

'Oh, pouf. Doctors,' his grandmother exclaimed while Sebastian positioned the pot in the miniature rainforest that was her pride and joy, adorning every available space. 'What do they know?'

She peeled off her gloves and reached up, tilting her soft, lined cheek for his kiss.

Sebastian obliged, declining to argue, knowing she worshipped the members of the medical profession as though their words were piped direct from heaven.

'Well, *glikia-mou*. Now, what are you about?' She settled herself into a high-backed wicker chair draped with shawls, while Sebastian sat facing her.

Filtered by leaves both inside and out, the afternoon sun slanted through the glass walls, bathing the room in a greenish light.

Sebastian made himself relax, aware he was being examined by an almost supernaturally astute observer of human frailty. 'Do you remember the Giorgias family?'

Her elderly brows lifted. 'From Naxos?' He nodded, and she said, 'Of course. From when I was a child. There was always a Giorgias in our house. My father and their father were friends.'

'Do you remember Pericles Giorgias?'

'Ah.' She gave a sage nod. 'Of course I remember him. He was the one who inherited the shipyard, and the boats. He married Eleni Kyriades. He was such a generous man. It was he who helped your father when the stores nearly collapsed back in the eighties.'

Sebastian tensed. 'How do you mean, he helped Papa? Are you sure?'

'For sure I'm sure. When the banks wouldn't help Pericles made your father a loan. To be repaid without interest over a very long time. No strings attached.' She shook her head in wonderment. 'Such a rare thing, generosity.'

Dismay speared through Sebastian. Such generosity was rare indeed. But there'd been strings attached, all right. Strings of honour. With grim comprehension he recognised the situation. The Nikostos were now under an obligation to the Giorgiases. For some reason Peri Giorgias required a favour, and he'd chosen to collect from the son of his debtor.

A son for a father. A favour for a favour.

He could almost hear the clang as the trap snapped shut around him. Chained to a stranger in wedlock.

In an attempt to break free from the vice sinking its teeth into his gut, he got up and paced the room. Another marriage was the last thing he'd ever intended. How could he dishonour Esther's memory with some spoiled tycoon's poppet?

'There were other brothers too. Three. At least three.' Yiayia's gentle voice filtered through his reflections. 'I remember the youngest, but the middle boys…' The old lady sat back in her chair and closed her eyes. After a moment she said, 'I remember young Andreas. He didn't care for the family business. I think he was an artist. He came out here, and married an Australian girl. Oh, that was a terrible tragedy. Poor Andreas and his wife.'

In spite of his resistance to knowing anything about the Giorgias woman's history, Sebastian's attention was arrested, and he turned to watch his grandmother's face. 'What happened?'

'A boat accident. Night-time on the harbour. You may not remember. Your parents, your grandfather and me, we all went to the funeral, but you'd have still been a boy. Only imagine a Greek being killed in a boating accident! They said it was a collision. Silly young people out skylarking. Andreas and his wife didn't stand a chance.'

He frowned, unwilling to feel sympathy. Unwilling to feel. 'They left children?'

His grandmother's face lit up. 'That's right, there was a child. A girl, I think. I'm nearly sure the poor little thing was taken back to Greece with one of the brothers.'

Sebastian grimaced and resumed his chair. After a smouldering moment he made the curt acknowledgement, 'Pericles.'

'Ah.'

A pregnant silence fell.

Sebastian wondered if by admitting he knew that one fact, he'd given away something crucial. Sooner or later, if he went through with this charade, they would all have to know. What would they think of their brilliant son then, snagged like a greenhorn in a duty marriage? Forced up the aisle with a woman he hated?

A flash of the Giorgias woman's drawn, anxious face at the last stirred a sudden unaccountable turmoil in his chest and he had to rescind the thought. No, he didn't *hate* her, exactly. He just felt—angry. What man wouldn't? To have his bride, his *life*, decided by someone else.

In the first flush of his outrage Sebastian had blamed—he allowed himself to use her name—*Ariadne*. He'd imagined her as a spoiled little despot, winding her doting uncle around her little finger. How had she come to choose him? Had he been listed in some cheap catalogue of eligible males?

Now, after hearing Yiayia's words he began to see it was almost certainly instigated by Pericles himself.

His grandmother studied his face, her shrewd black eyes revealing nothing of her thoughts. After a long moment, she said, 'You have met her? Andreas's daughter?'

Sebastian hesitated, then shrugged and said without expression, 'I have had that pleasure.'

The wise old eyes scanned his a moment longer, then closed, as if in meditation. 'I don't think Pericles and Eleni were blessed.'

Sebastian knew what she meant. Other people might be blessed with brains, beauty, talent, health or wealth, but to Yiayia children were the most worthwhile of life's gifts, so blessings referred only to them.

'They'd have wanted to take on the little one,' she continued. 'I expect they'd have been overjoyed. Eleni had nothing much else to fill her heart. That Pericles liked the business. He was the right one to take over the shipping because he had an eye for money. Clever, but not always very smart. Andreas, now... A thoughtful boy, I think. Sensitive.' She shook her head and clasped her lined hands in her lap. 'Oh, that was a terrible shame. The young shouldn't have to die.'

Was she thinking of Esther now? 'No,' he said shortly. 'They shouldn't.'

Again, her wrinkled lids drifted shut. She remained silent for so long Sebastian thought she must have nodded off to sleep. He was about to get up and cover her with one of her shawls when her eyes opened, as clear and focused as ever.

'Is she beautiful?'

Sebastian's gut tightened. Resistance hardened in him to the notion of Ariadne Giorgias's beauty. He opened his mouth to growl something, but nothing would come. Anyway, the less said the better. Regardless of how he felt, whatever he said now could come back to haunt him.

'Do women have to be beautiful, Yiayia?' he hedged. 'Wasn't there an entire generation of women who rebelled against that notion?'

The old lady made an amused grimace. 'They usually are, though, aren't they, *glikia-mou?* To the men who love them. A man needs something lovely to rest his eyes on.'

Again, he guessed she was thinking of Esther. And it was true he'd loved her as much as it was possible for a man to love a woman. People in his family rarely made reference to her now, not wanting to remind him of the bad times, all the losing battles with hope after each bout of surgery, the radiation treatment, the nightmare of chemo.

Even after three years they were still exquisitely careful of his feelings, even Yiayia, tiptoeing around him on the subject, as if his marriage were a sacred area too painful for human footsteps.

Sometimes he wished they could forget about all that and remember his wife as the person she'd been. He still liked to think of those easy-going, happy days, before he and Esther were married, before he'd started Celestrial.

A stab of the old remorse speared through him. If only he'd spared her more of his time. In those early days of the company…

With an effort he thrust aside the useless self-recrimination, thoughts that still had the power to gut him. Too late for regrets, now he'd lost her.

No one would ever replace her in his heart, but often he was conscious of a hollowness that his work, exciting and challenging as it was, didn't fill. He hardly spent any time at home now, even sleeping on the settee in his office at times. He could imagine his parents' amazement if he ended up marrying this Greek woman, after they'd long since given up hope and become inured to the prospect of his ongoing singularity.

The reality was, he might as well admit it, one way or another a man still needed a woman. Somehow, against his will, against all that he held decent, meeting Ariadne Giorgias in the flesh had roused that sleeping dragon in him.

Though she wasn't his choice, she was no less lovely than any of the women he knew. If he'd met her at some other point in time, he might even have felt attracted. But…

Resistance clenched inside him like a fist. He wasn't the man to be coerced.

He became aware of Yiayia's thoughtful scrutiny. What was it she'd asked? Beautiful. Was she?

'She probably is,' he conceded drily. 'To anyone who cares for her type.'

'What type is that?' Yiayia enquired.

Defensive, scared, fragile. Pretty. Sexy.

CHAPTER THREE

MIDWAY through winding her hair into a coil, Ariadne's hand stilled. What had Sebastian Nikosto meant by 'a start'? And how much of a start? Surely he wouldn't expect to kiss her. Or *worse*.

She remembered his cool, masculine mouth, the seductive blue-black shadow on his handsome jaw, and felt a rush in her blood. Panic, that was what it must have been, combined with a fiery inner disturbance to do with how little she'd eaten since she'd boarded the plane.

The man had revealed himself as a barracuda. Her feminine instincts told her he might want to try something, but she'd just have to hold him off. That shouldn't be so hard, given how much he'd disliked her at first sight.

She'd managed to hold Demetri at bay for months, even though they'd been engaged and she'd believed herself in love. She made a wry grimace at herself. What a fool she'd been.

Afterwards, Thea had hinted that that might have been where she'd gone wrong with her ex-fiancé, but Ariadne knew better. It was *because* he'd had the mistress that Demetri hadn't been concerned about making love to her.

And everyone knew that like or dislike didn't necessarily have much to do with a man's sexual desires. Take Demetri's case. He'd made love to people he didn't even *know*. And she'd been such a contemptible pushover, believing his lies every time, doubting the evidence her close friends had tried to give her. Making excuses for his lack of interest in her, because she'd wanted to believe it was all fine and everything was as it appeared. Until she'd gone for lunch at that Athens restaurant and seen him there with his girlfriend.

It had still taken her days to accept the reality, but she'd never be so naive again.

It would hardly make sense if Sebastian Nikosto wanted to kiss her, after the things he'd said, but nothing about this whole situation made sense. The more she puzzled over it, the more her confusion increased.

She felt as if she were locked in a nightmare. If only she could fall asleep she might wake up and find herself back in her bedroom in Naxos. Had Sebastian's anger been with her, or with the deal he'd struck with her uncle? He'd made it sound as if the whole thing had been her idea.

Some aspects were so ironic, she'd have laughed if she hadn't been in such distress.

Thio had probably thought she would suit an Australian Greek because of her Australian mother. Meanwhile, Sebastian Nikosto had taken one glance at her from across a room and had felt cheated. She'd never forget that frown, how it had speared through her like a red-hot needle.

Was it because she wasn't attractive enough? Had her uncle explained to him that the woman he was throwing in to sweeten his pillow had blue eyes, *not* the dark shining beautiful eyes most Greek women took for granted as their heritage?

She stabbed a pin into her chignon. Whatever happened, she would die before she kissed a man who'd been paid to take her. No wonder he judged her with contempt. She must seem like the leftovers on the bargain rack in the Easter sales, thrown in as an added incentive. She was almost looking forward to meeting the man again and showing him his mistake. She truly was.

Despite all her bravado, the coward inside her was tempted not to keep the dinner engagement. What if she were to lie low in her room with a headache instead? In the morning, simply check out of the hotel and disappear from Nikosto's life without a trace?

She would have to check out, anyway. She wasn't sure what the price would be, but with the grand piano and all in the suite she guessed she wouldn't be able to afford many nights here.

After the devastating conversation with Thea, desperation had inspired her with a survival plan. If she sold what little jewellery she'd brought and added the proceeds to her holiday money, provided she found somewhere cheaper to stay, she should have enough to get by on until she could find some sort of job. There must be art galleries in Australia. Under the terms of her father's will, unless she married first she couldn't inherit her money until she was twenty-five. All she had to do was to stay alive another fourteen months.

More and more throughout the afternoon her thoughts had returned to that beach house on the coast. She wondered if her mother's auntie still lived there. Would she remember the little girl who'd come to stay nearly twenty years ago? Would she even be alive?

It was tempting to just cut all communication with Sebastian Nikosto and his accomplices in the crime *right now*. That was what the man deserved. What they all deserved, she thought fiercely. She should just vanish into thin air. Trouble was, if she did that he might raise some sort of alarm. She shuddered to think of how it would be if she were pursued by the Australian police. She could imagine the sneering headlines back in Greece.

Ariadne of Naxos goes missing in Australia. Has Ariadne been eaten by crocodiles?

Ariadne, lost in the outback.

And one that made her wince. *The runaway bride runs again.*

No, disappearing without saying goodbye could not be an

option. And there was no one else who could fix her dilemma for her. She was on her own, in a strange country, and for the first time in her life there was no one else to rely on except herself and her own ingenuity.

She needed to go downstairs in that lift, face Sebastian Nikosto squarely, and tell him eye to eye that she would never marry him, under any circumstances, and that she never wanted to see him again.

A surge of nervous excitement flooded her veins. What if he was furious? She almost hoped he was. It would do her heart good to see him lose his cool control and spit with rage.

She highlighted her cheekbones with liberal application of blush, at the same time boosting her mental courage with some strong, healthy anger. Whatever he said to her this time, however cold and hostile he was, whatever bitter insults he fired at her in that silky voice, there was no way her pride could ever let him think she was afraid of him.

Let the barracuda do his worst. Make-up would be her shield.

She painted a generous swathe of eyeshadow across her lids. Even without it her eyes had appeared dark and stormy after the adrenaline-wired past thirty-six hours. Now they looked enormous, and with more adrenaline pumping into her bloodstream every second there was no disguising their feverish glitter. She smoothed some kohl underneath with her fingertip. Somehow the blue of her irises deepened.

The effect was atmospheric, almost gothic, and intensely satisfying. She felt as if she were in disguise. What to wear was more of a worry.

She hardly wanted to inflame the man's desires. A burkha would have been her choice if she'd had one to hand, but pride wouldn't allow her to appear like a woman in a state of panic, anyway. In the end she chose a black, heavily embroidered lace dress that glittered with the occasional sequin when she moved. Since the dress had only thin straps she added a feathery bolero to cover her shoulders. The lining ended a few inches short of the hem, revealing a see-through glimpse of thigh in certain lights, but with the feathers added she looked modest enough.

At last, dressed and ready for battle, her breathing nearly as fast as her galloping pulse rate, she surveyed her reflection.

Red lipstick, the only touch of colour. Black dress, feathers, purse. The sheerest of dusk-coloured silk stockings, and black, very high heels to lend her some much-needed height.

All black.

Well, he wanted his Greek woman, didn't he?

Sebastian shaved with care, keeping an eye on the clock. Not that he felt any guilt over failing to meet the plane from Athens. Not exactly.

He was a busy guy. If he didn't keep an eye on Celestrial, who knew how much of a tangle things could get into? He could hardly place himself at the beck and call of every heiress with a whim to make him her husband.

Still, manners dictated that tonight he should make the effort to be punctual. It didn't have to be a late evening. He could buy her a decent dinner, smooth over the jagged hostilities of the first meeting, and be away by nine to get in some work.

He hoped Miss Giorgias was in a better frame of mind. She'd have been jet-lagged, of course, which would explain her waspish behaviour.

He splashed his face with water and reached for a towel, avoiding meeting his gaze in the mirror. He hadn't really been so hard on her, had he? There was a lot more he could have said. Anyway, hadn't she thanked him at the end for being kind?

He felt that uncomfortable twinge again and brushed it aside. For God's sake, did he have to be a nursemaid simply because he'd agreed—*under duress*—to meet the woman and check out the possibilities?

He dried off his chest, dropped the towel into the hamper, then slapped on a little of the aftershave his sisters had given him. Lemon, sage and sandalwood, the label read. *Guaranteed.*

He made a rueful grimace. Guaranteed to soothe a princess?

As rarely happened to a man with his gaze fixed firmly on the stars, his eye fell on a green, moss-like growth around the base of the tap. How long had that been there? It was robust enough to have established quite a hold. Agnes must have missed it. More than once, by the look.

He supposed he could attend to it himself without threatening his gonads. He cast about for something to wipe it away with, and used the only thing readily available: one of yesterday's socks. The sock made no appreciable difference, so he gave up.

With grander things to attend to, how could a guy be expected to attend to the demeaning sludge of housework?

He frowned into his wardrobe, then surrendered to necessity and chose an evening suit. Was the shirt clean? He checked that it had a recent laundry ticket attached. Lucky he'd remembered at some stage to remind Agnes to empty the washing hamper. It was only to be expected she'd forget things when he was hardly ever here.

Scrubbed, dressed and polished, he gave his overall appearance a cursory check. Looked at from a certain point of view, he supposed, the Giorgias woman had flown across the globe to nail him. *Meet* him, in her words. Might as well grit his teeth and make an effort to show her a little respect.

He was, after all, he supposed, an eligible guy. A single guy. *Widower.* He flinched inwardly as the loathsome word surfaced from the deep to strike him down with all its connotations of dust and ashes, funerals and long black days and nights that rang with emptiness.

He wiped those horrors from his mind and walked downstairs, a single man free and unencumbered.

At the hotel he tossed the car keys to the parking valet, then strolled into the lobby, conscious, despite everything, of a certain buzz of anticipation in his veins.

It was the hush of the evening, the city poised to leap into its nightlife, with neon lighting its every billboard and high-rise. Wherever he looked people were hurrying off to their evening engagements: guys with their girlfriends, couples holding hands. For once he felt like a man with somewhere to go other than the office.

Ms Ariadne Giorgias would've had an hour or two to rest, so hopefully she might be less prickly. He wondered what she'd be wearing. Something slinky? Some little designer number from one of the couture houses, exhibiting more skin than fabric?

The lobby was busy, but there was no sign of her. After his lapse this morning he would hardly be surprised if she kept him waiting as a punishment.

He strolled over to Reception and asked one of the clerks to phone up to her room.

The clerk had scarcely lifted the phone before Sebastian saw her. She was emerging from the lift along with some other people, but he singled her out at once. Unaccountably his lungs seized. Even after one brief meeting, he recognised the characteristic way she held herself. She walked with her head high, as though to ensnare every available ray of light in her hair, her slender, shapely body graceful and erect. He must certainly have been too long without a woman, because he found his gaze riveted to the sway of her feminine hips, and felt stirred at some deeply visceral level.

Whatever else she was, she was all woman.

The rushing sensation in his blood heightened.

She caught sight of him and her steps made an involuntary halt, then picked up again, and she advanced to meet him, her expression now cool and wary. That tiny, undeniable falter, though, resounded through him and struck his guilty heart like a blow.

A man didn't have to be an aeronautical design genius to see that underneath the fantastic black dress, slim shapely legs and silky gleaming hair, Ms Ariadne Giorgias was scared. He suffered a jolting moment of self-insight.

Was this what he had become? A cold, angry man who frightened women?

Conscious of her nervous pulse, Ariadne steeled herself to the challenge, then plunged onwards. Sebastian Nikosto looked more handsome, if possible, in an evening suit with a charcoal shirt and a bronze-hued silk tie that found golden glimmers in the depths of his dark eyes. She conceded reluctantly that his colours were again excellent, though the tie was slightly skewed as if he hadn't given it a final check.

Perhaps it was her imagination, but did his expression seem friendlier? Less—hostile?

His dark gaze swept her, and again she felt that roaring sensation, almost like excitement. There was a look in his eyes that made her too aware of her curves and the shortness of the dress. A million wild thoughts assailed her at the same time. Why, oh, why hadn't she worn trousers?

While her fingers nearly succumbed to a mad itch to tweak that tie into place, her pulse was thudding in her ears so loudly she hardly took in what he said.

'…Ariadne.' The way he said her name made it sound as if it had been wrapped in dark chocolate. One of those liqueurs they gave you with coffee at the Litse in Athens.

'Cheri Suisse.' Her voice sounded overly husky. Oh, *Theos*, had she actually said that? Surely not. Where was the poise she so desperately needed?

It was another of those awkward moments when he would expect to clasp her hand, but this time he went one better. Before she could forestall it, he leaned forward and brushed her cheek with his lips.

It was so unexpected her heart nearly arrested. She felt the slight graze of his shadowed jaw on her skin, and the heady masculine scents, the powerful nearness of him swayed her senses.

Flustered, her cheek burning as if she'd been brushed with a flame, she had one coherent thought swirling over and over in her brain. Here was a man whose interest in her was purely financial. This wild fluttering inside, these uncontrollable sensations, needed to be crushed into extinction. *At once.*

'I'm thinking we won't go too far afield tonight, since you're probably jet-lagged,' he said, as smoothly as if he hadn't been insulting her only a few short hours previously. 'I know a little place not far from here. Do you like Italian?'

She drew a deep breath.

'Listen, Sebastian…' She raised her hands before her like a barricade. 'I don't want to marry you.' He blinked, and before he could reply she added, a tremor in her voice, 'So—so you might not wish to waste any more of your time. Thanks anyway for—for coming.'

'What?' He looked stunned.

'Yep, that's right.' Wound up and swept by a massive charge of adrenaline, she gave him a cool smile. 'As the song says, I'm holding out for the prince.'

Without waiting to watch him crumble into a heap of masculine rubble, she turned on her heel and swept towards the lifts, rather pleased with her exit line. Unfortunately for her grand moment, before she'd gone more than a couple of steps the persistent man recovered himself and caught up.

'Well, er—hang on there a second.' He moved around to block her path. He was shaking his head, amusement seeming now to have replaced his astonishment.

She had to wonder if he'd understood. Or was he so in need of the money, he felt driven to try some other way to talk her round?

'That's fine, Ariadne,' he said. 'That's just fine. But whether we marry each other or not, we still have to eat dinner, don't we?'

His lean handsome face broke into a smile that was far more dangerous than his earlier sternness and hostility. Charming little lines appeared like rays of warmth at the corners of his eyes and mouth, and crept insidiously through her defences to assault her too soft heart. Here she was, all geared to be brave, to foil his cold, cutting words with icy hauteur, and now he'd changed tack.

It was confusing. And unfair. She was so desperately in need of a friend, if she wasn't careful, before she knew it she'd be forgiving him. Complying. The very word evoked a shudder.

Thank goodness Demetri's legacy had died hard. She reminded herself that a man's smiles came easily, and this one could hardly wipe away the distress she'd gone through since she'd boarded that plane. She needed to be strong, and, after so much humiliation, true to herself.

'I'm not very hungry,' she asserted coolly. 'I'll be happy enough just to order room service. Anyway, it was—interesting, meeting you.'

'Oh.' Perhaps he'd picked up on the edge in her voice, because he dropped his gaze and his smile faded. When he glanced up again she saw remorse in his eyes. 'I deserve that. I know I wasn't very welcoming earlier. You'd had a long flight and I...' His deep voice was suddenly contrite. 'I'm pretty ashamed of how I spoke to you this afternoon. I'd like to apologise properly, and explain, if you'll give me the chance.'

His eyes had softened beneath his luxuriant black lashes to a rich, warm velvet. She had the ghost of an impression of what it might be like to be someone he admired. Someone he felt affectionate towards. He looked so sincere, her instincts, always weakly anxious to think the best of people, rushed to believe him.

She felt herself begin to melt, then just in time remembered all those occasions with Demetri and steeled her heart against him. Men could be such smooth liars. Especially if there was a financial incentive.

'Apology noted,' she said softly. 'Goodbye, Mr Nikosto. Some other time, perhaps.'

Like some other life. Some other universe.

'Oh, look, Ariadne… Are you sure I can't tempt you to a little taste of Sydney nightlife? You look amazing in that dress. It's a shame to waste it.' His dark eyes flickered over her, a sensual glow in their depths. 'We don't have to go far. As it happens, this hotel is said to have one of Sydney's finest seafood restaurants.' With a lean hand he indicated the other side of the lobby. 'Won't you let me at least buy you a glass of wine? Break the ice?'

An olive branch was so tempting. She'd never been the vengeful type. His mouth relaxed in a smile, its warmth reflected in his eyes. With his sexy, deep-timbred voice seeping into her tissues like an intoxicant, the man was a powerhouse of persuasion.

She lowered her lashes to avoid his mesmerising gaze, her pulse drumming. Shouldn't she have one drink with him? Even with the off-balance tie, he looked so darkly handsome in his evening suit. The beautiful cloth was so well cut, it enhanced his wide-shouldered, lean-hipped six-three to perfection. It was hard to imagine he was anything but what he appeared. Civilised, straight, honourable, decent…

Unfortunately, Thea's information about his company's need for a cash injection was still lodged in her oesophagus like a spike. The hurt pride and shame surrounding the notion of herself as a prize in a transaction welled inside her again.

'No, thanks,' she said hoarsely. 'I think I'd prefer to go to bed early and read up on Australia.'

Sebastian felt a spurt of good-humoured frustration. How far did a man have to grovel to lighten the mood of this difficult and, the more he saw of her, really quite desirable woman?

He drank her in, admiring her black dress. Wasn't it the classic dinner garb women wore? That feathery affair she'd added couldn't conceal the shape of her breasts, the pretty valley dividing them. It was hardly a dress to be lounging in.

Unless of course it was lounging on a man's bed, prior to being unzipped.

He had a sudden hot flash of smooth, satin breasts spilling into his hands, meltingly tender raspberries aching to be tasted, but he banished it. Still, the thought of them stayed there just below his awareness, like a wicked temptation, dreamed of but forbidden.

He cursed himself for having alienated her and making his situation more complicated than it needed to be. The irony wasn't lost on him. He was the one who was reluctant to be married. Who'd have thought he'd have to end up fighting to win his unwanted bride for even the smallest dinner engagement?

In every corner of his being, instincts of determination and masculine self-respect gathered in momentum and roused his red blood cells to the challenge. He was reminded of one of his more complex satellite projects. The harder it had been to resolve, the more fired up he'd been to conquer it.

Added to that, he had a vested interest here. If he didn't marry her, where did that leave his contract with Peri Giorgias? Now faced with the real danger of her slipping from his grasp, with a galvanising immediacy he suddenly realised how crucial it was for him to keep her. He could hardly expect to persuade her against her will, but his entire being grew charged with an urgency to win. This little tussle, at least.

'Read up on Australia?' he echoed, appealing to her with the rueful charm he'd known never to fail with women. 'You'd prefer that to sharing an excellent dinner with a guy whose only desire is to make amends?'

Her glittering blue gaze met his without wavering. 'Depends on the guy.'

Touché. The thrust was as unexpected as a punch in the gut. 'Oh,' he said, his insides reeling. 'Right.'

Ariadne sensed the impact of her words and knew they'd hit home. She tensed, waiting for some blistering response. To give the barracuda his due, he controlled whatever it might have been.

He merely nodded. 'Fine,' he said with a shrug. 'It's your call.'

His eyes gleamed and his mouth hardened to a straight, determined line, but he raised his hand in a cool farewell gesture, 'Enjoy your holiday, then, Miss Giorgias,' and walked away.

As Ariadne watched his rigid, retreating back the sudden relief from tension made her knees feel wobbly. She let out the breath she hadn't even realised she'd been holding. Spying a nearby ladies' room, she made for it, and pushed her way into the blessed sanctuary for a moment of private self-congratulation.

Her first triumph of the day. She leaned up against the washbasin console until her breathing calmed. In the mirror her eyes had a dark glitter, as though she'd been in a fight. In a way she had, she recognised, and she'd come off victorious.

He'd looked so shocked, as if he'd been savaged by a sheep. Serve him right for conniving with her uncle to snare her like a helpless little lamb. A fleeting image of the sincerity in his eyes when he apologised flashed into her mind, but she dismissed that.

Let him be sorry. Let him suffer.

For once she hadn't succumbed to a man's wiles. She'd carried out her plan, and felt better for it. Empowered. With relish, she watched herself in the mirror make a symbolic gesture of dusting off her hands.

Let Sebastian Nikosto know how it felt to be scorned.

Empowerment must have been good for the soul, because it no longer seemed necessary for her to spend the evening cowering in her room. In fact, her appetite came roaring back and she felt ravenous enough to eat a lion.

She swept from the washroom and sashayed in search of the restaurant. Guided by the chink of china and the unmistakable hum of a large number of people tucking in, she found the entrance without much trouble. She could hear the smoky voice of a singer performing some bluesy old love song, and delicious cooking smells wafted to her. Garlic, herbs and exotic spices mingled with the savoury aromas of char-grilling meats to taunt her empty stomach. All at once she felt nearly faint with hunger.

She approached the entrance, feeling glaringly conscious of not having an escort. At the host's desk she paused. 'Excuse me,' she said, lowering her voice to avoid attracting too much attention. 'A table for one, please.'

The portly head waiter raised close-set brown eyes to regard her, and arched his supercilious brows. 'Name?'

'Ariadne Giorgias.'

A subtle and strangely smug expression came over the man's face. 'Do you have a reservation, Miss Giorgias?'

'Well, no.' She smiled, and almost whispered, 'I'm a guest in the hotel. I didn't think a reservation would be required.'

'I think you will find, madam,' he said in crushing tones, making no effort to lower his voice to spare her embarrassment, 'that in the finer hotels with restaurants of renown, a reservation *is* required.'

She flushed. 'Oh. Sorry, I didn't realise. The finer hotels I've stayed in before haven't expected a reservation in their dining rooms.'

The man's sceptical gaze clashed with hers. 'And which hotels might they be, madam?'

'Well…' She thought back. 'There was the Ritz in Paris. And the one in London. And the Dorchester. I'm sure The Waldorf in New York was very welcoming…' Although, her uncle and aunt had been with her on those occasions. She supposed there wouldn't be many head waiters who would refuse Peri Giorgias a table. 'Oh, and there was the Gritti in Venice. Though I'm not so sure about that one now. Maybe we did have a reservation there.'

The man drew in a long breath and seemed to swell, while at the same time his lips thinned.

'Madam,' he stated, with austere emphasis, 'this is the *Park Hyatt* in *Sydney*. Our rules may differ from those of the less *moderne* northern hemisphere establishments, but they are crucial if our guests wish to experience the continuing superbness of our cuisine.' He gave her a moment to digest the information, then lowered his gaze and darted his plump fingers across the screen of his little computer, frowning and pursing his lips. 'As it happens, madam is fortunate in that we do have one remaining table.' He picked up a menu, tucked it under his capacious arm, and, pivoting on his heel, made a grand gesture. 'If madam would follow me.'

He raised his hand, and another waiter materialised from somewhere, bearing a water carafe and a basket of freshly baked bread. Thankful for her stroke of luck in not being turned away, Ariadne followed the procession across the crowded room. Through the glass walls she received an impression of the harbour lights, vessels on the dark water, the hard glitter of the city rising up behind Circular Quay. The pale shells of the Opera House floated in luminous majesty, seemingly a stone's throw from the terrace.

As she threaded her way among the tables, she couldn't help noticing the small, delicious-looking morsels on the diners' overlarge plates, and wondered anxiously if she should order double of everything.

She rounded a pillar after her guides and stopped short. Tucked into a corner between pillars and the step down to the terrace, was a small, round, vacant table, gorgeous with crystal, roses and pink and white linen. Right next to it, in fact, practically jammed against it, was another table, similarly adorned. Only this one wasn't vacant.

To her intense shock, lounging back in its single chair, his long legs stretched casually before him, Sebastian Nikosto sat perusing a leather-bound menu.

The host pulled out her chair and waited. Sebastian glanced casually up at her from beneath his black brows. His eyes lit with a curious gleam, then he resumed brooding over his menu.

Momentarily thrown, but loath to betray it or start a distressing scene, she hesitated, then submitted herself to be seated. With chagrin she noticed that her chair was positioned to face Sebastian's.

The head waiter deposited her napkin on her lap and presented her with her menu, while the other waiter fluttered to fill her water glass, offer her hot rolls.

She barely knew what she said to them. Questions clamoured in her head as Sebastian's dark satanic presence dominated the space. Had the man somehow guessed she'd be coming here after all and arranged this with the restaurant staff?

But how could he have known? Did he have some sort of diabolical clairvoyance?

The head waiter retreated, along with his small entourage. Almost at once a wine waiter advanced, who hovered, exerting polite pressure for her to make a choice. Conscious that this was something she'd never had to do herself before, she opened the wine menu and skimmed page after page of unfamiliar Australian and New Zealand names, hypersensitive to the unnerving presence of her neighbour.

She could feel his eyes on her, boring into her brain as if he knew, damn him, how distracting his presence was, how little she really knew about wine. Out of cowardice she considered rejecting it altogether, then noticed a bottle of red on the neighbouring table, its cork removed.

Allowing the wine to breathe, her uncle would have pronounced with approval.

Pride and prudence warred in her chest, and pride won the day. If Sebastian Nikosto could order wine, so could Ariadne Giorgias.

Still, she'd hardly ever been the person at the restaurant table who'd made the selection, except on a couple of lunch occasions with her girlfriends. Praying she didn't make a fool of herself, she murmured the most familiar name on the list.

The waiter's brows rose. 'Veuve Cliquot. Excellent choice, miss.'

The man whisked away, and she was left to face Sebastian alone. She held her menu up before her face, self-consciously aware he was now leaning forward with his arms folded on the table, watching her like a cougar poised to spring.

She felt a spurt of annoyance. His firm, masculine mouth— on another man she might have even considered it stirring—was gravely set, but there'd been a very slight flicker in one corner as if a smile was willing to break out. Except there was nothing to smile at. For goodness' sake, the man had just been rejected in marriage. Couldn't he accept it with dignity?

She was just winding up to say something to challenge him, when the waiter came back with a champagne flute, and presented a bottle with a yellow label for her approval.

As she'd seen her uncle do countless times, she nodded. The man set the glass before her, then without spilling a drop worked off the cork with deft fingers, and poured her a foaming taste.

As coolly as possible, considering she was under scrutiny, she swirled it in the glass, sniffed it, then took a small sip.

The buoyant liquid foamed its way to her stomach like a potent wave.

'Thank you,' she said, her eyes watering a little as the waiter topped up her glass. To crush any suspicions Sebastian Nikosto might have that she wasn't completely at ease and self-assured, she raised the sparkling liquid casually to her lips for a further sip. Bubbles shot up her nose and she couldn't prevent a sneeze. In the desperate grab for tissues, she reached blindly for her purse and accidentally knocked over her water glass.

Oh, Theos. A flood the size of Niagara Falls swamped her side of the table.

The waiter snapped into emergency mode, fussing over the pool with a napkin, helping her move out from the table to avoid the drips, enquiring if she was all right, if there was anything wrong with the champagne, trying to insist despite her protests that he must summon someone to change the table linen.

Shut up, she wanted to scream, burningly aware of Sebastian Nikosto's attentive face observing and listening to it all. *Get lost.*

'No, no, it's all *right,*' she hissed at all his mopping and tsking over the sodden spot. 'It's nothing. *Nothing.* I like it damp. Please,' she added with a heartfelt tug at his sleeve.

At last the guy took the hint, though unhappily, and edged away, casting uncomfortable looks back at her over his shoulder. The sheer irony of it, she kept thinking. Fate was so unfair. After her extensive experience in the grand restaurants of Europe, to appear now in her own country in front of the most unpleasant man she'd ever met as a gauche, clumsy fool was too much.

As soon as the waiter was out of earshot and she'd recovered some of her poise, Sebastian Nikosto drawled, 'Celebrating?'

She gave him a withering glance. There was an unnerving glimmer in his dark eyes, while that suspicion of a smile still lurked at the corners of his sexy mouth. He might not have personally upset the glass, but in her heart she blamed him. It was his fault for flustering her.

'That's none of your concern.'

At least her dress was black, she reflected. No one else had to know how uncomfortable she felt sitting with a wet tablecloth in her lap.

He leaned back in his chair and stretched with luxurious ease. 'Are you usually this snotty and touchy, Ms Giorgias?'

She drew a sharp breath and retorted, 'Are you usually this rude and annoying?'

He lifted his brows. 'Now, how fair is that? Here I am, a harmless guy, rejected by my date and forced to a lonely dinner, when by the most astonishing coincidence…'

She leaned forward. '*Is* it a coincidence?'

He narrowed his eyes thoughtfully. 'You know, just what I was wondering. I don't usually believe in coincidences. When you showed up here I was—have to admit it—gobsmacked. I have to wonder how it was arranged. It looks like a set-up to me.'

He made a sweeping gesture around at the setting. 'Here we are, in our own little intimate space, night-lights out there on the harbour, soft music, the terrace…'

She gasped. 'What are you implying? That *I* set this up?' She glared at his solemn face. 'That's ridiculous. I didn't know you were here. Why would I?'

He shrugged, shaking his head. 'Can't work it out. Unless you followed me because you felt—ashamed.'

'Oh, *what*?' she said incredulously. She rolled her eyes. '*I* should feel ashamed!' She glowered at him, remembering the way he'd behaved at their first meeting, even if he had made an apology since. 'Anyway, it wasn't a date.' She leaned forward again and added softly and distinctly, 'For your information, I wouldn't go anywhere with a man who had to use a business deal to catch a wife.'

His eyes glinted. 'Wouldn't you? But you'd come halfway across the world to meet him.'

The silky insinuation jabbed her and she retorted hotly, 'No, I would not, not if I had any—'

She pulled herself up in the nick of time. For all that her aunt and uncle had hurt and betrayed her into getting on that plane with their cruel trick, they were still her family. Still all the people she had in the world, though she could never forgive them. There was no way she could admit to Sebastian how cheaply they must have held her in their hearts all these years, even though she'd never before questioned their unconditional love for her.

His eyes sharpened. 'Not if you had any what?'

For the thousandth time that day she felt tears prick at the backs of her eyes. Blinking fast, she lowered them and turned away and pretended to look for something in her purse until the danger passed.

When she looked up Sebastian Nikosto's alert, intelligent gaze was still fixed interrogatively on her face. 'You were saying…?'

'Nothing,' she said huskily, grateful that food waiters chose that moment to swish up to each of their tables to take their orders.

Relieved that Sebastian's attention was diverted from her for the moment, she turned her attention to the menu and the efficient young waitress.

Since during her perusal she hadn't managed to take in a word of the menu, apart from one heartening glimpse of the dessert list, it took her a few moments to read it.

By the time she'd made up her mind, Sebastian had finished ordering his, and his waiter had hurried away. He lounged back in his chair, his long legs stretched out in idle relaxation. Though his gaze only drifted her way intermittently, she could sense his full attention trained on her like a million-megawatt spotlight.

With her cheeks growing uncomfortably hot, in the effort to exclude him she kept her voice at a low murmur. 'I might start with one or two chocolate truffles, and then the basil bruschetta.'

The woman looked surprised. 'The chocolate truffles are a dessert, miss.'

'Of course. I *know* that. Only one, then. And then could you cut me a really, really thin slice of that ricotta tart with the truffled peaches? Followed by the linguini…'

'Which one, miss? The broccoli or the prawn?'

She hesitated, weighing it up, then mumbled so softly the waitress had to bend her head to hear, 'Could I try a small taste of each? And I'll have the flounder with the artichoke and caper sauce.'

'That is a *whole* flounder,' a deep voice interjected from the other side of the neighbouring table.

Ariadne felt a sharp stab of annoyance. The man must have had supersonic hearing. Not to mention an insufferable nerve. As if he hadn't spoken, she kept her eyes firmly on the face of the waitress and murmured, 'And a garden salad to go with that, please. And vegetables.'

'Anything else, madam? Pommes Paris? Witlof gorgonzola salad with pancetta and Granny Smith apple?'

'Yes, yes, everything.' Ariadne leaned her head away from the direction of the Nikosto table and whispered, hoping the waitress would get the message and lower her voice as well. She smiled meaningfully at the young woman, wishing with all her heart that Sebastian Nikosto would implode and disappear. 'One more thing,' she said, barely moving her mouth.

The waitress tilted her head to catch her words. 'Yes, miss?'

Ariadne beckoned until the woman leaned her ear closer. 'I'm finding that the light is shining in my eyes here. Would you mind helping me to shift around to that side of the table?'

She could see it would be a squeeze, but it would have the advantage of her sitting with her back to Sebastian.

The woman eyed the space doubtfully. 'I'm not sure your chair will fit on this side, miss. It might be an obstruction when we try to serve the gentleman.'

The deep smooth voice intruded again. 'What if the young lady moves over here?'

Ariadne allowed herself a freezing glance at him.

He was indicating the space beside him, his dark eyes agleam, his smile exuding innocence and goodwill. 'Then she'd be facing away from the light, and she'd be able to enjoy the view. Since we're practically dinner partners already…' His eyes dwelled on Ariadne's face with a sensual, velvet intensity. 'I'd love to have you join me, Miss Giorgias.' His voice was awash with sincerity. 'And you'd be rescued from that wet tablecloth.'

The waitress's eyes warmed when she saw Sebastian. 'Oh, do you know each other?'

'God, yes,' he said heartily. 'Our families have known each other for ever, haven't they, Ariadne?'

Turning to Ariadne, the waitress caught sight of her tablecloth and her drooly expression changed to horror. 'Miss,' she exclaimed, 'this cloth is *soaked*.' She tested the sodden patch. 'Oh. You should have said. This table will have to be reset.'

She swivelled about, and had begun telegraphing across the room for reinforcements when Sebastian murmured something to her and pointed towards the lights.

Easily distracted if the distraction happened to be lean, dark-eyed with stunning cheekbones and a sexy, mocking mouth, the waitress turned to Ariadne, her eyes alight with meaning. 'What do you think, miss? Wouldn't you like to move?' With a lilt of her brows she indicated Sebastian. 'You shouldn't be bothered by the light over there.'

Ariadne was cornered in more ways than one, and her simmering gaze met Sebastian Nikosto's with sardonic appreciation. She wasn't sure how many of the staff he'd bribed, but that smile was anything but innocent. A refusal would make her look downright nasty, her request to move petty and insincere.

'Do you always have to have your own way?'

'I find it best.'

She glowered at him. 'Your tie's crooked.'

'Is it?' He smiled, as if he knew, damn him, how handsome it made him. 'Why don't you come over here and fix it for me?'

She folded her arms across her chest. 'I think you must enjoy punishment. I've already rejected you once this evening.'

His eyes glinted. 'You could always change your mind, though. I'm willing to bet you're pretty good at that.'

Her guilty past rushed to the surface. 'Why? What have you heard?'

His brows lifted with amused curiosity. 'What should I have heard? See? We're already talking. You might as well come on over.' He patted the spot next to him.

She exhaled a long, incredulous breath. Couldn't this man take no for an answer? On the other hand, her tablecloth was wet. And it couldn't hurt just to eat dinner with him, could it? He wasn't likely to whisk her away to his fortress and force her into a wedding ceremony at gunpoint in the dead of night.

'Oh, all *right,*' she said. 'Anything for peace.' The concession was barely wrung from her before Sebastian sprang up and, with help from the waitress, whisked her, her chair and place setting to the Nikosto table.

'There, isn't that better?' His eyes gleamed. 'Now we won't have to shout at each other to be heard.'

'I never shout,' she said coldly.

'No, and you never smile. I'm looking forward to removing that sulky expression.'

She smiled at him just to prove he was wrong, but, after all the horrors of the day, somehow the criticism wounded her already abused feelings. She clung to the smile as tightly as she could, her gaze fixed on a ferry chugging across the harbour in a blaze of lights while she fought the fatal thickening in her throat.

The silence grew charged. After a long tense minute he said gently, 'Ah... Now that I think about it, it might just be the shape of your lips.' He leaned closer and traced the outline of her lips with one lean finger, not quite touching them. 'They have that little pout. And they're very sensuous.'

His voice soaked through her nerve fibres like *kitro*.

CHAPTER FOUR

DINNER had a dizzily mounting tension, not unlike a ritual dance in which each move and countermove weren't known in advance, but had to be guessed at by the dancers.

Ariadne felt weird to be dining with a man she'd so recently refused in marriage, but probably as part of some diabolical master plan Sebastian made no reference to it at all. He drew her along in conversation, smoothly and skilfully, even warmly, though not about the sensitive issues between them. He just skirted the edges of those. *Flirted* the edges. Despite the chilly start, the temperature managed to pick itself up off the floor.

Still, the subject lurked in every glance and nuance of the conversation. What sort of man persisted in charming a woman after he'd been rejected so finally and utterly? Shouldn't he have slunk off into the night? Perhaps he was hoping to change her mind.

And he did have charm. With every comforting mouthful of the heavenly Hyatt food, she felt increasingly aware she didn't dislike him as violently as she'd at first thought. Perhaps he wasn't a barracuda. More a smooth, sleek stingray with a devastating five o'clock shadow. And midnight satin eyes that made her pulse quicken. And a mouth to ravish a woman's dreams.

Her conscience wasn't quite at ease with the new situation, but she quelled it by thinking of it as an emergency. Now she was cast adrift upon the world, for the moment this small table, in this pool of light, with this smoothly determined, dangerous and— she had to admit—extremely attractive man, was all she had to cling to.

It was risky though, feeling this rocky and emotional in the presence of a handsome man and a bottle of champagne. Heartsore, tired people with jet lag could easily switch from sexy enchanting laughter to tears. To prove it, there was a small jazz band across the room, and a singer with a voice like dark honey plucked at her heartstrings with every line of every plaintive old love ballad she sang. *Cry me a river*, she sobbed. *Willow weep for me.*

The setting might have been exciting, and picturesque, with the constantly changing light show on the harbour as traffic streamed across the bridge, and ferries chugged in and out of the Quay lit up like Christmas, but she didn't feel she belonged. She felt so out of place, it was no wonder she was finding solace in the company of her despised bridegroom. *Aspiring* bridegroom.

Every so often she reminded herself this was her country too, but had trouble convincing herself.

She withdrew her gaze from the harbour lights to contemplate Sebastian. If he was regretting transferring her to his table, he wasn't showing it.

His sexy mouth was grave, but there was an unsettling warmth in his dark eyes whenever they rested on her, making her insides curl over with an exhilarating suspense. Meeting his eyes ran her the risk of being scorched. She knew she was flirting with danger, yet she couldn't seem to resist it.

And what with the warm summer air floating in from the terrace, she was getting overheated. 'It's hot in here,' she breathed to Sebastian. 'Don't you feel hot?' She took off her feathery wrap and draped it over the back of her chair.

When she did that an appreciative gleam lit his eyes that made her conscious of having crossed some sort of safety line.

His glance made the skin of her chest and shoulders tingle and burn as if razed by a solar flare. Call her a needy tart, but the sensation felt thrilling to a woman that no man in Greece— probably *Europe*—would touch, even with a very long pole.

Her sexual receptors were madly spinning. He would touch her if he got the chance, she felt sure.

'You set this up, didn't you?' she challenged him, caressing the stem of her glass.

He smiled in acknowledgement. 'I've never really liked eating alone.'

She glowered at him, hoping he didn't guess how seriously that sexy smile was seeping into her bloodstream and melting her resistance. 'How did you know I would be coming to the restaurant?'

He considered her, his sensual gaze flickering with masculine expertise from her face and hair, down her throat to her breasts. 'You've put your hair up. And the dress. You went to so much trouble to look gorgeous, I couldn't see you wasting it all in your room. Even to spite me.' Amusement warmed his eyes.

'Oh.' She flushed. 'Well, I hope it cost you heaps.'

Sebastian watched the delicate tide suffuse her neck, then rise to her soft cheeks, and felt a dangerous surge in his blood. The knowledge that he had the power to evoke such a response was seductive, to say the least.

He restrained his eyes from wandering to her breasts, though he was aware of them with every fibre of his being.

Now the thaw had set in, there was a sparkle in her blue eyes, brought about by the champagne, or the electric charge pulsing between them, he wasn't sure which. Either way, tonight his edgy bride had shown him alluring glimpses of her true self. Bubbly, mischievous, funny, though every so often he heard the tip of some other emotion tinge her voice. Sometimes her smile had a feverish quality, as if her mood could be fragile. Or was she excited?

His *supposed* bride, he corrected himself, watching her lips close over the chocolate-laden spoon while her lashes drifted down in utter bliss.

Disturbed from her appreciation of the divine chocolate by that searing gaze, Ariadne looked at him. 'Do you ever accept a no?'

The sensual flicker in the dark depths of his eyes triggered an answering response deep in her insides. 'Depends who it's from. And how much I want to get to know them.'

'You didn't want to get to know me this morning. Or this afternoon.'

'That was before I met you.'

'Am I supposed to be flattered?'

He considered her. 'Not flattered. Just alive to the possibilities.'

What possibilities? The word floated in her mind like a scintillating mist. Truth to tell, part of her had been alive to some possibilities since the moment she'd rounded that pillar and seen him occupying the table. Or maybe even before then. Perhaps from the first time his eyes had connected with hers across the lobby this evening and started her heart hammering.

She risked a gulp of her champagne, knowing very well it could be a mistake. The stuff was already effervescing in her veins, and she needed to keep her head.

But it was magic, frothing away her misery and easing her anxiety, or at least changing its flavour. Now she felt like a beautiful, desirable woman riding a wild and fantastic whirlwind, and if it wasn't the champagne making her feel that way, what was it?

As if to heighten her turmoil, the singer wrapped them in a smoky embrace with a nostalgic lament for a lost past in some shining place.

She was used to good-looking men with dark eyes and gleaming white smiles, but Sebastian had another dimension that could cut straight through her defences if she didn't take care. Though tonight he was subtly flirtatious, every so often that serious, steel quality shone through. Like her first impression, but without the anger and the ice.

She risked another glance at him. Definitely, the ice had melted, but he was a different species from Demetri and friends, strutting the playgrounds of the world with their lazy, sophisticated boredom. If she hadn't known the truth, she couldn't have imagined he'd have accepted a bribe to marry her.

What had he been offered? she wondered. Shares in the Giorgias line, with the expectation of his wife being heiress to the lot?

She pushed the horrid thought away and concentrated on the positives. She was, in fact, feeling better after the bruschetta, the sliver of tart, the two delicious serves of linguini, the fish—not that she'd eaten very much of anything. She was in far too much of an uproar. The chocolate pudding had been certainly beneficial, although there was also that glass of champagne. Or had it been two? There was the one she'd had before she'd moved…

She peered over at the ice bucket and tried to see how much was left in the bottle. Whatever the level, it had shored up her spirits and helped her to feel warm and glowing and alive, even a bit reckless.

'So what are you doing here with me?' she challenged, fluttering her lashes. 'Is there a shortage of women in Sydney?'

'Not that I've noticed. What's your excuse?' he retorted. 'Are the guys in Greece all doddery and near-sighted?'

She hesitated, evading his smiling, but still penetrating glance, regretting laying herself open to that painful subject. This was a murky alleyway she didn't want to venture down. The last thing she wanted to admit to him was that she'd exhausted her options in Greece. She didn't doubt her uncle's declaration for a minute. No Greek man would risk engaging himself to her now. Not after Demetri's experience and all the publicity.

She said huskily, 'I don't plan to get married. Ever. In Greece or anywhere else.'

'What if you meet someone you fall in love with?'

She shot him a sardonic look. The sheer irony of *him*, of all people, talking about love. 'Are you kidding?'

His brows lifted and she said, waving her fork, 'Let me try to explain, though like all men I expect you'll scoff.' Ignoring his blink, she wrinkled her brow in concentration, and tried to bring it down to words of few syllables. 'You see, my problem is I'd need the person to be in love with me as well. So we would be equals. How can you make promises and accept the blessing of the church without sincerity on both sides?' She looked earnestly at him. 'Do you think you can try to understand that concept, Sebastian?'

His eyes glinted, but she went on, regardless. 'That's why I can never risk it. You imagine someone loves you, then you find out they only wanted to marry you because they mistakenly thought you would inherit the Giorgias shipping fortune.'

His tanned, lean hands stilled. He'd understood that bit all right.

'So you aren't set to inherit?' He scanned her face with an alert gaze.

She might have predicted his interest, but still she felt a stab of disappointment. Just when she was thinking he might be different from Demetri.

He'd made his own feelings on the issue so clear this afternoon, it made her wonder, if he *was* hoping to talk her round, what sort of marriage had he in mind? A marriage in name only, where they signed the register then went their separate ways?

Oh, it was all so humiliating. Did greed always have to outweigh honour and integrity in every man alive? She let out a frustrated sigh. She should let him know right now his chances of using her to improve his fortunes were zilch.

'I won't get a cent of it, as far as I know,' she informed him, watching his face while she dashed his hopes. 'I have older cousins, all male, and the company will go to them. Thio Peri doesn't believe a woman can manage a business. Well, he knows, of course, women can manage *some*, but he doesn't think a woman could manage *his* business.' She sat back in her chair to await results. Would he rise from the table, bid her goodnight and disappear into the distance? 'I'm only a niece, you see. And besides, Thio knows I don't want to have anything to do with it.' With a bittersweet smile she added softly, 'The only thing I'm set to inherit is a little bit of money my parents left. They weren't rich, I'm afraid. We lived in a modest little cottage. I don't think they even owned it. So you'd have nothing to gain.'

He was silent for several seconds, his eyes downcast, his lean face inscrutable. Then he looked up at her. His dark shimmering eyes meshed with hers, deep and unreadable.

'If I married you.'

'That's right. If you… But you can't now, can you? Now that I've—refused you.'

He continued to hold her in his veiled gaze. The moment stretched, while her heart thumped and questions clamoured in her brain. What was he thinking? She had no real idea what her uncle had offered him, what he'd said. Had her warning been enough to put him off? Did he think he could change her mind?

Was she really so innocent? Sebastian wondered. It sounded as if she had no idea of the means her uncle had used to bring him to this point. If she had been set to inherit everything, he felt sure the old magnate would have had no hesitation about dangling his empire before his eyes. The fact that Pericles had never mentioned it to him made her claim seem likely to be true. In a strange way, it even made the outrageous deal slightly more palatable.

He grimaced. He must be going insane. What was wrong with him that made him find something to prefer in being blackmailed in a business deal over being bought like a stud stallion?

The dessert courses were cleared, and he watched her lift her head and turn a little to ask the waiter to pass on to the chef her undying gratitude for the chocolate pudding. The line of her cheek and neck, the smooth curve of her shoulder riveted his gaze and sank into his awareness like a hypnotic. Desire quickened in his blood.

Yiayia was right. He'd been without something lovely to look at for too long.

Even her voice, low and sweet, fell on his ears like an intoxication. Supposing he did decide to marry her, how hard would it be to persuade her?

'Nothing else for me, thank you. Sebastian?' She turned enquiringly to him. 'Cognac?'

He pulled himself together and waved away the menu, asking for the bill, only part of his mind engaged.

The rest of it was imagining how it might be to have Ariadne Giorgias as his wife. To meet those luminous blue eyes, that luscious mouth across his breakfast table. To bury his face in the silken mass of her hair and fan it across his pillow. To plunge himself into the slick heat of her gorgeous body and possess her utterly, until she cried out in ecstasy, night after night after long, hot night.

He drew a long breath and smiled. 'Do you feel like stretching your legs?'

Ariadne looked up, met his darkly handsome face and her heart skittered. Was this where he made his pitch? She hesitated. She could excuse herself, say goodnight, goodbye, and flee to her room. It flashed in on her then though, that once she was alone in her room, she'd have to face the cold reality that this would be her last night's sleep in safety and comfort. All she'd have to look forward to when she lay her head on the pillow would be the morning—homeless, and on her own resources in a strange country.

That morning was racing towards her like a black horror. She felt a deep dread, like an offender staring prison in the face for the first time. With a little shiver, she rose from the table.

The terrace hugged the hotel like the deck of an ocean liner, the sea lapping at its sides. In one direction Circular Quay was a blaze of activity, while far and wide lights twinkled all around the foreshore. As she gazed across at the opera house, its luminous pale shells rendered magical by moonlight, Ariadne could almost have believed she was on one of her uncle's cruise ships, heading for some romantic destination.

Perhaps she wouldn't mind living here, once she'd settled with a job and a place to live. Once she got over the hurt.

They moved out of the spill of light from the restaurant, and she felt grateful for the shadows, not having to keep her smile on.

She could sense a tension in Sebastian, too. The intensity of the mood had ratcheted up to a higher gear, as if the looming goodbye had brought her uncle's deal back to scream silently between them. The suspense that he was about to ask her to reconsider marrying him kept her nerves jangling.

As they strolled the terrace, though, chatting about tastes in books and music, he didn't mention it, or touch her. Maybe she was being super-sensitive, but it seemed to her he tried extra hard not to let his hand or any part of his clothing brush hers.

Like Demetri, only not like Demetri. With Demetri, she'd never had this taut, smouldering awareness. Never felt so feminine and desirable.

Sebastian eyed her profile and wondered what devil had tempted him to suggest strolling out here in the dark. As soon as he had her away from the crowd, it was hard not to think about her breasts, and how long it had been since he'd kissed a woman.

It must have been the power of suggestion. If it had never been suggested to him that she could be his, he probably wouldn't need to keep looking at her. He wouldn't be itching to smooth his hand over her shoulder, or be so achingly aware of the creamy rises swelling the black fabric of the dress. And there was the explosive fact lurking in the nether regions of his mind that she had a room upstairs, and a bed.

His loins stirred and he willed his flesh not to react to his luscious imaginings any further. She was so slender and petite, he had to wonder if she'd be large enough to take him.

He sighed. As if she'd read his mind she sent him a quick, searching glance, and he made a resolute attempt to keep the conversation on the straight and narrow.

'Do you remember much about Australia?' he said.

She looked up. 'I have some images of our house, and the school I went to. Children I played with. When I drove in from the airport I saw some trees that looked familiar. You'll probably think this sounds silly, but seeing them made me get all misty.'

'No. I don't think that's silly. I guess this must be quite an emotional time for you.'

Ariadne lowered her glance. 'You could say that.'

She felt surprised. There'd been sensitivity in his observation, almost like a friend. How ironic that, having dreaded meeting him almost to the point of nausea, as he was the only person she knew in the whole country she now dreaded the moment of saying goodbye to him.

That poignant song wafted from inside, winding its way in among her emotions. As she fielded Sebastian's questions about her life in Naxos the singer brought the melody to a crescendo of yearning that tore at her heart like a cry from across the sea.

The silver moon, the evening tide…how they evoked Naxos. She was swamped by a flood of homesickness, made worse by the knowledge she could never go back there now. Not now she'd sinned and they'd packed her off to the other side of the globe. Not now they'd hurt her.

Sebastian leaned beside her, caught a faint whiff of some enticing flowery perfume, and moved a safer distance away. Her blue eyes were dark and unreadable, with an occasional glitter that came from within. He realised with a slight shock that a vein of sadness ran beneath her volatile mood.

Desire was singing a siren song in his veins, but he kept a tight rein on it. Beauty mixed with emotion and moonlight could tempt a man to do and say things he'd regret. If he didn't maintain strict control he'd be dragging her against him and kissing her, tasting her sensuous mouth, caressing her soft curves...

'So what do you plan to do on your holiday?' he said.

'I might travel around. See some of the country.'

'Do you have any relatives here from your mother's side? Grandparents?'

She gave a shrug. 'My Australian grandma died a couple of years ago. There are a few cousins I've never met. Just a great-auntie Maeve who lives somewhere on the coast. Well, used to. My parents took me to stay with her once for a holiday when I was very small.' She wrinkled her brow. 'It might have been called Noza. Nootza. Something like that. Is that a place?'

He frowned. 'Could you be thinking of Noosa?'

Her brows lifted. 'Could be. That sounds right, doesn't it? Oh, it was heavenly there. I remember the beach, and Mummy and Daddy being really happy.' After a second she said lightly, 'Is it far from here?'

Something in her voice made him turn to examine her face. 'Noosa's up north. In Queensland. About a day's drive from here, perhaps a couple of hours by air. It's a fairly popular tourist resort.'

'Oh, good, good.' After a second she cast him a veiled glance. 'Do you think Queensland has art galleries?'

He lifted his brows. 'Bound to, of some sort. But if you want to visit art galleries there are plenty right here in Sydney.'

'Oh. Yeah.' She lowered her lashes. 'Of course. There would be.'

'Are you interested in art? Your father was an artist, wasn't he?'

She looked quickly at him. 'How do you know that?'

'My grandmother remembers who's who in everyone's family.'

'Oh.' Even in the soft light from the restaurant he saw her flush. 'You checked up on me. They know.' Her voice grew hoarse, as if she was stricken with the news. 'Your—your family *know*. About the—the deal you made with my uncle.'

Shocked by the raw emotion in her voice, for a moment he couldn't answer, words were snatched from him. Then he said, 'No, no, they— They don't know anything. And I haven't signed anything.'

'Oh, you haven't signed. Great.' She gripped the rail as if to steady herself. 'So tell me, then, what did he offer you? Honestly, please.'

'You.'

Her flush deepened, then she covered her face with her hands. The strangled words were almost a cry. 'In exchange for what?'

Her pained mortification wrenched something deep in his guts. With shame he recognised he'd never once properly considered the transaction from her point of view. He'd always assumed she was compliant. Even when she'd told him she didn't intend to marry him, he'd assumed it had been out of pique and anger.

How had the uncle presented the deal to her? It was clear now it hadn't been her initiative at all, and she knew nothing about the blackmail. He tried to remember what she'd told him in the lobby. A holiday to see if they suited each other, wasn't that what she'd said? Was that how it had been sold to her?

Never mind that the deal was all but sewn up a week before she'd left home. She deserved to know the truth, but how much truth about her uncle could she take?

He said carefully, 'Peri has offered a contract to my company—Celestrial. We design satellite systems for all sorts of uses, including marine navigation. Your uncle wants to upgrade his fleets' equipment.'

'I see.' She held herself rigidly. Shadows under her eyes gave them a bruised look, but she maintained a stiff dignity, trying so hard not to betray her distress he felt moved. 'So—so what will happen now the deal's off? Without a wedding? Will that matter to your company?'

Again he felt ashamed. Here she was struggling with her own situation, and she was worrying about his. He had no right to place any more anxiety on her head, he saw now.

He gave an easy shrug, easier than the grim reality warranted. 'We have other clients.'

'Oh.' She expelled a breath. 'Good. Well, that's a relief, anyway.'

'So…' He glanced searchingly at her. 'When you said you came out here for a holiday, you were telling the truth?'

She glanced at him and he saw with a further shock that the sudden glitter in her eyes was a wash of tears. She lowered her gaze as if she couldn't face him and turned sharply away. 'Yes, ' she said in a choked voice. 'That was it. A holiday.'

A few strands of her hair were ruffled by the breeze. The sight of her vulnerable neck in the moonlight caused something to twist in his chest. He took her shoulders and turned her gently back to face him. 'Ariadne, listen… There's no need to…'

A ray of light caught the sparkle of a tear on her lashes, and he felt a dismayed, incoherent wave of tenderness, but how was he, a man and a virtual stranger, to comfort her? Unable to frame the appropriate words, he bent to brush her mouth with his. It was only the briefest of touches, but the contact to his starved lips was sizzling dynamite.

She didn't pull away. She stood absolutely immobilised as though poised on a heartbeat, her sweet face still turned up in the kiss position, her lashes fluttering down in languid expecta-tion. For an instant the planet held its breath.

God, it had been so long. Unable to resist such enticement, he kissed her properly.

He felt the shock ripple through her slender frame. Her mouth quivered under his, and he felt the leap of response ignite in her deliciously soft, fiery lips. He pulled her hard against him, his own lips ablaze, wild to feel her breasts in friction with his chest, greedy to have all of her at once with every part of him.

He urged her lips into parting, then slipped his tongue into the intoxicating seduction of her wine-sweet mouth. The scents and flavours of champagne, freshness, flowers and sweet, primitive woman rose and mingled in his senses, binding him in eternal, erotic enslavement. Stroking her mouth into arousal with his tongue was his own delicious torture.

He heard her make a small involuntary sound in the back of her throat, so evocative of passion the thrill of victory roared through him.

He deepened his demand on her mouth. And she responded, clinging to him and kissing him back with all the fire and fervour a man could dream of igniting in a woman.

All at once she leaned into him like a collapse, her soft curves so yielding and pliant it was another total seduction. He was swept with a purely masculine triumph as he recognised the slight loss of traction in her ability to stand upright. The more boneless and giving she felt in his arms, the harder and more focused was his lust to possess her.

With the strongest effort of will he fought to hold back his erection, but could anything be more irresistible than a desirable woman on the verge of surrender? Like a molten torrent the hot blood surged to harden him unbearably.

The wild notion stormed his fevered brain that he could take her, right there and then, up against the wall of the Park Hyatt.

But he wasn't altogether lost to reality. His desire filled him to bursting point but he restrained his yearning to grind his aching rod into the cleft between her thighs, though he was fast approaching the moment of barely being able to draw a line in his mind between imagining the rapturous pleasure and experiencing it.

He kept his lustful hands from plundering her ripe breasts, though his palms ached for their lushness.

He was a civilised man, and, though no one else was close by, they were in a public place. She must have become alive to that fact at the same time, because she suddenly stiffened in his arms, broke the kiss and shoved at his chest.

Regretfully he fell back, the feel of her warm, fragrant body lingering in his arms, in thrall to her fresh sweetness to the depths of his being.

She gazed at him, her eyes dark and stormy with that voluptuous, erotic knowledge women's eyes possessed when they'd just been thoroughly kissed. He could see her panting, her breasts heaving alluringly beneath the confining dress.

'Shall we go somewhere for coffee?' he managed to say, smooth as ever under pressure.

She stared at him for a second as comprehension clicked his meaning into place, then blue fire flashed from her eyes. 'We shall do no such *thing*. You listen to me, Sebastian Nikosto. That—*that* was a mistake. You shouldn't have done that.'

Her sultry mouth was even more swollen. It was so damnably seductive, it took his brain a moment to register her displeasure.

'You had no *right*,' she gasped. 'Just because my uncle offered me to you, doesn't mean *I* have. I'm not freely available to you. I'm not a—a—a goat or a donkey you can just–just *use* for your pleasure.'

'What?' He felt so rocked by the accusation his own voice sounded like a growl from the pit. 'That's not what I... Look, I *know* that, Ariadne. I wouldn't try to...I'm not the sort of guy who—who...' Anger, pride and masculine honour sprang bristling to his defence, but he damped down the bitter, blistering words that could have risen to his tongue.

With as much dignity as possible for a man in the grip of a hard-on, he said, his voice crackling with the effort, 'In case you didn't recognise it, what you just experienced was a kiss. A genuine kiss. The sort of kiss a man gives a woman he feels some sort of— *Admires*, for God's sake. And I'm pretty well certain you were appreciating it as much as I was. Sorry if you feel guilty about it.'

He waited to hear what she would say, but she'd turned her back on him and was smoothing herself down and tidying her hair, brushing down her dress with her hands as if she'd just been in the jaws of a wild foaming beast and needed to remove all traces of him.

He gave her an extra moment to lessen the charges, but nothing came of it. Sebastian Nikosto wouldn't wait for ever, however desirable the woman.

'Goodnight, then.' He clipped his punishingly polite words to give them maximum bite. 'Sleep well.'

He turned rigidly and walked back into the restaurant, a boiling chaos thundering through his veins of outrage, astonishment, guilt and bloody, bloody desire.

She swept up beside him in a flowery cloud of that perfume that would haunt him for the rest of his life, stalked to the table they'd shared, and snatched up her purse and wrap.

'And please don't insult me any further by attempting to pay for my dinner, Mr Nikosto.' Her sweet, low voice throbbed with emotion. 'I'll pay for my own. And it's not goodnight, it's *goodbye*.'

Sebastian drove to the Celestrial office, took the lift up to his floor and strode to his desk. Without a second's pause he typed the email he knew he should have sent a week since.

To: Pericles Giorgias

Dear Mr Giorgias,

At Celestrial we conduct our business contracts with honour and transparency. As CEO of this company, I reject utterly all hidden clauses, including 'gentlemen's agreements' that cannot stand up legally or morally to the light of public scrutiny.

Celestrial withdraws from all negotiations with Giorgias Shipping.

Consider our association at an end.

Sebastian Nikosto.

His cursor hovered over the send button while frustration and desperation boiled in his soul. Hell, but of course he couldn't send it. He slumped in his chair.

Now what? Work all night to eliminate the taste of her?

He got up and paced the office, striving to focus his mind on the challenges ahead of him the next day, anything to wipe out of his head the woman and her outrageous reaction to a simple kiss.

But it wasn't just the kiss, was it? his uncomfortable conscience nagged. It was the situation. It was his idiocy in suggesting coffee. Why had he done it? He cringed to think of how inept he'd been.

God, had he been so long without a woman he could no longer recognise one who'd been brought up in the traditions?

He cursed himself for a fool, blundering into that kiss with such blind abandon. How could he not have read the signs? He couldn't believe his error of judgement. She'd looked shocked, and revealed an utterly devastating lack of experience.

Where had she been for the last sixteen years? Had Peri Giorgias wrapped his niece in cotton wool and kept her in a tower?

He hadn't asked for her, but, whether he liked it or not, however furious and enraged and maddened he felt by the situation, she was here now, dammit. Proud, touchy and—

Soft. Fragrant. Yielding to any enchanted fool who took her in his arms.

Vulnerable, for God's sake.

Against his will, he'd been moved by her. And however unpredictable and explosive a package she was, he felt responsible for her. Not that she'd ever allow him to set foot near her again.

He winced with the acknowledgement that some of the accusations she'd hurled at him could have had some basis of truth. Would he have succumbed to temptation so rapidly if he hadn't at some stage thought of her as his for the taking?

He threw himself in his chair and flicked through his program files, stared for minutes unseeing at the screen, then gave up. A hundred laps of the pool were what he needed, followed by a long cold shower.

The situation looked irretrievable. Even if he wanted to risk taking the marriage option he'd wrecked his chances now. And admit it. He *wanted* to see her again. Wanted to talk to her, watch her eyes light up when she laughed, listen to her surprisingly husky voice.

Feel her softness. He closed his eyes while his senses swam in recollection.

If he could just think of some way to make things right with her.

CHAPTER FIVE

IT WAS too hot in Sydney, even in an air-conditioned hotel suite of the finer quality. And there was no use blaming the champagne. A woman suffering sleep deprivation and jet lag should have expected to be able to sleep, not to toss and turn on her pillow or lapse into fitful dreams about Sebastian Nikosto. Disturbing dreams. Sensual and erotic dreams.

Although, if she was still wide awake could they honestly be called dreams? Fantasies, more like. Fantasies where he kissed her and touched her in the places she'd been so wildly conscious of during that kiss.

But as for that crack he'd made at the end about her feeling guilty...

Guilty? Her? Was *she* the one who'd instigated the kiss? Certainly she'd been polite, and co-operated in the spirit of the moment, but that was because she'd been well brought up, she had good manners and he'd taken her by surprise.

Every time she thought of the moment his lips had touched hers her insides swirled helplessly with a warm, languorous pleasure. The experience had felt nothing like kissing Demetri. She'd thought she'd been in heaven kissing Demetri, but now she realised she might as well have been pressing her mouth to the mirror.

She smoothed her fingers experimentally over her lips. She'd read about that fiery sensation in romance novels, of course, but never imagined it actually existed. She'd known sexy kisses, sure, but she'd never experienced those little tongues of flame dancing along her lips. Privately, she couldn't deny it had been pretty overwhelming.

She wondered if Sebastian had felt the same sensation. Perhaps he had, because what else had he meant about going somewhere for coffee if not to bed with her? He'd wanted to make love, just like that, and for a wild moment, for just a brief, fleeting, minuscule fraction of an instant, she was tempted.

But he didn't know that, did he? Or did he? How could he have known? She realised then that she'd known pretty definitely that he'd wanted her, so he probably did know.

Oh, it was all so humiliating. How could she allow herself to feel the slightest bit of attraction to a man someone else had chosen for her? A man who stood to make a profit?

His stunned face when she was accusing him of taking advantage of her rose up in her mind and she grew hotly impatient with herself. For goodness' *sake*, if only she could stop dwelling on it. What did it matter? She'd never see him again, anyway, and that was how she wanted it.

She kicked off the covers and turned on her side, willing herself to fall asleep. She'd just closed her eyes when a weird vibrating buzz by the side of the bed alerted her to the fact that the hotel phone was ringing on its night setting.

Thea Leni? A reprieve?

She scrabbled for the phone, knocking nearly everything off the nightstand in the process. 'Yes?'

There was a very small pause, then the deep masculine voice sank through her. 'It's Sebastian. *Don't...*'

Her entire being sprang to vibrant, pulse-drumming attention.

'...hang up, Ariadne,' he was saying. '*Listen*, please. I just want to—say something.'

She shouldn't listen. She should hang up and avoid talking

to him ever again. But she held her breath and the phone with a faintly moistening grip.

'What—what is there to say?'

He sighed. 'Oh, Ariadne.' That sigh rustled through her and disarmed her utterly, so evocative it was of rueful, manly remorse and bewilderment. 'What isn't there to say? I haven't woken you, have I?'

'No, no, I—I'm in bed.'

There was a sudden dramatic silence, then another sigh. This one had a totally different quality.

'Are you? In bed?' Even without seeing him she could feel his slow sexy smile break out. 'Me too. I haven't been able to sleep for thinking of…tonight and…what happened.' His voice had deepened, and become darker and more velvet if possible, as if by proxy stroking her all over in lieu of his lean, bronzed hands. 'I just needed to tell you that—I'm sincerely sorry I upset you. *All*—all the times I've upset you.'

'Oh.' She struggled with whether or not she should forgive him. Would it be weak of her? Wasn't he just trying to talk her round? But she wanted to. She brightened at the thought that without anyone else in Sydney, possibly the country, she didn't have a choice.

Not to make it too easy for him though, she said sternly, 'Well, you know, you can't just go around kissing people.'

'I know.'

He sounded so contrite, she felt soothed enough to go on. 'Trapping people into having dinner with you, then talking them into walking in the dark with you, and…'

'I know, I know. It probably looked like that. Can you just consider for a minute that I might—that I just—sincerely wanted to get to know you?'

She was silent. 'Well, there's no way you can get to *know* someone from one dinner. Not enough to—kiss them. We were *strangers*. We're still strangers.'

'Not altogether. Not now. Now that we've…'

'Kissed?' The word came out so huskily she had to clear her throat.

This time she could feel his smile radiating down the airwaves like a warm Saharan breeze. 'Well, I *was* going to say broken bread together, but, now that you mention it, a kiss does rather focus your attention on a person, doesn't it? I think it can tell you a lot.'

A hot flush washed through her, possibly making her glow in the dark. What could he tell about her? She hoped he didn't guess she'd been lying here, unable to think of anything else except that kiss. Whether she'd performed her part well enough. How much better it might have been if she had more practice. How she might *achieve* such practice.

'Maybe,' she conceded. 'All right, then.'

'And—look, I have to say I don't think of you as being a donkey, or a goat.'

Suspecting that he might secretly be laughing at the passionate things she'd said, she retorted quickly, 'You knew what I meant!'

'I did, yes. I think I can understand. I wanted to tell you that I feel the deepest respect for you.' He exhaled a long breath. 'Oh. This is a damnable way to meet someone, isn't it?'

Her ears rang in disbelief. She was silent, straining to wrench the inferences from the words. Did he mean…*meet* someone? As in…?

After a while she ventured, 'What—do you mean?'

Now *he* was hesitating. 'I think you are aware that I find you very attractive.'

Her heart thundered into a drum roll. Now was the time to hang up on him. Stop him from saying another seductive, undermining word. But she held on, drinking in every gap, every pause and nuance of what came next like a swan under the spell of a sorcerer.

'Desire is an amazing thing, isn't it?' he went on, his voice grave now. Warm and serious and sincere.

She lay in the darkness, her heart thundering, breathing so fast, with no defences against the beautiful deep masculine voice vibrating through her body, playing on her emotions, saying the things she'd always dreamed a gorgeous man would say to her.

'...So stunning, and exciting, the way it hits you like a train. Even when you might expect to feel the very opposite, you see someone across a room and at once your body knows, even before your mind does. Do you know what I mean?'

She was knocked sideways, her heart a racing turmoil, her brain in shocked, incoherent confusion. 'Oh, well, yes, I know I guess, Sebastian, but...but I mean... I can't *say*... Anyway, look. I have to...I have to get up early in the morning. So...'

'Oh. So you'd better get some sleep. Goodnight, then, Ariadne.'

'Goodnight.' She breathed the last word so softly it was hardly more than air, while her racing pulse roared in her ears.

Sebastian closed his phone and lay in the dark, wondering how far he'd retrieved the situation, smiling to himself about the shyness and shock in her husky voice, imagining her lying in bed in her pyjamas. No, not pyjamas.

A woman like Ariadne would wear pretty, virginal night-dresses. Fine cotton embroidered by little Swiss nuns with lace attached. What did they call that stuff? Broderie anglaise. He supposed it would be pretty enough, but say she belonged to him, he'd have wanted her to wear delicate silks and satins with thin little straps. Filmy things.

The vision that had nearly overwhelmed him when she'd told him she was in bed came flooding back to swamp him. Her hair spread around her on the pillow, her slim body covered in something diaphanous. Sweet, pointed nipples through the gauzy fabric.

He dragged a pillow against him and groaned.

God, it had been too long.

* * *

Ariadne was up soon after dawn. After that call it had taken ages to fall asleep, but at least the jagged emotions of the disagreement had been smoothed away. Admit it, she'd been excited, going over every little thing Sebastian had said. At the time some of the things had moved her with their conviction, but now in the cold light of day she needed to try to be honest with herself.

What had really changed? Tempting as it might be to allow herself to be carried away, she mustn't forget that he had an incentive. Still, she wished she had at least said goodbye to him.

She was too worried about the bill to order breakfast, and besides, how could anyone eat with their life hanging in the balance?

When she was nearly ready to leave, she spread out the small collection of jewellery she'd thought appropriate to bring on a short holiday. Her earrings were all quite good, though she doubted she could get much for them, even if she found a jeweller who would accept them in exchange for cash.

She doubted her ruby pendant would buy her a bed for the night, let alone a plane ticket and a week or two's accommodation in Queensland. Then there was her watch. She laid it on the console table and tried to reconcile the idea of selling it with sentiment and guilt. It had been her mother's, one of the few reminders she had of that beloved face.

No, not that. Never. She couldn't bear to part with it.

The most valuable item was the sapphire bracelet Thio and Thea had given her when she'd turned twenty-one. The sapphires were finely matched Ceylonese, lavender-tinged blue and wrought with white gold. She adored the exquisite thing. The thought of selling it, when they'd loved her so much in the giving of it...

Her eyes started pricking again and she fought off the emotion and thrust those thoughts away. If they'd loved her, why had they done this terrible thing?

She fastened on the watch, and rolled the other items carefully back in their velvet pouches, slipping the earrings and the wrapped bracelet into her jacket pocket. She'd read of poor people selling their jewels to pawnbrokers, but Thea always dealt with Cartier. The bracelet had probably come from one of their boutiques, anyway. Surely they'd be happy to buy it back.

With her bags assembled ready for the porter, she located a phone directory, then reefed through it. There was a Cartier in Sydney, and hundreds of other jewellers, though she had no idea whether the addresses placed them near or far.

Perhaps the concierge could help.

Downstairs, she faced the reception clerk with a certain amount of trepidation. Her suite was opulent, even by the standards she'd been used to when she'd travelled with her aunt, so she could expect the cost to be high. Even so, when they handed her the account she was staggered.

She stared at it with disbelief, dismay clawing at her nape. Who'd have guessed champagne was so expensive? And why had she ordered so many courses without even checking to see what things cost? Guiltily, she realised she'd hardly even done justice to the meal, she'd been so churned up.

And why, for heaven's sake, had she needed an entire suite? Had Thio ever in his life been content to book a single room?

She stared at the invoice for a few moments, then looked the clerk in the eye and signed the credit-card slip as coolly as if she were rich and had the full backing of Giorgias Shipping.

Another night like this, though, and she'd be cleaned out. She'd have to think of something fast.

The concierge agreed to keep her suitcase safe until she returned. He obligingly scanned his computer screen for her when she enquired about jewellers, then produced a map of the city and ringed an address for her. Within walking distance, he said.

* * *

Sebastian made a deliberate effort to relax on his drive to work. In spite of a strenuous and bracing early-morning surf, the song that had haunted him through the night continued to echo in his mind. Ariadne, Ariadne…

How successful had he been in recovering ground with her? Perhaps she'd agree to meet him later. Maybe he could even take this weekend off to show her some of the sights. How long since he'd taken a weekend?

With an effort, he focused on the day ahead. Gloom had settled over the company, and it was becoming a difficult place to be. He knew his employees were asking questions about the Giorgias Shipping bid. Where was it heading? If there wasn't some sort of contract in the offing this week, any contract, he had some hard decisions ahead of him.

Trouble was, the place he really wanted to go right now was the Hyatt, to drown himself in blue eyes. This was hardly the way to deal with a crisis. The stress must have been getting to him.

Ariadne stalked numbly out of the pawnshop and into the street. She hadn't expected much cash for her earrings, but the amount the broker had offered for the sapphire bracelet had been pitiful. Surely they must be worth thousands. Thea never bought poor jewellery, not for a gift, not for anything.

If the salespeople at Cartier's hadn't been so suspicious and mistrustful when she'd offered to sell it to them, she'd have thought to have it valued so she'd at least know what sort of price to bargain for. As it was, she'd been lucky to escape from the shop without the police being called.

She broke out in perspiration as for a wild second she teetered on the verge of real panic. Conscious of an unpleasant sensation of nausea, she had to fight to steady herself enough to hang onto her control.

She leaned back against a shop window while she cooled down enough to think. There was no use sinking down onto the pavement. She could *earn* money, and when she had enough she'd buy her bracelet back from that sleazy pawnshop.

What she needed was to find a way to solve her situation. She forced herself to concentrate on her map, clinging to its solid reality like a lifeline. When her hot, scared pulse had subsided, she picked herself up and headed away from this dingy section of the city, back in the direction of the glossy shopping malls and department stores where she felt safer, enviously aware of all the happy-go-lucky Australians who took their homes and means and shelter for the night so cheerfully for granted.

Somehow, she would have to find work and a place to stay *quickly*. Surely accommodation would be cheaper outside the city?

The Centrepoint Arcade looked like a promising centre for internet cafés. She rode up and down escalators, tramped through the labyrinth of byways, until she found one and was able to log onto a computer.

Flights to Queensland weren't very expensive, she discovered, but accommodation in Noosa was. With a growing sense of dismay she scrolled through list after list of Noosa hotels. In Australia it was midsummer, the high season. There were a few vacancies left in cheaper places for backpackers, but she shrank from the idea of sharing accommodation with strangers. Did she even really want to go to Queensland now?

If she risked money to travel to Noosa and stay for the several nights, maybe weeks, it would take her to find a job, what guarantee did she have that Maeve still lived there? And how would she find her? She wasn't even sure of Maeve's surname. Her mother had been a Hughes, but a five-year-old would hardly have been aware of Maeve's family name.

And what would she do if she found her? Throw herself on Maeve's mercy? If Maeve had been the slightest bit interested in her existence, wouldn't she have contacted her after her parents died?

Without a secure money supply, the whole scheme started to look like a wildly impossible fantasy.

She spent a long time working out the intricacies of trawling through job registers, and saw with a sinking heart that it might not be as easy to find work in an art gallery as she'd hoped, even in a smaller centre. According to these websites, people needed as much documentation to prove their credentials and experience here as they did in Athens, and hers were all behind her in Naxos.

In desperation, she considered emailing Thea with an urgent request to send on her documents, then dismissed the idea. How likely was Thea to help her?

She slumped back in the chair. The naivety of her plans homed in on her. She knew one definite person in Australia, and here she was, rushing to get as far away from him as quickly as possible.

She needed help, but there was no way she could surrender to her uncle's plan by begging Sebastian for it. Her pride smarted fiercely at the thought of that. Unless she could think of some way to re-open negotiations without losing face…

One thing she'd learned during the Demetri crisis was that, whatever the fallout, she had to be true to herself. No matter how desperate she was, there was no way she would go on her knees to Sebastian in the role of victim.

And after that call last night, it was clear *what* he would think if she went to him. If he believed she was attracted to him…

Oh, please. Who did she think she was kidding? He believed it, all right. He knew it. Why else would he have said those things? He'd practically spelled it out.

If she went to him and told him she was without money, she'd have no bargaining power. What would he do—write her a cheque? She couldn't accept that. Anyway, he'd be much more likely to take her home with him. He'd be throwing her into his bed and having his way with her in no time, with no ring on her finger.

She'd be in an even worse position than a mail-order bride, reduced to being a casual fling, with no long-term security, her faith and upbringing betrayed, her conscience on fire for the rest of her life.

For the thousandth time the prospect of her own money sitting there in some solicitor's trust fund glowed in her mind with frustrating allure. If only she could get her hands on it. Even if it only amounted to a few thousand dollars, from where she stood now it would look like security.

She tried not to panic, but she knew she'd have to be quick. If she was in Sydney for long, last night had shown her how rapidly she'd eat up her little fund of money out of pure ignorance of the cost of ordinary things. Even when she'd been working in Athens, her flat and household expenses, including the domestic staff, had all been paid by her uncle.

She was green, that was her trouble. But no way was she a useless hothouse flower, as the tabloids had painted her, with no useful knowledge of the world except how to dress and how to look at a painting. Her aunt and uncle had seen her job as a nice little way to fill in time while she waited for her real purpose in life to be established, but she'd loved her career and taken it seriously. She'd run the acquisitions department at the gallery like clockwork until the scandal had caused her sacking. One rude assistant had described her as the fairy-floss tyrant.

Anyway, she could run a household and manage a staff of eleven, more if required. Thea had done her best to shape her as a potential wife, making certain she could cook, even if it wasn't very likely she would ever have to on a regular basis. And she was a fast learner. Some men found her attractive, even if Demetri didn't. Some even *admired* her.

Her uncle had often laughed at how she made every personal decision with her heart and not her head. She'd accepted his analysis with pride, preferring to be described as a passionate idealist than as some ruthless, calculating machine of a woman.

But it was clear that if she was to survive, this time she would have to dredge up her hard-headed negotiating skills.

Somehow, despite her attraction to Sebastian Nikosto, she would need to bargain with him as coolly and dispassionately as ever her uncle had.

She stared unseeing at the computer screen, then slumped forward with her face in her hands.

If only she understood more about men. How much had that midnight phone conversation meant? He might just have been trying to smooth things over after the restaurant. Sweet-talking her. But why? Did he still have hopes of the marriage?

Perhaps it really had been a genuine kiss, and he was sincere. How on earth was she to tell?

CHAPTER SIX

FEELING like an executioner, Sebastian listened to the discussion around the conference table with half an ear, his brows drawn. Which of his team would he let go? Shiny, fresh-faced Matt, who was only just starting out, straight from university, so thrilled to have found employment in the industry of his choice? Or Jake, with a wife and three kids to provide for? School fees and a mortgage. Then there was Sarah, a creative talent who showed real promise.

Once lost to Celestrial, the chances of replacing his carefully chosen designers with equal talents in some post-crisis future were slim. And how would they survive in the meantime?

He'd just roused himself to rejoin the discussion when Jenny, his warm, efficient PA, slipped into the room and caught his eye.

'Not now.' He frowned with a slight shake of his head.

'But…' There was hesitation in her hazel eyes, then with an unprecedented disregard for his rebuff, she leaned close and murmured in his ear, 'Mr Nikosto, she says it's urgent.'

Deep in Sebastian's entrails a nerve jumped. '*Who* says?'

Though he knew. With a soaring anticipation in his chest, he knew.

Jenny lowered her voice even further. 'A Miss Giorgias. She says she's leaving Sydney in an hour, but she's prepared to give you some time to talk if you come at once.'

'Thanks.' He gave her a nod, then rose and excused himself. He strolled to his office, still cool and in control though an exultant expectation was rising in him like foam.

He reached for his desk phone. Steady, he warned himself. He put the phone to his ear, said without expression, 'Sebastian.'

He heard her small intake of breath, the slight hesitation, and his pulse quickened with the most thrilling suspense.

'It's—Ariadne.' There was commotion in the background that suggested a busy public place. 'If you would— If you would care to, I have a little time to talk to you before I leave.' Her voice sounded breathless, as if she'd been running. Or felt nervous.

He was plunged into a turmoil of conflicting desire and responsibility. 'I'm involved here today. I can't—'

'Oh, well, it doesn't matter,' she said at once. 'I don't really have time either. I guess I'll just say—'

'Where are you?'

'I think it's…er…Pitt Street and Market. In a phone booth, near a café called The Coffee Club.'

For a wild, wavering instant he tossed up his competing urgencies. Glancing at the desk clock, he saw it was nearly morning teatime. Supposing he sprinted all the way…

He issued a command. 'Stay there. Don't move.'

He punched in a call to Jenny, gave her some brisk instructions, then took the lift down to the ground floor. As soon as he was on the street he broke into a run. With the adrenaline singing in his veins he hardly noticed the shoppers as he cut through the crowds like a home-running champion whizzing through the bases. He grinned at furious drivers pumping their horns when he dodged them at the crossings, and flew the five city blocks in a matter of minutes.

Once in the Pitt Street Mall, though, he paused to catch his breath, smoothed his hand over his hair, checked his tie was in place, shirt tucked in. Then, energised, his capillaries tingling to the scent of victory, he headed for the Market Street end.

The café was easy enough to locate. He zeroed in on her standing to one side of the entrance, her bag slung casually from her shoulder. At first sight of her desire quickened his blood like an aphrodisiac.

Her blonde hair rippled down her back and she was wearing sunglasses, slim, sand-coloured trousers that hung from her hips and a pretty white short-sleeved top. Simple, classy and sexy. Oh, so sexy.

He started forward, then restrained himself to a casual stroll.

Ariadne scanned the crowd, her nervous pulse bumping along. She was about to take the most enormous risk. The possibilities of humiliation were so extreme she felt almost faint. She was gambling on making her offer sound businesslike, a simple contract. If only she could manage to control her responses to him and stay cool and clear-headed.

'Hi.'

She started as Sebastian's deep voice cut through her anxious churnings and swivelled around. His handsome face was smooth and expressionless, his dark eyes veiled.

'Oh, hi,' she breathed, overwhelmed by the immediacy of his lean, dark sexiness in the raw, masculine flesh. She felt burningly conscious of those words that had thrilled down her spine during the midnight call. 'You—you didn't take long.'

His searching gaze swept over her, not missing a thing. She prayed she didn't look desperate, or too rounded in the hips and bust as Demetri had once criticised. Then his eyes lit with a smile, and she remembered what he'd said about desire hitting you like a train.

'It's not far.' He shrugged. 'People are waiting for me, so I can't give you much time.' He glanced at his watch, then indicated the café entrance. 'Do you want to go inside?' He made to take her elbow, but his hand just stopped short of touching her.

She walked into the café ahead of him, sensing his gaze scorching down her spinal column while she racked her brains for a way to begin. He was in a different mode from the man who'd talked so sweetly to her in the night. He looked serious and inaccessible, a CEO with his mind on his work.

He pointed her to a vacant table and she sat down, trembling all at once with the risk of the gamble she was about to take.

'So?' His acute gaze penetrated through to the back of her brain as if he could read all the lies she'd ever told, all her fears and failings, her empty bank account, the Demetri scandal, her uncle and aunt and their low trick.

Ariadne drew in a long breath and met his gaze. 'All right. I've made a decision. I'll do it.'

His eyes sharpened. 'Do what?'

It took her a moment to frame the words. 'Marry you.' She clenched her hands in her lap.

He stilled. The lines of his face grew focused and intent. Her words seemed to crash in the air around them. It was as if the entire café receded into the distance, and he and she were the only people in the world. She had a dim realisation of the enormity of her offer.

He sat studying her face with a frown. 'Let me get this straight. You're now asking me to marry you. What makes you think I want to get married?'

Thunk, went her heart, then started knocking against her ribs.

He lowered his black lashes, then gave a quizzical shrug. 'I'm not sure I know what to say.'

She felt heat flood her. The ground under her suddenly shifted. With a terrible embarrassment she realised she'd assumed too much, thinking he'd ever been willing. Aware of her cheeks burning, she tried to think of an excuse for her ghastly blunder. 'I thought you said—my uncle had offered your company a contract.'

'I didn't say I'd accepted it.'

He was playing it cool but alluring images were flashing through Sebastian's mind. The contract with Giorgias Shipping, signed and sealed. Celestrial on solid ground, his workforce safe and secure. He thought of the faces around the conference table that morning, the unspoken anxiety that hung over the office. How it would feel to tell them all the company's worries were over.

He contemplated the woman seated across the table from him and felt a dangerous excitement streak through him. Her blue eyes were cool and guarded, her delicious lips slightly parted, as if she was holding her breath. So kissable. He remembered the taste of her, the fragrance of her skin and hair.

Warning bells clanged Esther in some cautious part of him, perhaps he should pull back, but her sweet femininity drew the beast in him like honey. He tried not to dwell on her mouth, her satin throat, the smooth skin disturbed by one tiny, nervous pulse as she waited in taut anticipation of his response.

He mustn't let desire rule him. He'd vowed never to marry again, remember? He refused to be blackmailed. Still…

She was so mouth-wateringly desirable. And last night had demonstrated pretty clearly how far he was likely to get with her if it wasn't legal.

Ariadne held her breath, trying to read his face, intensely aware of his scrutiny.

He said softly, 'Do you propose to every man who tells you he desires you?'

His directness rocked her again, just as it had in the night. She felt intensely aware of his lean, supple hands relaxed on the table, the dark shadow outlining his chiselled mouth. But she needed to keep her head.

She gave a shrug, just as if her pulse wasn't racing. 'Only if they've just been offered a big fat juicy contract to take me on.'

He broke into a laugh, but there was ruefulness in its tone. 'Poor Ariadne.'

She clung to her cool façade. 'This is just a wedding I'm talking about. A business contract, pure and simple. No—'

The corners of his mouth edged up and he said, his voice softly mocking, 'No what? Passion?'

She felt a deep internal lurch. 'Oh. Oh, well…'

His mouth was grave, but his eyes were suddenly heavy with sensuality. She broke off, realising he was loving this, teasing her, saying sexy things he knew affected her, keeping her in suspense.

His gaze flickered over her and she felt singed. 'What happened to only marrying people on equal terms? Or did I dream that?'

'No, you didn't dream it. But you aren't the only one who has something to gain from the marriage. I—I do too.'

'What?' He examined her face, his dark eyes shimmering. 'Now you're sparking my imagination. What could possibly make it worth your while to become my wife?'

She risked meeting that scorching-hot gaze again. 'When I get married, I can claim my inheritance. From my parents. Otherwise I have to wait until I'm twenty-five.' The smile in his eyes was doused, and she added quickly, 'We'd only have to stay together a few days. After that, you can go your way and I'll go mine. You see? Everyone wins.'

She glanced up as a waitress approached with a notebook and pencil. Toast and hot chocolate, a flat white. 'Do you have orange juice?' she enquired.

Sebastian marshalled his critical faculties and considered the facts, such as they'd been presented.

Remembering her distress last evening, he was surprised. Why had she suddenly come around to the marriage she so despised? He doubted now it had much to do with his lust-driven midnight call. Could money be an issue with her? But how was that possible? Could she have fallen out with her uncle and aunt?

He drummed his fingers on the table, trying to reconcile his conflicting instincts, only too blazingly conscious of her blue eyes, the sweet lips that had haunted his sleep.

She had her hair tucked back behind ears as delicately curved as cockleshells. Her slim neck held her graceful head upright, like the stem of a flower, a proud, soft, heartbreakingly beautiful flower.

To have her for a few days, or not to have her at all?

Marriage sounded so final, but this one wouldn't be genuine. There'd be no emotional demands, no risk of loss here. No horror or heartache to weigh him down for years to come. A few days would pass like a flash.

What did the man who'd already lost everything have to lose?

Anyway, he hardly ever spent time at home. How badly could it disturb his comfort to have a woman waiting in that empty, soulless house for him for a few evenings?

A woman whose luscious mouth had opened to him like a flower?

The food came, and he watched her wrinkle her nose as she tasted the orange juice.

She sipped her chocolate next, then spread butter over her toast. With graceful manners she offered him a piece, and when he refused he watched her bite into hers with her pretty white teeth. He sipped his coffee, gave her a moment to assuage her hunger, only just suppressing a groan.

Would a few days suffice to assuage his? A few nights? A thousand and one nights?

'Don't they do breakfast at the Hyatt?' Desire deepened his voice almost to a growl.

'They do, but I—didn't have time.' Finished her toast, Ariadne wiped her hands on her paper napkin, then glanced up to be trapped in his smouldering dark gaze.

'So you aren't prepared to marry a man who wants you for your money, but *you* are prepared to marry for money.'

'For my *own* money.'

His mocking words gave Ariadne the dismayed sense that she'd failed. He might be burning her to the floor with his eyes, but that didn't mean he was prepared to marry her. He was just toying with her. So what now? Beg him to give her a bed for the night? But it would be his bed, wouldn't it?

Desperation had brought her to this, and pride was all she had now to fall back on. Time to get out before she made an even bigger fool of herself.

She found a note in her purse, laid it down beside her cup, then stood up. 'All right, forget I mentioned it. It was a mistake. I thought you wanted a—a deal. I must have—misunderstood.'

She was on the way to sweeping out when his hand snaked out and gripped her wrist. For an instant she saw something else in his eyes. Amusement. Kindness.

'Hang on. Sit down a minute longer and tell me more. Just how do you envisage this deal working?'

Her crushed hope quivered, then sprang back to buoyant life. She hesitated, conscious of the burn of his fingers on her skin, then allowed herself to sit down again.

He waited, his mouth grave, and so stirringly sexy she couldn't help thinking of how it had felt when he'd pressed his lips to hers. That fiery sensation still seemed to linger in her nerve fibres.

She drew a breath. 'Well, first I considered getting a marriage certificate somehow and faking it…'

He held up a hand, shaking his head. 'Stop right there. This is Australia. You can be done for fraud here as fast as blinking. For God's sake, never try to mess with a legal process that involves money *here*.'

She nodded. 'That's why I decided I might as well go through with the real thing. I don't want anything else from you. All I need is to marry you today.'

He blinked. 'Today?'

'Yes. Then I'll fax the marriage certificate to my uncle, he can notify the lawyers and have my inheritance transferred into my bank account, and I can get on with my life. And you can get on with yours.'

'Whoa, hold on.' The separate pieces of information lodged themselves into Sebastian's brain, but, focusing on the most immediate, he held up a hand. '*Today*. I don't think so. I told you, there are laws in this country.'

'No,' she said, her face as earnest and innocent as a nun's. A sexy, determined nun. A nun whose smooth breasts were screened by little more than a couple of thin layers of cotton fabric. 'I looked it up just now on the Internet. You can get the court officials to grant you a licence if you have a good reason.'

'Right.' He shook his head disbelievingly, although he had an inkling that what she'd said might be true. She'd done her homework well. It was clear Miss Ariadne Giorgias really wanted to marry him. Today. For whatever reason.

Even in thrall to lust, he had to wonder what the emergency was.

'Ah,' he said, his voice deepening, 'just supposing for a crazy moment I were to consider it, I'm not sure what that good reason would be. So I can assist a rich woman to get richer?'

'I'm not rich,' she said quickly. 'If you expect that you'll be disappointed. I just want what belongs to me.' Then she lowered her lashes and added quietly, 'Anyway, if you don't care to, it doesn't matter. I'll probably go back to Greece.'

Intrigued, he realised that for some reason, she needed to get married fast. And whether she knew it or not, her threat had genuine potency. He didn't want her to go back to Greece. Not yet.

His gaze drifted to her shoulders and arms. The feel of her ached in his memory. He itched to take her arms in his hands, feel their soft, toned resilience. Instead, he reached across and took her hands.

'So tell me. What's the big rush?'

Her slim hands trembled in his grasp, and her gaze flooded with an awareness that sent the hot blood coursing to his loins. Nothing could have been more seductive than to inspire that look in a beautiful woman.

But almost at once she pulled away and tucked her hands out of reach, her gaze guarded. No touching, he understood. Not until it was legal.

'Well, it's—it's just a matter of timing.' She evaded his eyes. 'I'm not planning to stay in Sydney long, so it makes sense to do it at once. The sooner I marry, the sooner I'll have my inheritance. Why wait?'

'What about your dress, the church, the photographer? They all take time. And don't you want to give your aunt and uncle plenty of notice? Surely you want them at your wedding?'

'*No.*' Her hands flew up in agitation. 'Absolutely *n*—' She pulled herself up and said in a low, firm voice, 'I—I don't want to bother them with it. I don't want to bother anyone.'

'I see.' He considered her a moment. 'As it happens, I have a grandmother, parents, two sisters and a brother who'd almost certainly feel cheated if I didn't invite them to my wedding.'

'Please.' Her blue eyes widened in horror. 'I can't do it at all if I have to have a big ceremony and all that publicity. I'd really much prefer it if we kept it a secret from people here.'

He raised his brows, then remembered her distress last night at the thought of the uncle's deal being known. Still, he couldn't imagine keeping a bride concealed for long from his highly inquisitive family. 'Are you sure you know what you're doing? Families have a way of finding things out.'

Her face tensed. 'Oh. Do you live with yours?'

'Hell, no, thank God. They live across the bridge, and I live at Bronte Beach.' He was touched with a slight discomfort then about what they would think if they knew any of this. Him taking up with a woman so spontaneously, after Esther and all she'd suffered. At least, that was how it would appear.

'Why? Don't you like them?' Her anxious blue glance drew him.

'I *like* them. It's just that I have to keep a distance from them or they'd kill me with kindness.'

Her shoulders relaxed and she brightened. 'Good. Then what's the worry? And anyway, how could you even *think* of wanting it in a church with the priest and the holy sacraments? We'll be divorcing just as soon as we can. It'd be a—*sacrilege.*' She gazed at him with scandalised reproach, then shook her head and sighed. 'Don't they have places here for things like this where you can just have a civil wedding? Without all the stuff? Just someone to say the words, then you sign something?'

He made a wry grimace. 'Sure. They have that. I thought it was the life goal of most women to have all the stuff.'

She looked quickly at him, and he realised he'd struck some sort of chord. She said emphatically, 'Not me.' Then she leaned forward, her eyes suddenly blazing, her cool thrown to the winds. 'Look, if you don't want to do it, it's all right, I don't either, not really. It was a stupid idea. Let's forget the whole thing.'

Sebastian heard himself say coolly, 'Relax. I'll do it.'

'Oh,' she breathed, sitting back. 'You will?' The relief sparkling from her blue eyes sent his curiosity skyrocketing. What was going on? 'Today?'

He shrugged. 'If I can organise the licence. There's no guarantee, mind, but I'll get my lawyer to give it a shot. You'd better give me your passport. There's bound to be miles of red tape.'

She handed him a slim zip-purse with her passport and travel documents. He slipped it in his pocket, then took her hand across the table and held it. The hand was warm and trembling, her shy, glowing eyes the same cerulean blue as the sky.

He felt a giddy burst of desire-driven euphoria. 'You won't regret it.'

'Of course not.' She gave him an unsure smile. 'We both have something to gain.'

But he could feel her palm zinging against his like a butterfly wing. His heart accelerated to a strong certainty that his instincts about her were correct. She wanted him, he felt sure of it. He could feel the leap of response in her every touch and glance. Despite her cool little negotiation, there was passion in her, and tonight it would be his to unlock.

A shadow hovered at the edge of his mind but he pushed it back and rose to his feet, glancing at his watch. Just about time to get back for his next meeting. Though God knew how he'd concentrate for the rest of the day on such mundane things as satellite systems when he had a wedding ahead of him. A wedding *night*.

He whipped out a card and wrote his number on the back. 'Here. I'll phone you at the hotel when I've arranged things.'

She hesitated, then said lightly, 'It might be better if I phone you.'

'Fine.' He touched her cheek, and made a gruff attempt to soothe away the aftermath of last night's angry exchange at the restaurant. 'I'm—glad you feel better today.'

Her lashes lowered. 'Well,' she murmured. 'At least we know where we stand now.'

Do we? he wondered on his athletic dash back to Celestrial. Where did *he* stand? Or was he floating on high above the moon? Wherever, it felt like a very unstable, rocky location, for a man used to navigating space without fear. But he was getting married in just a few short hours. Exciting, the night ahead. Crazy, perhaps even dangerous, but it was a long time since he'd felt so exhilarated.

So—*alive*.

CHAPTER SEVEN

THE lobby at the Park Hyatt was so busy with the midweek arrivals and departures of guests, that in all the bustle no one seemed to notice when Ariadne dropped off to sleep behind her magazine. Eventually something woke her, and her immediate panicked thought was that she'd forgotten to phone Sebastian. She calmed down when she realised it was only three, and made for the public phone.

The licence had been arranged, Sebastian informed her, and his PA had been working on the wedding all day long. A celebrant had been located, and Sebastian would pick her up just before five. Ariadne galvanised herself to action, retrieving her suitcase from the concierge and taking it to the Ladies' to search for a more appropriate wedding outfit.

The amazing success of her gamble at the café had left her feeling exhilarated at first, then caution had crept in. Her financial problems were all about to be solved, but the possibilities of what might happen after the wedding began to consume her. Sebastian was no preening butterfly, vacillating between mistresses. If he wanted a woman, she felt sure he'd be direct about it. She thought of his straight dark gaze, and a flame curled her insides.

He desired her all right, she realised with an accelerating heartbeat. Would he expect her to sleep with him when it was merely a marriage of convenience? Without the blessing of the church?

She should have talked about it to him at the café. She wished she'd had the poise to bring it up at once and deal with it gracefully. Somehow, she'd have to try to settle it before the ceremony.

How easy would it be to talk to him about the delicate subject? Last night on the phone he'd had no trouble talking about his attraction to her, but she doubted she'd ever be able to say things like that.

She'd always dreamed her husband would be someone she knew very well, someone who understood her and loved her, even so. With a grimace she realised that so far neither of her potential bridegrooms had fitted the profile.

She chose one of the little suits she'd had made in the Rue du Faubourg St Honoré for her intended honeymoon with Demetri. It was cream with the palest of pink and blue threads running through it, and thin edgings of cream lace at the cuffs and lapels. It cinched in at the waist and buttoned at her breast, with a hint of cleavage just visible. She'd never worn it, so it wasn't as tainted as some of the clothes she'd discarded from her trousseau.

This wasn't a wedding in the true sense but, even so, she wanted to look pretty. She wound her hair into a loose bun and threaded a blue ribbon through it.

When Sebastian arrived, for the first few moments she felt quite overwhelmed. He'd gone to so much trouble, she was momentarily speechless. He looked so handsome and austere in a beautifully tailored black three-piece suit, elegant white shirt and white silk tie with a silver stripe, like a genuine bridegroom. Somehow, though, the fine clothes only made her more aware of the raw animal man confined inside.

He swept her with a hot shimmering gaze that sent a wild surge through her veins.

When she'd collected herself, she said, 'You look *gor*— Very wedding-i-fied.'

Amusement gleamed in his eyes, but there was a searing sensual intensity in them that told her clearly what was uppermost in his mind. When he spoke his voice deepened.

'Likewise.'

Her nerves jumped. Maybe it was her imagination, but the air seemed rife with sexual vibrations. He bent to kiss her, and his sexy lips missed her mouth and just brushed her cheek. Even so her senses spun into dizzy overload.

He took her bags and piled them into the boot of his car, then held the door for her. 'Ready?'

As they swept out of the drive of the Park Hyatt into the maze of city streets she felt a moment of deep insecurity. She hardly knew him. What had she let herself in for?

After only a few twists and turns through the heavy traffic— hair-raising to someone used to driving on the other side of the road—he swerved into the kerb and parked. He hustled her out of the car and onto the street, and she was faced with the façade of the jewellery boutique she'd braved that morning.

She gulped. 'Oh. Are we going in there?'

'We need to pick up our rings. Come on,' he said, shepherding her relentlessly through the doors. 'They're expecting us.'

She reminded herself she was wearing different clothes. Perhaps they wouldn't recognise her. Once inside the glossy interior, she glanced about at the sales people, then tried to nudge Sebastian in the direction of one she hadn't dealt with in her morning visit.

The attempt was useless, because the manager of the boutique caught sight of them and came out of his office, rubbing his hands. He greeted Sebastian warmly, and looked keenly at her as if she reminded him of someone. To her intense relief, he mentioned nothing about their previous encounter.

Several trays of rings were placed before them. Sebastian was more careful and discerning than she'd expected, considering they were in a hurry. She was so anxious to escape from the shop she'd have agreed to anything, but they managed at last to find beautiful, plain bands in matching rose gold, Sebastian's heavy and solid, hers finer and more delicate.

The manager suggested they have them inscribed, and surprisingly Sebastian was keen to go to the trouble. There was a small discussion, and in the end it was decided to have their initials entwined, along with the date and the word 'Eternity'. She prickled with impatience, desperate not to wait the few extra minutes it would take.

'What about your engagement ring, though?' Sebastian said, advancing on a display case bright with diamonds. 'You should have one of these.'

'Is that really necessary?' she exclaimed.

He gave her a firm look. 'Absolutely, though on second thoughts… No, I think a sapphire. What do you think?' He smiled, the glow of desire in his gaze. 'Could there be a sapphire to match those eyes?' Before she could reply he turned to a hovering sales assistant. 'Sapphires. Do you mind?'

It was the same man she'd dealt with in the morning.

'By all means,' he said with an oily smile. He unlocked a cabinet and laid a tray of blue brilliants before them on the counter. 'Felicitations, Miss Giorgias. Oh, and…er…did you manage to find a satisfactory broker for your bracelet?'

Sebastian's surprised gaze swivelled around to examine her face, and she felt herself blush to the roots of her hair. 'No, no…well, yes…sort of, thank you,' she mumbled.

'Very fine stones,' the assistant murmured. 'Very fine indeed. Sorry we couldn't…er…accommodate you.'

The bland apology came too late, and at the worst possible time. She participated in the selection of an exquisite sapphire ring set in diamonds with her brain only half engaged. The other half was busy worrying about Sebastian having been alerted to her desperate situation.

She escaped from the shop, shards of blue fire flashing from her finger. It was a fine stone, and had cost no mean price for a temporary arrangement. She felt guilty at causing Sebastian such expense, and hoped he could afford it. But at least now he would be able to benefit from her uncle's deal.

He returned to the car and tossed the package into her lap. He turned to scan her face with his acute dark gaze, but didn't question her about the sapphires. She might have been imagining it, but he seemed extra silent and thoughtful for the rest of the journey.

After that everything took place at high speed. It was only a brief journey to the home of the wedding celebrant, where Sebastian's lawyer, Tony, and a woman from his office he introduced as Jenny, were waiting in a small courtyard at the front.

'Witnesses,' Sebastian explained.

The men shook hands, and Tony and Jenny kissed Ariadne, just as if she were a real bride. It was just a marriage of convenience, she kept reminding herself. She had made that clear, hadn't she?

They were about to ring the doorbell when Sebastian made a small exclamation and hurried back to the car. He returned with a bouquet of pink and white roses, fragrant with white stars of jasmine and orange blossom.

'Here,' he said. 'Hold this.'

While Ariadne clutched it, he nipped off a rosebud and tried to thread it through his buttonhole, his sculpted, masculine lips pursed in concentration. Everyone watched while he struggled. Eventually he stuck it in place at a slightly crazy angle. No one else offered to fix it, and in the end Ariadne was forced to give the bouquet to Jenny and fix it herself.

She stepped close to him, searingly conscious of the thinness of the layers of clothes between her breasts and his bare chest, the seductive shadow on his smooth-shaven jaw. As she performed the intimate little task before the interested onlookers, she felt his sensual gaze on her face, and knew she was going pink.

'There,' she said, risking meeting his eyes for a soul-scorching instant. He might have kissed her then, but he didn't. He was thinking of it though, she knew with a sudden certainty. Thinking of that, and the time after the ceremony when she would be his legal wife.

The celebrant, a middle-aged woman with a pleasant face, greeted them and ushered them all through the house to the garden in the rear.

The small party stood on a smooth velvet lawn in the rays of the setting sun. The hill sloped down to the sea, but Ariadne hardly registered the beauty of the surroundings. The entire event had taken on a surreal quality.

Sebastian was quiet, his face grave, but every time their eyes met his held a dark, possessive gleam that reached into her in some deeply stirring, primeval way she'd never experienced before with a man.

She was in such a haze she was hardly aware of the words of the ceremony. 'I, Ariadne Sarah Christiana…' she said at one stage. Then there was the moment when Sebastian slid the ring on her finger and promised to love and honour her. The look in his eyes was so intent, so serious, she felt a thrilled clench in her chest.

The celebrant pronounced them man and wife. There was a pause, while all held their breaths. Or it might have been that she was holding hers. Then Sebastian tilted up her face and kissed her. It was a gentle brushing of lips to begin with, then he subtly deepened the pressure. Her senses swayed as she felt him move a hand to her ribs and another to the small of her back.

A slow, sly flame licked through her lower abdomen. Her knees turned to water, and she melted into him, just as she had the night before.

In the nick of time Sebastian broke the kiss before it grew too intense to draw away from. Even so, that licking flame had infected her blood and she was left breathless, and just the slightest bit intoxicated. She became aware then of cameras flashing, someone throwing rice and confetti, and the dark triumphant gleam in Sebastian's eyes before his lashes flickered down to screen his gaze.

The wedding feast was in a private room at a restaurant, where toasts were drunk and course after course was placed before her, including a glistening slice of chocolate cherry torte. Tony and Jenny, strangers a few short hours since, were friendly and open and funny, and warmer to her by the minute, though she sensed the slight distance between Jenny and Sebastian that went with boss-employee relationships. Jenny was quite wary of him, Ariadne realised. Perhaps he was an exacting boss.

There was no dancing, no joyous bouzouki and loving cele-bratory family, but a chance to laugh with some new-found friends soothed her wounded heart and gave her worries some much-needed relief.

Added to that, seething somewhere inside her was a deep vein of excitement, a fever that grew in her blood every time her eyes fell on Sebastian's hands, or the lean, sinewy wrists bound by his elegant cuffs. Eventually the laughter and conversation reached a point when he said, 'Come, my sweet. I think it's time we left, and allowed Tony and Jenny to get on with their evenings.'

My sweet. That was what men called their wives. Their lovers. His gaze captured hers across the candle flame. He was smiling, his midnight satin eyes aglow with a dark sensual fire.

CHAPTER EIGHT

ARIADNE stood before the front door of a cliff-side villa with a giant telescope on its roof, while her husband slid a key into the lock. Her legal husband.

During the feast, carried along by the atmosphere, she'd looked forward to being alone with Sebastian, but, now she was, misgivings had set in. How married were they? And how much of a wife would he expect her to be? The situation was so tenuous. Once she had her inheritance she would be on her way.

On the other hand, there had been something quite definite about that ceremony they'd been through. From his point of view, she supposed he'd carried out his side of the bargain. Her turn now, some inner voice prodded.

He opened the door and looked down at her with that fire in his eyes. 'Welcome home,' he murmured, slipping his arm around her waist.

Even smiling, his mouth looked so firm and capable. Capable of delivering ecstasy, she thought with a plunge in her insides.

His possessive hand on her ribs actually felt pleasant. He was in such a buoyant mood she wondered if she should remind him their marriage was only temporary.

'Thanks.' She drew in a breath. 'Do you...do you have a fax machine?'

His brows shot up, then came down again rather hard. 'Can't you worry about that tomorrow?'

'No,' she said firmly. 'Right now's the best time. Thio will be reading his messages now.'

'To hell with Thio,' he said forcefully. 'This is our wedding night.'

Without any warning he lifted her off her feet and into his arms, laughing at her shocked cry. Pressed against the wall of his chest, her sensitive flesh fairly tingled with electrical impulses. Even the sensation of his jaw grazing her forehead was distinctly pleasurable.

He carried her inside, pausing at some point to touch a switch with his elbow. Lamps came on in all directions.

As he strode with her through the house she got a confused impression of large airy rooms with high ceilings and wide windows, which revealed glimpses of the cliffs undulating around the shoreline, peppered with twinkling lights. He swept her up a flight of stairs, down a wide hall and through double doors into a huge bedroom, and halted there, holding her in his arms a second longer, his eyes agleam with triumph. His glance flicked to the bed, and for a nerve-racked second she thought he was going to toss her into the middle of it. She braced in readiness, then he checked the impulse, lightly kissing her lips before planting her on her feet on the rug instead.

'Just relax,' he commanded, his deep voice rich with satisfaction. 'I'll be back.'

Relax! She gazed around the alien space, intimate with another person's occupation. A male person's. The room had an extremely masculine feel, with solid, hard-edged furniture. On either side of some French doors, windows reached to the floor, with soft filmy white curtains adrift on the breeze while heavier dark red satin ones were bunched back. But what dominated the room was a large bed, luxuriously attired in rich dark red fabrics.

It had big snowy pillows, heaped to look inviting. And it was inviting. Its insidious message would have enticed even the wariest virgin to dive in, roll on its plush covers and wallow in its springy embrace.

Maybe it was just her, but that bed seemed to glow and vibrate and command attention. She noticed a black satin dressing robe draped over the end, and the large masculine slippers neatly aligned on the floor beside it. Someone had placed them there with care.

Sebastian returned with her suitcase and set it down inside one of several doors leading off from the bedroom. She followed him and saw it was an unoccupied dressing room with long glass mirrors. Adjacent to it was a rather sumptuous bathroom, also unoccupied.

'Oh. Is there—another bedroom through here?'

He undid his silvery tie, his eyes shimmering, then slipped it off and dropped it on the floor.

'Several, but ours is the only one fit for occupation.' A lazy, amused smile played on his mouth. 'No need to worry.' His voice grew husky as he took her wrists and ran his hands up her arms, sending thrills through her nerve endings. 'I think you'll find everything in *this* room more than adequate for your needs.'

Her skin cells seemed to have developed a will of their own. They were loving his touch through the jacket sleeves, were tuned into it one hundred per cent. Unfortunately, she needed to get some things clear in her head before things zoomed out of control.

He lifted his lean hands to cradle her face, but before he could press his lips to hers she seized his wrists to still them, and slipped from his grasp.

'I think we need to sit down and have a good chat,' she said, her voice rather higher-pitched than usual.

Sebastian narrowed his eyes and examined his bride. Though deliciously flushed from the champagne and the excitement, while she was clearly attempting to preserve her poise, her eyes were conveying a dark uncertainty.

He felt a pang of misgiving. Last night's choking moments after the kiss were etched into his soul, moments he would prefer never to revisit. The charge that he'd taken advantage of her had cut deep. For God's sake, he was hardly a wild animal. He was aware that a civilised man didn't ravish a tender woman at the first opportunity. And if she was as inexperienced as he suspected, it was only natural she'd be feeling a few nerves. Still, it was their wedding night, and anxiety should never be unnecessarily prolonged.

'Of course,' he said politely, bracing for the challenge. He stood back a little to give her some space. 'Are you—nervous about anything?'

Her chin came up. 'Nervous? I should say not. I just—just need to be clear about things.'

Ariadne saw determination settle into the lines of his chiselled mouth, and she was reminded of last night when she'd refused to have dinner with him. During the day she'd been so worried about her precarious situation, then so relieved to think she'd solved it, she hadn't had enough time to crystallise a plan.

Everything had happened so fast. But now that the moment had arrived, whatever her primal instincts had earlier been whispering, she had a conscience. A celebrant wasn't a priest. A garden wasn't a church. And despite the certificate Sebastian had slipped into the inner pocket of his jacket, their reasons for being married had very shaky foundations.

Looked at in the cold light of objectivity, a financial contract between virtual strangers was hardly an excuse for making love. Although, did she really need to look at the situation in the cold light of objectivity?

As she met Sebastian's speculative gaze, even thinking the words *making love* cast her insides into a swirling hot chaos. She wasn't exactly tipsy, but she wished she hadn't joined in quite so many of the toasts and could weigh the moral issues with more clarity.

Before he decided to pounce, she backed from the room, then turned and found her way rather quickly down the stairs and into a large sitting room.

Despite her inner upheaval, she couldn't help noticing that the house looked a little dishevelled. There was potential there though, in its high ceilings and harmonious lines. The sitting room was handsome enough, with pleasing antiques and several graceful lampshades casting warm pools of light, but the elegant, capacious sofa and the cushions on the comfortable-looking armchairs all looked as if they could do with a good plumping up.

She could tell which was Sebastian's favourite chair because his imprint was squashed into the cushions, and there was a space in the dust on the beautiful old coffee table between the laptop and numerous coffee mugs where two large male feet might comfortably rest.

The room had a neglected sort of comfort, as if someone with taste had started moving in, then been waylaid. She made for the safety of the sofa, hesitated, then gave the seat cushions a wipe before risking her suit.

Sebastian strolled in behind her with leisurely, confident calm, and at once her eyes zeroed in on the unmistakable fact that he'd taken off his jacket and waistcoat. In his shirtsleeves it was easy to see his lean angularity and the powerful outline of his shoulders.

He hesitated a moment, then to her relief made for his armchair, dropping into it and stretching out his long legs with idle ease.

Burningly aware of seeming like a craven coward, she attempted some light conversation. 'Er… Is this your primary residence, or just a beach villa?'

Amusement tinged his expression, but he replied with solemn politeness, 'Both. You get a better night-sky out here. Not that I'm always in residence. In recent months I've often needed to work so late I've found it easier to stay over at the office.'

'Oh.' She seized on the potential escape hatch and said eagerly, 'Well, if you'd rather do that tonight, don't you worry about me. I can look after myself.'

His brows shot up and his eyes gleamed. 'But it's your wedding night, Ariadne.'

She flashed him a brilliant smile. 'I know, but, heavens, I'm not so hung up on all those old traditions. If you need to go somewhere and do things with your satellites, go right ahead.'

His brows drew together, and he said silkily, 'There are *some* traditions that shouldn't be ignored.' His sexy, heavy-lidded gaze flickered over her face, and she realised she might have given away her very slight case of nerves.

A kiss, even a very hot kiss, was one thing, especially if it happened unexpectedly. A woman's natural instincts took over. But a wedding night was something else again. Something official, formal, that required a certain poise and graceful expertise. Should she inform him she was a virgin, or would he just take it for granted? She had no idea what his attitudes were about such things, though last night he'd clearly expected her to be free and easy about sex. What if she confessed her inexperience and he laughed?

She didn't think she could bear it if he laughed. There were some things a woman just couldn't discuss with a man.

She felt so naive and out of her depth. And the nervier she felt, the more relaxed and idle he seemed to become. Maybe he wasn't thinking about sex at all?

She met his dark gaze then and a major earthquake rocked her insides. A lazy, wicked smile was touching his mouth, and she was reminded of a big patient panther in the mood for play. He was thinking about it, all right.

'Now, what was it you wanted to talk about?' His black lashes had developed a sleepy languor. 'Can I get you something to help you relax? Some chocolate?'

'No. No, thanks. I—don't need to relax.' She got off the sofa and started pacing about, clasping her hands in front of her. 'Look, er, I'm not sure what you expect. I probably should explain that I'm...' She was just winding up to expand on the difficult subject when her foot connected with something on the floor. She tripped, only just managing to maintain her balance.

'Oh! Tsk.' She glared down in irritation at a thick heavy book entitled *Time Drag: Was Einstein Right?* lying where some lazy person had left it by Sebastian's armchair.

He sprang up. 'Sorry. That shouldn't be there.' He picked up the book and tossed it carelessly across the room onto a large pile stacked by an empty bookshelf. The pile collapsed and books scattered, sending up a mushroom cloud of dust.

Besides the heaps of unshelved books, she noticed several paintings on the floor leaning against the wall, and a couple of packing crates he was using to prop up his stereo system. Momentarily distracted, she enquired, frowning, 'How long since you moved in here?'

He shrugged. 'Oh, must be three years.' He glanced about as if for the first time, looking rueful. 'I guess I should have... I didn't have a chance to warn Agnes I'd be bringing you home tonight. There should be flowers. Oh, and I meant to... These ought to be shelved.'

He strolled across and gave the pile of books a desultory kick to shove them out of the way. More dust rose in the air.

'Sorry.' He gave an amused laugh. 'Agnes doesn't get time for the finer touches.'

She delved into her purse for a tissue, and held it to her face until the dust settled. 'How many staff do you have?'

'Just Agnes.'

'In *this* big house?' She arched her brows. 'Does Agnes have cooking duties as well?'

He looked evasive. 'Well, she has cooked, but...I don't often eat here, anyway. I'm sure we can get her to rustle up some meals.'

She felt curious to know what sort of relationship he had with his housekeeper if he wasn't certain he could persuade her to cook. 'Anyway,' she murmured, almost to herself, 'it doesn't matter. Really. I'm hardly going to be here long enough to notice.'

He turned and looked across at her, eyes glinting. Then he strolled back, determination in his smile. 'We'll see. No, no, not there, come and sit down here.' She'd been about to relocate to the strategic safety of the other armchair, but he drew her inexorably back to the sofa, and dropped down beside her.

'Now, what was it you wanted to chat about?' He lounged back, angling his body to face her, one arm resting along the sofa back behind her. Absently, almost unconsciously, he began to caress her cheek with his lean, tanned fingers. 'Was it something about your uncle and aunt?'

She felt a wary surprise. 'What about them?'

'Well, you seemed a little reluctant to have them at your wedding.'

'My *convenient* wedding.'

He smiled. 'I was surprised. I'd have thought you'd be pretty fond of them.' The touch of his fingertips on her cheek caused a delicious tingling that radiated to her ear and down her neck.

She lowered her lashes and crushed down the jagged spike in her private family emotional register. 'I am fond of them.'

'Aren't you the apple of their eyes?'

'Perhaps. Well, I was… *Thought* I was…' She smiled to cover the unwelcome pricking at the backs of her eyes. 'You can be mistaken about people. Even people you think you know very well.'

He shot her a keen glance, and she had the mortified feeling her voice might have given her away. She prayed he hadn't spotted the pathetic shimmer suddenly misting her vision. All at once she felt so weary, as if she were weighed down with all the miseries of the world. And she could feel the searchlight of his sharp intelligence probing her sad little secrets like a solar flare.

But he said quietly, 'Yeah, I guess. So…is there anything wrong over there with your family? Anything worrying you?'

As if she could tell him any of that. *Theos*, he'd done the trading deal with her uncle. They were probably in daily communication. Sure, Sebastian Nikosto looked reassuringly strong, and right now sympathetic and sincere, but he was the last person on the planet she could trust. No, the third last. *No, no*, she reflected with a dreary sigh. She'd been forgetting Demetri. Fourth last.

'Wasn't there something you wanted to tell me?'

She crashed back to earth. 'Oh, right. Well. I—I think we need to discuss… I think you know… You—you *should* know…' His fingers traced a soft searing trail down the side of her neck. Should she have stopped him? Though *he* might not have been conscious of it, she was. But it was only a caress, barely that. A harmless, friendly caress. It wasn't as if it were anything sexual.

'You do know this is just a marriage of convenience.' She swallowed. 'In fact…I—I'm not sure we're properly married at all.' She couldn't help closing her eyes briefly to savour the ongoing sensation. Her breath grew short and made her voice huskier than usual, her words disjointed. 'You must see…see that…in the eyes of the church, we…we haven't been properly joined.'

The smile gleamed in his eyes. 'That can very easily be fixed. We can be joined just as soon as you like.'

'*Oh*. You know what I mean. I'm not sure that we should—sleep together.'

He said very firmly, 'Yes, we should.'

'No, well…I'm a very light sleeper.' She searched his face in an attempt to gauge his reaction. 'I think I'll feel better if I sleep here on the sofa.'

'I don't think so.'

He stopped stroking her cheek, leaving her skin feeling bereft and yearning. *Aching* for him to start it again, she edged her cheek a little closer to him. With a grave expression, this time he stroked some hair back from her ear, then circled her ear with his fingertips.

Her entire being melted into swoon as thrills shivered through her scalp and down her spine.

'I think I can promise you'll feel much better if you sleep in the bed.' There was a suave, confident finality in his tone.

'No, what I'm trying to say is—that I'm not sure I feel married enough to—you know.'

'Make love?' he supplied, lifting his black brows and smiling like the very devil.

She gave a nod. 'Without the blessing of the church.'

'Oh, but...' his expression grew solemn '...what could be a holier place to wed than a garden? I have to say I felt *very* blessed.' He made an expansive gesture. 'There we were, at one with the earth, the sea and the sky, kissed by the rays of the setting sun.'

'Oh, well, *perhaps*...' Had there been some special deeper inflection in the way he said 'kissed', or had her hypersensitivity to the hot, strong current she sensed emanating from him made her imagine it? 'It was lovely, I know, but...' she had to give her conscience a proper hearing '...just because we're married doesn't mean we *should*.'

He pinned her with his compelling glance and said softly, and very definitely, 'No, my sweet wife, we *should* because I want you and you want me.'

She met his hot dark gaze and all her arguments dried on her tongue while her heart slithered into emergency pounding.

Suddenly he bent his head and planted a soft little kiss at the base of her throat. It was so thrilling and unexpected, she couldn't restrain a gasp. Then he trailed more kisses down her chest, all the way to the valley between her breasts. She felt them surge with warmth under the lapels of her jacket.

If only he would push her lapel aside and kiss her *there*. Imagining it sent a hot helpless rush to her nipples.

He smelled so attractively male, and his hot hungry lips on her skin ignited such arousing little fires, her breathing grew increasingly shallow. Still, she struggled to retain some control.

'All right, fine,' she panted after a second. Despite what Thea had said, she was quite willing to compromise. 'Perhaps...I *could* feel okay about a kiss.'

He drew back from her, leaving the skin he'd recently aroused ablaze with yearning for more.

'A kiss?' He considered it, scanning her face with a narrowed gaze. Then he nodded. 'Hmm. A kiss is fairly harmless. That shouldn't disturb your conscience too much.' He continued his meditative scrutiny for a while, then grinned, so wickedly her insides turned over and a hot hungry flame flared low in her abdomen. 'Anyway, since we've already kissed once, I guess that genie is out of the bottle now.'

'*Twice*.' She gazed at him from under her lashes. 'Remember? We've kissed—twice.'

His voice was darker than a cavern. 'I remember.'

The gleam in his eyes grew so piercingly sensual, she held her breath in suspense, her heart madly pounding. Then he brought his mouth firmly down on hers.

At first it was a fantastic collision of lips, until he took first her upper, then lower lip between his, sliding each one gently through his teeth as if for the maximum knowing of them.

Theos, it was *so* slow and sexy.

A heavy, voluptuous heat beat to her breasts, and she felt her nipples and other erogenous zones rouse to a moist yearning. Then his tongue slid into her mouth, tickling the delicate tissues inside and igniting little snakes of fire there that somehow wound their way through her bloodstream, inflaming her longing to be thoroughly stroked *everywhere*.

She found herself clinging to him. He deepened his possession of her mouth, his hot, wine-flavoured breath mingling with hers in intoxicating intimacy. Then she felt his hand slide under her lapel, and she felt him squeeze then gently caress her breast through the lace of her bra. Thrills shivered through her.

She was seized by the most urgent need to be rid of the bra, to allow her breasts to be free and bare to his clever, devouring hands. And all the while, down below between her legs, a wilder urgency burned.

Just when she felt all hot and afire, he broke the kiss and drew away from her. She dragged in some air, her skin tingling and crazy to be touched.

'There,' he said, his voice deeper than a growl. 'One kiss. How do you feel now?' His eyes were hot and slumberous, with a dark sexual flame that somehow exacerbated the hunger in her blood.

His shirt collar was unbuttoned, opening to a triangle of bronzed skin at the base of his strong neck. Her mouth watered with a sudden insane need.

'Fine. Just fine. Only… Who said it had to be just one?' Her voice was smokier than a Naxos taverna.

It was only a kiss, after all. Giving him little chance to protest, she placed her hands on his shoulders, and leaned forward to press her lips to that bare triangle. A tremor passed through him, delivering her a thrilled satisfaction. His skin had a faintly salty, masculine taste that was distinctly moreish to her hungry lips. With her breasts rising and falling in the upheaval of a new and heady exhilaration, she slipped undone the next couple of buttons of his shirt, revealing a deeper expanse of masculine chest.

A sultry pang roiled through her as her glance fastened on his alluring whorls of black chest hair, just begging to be explored. She bent her lips to his hot satin skin, then almost of its own volition her tongue licked a trail all the way to his neck. She felt another satisfying shudder rock him.

He grabbed her upper arms then and held her a little away from him, but her hunger wasn't appeased. In fact it intensified. Her avid gaze flicked to his mouth, and it was as though she couldn't help herself. She just *had* to.

She leaned forward and pressed her lips to his, feeling his thrilling leap of response, tasting and savouring and exploring with her tongue until she felt so hotly aroused with pleasure, she was aflame. Then he took charge of the clinch, his hands suddenly becoming rough and urgent to explore her willing curves. Her hands were infected with the same mad thirst. They couldn't keep from roaming, craving to feel his shoulders and powerful chest, sliding under his shirt to explore the lean hard contours of muscle and bone.

Somehow she found herself lying down, ablaze, her head on the cushions against the armrest, with Sebastian's long lean frame half lying on top of her. But it was still only kissing. Somehow they each adjusted their bodies, his so lean and angular, hers softer, more yielding, to find a way to kiss on the limited space without interrupting the steamy progress.

To her sinful delight, Sebastian was an expert at creating pleasure with his hands. She wasn't sure when her jacket became unbuttoned, but the kiss grew even hotter and sexier as his clever fingers stroked her yearning breasts and sent tingles resounding through her body.

Far too soon though, he broke from her. She waited, her momentary disappointment quickly changed by his scorching gaze to a limbo of thrilled suspense. What next? With a searing glance, he bent his lips to her breasts, and to her shock deliberately sucked each yearning nipple through the lace of her bra.

Ah-h-h, *bliss*. The gentle friction of the cloth and his mouth on her sensitive peaks was so arousing, her desire blazed to an inferno. Her convulsive fingers mauled his shoulders, kneaded his arms, tangled in his hair as she gasped and cried out in pleasure. Then just when she was ready to melt into a molten puddle, he drew away from her and sat up.

Panting, she eyed him hungrily. Far from being satisfied, her appetite to taste his kisses seemed to have escalated to an evil obsession.

'Come here,' she rasped throatily, surprised by her own boldness, half sitting in the attempt to grab him and pull him back to her.

But he placed a light but firm hand on her chest. 'Stay there.' His dark drawl rippled down her spine like the devil's breath. For a second he sat very still, the gleam in his eyes darker and more seductive than she'd yet observed.

Her blood seethed with the most delicious anticipation.

He made sure she was comfortable, arranging her cushions securely against the arm of the sofa, lifting her feet to rest on his thighs. A wild and pleasurable suspense fluttered inside her.

He caressed her feet absently for a moment, watching her face, then traced a lean hand along her leg to her knee. 'Ah, these gorgeous legs,' he growled, bending to kiss her knee.

It was so flattering. She bent her knees up to make it easier for him if he felt like kissing them again. And he did. Though next time, he kissed her *above* the knee, on the inside of her thigh.

Her excitement intensified.

He stroked her legs with increasingly long and sensual sweeps, his fingertips rousing fire wherever they connected with her willing flesh. How far would he dare to go? Then his caressing fingers slipped under her skirt and travelled softly, gently, all the way up to the silken skin at the top of her inner thigh. Close, so scintillatingly close, to the holy of holies.

It was explosively dangerous, it was hardly a kiss, but the sensations were so thrilling, what else could she do but give herself up to voluptuous enjoyment?

And all the time, while rivulets of sheer pleasure radiated through her flesh, a very short distance away, covered only by the delicate cotton of her pants, her most intimate, secret parts burned to be included in the orgy. In truth, *Theos* pardon her weakness, the closer his questing fingers roamed to the strictly forbidden zone, the more she ached for him to caress her there.

While he gazed at her, his hot, slumberous eyes as dark as Lucifer's, she looked back at him, knowing her own eyes must reflect the pleasure she was feeling, at the same time hoping he'd somehow read her desperate yearning.

Then all at once his traversing hand moved a little further afield. She tensed in anticipation. A low, throaty moan escaped her as with the most thrilling pleasure she felt his fingertips softly glide across the flimsy fabric of her pants.

Ah-h-h.

He caressed her, so lightly, so tenderly it was the purest chocolate, the sheerest rapture, it was the darkest, most sinful black magic.

She was gasping, moaning, hardly able to keep herself from writhing out of control, when all at once he nipped down her pants, leaving her utterly exposed.

For a second she stared at him in complete shock. He gazed on her naked triangle of dusky curls with a riveted gleam in his eyes, then with a bold, determined smile he changed position, unhesitatingly parting her thighs to expose her nakedness even further. Then he bent his dark head right there between her legs.

Theos, it was so *erotic*. Having laid her completely bare, he stroked his divine tongue across the sensitive, most secret yearning folds of her body, with exquisite artistry connecting with her sweet spot and sucking.

'Oh-h-h.' How could he have known? She shuddered in ecstasy as wave after wave of liquid pleasure roiled through her with every delicious, forbidden touch.

But that wasn't all. Strangely, while the rapture was white-hot and intense, somehow her hunger grew and grew, until she reached some kind of pitch of maddened erotic need. Just when she thought she must scream, he thrust his heavenly tongue inside her and flicked it around the tenderest, most yearning tissues of all. Her wild pleasure escalated to a dizzy, suspenseful pitch, then crashed into shards of exquisite relief.

It took her some seconds to recover. Sebastian waited, his eyes so wicked and aroused, his brows lifted in amused query for her comment.

'Oh,' she said, when her breathing had slowed enough for her to speak, her voice hoarse and deeper than the Katherine Gorge. '*That* kind of a kiss.'

Ignoring the scruples she'd already thrown to the wind, she contemplated him with enthralled appreciation, speculating on what other pleasures she'd read of that he might be equally expert in delivering.

'You know, Sebastian,' she panted, 'it's cramped here on this sofa. I might—sleep better in the bed.'

CHAPTER NINE

SEBASTIAN contemplated his bride with satisfaction. Her passionate writhings on the sofa cushions had mussed her blonde hair into an enticing state of disarray, and her already full mouth was so plump and voluptuous from kissing, it was as much as he could do not to flatten her to the bed and devour her at once.

But unless he was mistaken, he had an instinct, unchanged by his initial lustful exploration of her honeyed flesh, that his proud bride was a virgin, a condition it would be his fiercest pleasure to correct, though tenderly, as befitted a princess on her wedding night.

She stood before him on the rug, eyeing the arrangement of the pillows on his bed. 'You know, Sebastian,' she said, with an uncertain laugh, 'I know I seem incredibly cool and casual about all this…negotiating this deal to marry you, then doing it all in a hurry, going through with the wedding and kissing you so…so…*often*. But the truth is…'

There was the faintest tremor in her voice, and he stilled in the act of tearing off his shirt. 'I can assure you,' he said, 'the linen's clean. It only came back from the Holy Cross Laundry this morning. Agnes was making the bed as I left.'

'Was she?' Ariadne frowned slightly. At least Agnes performed some part of her duties with passion. 'Where does Agnes sleep?'

'At her place,' he said, smiling.

She was about to question him further when she caught sight of the uninterrupted expanse of his gorgeous chest. Her mouth dried at the impressive proportions of his hard pectorals, his muscled arms.

'Goodness, you're very athletic,' she exclaimed. 'I hadn't realised quite how big you are.'

Startled into a grin, Sebastian let his shirt drop. Surprisingly, she'd rebuttoned her suit jacket after he'd carried her back in and deposited her on the rug, suggesting a back-pedalling in the momentum he'd so artfully established. Was his bride losing her nerve?

'Now,' he murmured, taking her arms and drawing her to him. 'Forget Agnes. You were saying something about the truth...?'

She closed her eyes. 'I—I think you understand that I won't be staying here long...'

Her brow was creased in worry, and he had a sudden inkling of the most immediate cause of her concern. He felt a rush of tenderness for her as she went on, 'You weren't hoping for a wife with the beautiful dark eyes, were you? Because, I truly think...'

He tilted up her face. 'Just relax,' he murmured. 'No need to think. Leave it all to me. Tonight is a night to feel.'

'But...' Ariadne was about to try again with her confession, when he took her mouth in a hotly demanding kiss. As his intoxicating flavour again invaded her senses, her overactive brainwaves, stressed by the rapid flow of events, calmed to a low, sultry purr.

She linked her arms around his neck and responded in kind, locked in like an electrocution victim to his high-voltage sexual power.

As she opened to him and she felt the virile length of his erection push against her abdomen, some primitive instinct tempted her to writhe her pelvis against him in sensual encouragement. The effect must have been potent, because the kiss intensified to a sizzling firestorm.

Drowning in tastes and sensations, compelled by the iron-hard demands of his big, masculine body, she clung to him, excited by his bronzed bare chest, his hot, roving hands, and wired to the thrilling beat of his big powerful heart against her breasts.

At last the kiss broke, leaving her panting and breathless, and hungry, oh, so hungry for more of him. His eyes were black, with a golden shimmer of lust tingeing the dark flame in their irises.

He set her a little away from him, watching her face as he undid her buttons one by one. Anxious now for skin contact, she wriggled out of the jacket and turned her back to allow him to unfasten her bra.

Slowly, gently, Sebastian traced the ridge of her spine with his thumb, feeling the electric quiver of response under her skin. His heart clenched at the beauty of her slim pale back. He located her skirt zip and drew it down, hardening in anticipation for the moment when she would be totally nude.

Ah. As smooth and delicately shaped as a violin.

His underwear tightened beyond endurance.

The skirt fell to the floor. She gave a small gasp, as if she'd forgotten she'd already lost her pants in the first round. The fierce blood beat a torrid path to his groin as his lustful gaze took in the graceful curves of her neck and waist, the delicious flare of her hips and smooth, satin bottom. He ached to plunge his burning length into her then and there, but with iron self-restraint merely bent to kiss the alluring dent in the small of her back, then turned her to face him.

Ariadne burned under his scorching regard of her nude body. Adrenaline, or desire, had dulled her anxiety. She felt bathed in a feminine glow, a primeval woman facing her mate.

He pushed her onto the bed, and she stretched out in the middle while he stripped off the rest of his clothes.

He was so beautifully made, a lean, bronzed, hairy symphony of muscle, sinew and masculine power, but when her eyes took in the massive extent of his thickly erect penis, her nerve jumped and she could almost feel herself shrink.

'I think I should tell you,' she quavered without further delay, 'I'm a virgin.'

'Yeah?' he said, smiling as he came down beside her with such tender warmth she felt her heart lurch. 'Who'd have guessed?'

Sebastian gazed down at his bride, her hair wild on the pillow, her luscious breasts with their raspberry-pink peaks straining for his attention, and his grin faded as he was seized with a solid-steel conviction that he wouldn't be letting her go any time soon.

'You're such a beautiful woman I can't believe some guy hasn't snapped you up,' he said, his voice so deep it was a primal growl from the earth's core. A shadow, so fleeting he might have imagined it, crossed her face, and he thought of what she'd told him about her past suitors. Someone had hurt her along the way.

She lowered her lashes, then smiled at herself with such shame and self-doubt he felt a sharp tug in his chest. 'It's me. I always choose the wrong ones.'

'Not this time,' he said with a fierce, tender certainty. 'This time you've chosen the right one.'

Ariadne felt shaken by the warmth and sincerity in his eyes, then as she continued to scrutinise him they flamed and all she could read in them was sizzling hot lust.

He bent his head, then softly, lightly ran his tongue-tip over her lips in a sexy little tease. Then he crushed her mouth in a fiery kiss, compelling her with the force of his passion to leave everything else behind, summoning her to this one moment in time and space.

Their hot breath rushed and mingled. As she lay in his powerful arms his chest hairs grazed her tender naked breasts, setting her skin alight with tingling little explosions of pleasure.

Possessed by his demanding lips, his hair-covered legs brushing her smooth skin, his rock-hard rod tickling her sex, she felt her veins flow with fire.

He broke the kiss first, in the nick of time to save her from drowning in sensation. But her body had sprung back to life with a primitive thirst that couldn't be ignored.

When he bent his head to her breast and took her nipple in his mouth, she mewled with pleasure. Then he explored her with his hands and lips until she was mindless and wild, a moaning, writhing creature incandescent with desire, a willing, wanton prey to a mutual, insatiable passion.

As the sensational storm raged she burned with a potent yearning. She tried not to obsess, but his arousal was so straight and strong and masculine, and in some way so *right*, springing from those crisp, little black curls, every fibre in her body was on edge.

At last Sebastian paused to take a foil packet from the bedside table. He tore it open, and she watched him slide the sheath onto his rosy, throbbing length, hoping against hope she would stretch half as well as the condom had. At the very thought she felt a tingling rush of moisture between her legs.

'Now,' he said, passion in his dark eyes. He parted her thighs, and traced the delicate folds until they felt as plump and full as a peach and she was reduced to a quivering, burning mess. Her need for release reached a desperate pitch.

'Sebastian,' she breathed shudderingly, arching up to him. 'I'm on fire here.'

With intense satisfaction in his hot eyes he slid a finger inside her. 'And you're tight,' he murmured, gently stretching the entrance to her moist channel, his voice like thick husky gravel. 'So fabulously tight.'

She wrinkled her brow. 'That's a good thing?'

'It's a *great* thing,' he said, then positioned himself between her legs and firmly pushed inside her. She felt filled to bursting point.

'*Theos*,' she cried, digging her fingers into his hard, muscled arms. '*Sebastian*.'

He withdrew at once, soothing her with his voice, 'Sweetheart, sweetheart,' he crooned, stroking her hair. 'It might be uncomfortable the first time. But it'll get better. Trust me.'

Trust him? He looked supremely confident, but there was a concerned little frown between his eyes. She had a vague realisation that he'd already given her one fabulous moment of blissful release. What about his? And did she really want to draw back after going this far down the road to losing her virginity?

She knew what to expect, after all. Her girlfriends had told her in graphic detail, and she'd read enough about how it would hurt. Clamping her eyes shut, she steeled herself to the agony. 'Go on, then. Get it over with.'

He bent to kiss her lips, then when she was least expecting it gave an almighty thrust, and she felt a raw little pinch that tore a pained gasp from her.

He froze all action, then withdrew from her, his face taut with concern. 'Are you okay?'

The smarting eased almost at once. 'Well, *now*.' She made a check of her bodily sensations, but could find no lingering pain. 'Is that it?' she said tensely. 'Just that?'

His anxious expression lightened and he smiled, while the dark flame smouldering in the depths of his eyes reached deep into her womb. 'That's just the beginning. Now it's the good part. Just relax.'

He eased into her again, and this time the sensation didn't feel quite so strange.

'See how we go, Ariadne Giorgias.' He watched her face, a sexy little smile edging up the corners of his mouth as he started to move his lean hips, stroking inside her with seductive, sinuous little movements that weren't as uncomfortable as she'd expected.

'How does that feel?' he said huskily, his eyes tender and

warm and desirous. 'I'm inside you, and you're opening to me…' He eased her into a gentle rhythm. 'Like a glove. A beautiful tight, hot, velvet…' His scorching hot eyes flared and he increased the rhythm. At first it just felt athletic and very intimate, but then every so often, amazingly, she felt his hard rod touch some spot inside her that ignited like a sunburst, sending streaks of the most intense and fabulous pleasure throughout her entire body.

'Go on,' she urged, wanting more of them. 'Go *on*.'

He rocked her even faster, then she could tell by his increasingly concentrated expression that he'd become locked in a rapture of his own. She let go of her fears and gave herself up to the rhythm entirely, each stroke igniting more and more pleasure points inside her until she was a river of blissful sensations.

She wrapped her legs around him, relishing all the physical sensations of his hard, lean masculinity, the intimacy and warmth of the amazing connection.

Feeling his hard, sensitised flesh swell with unbelievable bliss inside her slickly tight sheath, Sebastian gritted his teeth with the sublime pleasure.

Locked in his arms, Ariadne strove faster and faster, harder and higher, until before she knew it he was once again zooming her up that wild, hot, delicious incline to an even higher, more glorious summit than before. She hung there in a desperate trembling suspense, then her moment came and she dissolved into waves of ecstatic, rapturous pleasure.

'Oh, *Theos*,' she gasped as the ripples subsided.

Sebastian reached a climax of his own, then collapsed upon her, his lean bronzed body sheened with sweat. After a few seconds he lifted himself off her and rested quietly with his eyes closed. Then he hauled himself up and went into his bathroom. She lay bathed in a slumberous glow, her body purring in relaxation while she listened to the flow of the taps.

Soon he came back and stretched out beside her with his eyes shut. She'd started to think he'd fallen asleep, when he rolled on his side to face her. He smiled down at her, his warm gaze a mixture of triumph and tenderness, reaching out to trail a gentle finger over her shoulder and along the line of her body.

'I'd have thought you might have at least said, "Oh, *Sebastian*."'

She gave a low throaty laugh. 'Sorry. You *were* good.'

'Thank you,' he said modestly.

She smiled into his eyes. 'My aunt told me you were a genius.'

His deep laugh rumbled, then he planted a little kiss on her breast. 'From this point on, we only get better.'

'With practice, you mean?' She fluttered her lashes at him. 'How much practice?'

'Plenty,' he growled. Then he grinned and pulled her into his arms. 'Aren't you glad we got married?'

After a while, in which she floated in a sort of dreamy glow, relaxed and intimate in the soft dark, he said, 'So what happened with that guy? The one who broke your heart?'

'I didn't say that.'

'As good as.'

Had she, though? She thought back to the night before. She'd said so many things at that restaurant. She must have been out of her head. Still, here and now in the most intimate and blissful cocoon she'd ever been wrapped in, honesty had never felt safer. 'Demetri Spiros,' she said after a while. 'I was engaged to him.'

'*Engaged?*' He sounded astonished.

'Well, it was one of those things. I met him on this cruise on Thio's yacht. You know how it can happen. *My* family wanted it, *his* family wanted it. He seemed really cool. Anyway, I found out he had a girlfriend in Athens. This older woman.'

'Older than him?'

'No, older than *me*. A few days before the wedding I saw him with her in a restaurant. She was really sophisticated. People said he would drop her after the wedding, once he had me, but I couldn't forget about it.' Some of the remembered pain must have leaked through into her voice, because he squeezed her a little tighter. 'Then on the wedding day when I was all dressed up in my white dress, I couldn't force myself to go through with it.'

'Hell. What did you do?'

'When they were all rushing about busy with things, I went down to the beach and stayed there all day, in my dress and everything. *Ruined* the shoes.'

'Your aunt and uncle would have been upset.'

Her stomach clenched with the old guilt, then she sighed. 'Oh, yes. Well, the whole world was there waiting in the church. I can't really blame them. Prince Philippos. The King and Queen of Sweden. The Grimaldis.'

He made a silent whistle. 'My God. All hell must have broken loose.'

In the dark, still bathed in the afterglow of passion, confession was easier. 'It was in all the papers. Thio said he was ashamed to walk down the street. Thea cancelled all her committees. And I lost my job. The gallery said I was too controversial.'

There was a long silence, though it felt warm and uncritical. His arms tightened around her and she felt his big strong heart beating against hers. Then his deep, comforting voice murmured in her ear, 'That guy was a damn fool. Fancy wrecking his chance with *you*.' He kissed her ear. 'I'm glad you did it, though. That took real courage. You're the bravest girl I ever met.'

After all the recriminations she'd suffered, the words were a soothing balm to her tortured soul, and she felt a flow of joyous relief. Her heart swelled with love for Sebastian Nikosto.

Ridiculous, maybe, stupid, obviously, but she was in love.

He sounded so brisk and efficient. Was she imagining it, or was he avoiding meeting her eyes? In no time it seemed he was heading downstairs for the door.

'What? No coffee? No breakfast?' she couldn't prevent herself from calling after him in a last bid to keep him.

He arrested his stride and half turned. 'There's stuff in the fridge, I think.' Then his eyes narrowed. 'Er... Now that I think of it, you might want to go down to one of the cafés. I'll catch something in the city.' He hesitated as if he wanted to say something more, then seemed to think better of it. 'Well...anyway... have a great day.' With a backward wave over his shoulder he strode for the door.

Was he so eager to get to his satellite designs? It gave her a bit of a cold burr. She couldn't imagine Thea allowing Thio Peri to leave for his office without sharing breakfast with her.

Disappointed, she turned back inside and gave her bath a careful rinse, then filled it and climbed in for a long, hot soak in the rosemary-scented bath bubbles she'd brought from Naxos.

In truth, she was sore, though it was a good and useful soreness. The sort that came from having given and received the most bounteous of pleasures as a warm and passionate woman. A real woman, at last. She kept wanting to hug herself with the precious knowledge of her new self.

Fresh-scented and relaxed after her bath, she applied some soothing moisturiser to the areas most affected, then slipped on a tee shirt and went downstairs to investigate the kitchen. There was hardly anything in the fridge, apart from a number of plastic containers holding strange-looking leftovers, and a few bottles of beer. She sniffed a tub of ancient yoghurt and wrinkled her nose in disgust. Nothing like the yoghurt at home. The freezer, on the other hand, was packed with frozen dinners.

No fresh fruit. No vegetables or salad, and where was the coffee? Who could survive on such food?

Postponing the problem, she drifted back upstairs and

crawled into the bed to luxuriate in recollections of every fantastic thing Sebastian had done to her, and the gorgeous things he'd said. Every time she thought of how warm his eyes had been her insides swirled. With a twinge she wondered if it was natural of him to have retreated into himself and become rather remote this morning. Perhaps he simply wasn't a morning person.

She was just drifting into a blissful doze when she was startled back into wakefulness by sounds in the house. Someone was downstairs. Sebastian?

She bounded out of bed and flew down the stairs, only to be brought up short by the sight of a large grey-haired woman in the hall, bucket and mop beside her as she propped herself up against the wall and inhaled from an asthma puffer.

The woman started with surprise when she saw Ariadne. She finished dosing herself and slipped her puffer into the pocket of her capacious overall. 'Oh, heck,' she wheezed. 'I didn't know anyone was here.'

'Hello,' Ariadne said, smiling. 'Agnes, is it?'

'That's right, love. I…' Agnes broke off again to breathe deeply. 'Sorry. I just have to catch me breath.' After a few heavily breathing seconds she inspected Ariadne with curiosity. 'You must be a friend of Seb—Mr Nikosto.'

Ariadne nodded, noting that Agnes's face had a high unhealthy colour, as if from major exertion. She held out her hand. 'Ariadne.'

She'd been about to say Ariadne Giorgias, but wasn't quite sure where she stood with that now. She clasped Agnes's rather clammy hand with some concern. 'Are you feeling quite well, Agnes? Would you like to sit down and have a cup of tea?'

'Oh, no, love. I'll be fine in a while. It's just me asthma. It's this humid weather. I'm all right if I don't have to do anything too strenuous. Times like this I just do a bit here and there, and wait for a good day so I can fix up the rest.' She wheezed in a few breaths, then added, eyeing Ariadne's tee shirt and bare legs, 'Staying here, are you?'

Her eyes lit up when Ariadne nodded. 'Good, good. It's about time. Don't like to see a good man go to waste.' She grinned.

Ariadne smiled uncertainly. 'Fine. Well, thanks, Agnes. I'll just…' She gave a little wave and turned for the stairs.

Agnes bent to pick up her bucket, talking and puffing at the same time. 'That's okay. Just leave it with me, love. Though I don't think I'll be making it up the stairs today.'

Ariadne walked back up, thinking fast. That bucket looked heavy. Poor Agnes needed help. A villa of this size really needed more staff to do it justice. Sebastian hadn't seemed very concerned about it last night, though, of course, he'd had other things on his mind. She smiled in recollection of those other things.

Still, if she'd been in charge here, she'd have enjoyed bringing the chaos into order and making everything shine, showing him how comfortable and beautiful his home could be. Heavens, she was even starting to think like a wife. Thea would be so proud to see her life's work paying off. She grimaced.

A little later she descended again, clad in jeans and a shirt. Agnes was in the dining room, supporting herself by leaning with both hands on a chair back while she caught her breath. She gave Ariadne a wave, clearly unable to speak.

Ariadne took one look at the suffering woman and was inspired, partly by her conscience. 'How would it be, Agnes, if I gave you a helping hand?' Agnes's mouth dropped open, but she insisted. 'Come on. Where do you keep all your cleaning potions?'

Vacuuming was strenuous work, Ariadne discovered, and so was washing floors, dusting and polishing. Domestic work had clearly been underrated as an exercise regime. But she'd never have guessed what satisfaction there was in personally being the one to make surfaces gleam and bring the subtle glow of cleanliness to rooms that had formerly been dull and dusty. She could hardly wait to see the surprise and pleasure in Sebastian's eyes when he came home that evening and saw his villa looking bright and neat and shiny.

Agnes managed some dusting in the downstairs rooms, and, though she'd been worried to be assisted at first, now she seemed grateful to have the load of responsibility shared. In a mounting frenzy of domestic enthusiasm Ariadne attacked the bathrooms with sponges, scrubbing brushes and fresh-smelling germicidal sprays.

Windows, she mused, standing with her hands on her hips to survey her handiwork. Should she clean windows? *Theos*, married a day and she'd turned into a housewife. If Naxos could see her now!

Agnes went home early to rest, to Ariadne's secret relief.

After several athletic hours she changed into fresh clothes and prepared to solve the food problem. If she was to stay in Bronte a few days, for those few days she would try to somehow alter the breakfast situation to eat with Sebastian. Perhaps outside on the kitchen deck? By the pool? In bed?

Her insides flipped over when she thought of bed, then she experienced a tinge of regret. Bed might have become a whole new universe of excitement and delight, but it was one that couldn't last.

It was a pleasant downhill walk to the shops. People greeted her and said, 'Good morning,' several elderly souls stopping to chat about the weather. Exactly like Naxos. Among the restaurants she found a café with Danish pastries and quite good coffee. Disappointingly, their orange juice was the same fake stuff she'd been given at the airport and elsewhere.

There was a busy little delicatessen, with a fruit shop attached. She managed to fill a trolley, though remembering the hotel experience this time she carefully tallied the prices as she went. Feta and Greek yoghurt—so they *said*—eggs and bacon and tomatoes, in case Sebastian liked Australian breakfasts. Cereal to cover all contingencies. Olives and filo pastry, although she couldn't find any real myzithra cheese to bake inside the layers, and had to make do. Italian coffee beans, tea from India. Oranges, honey and pine nuts, spinach and salad vegetables, and the best olive oil available, though it wasn't Greek.

And what about Sebastian's dinner? she thought with a surge of excitement. A man needed a nourishing diet. Simple Greek food, Thea always said, was the best in the world. Ideas for the dishes she might cook crowded into her head.

In the end she had to negotiate with the shop proprietor to deliver all the supplies to the villa. Delivery cost only a little more, though luckily she'd be getting her inheritance in a few days, because her funds were now quite alarmingly low.

After the walk back, she found the boxes of groceries ready and waiting on the doorstep. Excellent. She braced herself. Time to attack the kitchen and make it fit for haute cuisine.

Sebastian closed the Thursday meeting, conscious of the worried faces of his colleagues. Athens would be sleeping at this time, so, although he'd sent the proof of his marriage first thing, it would be several hours before he heard from Peri Giorgias and could relay the good news. His team deserved something to cheer them up.

When the contract came through, signed, sealed and delivered, he'd give everyone a substantial pay rise, extra time off and a bonus for their work on the Giorgias project. In the meantime...

In the meantime, he was glad when the seemingly excruciatingly long meeting was over and he could concentrate on the issue possessing his soul.

He'd married a woman. *Another* woman. A beautiful, sexy woman was in his house, waiting and available.

Every so often his conscience tried to throw in sly glimpses of Esther towards the end to torture him, her eyes and cheeks sunken, her skin like paper, but replays of the previous night had stormed in to dominate his head-space. Throughout the entire day he'd found himself stopping every so often and closing his eyes so he could savour the stirring images. Ariadne's lovely body, her smooth satin limbs. Her blue eyes, heavy-lidded and languorous in the lamplight, with that devastating mixture of naivety and arousal.

So trusting, so—*giving*. Her sensual beauty had promised passion, and he hadn't been disappointed. Far from it. She'd surrendered herself to him with total generosity and he'd immersed himself in her until his senses were saturated with her. And still he'd craved more.

While afterwards… His thoughts kept straying to her sweet low voice confessing her secrets in the dark. No wonder she'd seemed fragile, after that painful wedding scandal. Again she'd managed to pierce his emotional armour to move him. He'd felt such a fierce need to protect her, to hold her to him, and…

He clenched his fists. For God's sake, what was he *doing*? His *wife*, his true love only three years in the ground, and here he was lusting after another woman, imagining he was feeling things, emotions his conscience told him he had no right to feel.

In a rational sense he could diagnose the situation, of course. He'd been working too hard. Worrying too much about the crisis. Add to that having been deprived of feminine company for some time, it was only natural his senses should have woken up with such a vengeance. He was in the middle of a firestorm, and he'd just have to douse the flames.

Unless, of course, he could think of some safe way to ride them out?

No, it was clear the only way to deal with these few days would be to hold Ariadne Giorgias at arm's length. Already she was creeping into his mind, twining herself around his emotional nerve centre like some sort of addictive drug. It wasn't as if she were even his choice. The less he saw into her and her little issues, the better.

His last glimpse of her this morning flashed into his mind.

She'd looked so utterly desirable wrapped in the overlarge robe, her hair all in a tangle. The surprise in her eyes when he'd been a little curt with her had somehow twisted its way into his guts and stayed with him all the way into the city. But he needed to make it clear to her nothing had changed. Having sex meant nothing more than that. Sex, pure and simple.

Ms Giorgias needed to understand. She was temporary. Esther, *Esther* was the lodestar of his life.

He couldn't help wondering, though, what Ariadne would be doing with herself all day out at Bronte. How did a princess kill time in an empty house? He'd actually considered phoning her at various stages to see if she was all right, but thank God he'd conquered that weakness. Would he have been able to trust himself not to rush home and bed her all over again?

The strange look Jenny had given him when he'd bowled in this morning earlier even than the usual time flicked into his head, and he frowned to himself. Jenny should stick to worrying about her job.

As knock-off time approached people said their goodbyes and hurried off to their homes and families. The building gradually grew quiet. Lights started flickering on all over the city, but he didn't bother with his desk lamp. The dark made for better brooding, and he needed to get his head around things.

Esther's life and joy had been snatched away from her. God forgive him for the selfish bastard he was, but he had to grit his teeth and acknowledge the truth about himself at last. Shameful, despicable, but he'd actually felt relief when her dreadful battle was over and she was gone.

He heard the cleaners' cheerful clatter, then even that diminished. He stayed frozen at his desk, trying not to imagine the vivid woman at home, his soul in a vice.

Ariadne checked the oven for the umpteenth time. The potatoes looked scrumptious, and the aroma of the resting lamb reminded her it had been a long time since lunch. The salad had been sitting there ready for some time, and a simple *avgolemono* soup simmered fragrantly on the stove. She hoped Sebastian was hungry.

She'd unearthed a cloth, and set the dining table with silver and the only glasses she could find. In the absence of flowers she'd picked a leafy spray from a shrub in the garden.

She looked anxiously at her watch. Nearly nine. She remembered him saying he didn't always come home for dinner, but he would tonight, surely? Maybe she should call him. She gave him another twenty minutes, then headed for the study.

Sebastian's study was surprisingly well organised and quite atmospheric, with books neatly tucked into their shelves, and, on the walls, huge, glowing maps of star constellations to vie with the evening sky visible through the wide windows. At some point he must have intended to work in here, she thought, preparing to dial his mobile number. Her eye fell on a framed photo and she stood stock-still.

It was of Sebastian, on the steps of a church with a bride. A red-hot needle jabbed Ariadne's chest in that initial instant of shock, and her wild heart revved up for a few pounding seconds, so that she had to sit down until her brain caught up with her body.

So, he was married. *Had* been, she presumed, since he didn't seem at all like the sort of guy to commit bigamy. Although what did she know of him, really?

When her heart had slowed down she studied the picture. He was quite a bit younger there, his handsome face split with his gorgeous white grin. The bride was quite lovely too, she supposed. Dark-haired, although clearly not Greek. *She* didn't have the big, dark shining eyes, either. They had that look people in love had, joy and euphoria pouring from every pixel.

Ariadne's heart suffered another jab as she noticed his arm around the woman's waist. How silly though. How absurd to feel jealous about something she knew nothing about.

Where was his wife now? If they'd divorced, would he have kept a wedding photo on his desk as if he cherished it? Cherished *her*?

Ridiculous maybe, but she hesitated to phone him now, as if that would be presuming an intimacy she had no right to claim. She grimaced. Might as well face it. He wasn't coming home.

Feeling deflated, she went back to the kitchen and turned off all the heating rings. All at once then the exertions of the day seemed to catch up with her and she nearly buckled to a wave of fatigue. She surveyed the kitchen in despair. Now there was the problem of what to do with all the lovely food she'd prepared. At home, she'd have simply handed the kitchen over to someone else to restore after she'd cooked a meal, but here…

Here, she was on her own.

It took longer than she'd expected, deciding on suitable storage containers, packing it all into the fridge, then clearing the utensils, scrubbing the roasting pan and wiping down the surfaces to remove all signs of her idiotic endeavour. She paused to wipe her forehead on her sleeve. How could anyone even *want* to be a wife? It was just unremitting hard labour, and what was the point? To make a man happy when he couldn't care less?

What an absolute fool she'd made of herself, trying to act the part when she was only a temporary arrangement. A business deal.

Even so, as she hauled her exhausted self up the stairs an hour later she couldn't help thinking he *could* have come home to be with her. After those things he'd said to her last night, after he'd made love to her so passionately, being ignored just didn't feel right.

CHAPTER ELEVEN

SEBASTIAN let himself quietly in his front door. It was nearly midnight, the house dark and silent. His nostrils twitched at an unusual scent in the air, like furniture polish mingled with the sort of clean household smells his mother's place always had.

For some reason he hesitated to switch the lights on, and when he walked quietly up the stairs found himself tempted by an absurd desire to take his shoes off. But why should he, for God's sake? It was his house.

There was no light on in his bedroom, and he blundered into a chest of drawers. He stilled, wincing, waiting for some reaction, but there was none. With a sharp lurch in his gut he realised there was no sleeping woman in the room. A sensation bordering on panic speared through him, and he hastened to switch on the lamps. Had she packed up and gone? Left him, for God's sake, even before he could get to know her properly?

In the lamplight the bed was smooth and untroubled. Then through the half-open door of her dressing room he glimpsed a corner of what looked like a suitcase. He sprang to push the door open further and with a flood of almost overwhelming relief saw that her clothes were there, hanging in the closet.

So, still in residence. He closed his eyes and let out a long breath. Not in his bed, where he'd expected, but some sort of tautness he sensed pricking in the atmosphere suggested she was almost certainly nearby. With questions clamouring in his brain he walked quietly along the hall, opening doors, and stopped short, his triumph mingling with bemusement when he discovered her sleeping form in the room across from his. At least, in the spill of light from the hall she *looked* as if she was asleep.

He paused, his hand on the doorknob, listening for her breathing.

'Ariadne?'

After a long, somehow nerve-racking moment, she stirred. 'Yes?'

Something about that husky *yes* confirmed his suspicions she hadn't really been asleep. She'd been lying there, listening for him. The question then arose as to *why* she wasn't in his bed. A guilty possibility sprang forcibly to mind, but he rejected it utterly. No, he'd done nothing wrong. Everything was good. Let her sleep alone if that was what she preferred.

'Er…' He took a few steps into the room, seized by a sudden concern. 'Did you manage to get some dinner?' In the dim light from the hall he could see she was on her side, her pale hair flowing loose, her smooth, bare shoulder exposed by the down-turned sheet.

'I wasn't very hungry, thanks.'

'Right. Okay. Look, er…sorry. Sorry I'm so late. I was—held up.'

There was no reply, and he tried another tack. 'Feel like a beer?'

'No.' She pulled the covers higher, and settled deeper into her sleeping position in what was clearly a dismissal.

He shrugged, backed out, then strolled downstairs. In point of fact, this cool statement of independence was a relief. It was better he didn't sleep with her. Wasn't that what he'd decided? Sleeping with her could only escalate his addiction, then how would he manage when she left?

The kitchen looked and smelled somehow different, the tiles seeming brighter and shinier, though it had been so long since he'd really noticed the room it could have just been his imagination. He opened the fridge door and stared in surprise. The shelves were packed with food. Genuine food. Fresh milk, oranges, leafy green things poking from the vegetable crisper. He investigated a large plastic container dominating the middle shelf and was astonished to find a roasted joint. He tore off a bit and tasted it. Despite being cold, it was as tender, succulent and delicious as anything his mother kept in her fridge.

He investigated further and found other containers: salad, potatoes sprinkled with oregano, some sort of herb sauce. And he was starving, he realised. He'd been so engrossed in contemplation at the office he hadn't thought to order in dinner. Without wasting any more time he took down a plate and served himself hearty portions of the leftovers, then sat at the kitchen counter and wolfed it all down, along with occasional sips of beer, thinking deeply as he ate.

She could cook. Who'd have thought it? The kitchen had been pulled into sparkling order, he could see, with the sort of attention to detail that had never been poor Agnes's strong point. He owed her his thanks, that much was certain, though why she must transfer to another bed was curious.

It wasn't bothering him exactly, but he had to admit it had come as a shock. If she was *tired*, if she wanted to sleep, she could have done that perfectly well in his bed. He was a civilised guy. He was hardly a gorilla, unable to keep his hands off her. He'd have made no demands on her, if that was what she truly wanted.

Maybe it had simply been the steamy summer night that had made her decide it would be more comfortable to sleep alone. That bare shoulder he'd glimpsed suggested she might have been wearing next to nothing.

He frowned. Surely she realised state-of-the-art air-conditioning was available at the flick of a switch. Maybe he needed to inform her of it. Encourage her back to her rightful place with a little tender persuasion.

Though ashamed of such a backsliding thought, he couldn't deny another rueful reflection. However proud and icy Ms Ariadne Giorgias might try to be, whether she knew it or not, persuading her into his arms would be so meltingly, deliciously easy for a sinful male animal like himself. He could start with kissing her throat…

He gave his jaw a thoughtful rub. Of course, if he intended anything like that, the considerate thing for him to do would be to shave.

He finished his meal and pushed his plate away, then, unusually for him, something about the clean state of the surfaces impinged on his brain. He rose and made an unprecedented effort to rinse the plate in the sink. God, if he wasn't careful he'd be turning into a metrosexual. Then his thoughts switched to her lying upstairs, possibly naked. No. No, he wouldn't. No chance of that.

He shrugged off his lascivious thoughts and made an effort to recapture the mood of resistance that had sustained him at the office. He'd embrace this opportunity to sleep alone. He could use it as a test of his endurance. Though he might have to resort to taking some good scientific reading material up with him to send him off to sleep.

He started for the study, but as he passed through the dining room something caught the periphery of his vision and he checked.

Oh, God. Oh, *no*. The dining table was set. Charmingly, intimately set for two. If Esther had been able to see that. He stared at it, aghast, then something about the brave little optimistic bunch of leaves in the middle of the table hit him like a punch in the chest.

He closed his eyes. Bloody hell, how dumb could a selfish bastard get?

The enormity of his day's behaviour swept through him in a tidal wave, and he stood for a minute, paralysed.

On the floor above, Ariadne lay thinking about the pathetic lies men told. Held up at work. *Who* needed to stay at work until midnight? Prime ministers, maybe. Presidents, just possibly, although she couldn't see Michelle Obama allowing it to happen too often. But CEOs? She strained her ears for sounds from below. There'd been a bit of clattering, followed by silence. Then suddenly she heard Sebastian bound up the stairs. She tensed as his energetic step rang out in the hall and inexorably, for the second time, approached her bedroom door.

'Ariadne?' he said softly. 'Are you awake?'

She frowned. 'Well, I am *now*.'

He advanced into the room. 'Look…I'm sorry I didn't manage to make it home for dinner. I didn't realise you'd cooked a meal.'

'That's all right,' she said at once. 'I know you didn't know.'

'I guess I should have thought,' he floundered. 'I didn't…er… I should've…'

'It really doesn't matter. What's a bit of food?'

'Oh, look. Look, sweetheart…'

He advanced a little further into the room and hovered there a moment. The air throbbed with sexual vibrations. Though her lids were shut tight she could feel his eyes devouring her. She clutched the sheet to her breast, fighting her own weak desire for him to tear it away.

'Do you mind…?' She could hear the smile in his voice. 'Can I just turn on this lamp?' She felt the side of the bed depress as he sat down.

'What do you think you're doing?' she said sharply, blinking in the sudden light.

His smile flashed. He'd undone his tie and it was hanging loose. In his shirtsleeves with his five-o'clock shadow, he was so stirringly handsome her insides melted dangerously, and her treacherous body suddenly felt alive and wanton with desire.

His voice was as smooth as butter. 'I just wanted to thank you for cooking that delicious food. I don't think I've ever had such a great meal in this house.'

'It was greater five hours ago.'

'Oh, I know, I know. It must have been. You're a fantastic cook.'

'I'm just an ordinary *plain* cook, Sebastian.' She could feel the warmth of his knee touching her through the sheet, and piled up the pillows so she could lean up on them and not be at a disadvantage.

'Oh, no, you're not. Not ordinary. And not plain. Certainly not plain.' His dark eyes were smouldering in that way she recognised, drifting to the plunging bodice of her pretty satin nightie with the rosebuds on it and the thin straps.

'Thank you, you're very kind,' she said coldly, sweeping down her lashes, 'but I hope you don't think I cooked that food on your account. I just happen to have been brought up to prefer nourishing home-cooked meals myself.'

'Of course, of course.' He nodded. 'And it *was* nourishing. Thank you. Oh, well.' He got up and casually stretched. His shirt tautened to the max and she noticed a little gap appear in the opening just above his belt buckle. 'I'm heading for the shower.'

Paradoxically, she felt an almost overwhelming disappointment. Didn't he want to at least try to overcome her resistance? She'd had some wonderful things lined up to say about being a chattel, a convenient sex-slave and a domestic workhorse.

He made it to the door, and before she could stop herself she said, 'I think you might have at least mentioned you were married.'

He froze, then turned to her, a strange rigidity in the movement. 'I *was* married,' he said coolly, something a little scary in his voice. 'But it has nothing to do with anything here.'

He walked away, and she was left feeling rebuked, her imagination running riot. Anything *here* obviously referred to her. *Theos*, she regretted ever mentioning it. How could she have been so brash?

She switched off the lamp and lay there in the dark, listening to the sounds of the shower across the hall, her brain racing. All right, so his life had nothing to do with her. But she had some rights, didn't she? Even as a temporary wife? All her good instincts about last night, and making love and feeling that fabulous current of connection with him, seemed to have been cut off. But why? What had she done wrong?

Was it something she'd said this morning?

The water stopped flowing, and eventually everything fell silent, though it was a deafening sort of silence, filled with vibrations. She wished she could go to sleep, but she had a big aching lump in her chest. Her husband had wanted her once and once only, it seemed. Even as a temporary wife she was a failure. She could never go back to Naxos. Her aunt and uncle were fed up with her, and she was a stranger in her own country.

She was lying there in the unfriendly alien dark, realising she had nowhere in the world to belong, when the silence was shattered by a ringing phone. It stopped almost at once. She guessed Sebastian must have answered it. In a little while he opened her door and put his head in.

'It's your uncle. He wants to talk to you.'

'No.' Emotion welled in her throat and she turned away and covered her head with the sheet.

'But—I really think you should talk to him. He sounds very concerned. He says your aunt's frantic with—'

That cut her to the quick. '*You* talk to him,' she said through the sheet. 'He's your friend.'

'He's not my friend,' he said tersely, then walked away, speaking into the phone, his voice grim. 'Look, Giorgias, it's late here. Ariadne can't come…'

After a few minutes he came back to her door and said more

calmly, 'He's left the name of the solicitors in the city who manage your trust. You need to make an appointment to see them, and they'll arrange the transfer of your inheritance.'

She didn't answer, and he came up to the bed, frowning, his hands opened in query. 'Look, whatever it is that's happened between you and them, can't you—?'

'No, I can't.' Her voice gave away her emotional state. Or the way she was lying all hunched up in the foetal position with the sheet bunched to her chest. It must have, because he lowered his big frame to the bed, his eyes warm with concern, his voice gentle.

'Oh, sweetheart…'

Oh, she was a weak fool, but he shouldn't have said that. Sympathy was always her undoing, and she already had a very tenuous hold on her control. Tears rushed into her eyes and she was forced to surreptitiously dab at them with the sheet.

'Oh-h-h, no. No.' He reached and grabbed her, taking her into his strong arms, holding her against his bare chest, murmuring soothing things to her while he stroked her hair, planting little kisses on her face and throat and shoulders.

'I'm sorry,' she moaned after a while. 'I don't mean to cry.'

'No, no,' he soothed. '*I'm* sorry. I'm sorry I was such a selfish bastard today. Leaving you all alone like that.'

'I knew you couldn't help it. I knew you had to go to work.'

His hold tightened on her, and his caresses developed a different sort of energy. Soon he was kissing her, tenderly, and then passionately, and she was clinging to him and giving him her all as if there were no tomorrow. Then before she knew it, to her thrilled excitement, he was hoisting her up in his arms and carrying her into his bedroom.

She was so glad he'd shaved.

CHAPTER TWELVE

BREAKFAST was beautiful. After a night of passion, and long slow love as the dawn was breaking, Ariadne's husband chose to make her fresh orange juice and toast and bring it to her in bed. Then later, while he was showering, she cooked him some of the delicious little *bougatsas* with custard Thea often made for her uncle, and a nourishing spinach and feta omelette to sustain him in the workplace.

'Being married has its compensations,' Sebastian observed. As he smiled at her across the breakfast table, admiring her with his eyes in her shorts and pretty top, she allowed a wild, little hope to lift its head. What if they decided to play it for real? What if he asked her to stay?

When it was time for him to leave for work he kissed her long and deeply, though their lips were already bruised with kissing. 'I'd love to stay with you today,' he murmured. 'But I have some news for my employees that can't wait.'

'Is it about Thio's contract?' she guessed.

He nodded, scanning her face, and said carefully, 'It means quite a lot to Celestrial. There have been some worried faces in the office. I know you aren't comfortable with the circumstances, but the outcome has been very good for us. And...' he squeezed her hands '...let me know how it goes with the solicitor.'

After he'd gone and she'd cleared the breakfast dishes, she

found the firm of solicitors in the phone directory and booked an appointment. She had the option of Monday or Tuesday, but Monday seemed too close, so she opted for Tuesday. Fingers crossed there'd be something to inherit. Of course she was curious to know, but she couldn't suppress the thought that, once she had her inheritance in her possession, there was nothing to keep her here with Sebastian. It would be time for her to leave.

And go…where?

Sebastian drove into work whistling along to songs on the radio, preserving the buoyant, relaxed mood another night of passion had created by carefully controlling his thoughts. Some apprehension of having slid deeper into his glorious entanglement with Ariadne Giorgias lurked at one corner of his mind, but not to worry. He'd been moved by people before, and no doubt he would be again. The trick was not to get emotionally attached.

So she'd had a rift of some sort with her uncle and aunt. Families had conflicts, that was life, and there was no point letting a woman's distress play upon his heartstrings. An utterly impermissible notion had crept into his head while he'd been comforting her in the night, and he worried he might have said something reckless in the heat of the moment. She hadn't mentioned anything about it this morning, so perhaps he'd dreamed it. But there'd been a look in her eyes, a certain look he knew he must not encourage.

He doubted if *he* had that look. He'd never been a very emotional guy, despite what his family seemed to think.

Anyway, today was a day for celebration. He could hardly wait to assemble his employees and break the news.

A cheer went up at the meeting when he told them. If he'd been a different kind of boss they might have dared to pop a few champagne corks, but they restricted themselves to grinning, back-slapping and general loony happiness.

By mid-morning, it was clear not much work was likely to be

done this day. And with his own obsessive need to luxuriate in recollections of the night, he could hardly hold it against his workforce. He could have spent the day watching Celestrial's share price zoom on the stock market, but he kept wondering what Ariadne was doing. Cooking? He grinned to himself. That perky little vase filled with pretty leaves came back to him. He resisted as long as he could—it wouldn't be kind to give her any false ideas—but then he sprang up suddenly and grabbed his jacket.

'I'm leaving for the day,' he told a startled Jenny on his way out. 'Oh, and…hey, why don't you take the rest of the day off?'

He wasn't a romantic guy, by any means, but flowers should have a presence on other occasions too, not just funerals.

He stopped off at a couple of places on the way home. Searching for his wallet to pay the florist, he came upon Ariadne's passport in the inside pocket of his jacket. He patted it. At least he could definitely certify she was still in the country.

Agnes had phoned to say she didn't feel well enough to come in. Ariadne had the villa all to herself.

Feeling lethargic after her late night, she took Sebastian's laptop up to bed with her, propped herself up on some pillows, and composed a letter to her old university requesting a reissue of her degree certificates. Then she spent some time scrolling the ads on one of the major Sydney job network sites. Perhaps once she'd assembled her testimonials, she could find employment in Sydney. If she could find a flat not too far away, perhaps she and Sebastian would stay in touch. He might take her out some time, to dinner, or a movie. They might meet for coffee, or…

Her heart panged. What a fool she was. As if people who'd been lovers ever met for coffee.

Sounds from downstairs startled her, and before she could shelve the laptop she heard the familiar footsteps bounding up the stairs.

'Oh, there you are.' Sebastian's tall form appeared in the doorway and her heart leaped up in surprise when she saw he seemed to be laden with flowers and packages.

'What are you doing?' He deposited his armful on the floor and sprawled on the bed beside her.

'Job hunting. What are *you* doing?' She craned to see the flowers. Roses interspersed with white alyssum. 'Are they for me?'

'For the house.' His thick black lashes swept down and screened his gaze. 'It's such a shemozzle at work I've taken the day off. Here, let me see that.' He peered over her shoulder at the screen at the advertisement she'd been investigating. 'Ah. Have you done this sort of thing before?'

She nodded. 'In Athens. And I've done a bit of study and training in antiquities. I *could* work in a museum.'

'Well, you shouldn't have much trouble finding something you like. *I'd* give you a job. Like *that*.'

She smiled and raised her brows flirtily. 'What as?'

He kissed her neck. 'I'd think of something. That reminds me.' He glanced appreciatively around the room. 'I've been meaning to say, everything looks—fantastic. In fact, last night I could have sworn my mother had been here, though I don't think even she makes the *walls* sparkle. Agnes must have been inspired.'

She nodded without speaking, and he continued to hold her in his dark, smiling gaze. 'It wasn't Agnes, though, was it?'

'Some of it,' she said with a shrug. 'I just gave her a helping hand. She isn't very well, you know. Her asthma's pretty bad at the moment. It's a large villa for one elderly woman to clean on her own.'

'Yeah.' He frowned, and let out a sigh. 'I should have thought. I s'pose it's too much for her. I did notice she wasn't performing up to scratch.'

'You did?' She widened her eyes in mock astonishment.

He laughed and gave her a little shake. 'Yes, I *did*, but I didn't want to sack her. I think she relies on the money, and…well, you know, Esther was fond of her.'

There was a beat of silence. 'Esther. Your wife.'

He met her gaze, then lowered his thick, black lashes. 'Yeah.'

She screwed up her courage to say carefully, 'What happened with Esther? Did—she die?'

His face smoothed to become expressionless. 'Cancer. Three years ago.'

'Oh.' She had the sensation of walking on extremely fragile eggshells. 'That must have been—awful for you.'

'It was awful for *Esther*.'

'Oh, of course it was, of course.' She could see talking about it was painful for him, but wasn't sure how to back out of the topic gracefully. 'You—you must have suffered a lot too.'

He shot her a glance, then lowered his gaze and said harshly, 'I was absolutely fine. Esther was the one who suffered. I was the selfish bastard who survived.'

'Oh, oh.' Her heart clenched. She stared at him in distress, urgent to think of some soothing thing to alleviate the excruciating moment. In her desperation she risked touching him, and stroked his arms, relieved when he didn't draw away. 'Someone—someone has to survive to tell the story.' He didn't answer, and, still stroking him, she babbled on to fill the silence, 'The story of Esther, I mean. Who she was, and what she was like.'

She held her breath. Had she said the wrong thing?

He glanced up at her then with a shrug, and his grim expression relaxed. 'That's truer than you know. But let's not worry about it right now. See what I've brought you.'

He reached for the roses and put them in her arms, then piled a wide, slim black box on top.

'Oh, thank you. They're *heavenly*,' she breathed, inhaling their sweet heady fragrance. 'And wow. Not chocolates! *Wicked*.

Look at the size of this box. *Theos*, these are my downfall. How did you know?' She lay the roses down beside her and lifted the chocolates to smell the box.

He smiled, a sexy, sinful smile, his dark eyes flickering over her with a hungry, wolfish look. 'Well, I *am* a genius. You said so yourself.'

She laughed and he took her in his arms and kissed her, rolling her onto her back, oblivious of the gifts they were crushing in an embrace that grew hotter and steamier by the second. Desire flared in her again with an almost scary readiness as he undid the buttons on her top for an urgent and delicious exploration of her breasts.

The more she had of him, it seemed to her, hungrily releasing *his* shirt buttons, the more she had to have of him. After a long, writhing, mindless time she grew conscious of things sticking into her side, and broke from his arms, gasping in air.

'Oh, no,' she said when she could. 'The chocolates. They'll be crushed.'

He reached for the roses and lifted them to safety. The box wasn't too badly squashed, apart from the corners.

She examined it. 'I think it's only the box that's damaged.'

They surveyed each other, shirts hanging open, pleasure still tingling in her veins, desire shimmering in the air, unappeased.

She smiled. 'Hungry?'

His eyes gleamed. 'Not for chocolate.'

She flicked him a glance from beneath her lashes, then tore off the cellophane wrapper. 'Oh,' she sighed, opening the box and viewing the sumptuous array. She closed her eyes to inhale the intoxicating aroma. 'I'm so glad you've taken the day off.'

'The whole weekend. First time in—ages. Feel like doing a little sightseeing tomorrow?' He leaned forward and planted a sexy little kiss on her shoulder.

'Yeah! That'd be great.' She smiled, pretending to consider the chocolates, enjoying the play as he delayed the moment of pouncing on her with a little conversational chit-chat.

'What would you like to see?'

Aware of his fingers stroking a shivery path down her spine she murmured hazily, 'The Katherine Gorge.'

His brows twitched. 'How about the Opera House?'

'Seen it.'

The chocolates looked a little on the soft side, but were silky and succulent notwithstanding. She bent her head to study the key to the varieties. 'Nougat, almond or strawberry liqueur?' She glanced up at him. 'What I'd really like, if you had the time would be to see my parents' cottage.'

He was watching her with a sensual gleam in his eyes, but when she said that his brows lifted. 'Great. Do you know the address?'

She popped a cherry liqueur into her mouth, closing her eyes as its deliciousness melted on her tongue and mingled with her mouth juices. After a blissful second she said, 'Off by heart. It's in wobbly writing in all my old story books.'

'You've never been back since, have you?' A dark flame smouldered in his eyes.

'No. I've often longed to see it again. I'm quite excited.'

His lids were heavy and slumberous. 'Are you?' He ran his finger from her mouth to her shorts' zip and said huskily, 'Well I'm *very* excited.'

She could see by the bulge in his groin that he wasn't exaggerating.

Excitement was infectious. It turned her voice to a throaty purr. 'Sure you won't join me in a little Cheri Suisse?'

'That's exactly what I intend.'

He bent and slipped his tongue into her mouth at the same time as his rough, urgent hands finished unbuttoning her top, and slid around her back to unfasten her bra.

She felt her blood ignite. A hot, sexy kiss mingled with chocolate was almost too much pleasure to endure at one time. While his clever tongue tickled her sensitive mouth, her hungry hands convulsively enjoyed the textures and contours of his bronzed chest and washboard-hard abdominals.

'Delicious,' he said after another steamy while, drawing away from her.

She bent to lick off a chocolatey smear she'd left on his right nipple, causing his skin to shiver and the flat little bead to perk up. 'Ooh,' she said, savouring the flavours of chocolate and raw salty man. 'Your nipple likes chocolate.'

'You're a little tease,' he rumbled, his voice a deep, sultry murmur. She made a move to take another chocolate but he swiftly grabbed her hand and held it still. 'My turn.' He reached for the box, and his long, tanned fingers hung poised over the selection. 'Ah. What else but raspberry?'

He held his selection between his palms for a second, his eyes gleaming wickedly. 'Now let's see what happens.'

In a rapid movement he smeared the chocolate over her breasts, then, with a laugh that was halfway a growl, bent to suck each of her nipples. She shivered with delight as lightning raced along her nerve endings, tightening the tingling points and igniting them with an explosive hunger.

Her shorts came off in the sexy tussle. When his marauding tongue and ruthless, ravaging hands had turned her blood to wildfire and she'd cried and moaned her pleasure, it became her turn again.

Perhaps she was running a fever, because in a surge of reckless daring she sat up and placed her hands on his belt buckle, and purred, 'Let's see what we have here.'

With hands that trembled at their own unaccustomed boldness, she released the button and eased down his zip. He watched her face, sensual amusement dancing in his aroused eyes like searing points of flame. He lifted his lean hips a little to assist her in dragging off the confining clothes, then kicked them away altogether.

'Oh, my goodness,' was her sincere reaction.

His erection sprang thick and proud and virile, swelling and pulsing before her wide eyes. She stared, not missing the full and violent impact of its message.

Daunted, almost unconsciously she licked her lips.

Politely, but with a wicked grin, Sebastian offered her the chocolate box. She blinked. In truth, for a cowardly instant she nearly blenched at the challenge.

But what was she? An inexperienced virgin, or a married woman able to give and receive pleasure in the privacy of her husband's bedroom? The bravest woman he'd ever met? With grave care she selected a couple of chocolate caramels, then, with a long glance at him from beneath her lashes, melted the rich creamy beauties between her hands.

It took her a while to come to terms with what she was about to try, so she held the smouldering guy in suspense for seconds, letting her eyes flicker to his rampant penis, rubbing her hands together while she slicked the gooey, sensuous chocolate over her palms.

Her playmate waited, immobile apart from the barely perceptible rise and fall of his bronzed chest, his black eyes glittering with fever, and the air in the room seemed to tauten to a dangerous pitch.

As she eyed his virile length a tiny, expectant drop of pure masculine essence pearled on the tip, and she felt her mouth water and her folds moisten in helpless excitement. Then, just before the tension reached flashpoint, she smeared her mouth voluptuously with chocolate, then gripped his rosy rod and held him tight, sliding her hands up and down the throbbing shaft.

Sebastian let out a small groan, and to her intense satisfaction she felt him swell and become even harder in her grasp. Sympathetically, her nipples, her breasts, her sweet tender place all swelled too and yearned with desire.

Shudders of pleasure roiled through Sebastian's big frame, and though he held himself quite still she noticed a seductive line of sweat appear on his upper lip. Not to be called a coward, she knelt down then and stroked his amazing length from base to velvet tip with her tongue, smoothing the chocolate off as she went.

She felt so unbelievably hot and sexy and reckless, she was revelling in her brave exploration of the situation, but at that point things escalated beyond her control.

As though all at once driven crazy by her ministrations to his throbbing rod, Sebastian suddenly grabbed her and flipped her onto her back. He scrabbled at the side of the bed for the condom packet, ripped one open with his teeth, then with swift hands rolled the sheath on.

For a suspenseful, exhilarating second the hungry, hard, rapidly breathing guy softly combed her curls with his lean, smooth fingers, his dark eyes devouring her chocolate-smeared nudity like molten fire while he magically tickled her already moist delta into a state of electric wildness.

Then with a possessive little growl he covered her with his gorgeous lean body and plunged himself into her willing flesh.

CHAPTER THIRTEEN

ARIADNE cooked dinner that night and made Sebastian her kitchen-aide. She had no doubt he surprised himself with his ability to wash herbs, to peel, chop and dice to her rigorous standards, but she wasn't surprised. She'd had experience of the guy's artful fingers.

The preparation of dinner was really a pleasant extension of the bedroom and the subsequent bath, in which she'd learned so much more about giving and receiving. And the meal didn't suffer from the flirty camaraderie that had seemed to spring from their intimate adventures.

'There's something so sexy about watching a woman cook,' her husband said, kissing her neck as she stood at the sink.

'What's really sexy is a man *helping* a woman to cook,' she threw over her shoulder.

She'd decided on the simple, nourishing peasant food Thea believed every Greek husband thrived on, from the humble fisherman to the shipping magnate. When Sebastian had performed his part of the chopping, he perched on a kitchen stool and watched her toss some delicate calamari rings in the pan for their first course, in the absence of retsina sipping a glass of chilled white wine. She placed a little platter of nibbles at his elbow, plump olives and rice-stuffed dolmades that he dipped into a tzatziki she'd whipped up with some yoghurt, cucumber and lemon juice.

She could feel Sebastian's curious gaze appraising her in her pretty skirt and top, watching her reach for things, pause and check things, open the oven door to inspect the progress of the moussaka. He was still surprised, she guessed. He hadn't expected his mail-order bride to know her way around a kitchen. And he seemed warmly receptive to her ideas, including the one of hiring more staff to assist Agnes.

It gave her a surge of hope. He clearly enjoyed seeing his home glowing and comfortable and cared for. Perhaps he would start to see how lovely it could be to have a woman always here at the heart of things. Someone to keep the love fires burning.

On Saturday he drove her to her old street, as promised, but the cottage she dimly remembered from her early childhood had been replaced by an apartment block. Still, she took some photos of the street sign, and a tree she convinced herself had been there all along. Disappointed, she asked Sebastian if he would mind taking her to see the place where her parents were buried.

Something flickered in his eyes at her request, as though he felt taken aback, then he agreed readily enough. They took a little time to find the location on the Internet, then drove to Waverley, which she was surprised to see was very close to Bronte.

The modest headstones they sought were on a cliff, stalwart against the ocean breeze, if a little stained by the weather. Ariadne read the sad little inscriptions, shaken by the peaceful solemnity of the place, and laid some purple flowers at their base. Here were her roots, in *this* earth, this grass, this sacred ground.

When would she feel she belonged?

She saw Sebastian's watchful gaze flicker from her to her sur-roundings, and had the uncanny notion he'd read her mind.

He observed, 'Your father must have loved Australia to choose to be buried here.'

'He was dead,' she snapped. 'He had no choice.'

Shocked at her own terseness, she turned away, misting with tears all at once. How pathetic she was, grieving for a *place* when she was young, alive and had her health, while her parents' youthful lives had been so rudely interrupted.

She wiped her eyes, then felt a strong arm slip around her waist.

'He chose to live here,' Sebastian said firmly. 'He chose an Australian wife. He chose this as his child's homeland. *Your* homeland.'

'I *know* that, all right? I know.' She slipped from his grasp.

'Hey. Steady there.' He touched her bare arm, sliding his hand around the muscle as though unable to keep from savouring the texture of her flesh. He frowned. 'Isn't there anything in this country you like?'

He looked so mystified, with his dark eyes so serious and intent, his black brows bristling in puzzlement, her heart shook all at once with love for him.

She said softly, 'There is, lover. There's *you*.'

She stood up on tiptoe and kissed him on the lips, her hands on his ribs, relishing the charge of response in his lean, vibrant body as he held her hard against him and took command of the exchange.

The flare-up was smoothed away, and afterwards she couldn't remember why she'd been upset. She smiled wonderingly down at the graves.

'It's been good to see this place. I've often imagined it. Now I have, I don't really feel they're sad, you know, Sebastian? I think somehow they're up there in the ether, smiling and wafting around like clouds. Do you...?' She turned to look at him. 'Do you feel like that when you go to visit Esther's resting place?'

His eyes slid away from her, and he bit out rather curtly, 'I don't go.'

On the way back to the car, Sebastian held her hand, but he was silent on the way home. He'd withdrawn a little, and she couldn't help brooding. She'd told him she liked him, but despite his warmth he hadn't responded in kind. Had *like* been too close to that other word? The one she longed to hear?

That evening they drove up into the Blue Mountains for some star-gazing through a giant telescope belonging to a friend. They stayed overnight in a chalet, and the next day explored some of the little villages interspersed with the magnificent scenery, including some truly awe-inspiring gorges. But as the weekend drew to a close, though there'd been good times, she'd had anxious ones as well. Times when Sebastian was with her in the flesh, but was it only the flesh?

Could her instincts be so wrong? Did such a passionate, tender guy only feel desire?

On Monday evening, the day before she was due to receive her inheritance, he arrived home earlier than usual.

'Hello, beautiful,' he said, embracing her. 'Good day?' Though he smiled his dark eyes were searching, as if he had something on his mind.

As she served the meal they chatted about small things, the minor comings and goings of each others' days, but Ariadne was conscious of him being preoccupied.

Was it her imagination, or was he cooler than usual, though he praised her for the dinner? When the meal was over and she was about to put the tea on, he took her arm. 'Leave that. Come and sit down. I need to ask you something.'

His lean, dark face was serious, and she felt a stir of anxiety about what was coming, especially when he chose his armchair rather than the sofa next to her.

He dug into his jacket pocket, and produced an opaque plastic bag and handed it across. 'I picked this up this morning.'

He watched her so intently she hardly dared open it. Wonderingly, she shook out a slim parcel of tissue paper. As she unrolled the paper, with a flash of blue something cool and heavy slipped into her hand. She gasped to see her own bracelet of sapphires, their glittering fires as brilliant as ever.

'Oh.' Stunned, she stared at it for seconds, then looked quickly up at him. 'How? Where'd you get it?'

He reached into his jacket pocket again and fished out her passport holder. 'I found this in my pocket the other day. I'd forgotten all about it being in this suit. Today I took the passport out to flick through and the receipt for the pawnbroker slipped out. Then I remembered something the jeweller mentioned on our wedding day.' He made a sardonic grimace. 'Lucky you only hocked this. They ripped you off pretty disgracefully, I'd say.'

She flushed. 'I know they did. But there was no need for *you* to worry, Sebastian. At the time I just needed some—temporary funds. I always intended to redeem the bracelet myself. Once...'

'Once you had your inheritance.'

She blinked. 'Yes.'

He continued to scrutinise her face. Her heart started to thud and she felt a flush mount to her neck. 'Ariadne...'

He leaned forward in his chair, his dark eyes grave and compelling. 'I don't want to pry into your private affairs, but I need to understand. You said you weren't rich. But how so? How can a Giorgias be so short of cash she has to hock her jewellery?'

She tried to sidle out of explaining. 'Being a Giorgias doesn't mean I'm rich. This bracelet was a gift. An art gallery doesn't pay its employees massive salaries.'

'Even so...' He levelled his intent dark gaze at her, and pinned her to the point. 'You flew out here to meet me, you rejected me at first, then you were keen to get married the very next day. What was suddenly so urgent?' His intelligent dark eyes scoured her face in an uncompromising probe. 'It's time for the truth, my sweet.'

The implication stung, and she stiffened. 'What do you mean, "it's time for the *truth*"? I've never lied to you.'

'Well…you have to admit you weren't exactly open about your reasons.'

She could feel the walls closing in, and when she didn't answer, he said quietly, 'It's to do with your uncle and aunt, isn't it?'

She gave a shrug of admission. 'I suppose.'

'If you were short of funds, though, *why*…why couldn't you apply to them to bail you out?'

Her flush deepened as she felt herself twisting on the spit. 'I have told you most of it already.' She braced for deep humiliation. 'This is hard for me, Sebastian. Are you sure you want to…?'

His gaze was firm and unequivocal and capitulated. 'All right. It's true that I flew here for a holiday. At least, that was what I *thought* I was doing.' She saw his eyes flick to her suddenly shaking hands. 'I—I just couldn't bear to tell you the worst part. I feel so—embarrassed.' Her voice croaked in her throat, but she forced herself to expose her humiliation with as much dignity as she could muster. 'It was Thio who booked my holiday. It was supposed to be a gift. I didn't understand his real intention until I was on the plane.'

He frowned. 'His *real* intention. You mean, that you were coming to meet your prospective bridegroom?'

She lifted her shoulders in wry bitterness. 'I didn't know I had one. They mentioned I'd be meeting the Nikosto family. I didn't realise my uncle had struck a deal with *you* until something he said when I was getting on the plane. So I phoned him from the plane. That's when I—found out.'

There was a stunned flicker in his eyes. 'My God.'

She nodded. 'You see? When I arrived here I discovered nothing had been paid for. I had some money of my own, of course, to pay for meals and taxis, that sort of thing, but the big costs, the hotel and the tours, had never been paid.'

'And then you met me,' he said grimly. 'And the trap was complete.' He said in a constrained voice, 'And I—wasn't very kind to you at all.'

She shot him a low glance. 'Perhaps not,' she said, and saw him wince.

She spread her hands. 'I have to admit I panicked. In a strange country, with hardly any real money, I didn't have many choices. And it seemed clear to me...' She met his appalled gaze, then cast down her lashes. 'You didn't want to marry me, anyway. Not really, but you were just prepared to grit your teeth and go through with it for the sake of your company.'

He compressed his chiselled mouth into a straight, grim line, then nodded. 'I admit it. Your uncle—had made me very angry.'

She nodded, clasping her hands, her heart aching with mortification and pained love for her uncle and aunt. 'When I rang Thea to find out what had gone wrong, she said...' her voice wobbled '...you *needed* to marry me.'

'Oh, hell.' He sprang across to the sofa and grasped her arms. 'Why didn't you tell me any of this?'

'Oh, well.' Her throat thickened, emotion rendering her voice gravelly. 'Try to understand. They're my *family*. I didn't want you to think badly of them. Thio doesn't mean to hurt, truly. They're old, you know. And they—they do love me. They do.' Tears washed into her eyes.

Sebastian looked sharply at her, comprehension and compassion colouring his eyes, then they veiled almost at once and he shook his head, frowning. A muscle twitched in his lean cheek.

She fought for control. 'I know what you're thinking, but they still cling to so many of the traditions, you see. Thio has always had so much power he thinks he can do as he likes. He just bulldozes over people, and Thea lets him get away with it.' She dashed a tear away with the back of her hand. 'After the scandal he thought he had to rescue my honour. He probably thought by forcing me into marriage with some eligible guy, as far away as possible, he was doing the very best thing for me.' She realised how that must have sounded, and quickly touched his hand. 'It's only by the greatest good luck the guy turned out to be *you*. It hasn't been such a bad thing after all, has it?'

With a thud in his chest Sebastian heard the note in her voice. Her tentative blue gaze, so warm and shyly questioning, pierced straight through his steel-plated resistance and touched some yearning part of him with a dangerous potency. God, but she was sweet. Everything a man could dream of in a woman, surely. For an instant he was intensely tempted to lower his guard, drag her into his arms and hold her vibrant lusciousness to him. But with a roaring pressure in his temples visions of Esther and all the nightmare days and nights crowded in on him, reminding him of how it could turn out.

There was no way he could risk it. Never again.

Luckily, adrenaline lent him the necessary iron to deal with the situation before it got out of control.

'No, not at all it hasn't,' he replied without blinking, 'but when did you say you were seeing that lawyer?'

'Tomorrow.'

'Good.'

Ariadne searched his cool resolute gaze and the blood drained from her heart. 'Oh.' Her smile was so tight it hurt. She stood up and stuttered, 'I—I s-suppose you've been thinking I've overstayed my welcome.'

He lowered his lashes. 'No, no, not at all, but…' He hesitated, then chose his words with great care. 'It's been—fantastic having you here, but you need to have your money and your freedom of choice. Then you can decide what you want to do, and who with.'

She swallowed, half comprehending that the ground was sliding away from her. Desperation tempted her to say things her instincts were clanging alarm bells against. 'But what if I say now that I'd like to stay with *you*? What if I tell you that I…I'm in love with you?'

He closed his eyes then stepped backwards, increasing the distance between them. 'No, please… *Don't*…' He held up his hand as if to ward something off, and drew a deep breath. 'Look, Ariadne, it's better if we don't try to complicate what's been a fantastic time. We were both forced into this, and…I guess, we've naturally—bonded—to some extent.'

She opened her mouth to speak but he held up his lean hand again.

'No, we need to be realistic. Sweetheart, I'm very conscious I've been your first—lover.' A dark stain spread across his cheek-bones. 'People—people often think they've fallen in love with their first. It's all new, and it seems…' he made a jerky gesture '…*special* somehow. You know, you start seeing the world through rose-coloured glasses. Everything starts to look hopeful again. You can't wait to get home and see the person every day. You think about them all the time. *Worry* about them, all their little… But it can't last.'

The blood thundering in her ears made her head swim. Lighting on the one thing coming through loud and clear, she said, a treacherous tremor in her voice, 'You—don't want me, then?'

His dark face twisted and he turned his eyes away from her. 'Ariadne, think of this. Soon you'll have your money and your freedom of choice. And you'll look back on this inter-lude and think how lucky you were to escape from such a selfish bastard as Sebastian Nikosto.' He smiled, but it was more like a grimace.

Her heart ached so cruelly she could scarcely breathe but, gathering the last thin remains of her dignity about her, she croaked, 'I guess you'd prefer it if I left tomorrow.'

'No. *Hell*, no. Take as long as you need to find a job, and get settled. I'm very conscious of owing you a debt of gratitude for all you've done here. But, you know, *this*—' he waved his hand, and looked ruefully at her '—*us*, the way we started, it's been lovely, you're a gorgeous girl, but whatever it is we think we have between us is built on sand. Sooner or later you'll end up leaving anyway.' His voice rasped. 'Everybody does.'

CHAPTER FOURTEEN

SEBASTIAN stared out at the rain squall sweeping across the harbour and wondered if Ariadne had reached her appointment without getting soaked. Things had been strained after their discussion, but when he'd offered to leave work to come home and drive her this morning, she'd asserted politely that she could get there under her own steam.

He'd felt gutted when he saw her morning face. Since last night he'd had a jagged feeling in his chest, as if he'd kicked something fragile, or done something very stupid.

In fact, she'd slept in the other room. He still felt raw when he thought of the savage night he'd endured, but, in truth, in some ways he'd been relieved. At least he hadn't taken advantage of her last night as well.

A concept was lurking on the edges of his mind, something so simple, so bright and elegant. If only he could grasp it firmly.

The afternoon in the office seemed interminable, and on a sudden what-the-hell impulse he grabbed his car keys and headed for the door.

On the way home he tried to think of some things he could say to reduce her hurt. The trouble was, he was a blundering fool where women were concerned. Take Esther…

In a strange coincidence, he'd nearly reached the turn-off to Waverley. For some reason, on an absolutely unprecedented impulse he took it, and drove slowly along the street until he found the entrance where he knew Esther's ashes had been slotted into a wall, along with those of thousands of other souls. He got out of the car and stood a while, perhaps an hour, wondering if he was facing some crazy sort of widower's crisis, then walked along the avenues, hunched against the rain, until he came to the one he'd visited that one time before.

There was a little brass plaque set in the wall with Esther's name on it. He stared at it for an age, trying to sense if Esther was present, remembering what Ariadne had said about her parents. He wiped the raindrops off the plaque with his sleeve, then took out his handkerchief and gave it a firmer polish.

The truth was, Esther wasn't there. Not that he could sense. She wasn't anywhere any more, except perhaps up there in the ether, smiling with the other clouds. He saw it then, the simple dazzling truth.

Ariadne was here and now, warm and alive and smelling of flowers. Seized with a buoyant burst of energy and purpose he sprinted to the car, his feet squelching in his wet shoes.

'You're a very rich woman,' the attorney said, his rainwater eyes and thinning grey hair in perfect harmony with his grey suit, pearl silk tie and dim, grey humour. 'Didn't your uncle ever inform you of your father's stake in Giorgias Shipping?'

Ariadne shook her head.

'Your dad inherited his small stake from his grandmother, while your uncle inherited his larger one from his father. Lucky for you, Giorgias Shipping has gone from strength to strength.' He smiled a watery smile. 'There's nothing stopping you from doing whatever you wish with your life, Mrs Nikosto. You can buy the Harbour Bridge if you like. Travel anywhere in the world.'

Anywhere except Naxos.

'Thank you.' Ariadne pasted on a smile, just as though she

weren't a creature composed almost solely of pain. She gathered her handbag, then rose and shook hands with the lawyer. As she made the descent in the lift, then walked free and rich into the Sydney rain, she realised she didn't want to go to Naxos anyway. There was no one for her there now.

Or anywhere.

Still, she had choices. Billions of them, it seemed, all of them empty. What did a woman do when her husband couldn't accept her love? She probably should find a taxi to take her home in time to cook his dinner. Instead, she turned listlessly in the direction of a travel agent she'd noticed in the Pitt Street Mall.

Sebastian closed the door behind him and tossed his keys on the hall table. He paused, listening. The house seemed curiously quiet. He strolled through the house and into the kitchen. Everything was neat and orderly, clean and pristine, but there was no aromatic pot simmering on the range. He opened the oven door.

Nothing.

No crisp salad waiting on the bench top. No cooking. No wife. Could she be sleeping?

With a sudden dread he bounded up the stairs two at a time, calling, 'Ariadne.'

In every direction emptiness met his gaze. No trace of her in his bedroom, or in the other room she'd taken to sleeping in since the fateful discussion. Her wardrobe was bare. No bottles on the vanity. No combs or brushes on her dressing table. His house, his life, back to a threadbare shell.

A single silky scarf hung from her doorknob, drifting softly on the breeze. Something about its soft fragility devastated him. He snatched it up and held it to his face to inhale the last trace of her perfume. With a tearing pain in his chest he tried to come to terms with the possibility the worst had happened. She'd left him.

Although where would she go?

It was too late to call the lawyer at work, so he phoned the guy at his home. No luck there. The man couldn't say where his beautiful wife had gone after he'd handed her the keys to her inheritance.

His bed had never felt so desolate. He was still awake when the dawn broke. A little after six, haggard and unshaven, he hastened for the front door at the sound of the bell. Ariadne? The silly little hope rose in his heart. Maybe she'd forgotten her key, been held up somehow and stayed in a hotel.

He opened the door and stared. Two elderly Greeks were on the porch, issuing a stream of conflicting instructions to a chauffeur who was unloading suitcases from a long black limousine. The Greek man was portly and moustachioed, his wife formally and expensively dressed for so early in the day, her warm pleasant face creased in anxiety.

'Careful with that, you fool,' the man blustered. 'No, no, not there, idiot. *There*.'

'Just a moment, Peri. *I'll* handle this. Bring the black one first, will you, my dear young man? I'll need that first. Then find the brown one with the pinstripe. Ah, excellent. Thank you, thank you.'

The elderly man turned. When he saw Sebastian his eyes widened, and at once he threw out his hands. 'Ah, my boy, my blessed, blessed *boy*.' He seized Sebastian with enthusiasm and kissed him on both cheeks. 'It's me. Peri. Your uncle, and you must call me Thio. And this is your Aunt Eleni.' He beamed and rubbed his hands. 'Where is my girl? Where's our Ariadne?'

As Sebastian dredged up the bald words and delivered his tidings, it was the wife who broke the ensuing silence. 'What? Are you saying she isn't *here*? Where, then?' There was a note of panic in her voice. 'Where in the world is she? What have you done with my *toula*?'

CHAPTER FIFTEEN

ARIADNE adjusted her beach bag to cushion her back, and leaned on her elbows to watch the early morning surfers. Far out beyond the first line of breakers, a lone swimmer powered through the water in a leisurely freestyle, barely raising a splash. For a minute she watched, envying that assured, lazy crawl.

How she wished she could do it. It reminded her of a precious morning spent watching Sebastian in the surf on Bronte Beach. Though that was history now, just a bright, fleeting moment in time. Still, she'd done the right thing in leaving. She knew that with a deep certainty. If they'd gone on as they were, without a commitment of love on both sides, they'd have ended in tears sooner or later.

Better for it to be sooner, before her love had grown too deep for her to have the strength. The well of emotion connected to thoughts of her brief, disastrous marriage threatened to overflow again, and she was obliged to lift the corner of her tee shirt and dab at her eyes. She'd really have to stop giving way to this grieving soon. It was time to straighten her shoulders and do something worthwhile with her life.

Perhaps this place might help, with its echoes of that magic time in her childhood. Beaches might have been much the same the world over, but Noosa had a charm all its own. Perhaps it was the bush-scented air. She inhaled an aromatic whiff of it.

Tea tree, casuarina and eucalypt, mingled with salty sea. A unique blend of wild things. Or it might have been the emerald and turquoise waters, or the smooth black waterstones lining the pretty shores.

Sebastian was doing brilliantly, she'd read in the papers. Celestrial's share value had rocketed on the Stock Exchange. Thio would be impressed.

Sebastian wasn't the only one who'd racked up achievements. She'd travelled quite a lot of her homeland in the recent months, though there was still much left to see. She'd jolted along red-dirt outback tracks in a four-wheel drive, and slept by a campfire beneath the southern cross. She'd kayaked along the river of a red desert gorge carved out in primeval times, and swum in the pure, crystalline waters of a bottomless lake.

She'd slept in sleeping bags, buses, on hard dry ground and in hostels pared down to offer none but the most basic of human amenities. All of it had been rare and beautiful and exciting. She'd plunged into every adventure with all her heart, what was left of the battered thing, though the beauties she'd seen had been blurred often by tears and her yearning for the wonderful man who'd taught her how to love then at the last minute rejected her.

Now she was waiting. She'd done some research and found that her great-auntie Maeve was still a resident of Noosa, though currently away visiting relatives in Tasmania. Every time Ariadne thought of that her toes clenched in pleasure.

Relatives in Tasmania. Chances were, they were her relatives too.

The swimmer who'd been far out beyond the breakers had changed tack and was heading in now. He disappeared in a trough, then his dark head bobbed up and she saw him pause and look around, waiting. He caught the next wave with effortless ease, riding it in like a dolphin. Every flash of his powerful arms suggested he was lean and deeply tanned.

He vanished again for a couple of minutes. Next time she spotted him he was much closer to shore.

She narrowed her eyes behind her dark glasses. He was nearly level now with the braver surfers, the ones who weren't afraid of swimming out of their depths. Soon he'd be able to stand. His hair looked black, as black as Sebastian's, though from this distance the water darkened everyone's hair.

He body-surfed the next wave in and she saw him stand suddenly, steadying himself against the swell with his arms. He started to make his way in. She leaned forward, and her heart started a wild hammering.

She pushed up her sunglasses for a clearer look. The man was tall and beautifully proportioned, like an athlete. He was wide at the shoulders, narrow at waist and hips, and she could make out more of his features.

For heaven's sake, she *must* be insane. Incredible, but the further he advanced, the more he looked like Sebastian.

Her painfully thundering pulse thought it was true, but it couldn't be. She must be imagining things. Sebastian was in Sydney managing Celestrial, not rising from the sea before her like Poseidon. As she stared, frozen, other sights, sounds, everything else faded from her consciousness. All she was aware of was her lean, hard, beautiful husband, striding from the shallows and onto the beach, dripping, his gaze focused ahead.

A small silence fell around her. With a sense of unreality, Ariadne turned to watch him walk past her and continue on a further thirty metres to the rinse-off shower at the edge of the beach.

Apparently unaware of her presence, he rinsed his hair and smoothed his hands over his virile chest and arms. Arms that had once been hers. Then he turned off the shower and strolled a little way to a small heap on the sand, muscles rippling in his long back and powerful thighs as he stooped to pick up a towel.

Ariadne's heart made a savage thud. Hadn't he noticed her?

She couldn't imagine he wouldn't have, when he stood out to her in any crowd. In fact she was forever seeing him in impossible places. And why was he in Noosa? He never took holidays. A horrible thought struck her. Could he be here with someone? Someone *new*?

She could hardly expect him to feel kindly towards her, but if he walked away without acknowledging her she'd die. She sat up straight and still, eyes closed, hardly daring to hope, her tremulous heart on a precipice, her nerves as tense as wires.

A shadow fell between her and the sun and she opened her eyes, to be momentarily dazzled. 'Ariadne.' When she adjusted to the light she looked up to meet her husband's dark intent gaze.

Every instinct in her being rushed heart and soul to welcome him, but she fought back the impulse to leap up and throw herself into his arms.

'Hello, Sebastian.'

He hesitated a second, then dropped down beside her on the sand. As he leaned to kiss her cheek his familiar masculine aura swamped her and the old sexual connection impacted on her with massive, weakening force.

She closed her eyes and said faintly, 'What—what are you doing here?'

'Passing through. How about you?'

As he examined her sunlight caught the gleams in his dark eyes. He was dressed now in shorts and a loose white tee shirt that enhanced his tan. Drops of water sparkled on his brows and lashes. Perhaps she imagined it, but he seemed thinner. Even his face appeared leaner, the lines around his mouth more deeply etched.

'Me too. I'm just here—temporarily.'

'Oh.'

She cast down her lashes. 'I've been—doing a bit of travelling around Australia. Reconnecting with my birthplace. Thought

I'd stay here in Queensland a while, since winter's just around the corner.'

There was a strained silence. He broke it first, nodding. 'Right. Good. Well, you've always wanted to see the country. So tell me. Is it up to your expectations?'

Thinking of the places she'd visited, her heart swelled with inexpressible emotion. 'Oh-h-h. *Better.* Better than I could ever describe in a million years. It's stunning. Spectacular. Who'd ever think a desert would be so beautiful? And the people. Everyone here is so kind and friendly and warm.'

'Warmer than the Greeks?'

'No.' She gave a shaky laugh. 'Not warmer than the Greeks. No one is warmer than Greeks.'

There was another silence, then he said lightly, 'I guess I thought that since you're a rich woman now you might have chosen to wing your way back to Naxos.' He looked keenly at her.

She met his narrowed gaze. 'No. My long-term plans are for here.'

His brows shot up. *'Here?'*

'No, no, not Noosa. Sydney, I think.'

His eyes lit, then veiled almost at once. 'Sydney? Oh. Good.' He nodded. 'That'll be—great.'

His black brows drew together. The air thundered with vibrations. She was dying to ask what he was really doing in Noosa, but she was too afraid of the answer to risk it.

The silence grew thick with unaskable questions, and this time it was she who broke it. 'I see that Celestrial is doing very well. I read all about you in the paper. They're calling you a whizz-kid. Congratulations. You must be celebrating.'

He gave a shrug. 'Thanks, but—' he glanced at her '—since I lost you, nothing seems worth celebrating.'

Emotion welled in her throat. 'Oh. I—suppose we lost each other.' Her voice was so husky it could have been shovelled up.

He stared down at the sand, then looked at her with an intent, serious glance. 'Look, would you consider coming up to the hotel and having breakfast with me? There are some things I need to say to you.'

Her heart thrilled with an anticipation so intense it was hard to determine whether it felt like joy or anguish. Still, she had to protect herself. Had to beware of his capacity to hurt her. What if it was the divorce he wanted to discuss?

'Breakfast sounds good,' she said. 'Where—are you staying?'

'The Sheraton.'

'Yeah? That's a coincidence. That's where I'm holed up.' She looked sharply at him, then said, all at once out of breath, '*Is it a coincidence, Sebastian?*'

He hesitated. 'Not exactly.'

He stood up and held out his hand. Nervous of touching him with her senses already haywire, she disregarded the offer of assistance and scrambled up herself. The quick movement made her slightly giddy, and she swayed a bit.

His hand snaked out to grasp her arm and steady her. 'Careful.'

Predictably, his fingers left a ring of the dangerous old fire burning on her arm like a brand.

As they strolled along Hastings Street, under the poinciana trees, past all the tourists breakfasting in the sidewalk cafés and thronging the gelaterias, she babbled on about her travels, wondering what it was he had to say to her, her brain in a haze, though her body seemed to be so sharply, vibrantly attuned to every part of him. Was it actual months since they'd been lovers?

He hardly said much, just kept nodding and gazing at her as if he couldn't look away, drinking her in from head to toe in her tee and shorts and sandals, his eyes glittering as they did when he was in the grip of strong emotion.

'You have a tan,' he observed at one point, his voice deep and gravelly.

She nodded.

His eyes flickered over her. 'You look—more beautiful than ever.' He shoved his hands in his pockets. 'Sort of glowing. So—what are your long-term plans?'

They'd paused in front of the lifts at the Sheraton.

After a second's hesitation, she said, 'Well, I've decided what I want to do in Australia. I'm thinking of building shelters for homeless people.' His brows shot up and she added quickly, 'Oh, I know Sydney already has shelters, but I want to make my own contribution. I can easily afford it. I'll start with one. Find some good people to work it so I can learn the ropes of running a charity.' She met his gaze fleetingly. 'Well, you know, it's terrifying not knowing where you're going to sleep the next night.' Her chin wobbled. 'I'll never forget how that felt.'

'I know,' he said, his eyes flooding with warmth and remorse. 'Of course you won't.' He clenched his jaw, and turned sharply away from her. After a moment he added, 'That's—that's a wonderful idea, I think. You'll—you'll do it very well.'

'I hope so,' she mumbled, her throat so tight her voice was a croak. 'I know I'm pretty green. I have a lot to learn.'

He grimaced. 'Don't we all?'

In the lift, their close proximity became quite agonising, with all the unspoken emotion fogging up the airwaves. She wished she could talk to him properly, open up her heart and voice the real things between them. Instead she said, her voice wobbling with the effort of sounding calm, 'Did you know, Sebastian, that Fraser Island is made entirely of *sand*? And there's a lake there, so deep no one has ever plumbed the bottom, but its water is as clear and fresh and pure as a mountain spring. Held there absolutely by sand. Did you know that?'

He stared at her, his eyes so dark they were black, then with a little groan he grabbed her and dragged her against him.

He held her against his lean, hard body for a long glorious time, stroking her hair, his bristly morning jaw grazing her forehead. Tears of loss for the love they might have had welled up from the bottomless spring in her heart, and she had a good weep against his chest. She could feel his big, strong heart beating against her cheek.

At last, after soaking up the strength of his healing essence for a while, she noticed that the lift doors had opened and people were outside, gawking in.

'Oops,' Sebastian rasped. 'Our floor.'

Sebastian's suite was much like hers, she noticed through her misty haze. Opulent. Enormous bedroom, plush sofas, views across the sea to heaven, and a delightful balcony where breakfast could be set, if there was a point when one was eating alone. Clothes were spilling out of his suitcase, and he had the bedroom in a bit of a shambles already.

Recovering from her shameful excess of lift emotion, she said brightly, 'How—how did you know I was here?'

'I remembered you told me once about your parents bringing you here for a holiday. I thought it was worth a try. I'd tried everywhere else I could think of.'

'Did you?' She dropped her gaze and mumbled, 'I should have left a note, I suppose. It was a—a spur-of-the-minute thing. You know, I just—just…'

'I know.' A flush darkened his tan. 'I hurt you.'

There was nothing she could say to express how much, so she just looked away, pained at the memories.

He said fiercely, his voice rough and deep, 'I'm so sorry. I think when I met you I got—caught up in a tangle over my first wife. I guess you could say I had guilt about falling in love again. You know, unresolved grief, or whatever it is they call it.'

Falling in love again. Had he, though?

'You know, when I met you, I was—overwhelmed.' His voice grew deep and gruff and thick. 'I couldn't believe my luck when you asked me to marry you that day. And at *once*. God, I was euphoric. I'd have done anything to have you. *Anything.*'

Her stomach clenched and she said in a low voice, well, it was wonderful of you to take me on. I was so very grateful.'

'I guess.' The strong lines of his face tautened. 'Though if I'd had any *idea*… It was clear you were worried about money, but if I'd known the full extent of just how desperate you *were* that day…' His jaw clenched, and he said fiercely, 'I'd have found some way to…' He punched a fist into his palm, and the muscles bunched in his bronzed arms. 'That old devil. I still feel as if I've let him off the hook too lightly. But only because of Eleni.'

'Eleni?' She looked quickly at him. 'Do you mean *Thea*?'

He nodded. 'Thea, yes. And, oh…' He flicked his forehead in sudden remembrance. 'Yeah, that's right, that's what I had to tell you. They're here.'

She started away from him and her eyes sprang wide. She glanced involuntarily about her as if her uncle and aunt might suddenly pop out of the furniture. '*Here*? In *Noosa*?'

'No, no, not *here*, thank God.' He pulled himself up at once. 'Oh, sorry. I know they're your family.' He looked apologetic, though his eyes glinted with sudden amusement. 'They're in Sydney. They stayed at our place for a few days until Agnes got sick of them, so they moved to a hotel. They must have flown out from Athens almost as soon as they heard we were married.'

'*What?*'

Her legs suddenly turned to jelly and she was forced to plump down on the bed. 'You mean, they've been here all this time?'

He sat down beside her, and slipped his arm around her. 'Indeed they have. They've been worried sick. Peri's hired every private detective on the eastern seaboard, and your aunt is nearly beside herself. She says she blames herself for your engagement to that rich guy in Greece.'

'Really?' She gave a sardonic shrug. 'Well, there's a turnaround. After the way they complained I was difficult. You're too spoilt, they said. On one occasion Thio actually accused me of being a *princess.*'

Even recalling the insult could still make her burn with indignation.

Something flickered in Sebastian's eyes, then he frowned and shook his head. 'He said *that*? Tsk.' He patted her shoulder sympathetically. 'I *think* they said there's been some sort of scandal about the guy since the wedding.' He narrowed his eyes in vague recollection. 'Oh, yeah, that's right. He came out.'

She gasped in incredulity. With the shocks coming so thick and fast, could she be hearing right? 'Are you sure?' she screeched. '*Demetri*? You mean he's gay?'

'Yep.' He nodded, frowning. 'I think that's what it was. You've been totally vindicated for defending yourself, Peri says.' He smiled. 'In fact in Greece you're practically a national hero.'

She stared at him in astonishment, then held her face in her hands and rocked backwards and forwards. '*Oh*. Oh, look, I just can't *believe* this. Demetri *gay*? So why did he want to marry me? Oh, you've no idea how the press bashed me over that. I went through an absolute *purgatory.*'

'Oh, well,' he said soothingly. 'That's all over now. I guess the guy had his reasons. The press are saying now that you've been given a raw deal. And you know, your aunt really had no idea your uncle had played that trick on you with the finances until you rang her. She's been giving him hell over it.' He dropped his gaze, grimacing. 'Especially since you married *me* and I wrecked your life.'

She gave him a quick look. 'Is that what she said?'

'Something like that.' His lashes flicked down and he looked embarrassed. 'Yeah, well… There's been some fairly heated family discussions, as you might imagine. Your aunt can be quite a formidable woman. At one point I actually came close to feeling sorry for old Peri. I shudder to think what it must be like in their suite at the Hyatt.'

It occurred to her that some of their old camaraderie was back. She beamed at him, so overjoyed to be actually sitting there with him again in the flesh, hope frothing in her heart like the eternal Aegean.

'I hope she *is* giving him a hard time. Still, I'm not sure I can face seeing them for a very long time.' She lifted her shoulders. 'You know, I thought they sent me out here to get rid of me. I don't think I can ever forgive them.'

'No one would blame you if you didn't.' He gazed down at her with tender concern. With a gentle movement, he stroked her cheek with lean fingers. 'But I don't honestly think that *was* ever their intention. They've been breaking their hearts over you.' He hesitated, then said softly, 'Almost as much as I have.'

'Oh.' Her heart caught with a tremulous hope and she drew a long shivery breath. 'Have you?'

He blinked, and the lines of his face tensed. 'I've been in hell.'

Theos forgive her, she didn't ever want to see Sebastian suffer, but it was good to hear that he'd cared when she'd suffered so much pain.

His lean, handsome face from cheekbone to jaw was set hard. 'I'm hoping—you can forgive *me*. I know you're enjoying your freedom. You've got the world on a string now. You can do whatever you like with your life.' He met her gaze, his dark eyes serious with sincerity and warmth. 'I'll do my best to tell you now without making a mess of it.' He hesitated, searching her face for reassurance, and she nodded encouragingly, hardly daring to breathe. 'I realised the truth the day you left. I rushed home to tell you, but like a fool I was too late.' He made a rueful grimace. 'Whatever you choose, the truth is, I love you, Ariadne. I can't pretend I don't want you to come back home and be my wife.'

She was moved to her soul. Her entire being filled with such thrilled, joyful relief she reached out to stroke his beloved face with both hands. 'Oh, Sebastian.'

'Do you—think you could love me?' His voice was as deep as a well, and though his eyes were uncertain his fingers strayed to her neck, and stroked the tender spot in her nape with a rock-solid surety she recognised. The sensation was so delicious it required an effort to talk. 'Even after the way I hurt you?'

'Yes, I do,' she breathed, thrilling all down her spine. 'I love you. I love you like mad.'

He closed his eyes. 'Thank God.' Then he kissed her long and deep.

She moulded herself to his familiar frame and surrendered herself to the rapturous mingling of love and mutual belonging. By the time she surfaced again she was giddy, from happiness as much as the lack of oxygen.

It didn't look as if breakfast was about to happen any time soon. Once started on a certain divine course, in typical fashion, Sebastian wasn't anxious to stop.

He sprawled on the bed and pulled her to him, murmuring, 'Why don't we start our honeymoon straight away?' He kissed her throat. 'We could go to Fraser Island if you like.'

'Oh, I'd *love* to go there with you.'

He adjusted his big lean frame so that they were each lying on their sides, heads supported on their elbows, face to face, chest to chest, hands to seeking hands. 'And afterwards, we could, if you liked, have a proper wedding in a church. But only if you want that, my darling. With the music and flowers, and all the families and everyone. Then if you want to we could visit Naxos. Make a grand triumphal tour.' With a thoughtful gleam in his eye he added, 'Lure your aunt and uncle back home.'

My darling, he'd called her. She imagined it all, being loved and accepted by Sebastian's family as a proper bride, not a bartered woman with no autonomy or equality. Mrs Nikosto. Mr and Mrs Nikosto. Her husband. Her proud, darling husband.

The words sang in her ears like music.

'What do you think?'

'I think yes, my darling Sebastian. Yes, and yes, and *yes*.' Unable to help herself, she punctuated each yes with a fervent little kiss.

Somehow then she found herself lying on her back, being kissed in every little nook and cranny by the lips she most desired in the world.

Sebastian ran out of things to say very soon, but she had no doubts about his enthusiasm. He expressed his feelings in other ways, convincing her of his wholehearted sincerity with the most passionate and ardent means at his disposal, to her intense and delightfully long-lasting pleasure.

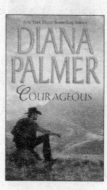

The World of Mills & Boon®

There's a Mills & Boon® series that's perfect for you. We publish ten series and, with new titles every month, you never have to wait long for your favourite to come along.

Blaze.
Scorching hot, sexy reads
4 new stories every month

By Request
Relive the romance with the best of the best
9 new stories every month

Cherish™
Romance to melt the heart every time
12 new stories every month

Desire™
Passionate and dramatic love stories
8 new stories every month